Expectations are never realistic. Outcome Wishes rarely come true.

None of that has ever stopped Abram Hoffman from meeting every goal he's ever set. In a world full of constants—his pace per mile, daily caloric intake, number of isolated bicep curls—the balance of Abe's delicately crafted life topples when his childhood best friend Cassie Montgomery unexpectedly moves back home with her new boyfriend, Jared, whose lingering touches and ambiguous actions make Abe question his true intentions. To top it off, Abe's ex, Harris McGee, also makes a sudden splash back into Abe's life.

As each of them suffer through life's obstacles, they are forced to face the fact that control isn't always an option and words, whether true or false, can't always save you. Set in Buffalo, New York, NEW YEAR, NEW YOU deals with life and death—and the love that flourishes in between—told from three powerful perspectives.

A NineStar Press Publication

Published by NineStar Press
P.O. Box 91792,
Albuquerque, New Mexico, 87199 USA.
www.ninestarpress.com

New Year, New You

Printed in the USA
First Edition
April, 2018

Print ISBN: 978-1-948608-56-5

Also available in eBook, ISBN: 978-1-948608-51-0

Warning: This book contains sexual content, which may only be suitable for mature readers.

Disclaimer: Though this book includes many places and street names actually existing in Buffalo, fictional elements have also been worked into the story.

Dedication

To Mike, for your endless support of my writing, my singing, and my dancing.

To Cindy, for inspiring me to write in the first place, and for your consistently brilliant input.

One: Abram

"New Year, New You!"

Abram rolled his eyes and let out a brief but exasperated grunt as those words on the sign stuck to the front of Vitality Fitness became visible through the wind-whipped flurries.

The welcomed warm weather of December had faded away with the start of the new year, and knowing this was likely the last time he could make the two-mile run to work, Abram kicked it up a notch and reached a full-on sprint as he hit the parking lot. He quickly and carefully skipped across the winter-soaked pavement, catching a reflection in the window of the light snowfall caking his perfectly parted hair. Abram always thought he'd look good with a little bit more salt mixed into his pepper hair, a belief that only solidified on this brutally cold morning.

The jangle of his keys opening the door and the quiet hum of the gym's lights comforted him. At 4:00 a.m., he knew the next hour would signal his final moments of solitude for the day. Because it was January 2, a day Abram coined January Fools Day, when the impostors began their infiltration complete with unrealistic timelines and unattainable wishes for their bodies. He hated this day.

Maybe it was an Upstate New York thing. Everyone there wanted everything so quickly, tossing aside the notion that the only way to achieve washboard abs or rock-hard pecs was actual work and commitment. In Buffalo, football was more important than fitness, eating more important than exercise. At no point was that more evident than the start of the year. Abram suspected this wasn't the case in San Francisco or Chicago or Brooklyn.

He couldn't remember when the thought of a busy gym full of people with healthy aspirations turned from a thrilling challenge worth tackling to an annoyance he'd rather avoid. Maybe it was because Vitality would be marking its seventh anniversary this summer, and for seven Januarys in a row, it was the same shit: a full house the first week of the year, followed by fewer people the next week, and even less the week after that. The purge continued until only the regulars were standing at the end of the month.

"New Year, Same Shit!"

He wondered if that slogan could be printed for next year.

Correcting the annual January attrition was one of the things Abe had worked on over the years by setting up programs designed to turn the slightly interested and motivated individual into someone wholeheartedly dedicated to fitness. But he knew that goal was futile. He had learned personal trainers and fitness programs could only do so much. A person only had the ability to change when they actually wanted to change, and there was nothing any outsider or any *The Wealth of Health!* class could do to change their mind. Being healthy was a lifelong obligation that very few people chose.

Abe glanced at his watch: 4:37 a.m.

It was way too early to be so philosophically negative.

He really had no reason to be bitter. The energy inside the gym that day would be electric. And the stability of owning Vitality was oddly comforting. No surprises meant no new disappointments. And at this point in Abe's life, no fresh disappointment equaled happiness.

Where had the morning bitchiness come from? He blamed it on his lack of caffeine. Eliminating caffeine—one of his three New Year's resolutions—had not been as easy an undertaking as Abe had envisioned. But he was determined to make this year the one he would become entirely independent of addiction. For as long as he could remember, coffee was the only thing Abe physically needed.

Sugar? He'd been ten years without it this spring—having none since the weekend of his twenty-third birthday.

Television? Down to about two hours a week, usually while squeezing in an ab workout.

Alcohol? Two and a half years without a drop and going strong.

Sex? Abram winced at the thought. He didn't feel like counting the months.

Wait, has it been years?

A quick headshake followed by a sudden slap to his face and Abram successfully dug out of that wormhole. The thoughts of the previous years would not continue to creep into his daily life and slowly gnaw away at the positive future. That was New Year's Resolution number two: don't let the past dictate your future.

Besides, today wasn't the day to be irritated. It was the day he finally got to meet Jared, Cassandra Montgomery's new boyfriend. Cassie had been Abram's best friend through and through since the first grade and the amount of love he felt for her wasn't quantifiable. From the age of eight to the time Cassie left Buffalo at twenty-three, they had lived life parallel with each other. No one in town had talked about the two without referring to them as a pair. "Cass and Abe" had become local legends during their high school years. It'd started after saving Olivia Davidson's life outside the local Dairy Queen when the six-year-old choked on a piece of bubblegum as they were working. When it happened, Cass and Abe looked at each other and sprang into action without even speaking. Abe hopped over the counter, ran out the front door, and began the Heimlich maneuver while Cassie called 911. By the time he forced the gum out, Olivia was powder blue. Abe would never forget the hue Olivia's face turned, or the color of the burns Cass suffered from kneeling on the scorching blacktop while administering CPR.

Every now and then, he popped in the VHS tape of their interview on the local news, chuckling to himself at Cass's ridiculously large scrunchie and the way his uniform hung on his gawky body.

That event only started their list of accomplishments as teens: the two were New York State Champions in their age group for Science Olympiad every year of high school; they became the first—and to this day, the only—couple at Kenmore East High School to be crowned Homecoming King and Queen and Prom King and Queen in the same year; and they even were valedictorian and salutatorian, with Cass beating Abe by a mere .013 in their final GPAs. That fact didn't even sting for Abe; he was happy to once again be linked with Cassie on a grand scale.

Everyone thought they'd end up married, but destiny had other plans.

It was Cassie who had encouraged Abe to come out to his family freshman year of college. She told Abram she "always knew" he was gay, but he suspected that wasn't entirely accurate. Deep down, Cassie had thought they would end up married, living the highly sought-after picture-perfect existence arising from innocent daydreams. And despite his sexuality, Abram had felt the same way. The two were inseparable and entirely on the same page in every aspect of life, from the type of house they wanted (a redbrick Colonial) to the number and the sex of potential children (three kids: two boys and a girl).

If life was about finding your soul mate, Abe had found his in Cassie.

Abe had never let being gay define him as a person, but he often thought about how much it changed his path. And every time he saw Cassie, he recognized if that one thing was different, the two of them would've achieved Happily Ever After.

Like most friends growing older in separate cities, Cass and Abe had slowly grown apart as time progressed. She'd moved to Charlotte after getting a teaching job, and, naturally, their relationship in the decade since wasn't the same. Abe still loved her like a sister. Hell, he loved her more than Susanna, his actual sister. Cassie was perfect.

Her only flaw? She had a penchant for picking the wrong guys. Six years ago, she had been engaged to Edward Shanahan, defense lawyer extraordinaire. Ed was fourteen years Cassie's senior, and if he had one memorable or noteworthy quality, Abe had never seen it. Ed was rude, dull, arrogant, a slob, and quite frankly, not in Cassie's league in the looks department. Thank God, that hadn't lasted.

Then there had been Brock Blount, another dud who had no business ever dating Cassie. She'd met him at a bar shortly after she and Ed split, and though Abe assumed he'd be a rebound guy, Cassie had floored everyone when she proposed to Brock a year into their relationship. Their engagement ended seven weeks later, when she'd found him in bed with her twenty-one-year-old student teacher, Jessica Herbert.

So, when Cass texted last week asking to stop into Vitality so Abe could meet her new man, Jared Pfeiffer, he hadn't been able to help but be skeptical. They had been dating since the spring and would have just enough time to stop in and say hi during a layover on their return home from a New Year's Eve trip to Vegas. It wasn't exactly the ideal reunion for Abe, but he would gladly take any opportunity to see her.

He sat stationary in his office, only snapping out of his Cassie coma after the hollow echo of a knock on the door filled the empty gym.

Abe sprang from his office, jogged to the front of the gym, and unlocked the door. As expected, Maureen Jacobs and Deirdre Schermeyer stood eagerly outside, water bottles and duffel bags in tow.

"Happy New Year, ladies," Abe said.

"Happy New Year!" they said in unison, making their way to the locker room.

Holding the door open, Abe lost himself in the winter wonderland before him. The snow had picked up a bit, leaving a heavy coating on the nearly empty parking lot, save for a few cars, a moving truck, and a boat. As much as he hated the cold, he had to admit the presence of a fresh snowfall was a pristine sight he had grown to love. Abe was so busy intently watching a snowplow disrupt the white blanket on Niagara Falls Boulevard, he almost shut the door on another gymgoer.

Without even looking, he knew this was one of the interlopers. Maureen and Deirdre were the only two to ever be there at five o'clock on the dot.

"Oh! So sorry about that. Happy New Year," Abe said. "Welcome to Vitality, I'm Abe."

Abe extended his arm for a handshake as the man made his way inside, unzipping his puffy platinum-silver jacket and lowering his hood.

"Hi," the interloper said, flashing an impeccable, megawatt Tom-Cruise-before-he-went-crazy smile.

Having never perfected his poker face, Abe could feel his eyes widening and his jaw dropping. The man before him looked like he was ripped straight from the pages of *GQ*. Flawless skin, high cheekbones, perfectly coiffed hair, deep-blue eyes, the right amount of stubble. Time stood still as the two locked gazes. Prior to this moment, Abe hadn't been a believer in love at first sight, but there was something about the aura radiating from this man that made him question everything he'd ever known about love.

Once again, Abe knew it was way too early to be so philosophical. At least this time, it was positive.

He has to be gay. He's definitely gay. Please be gay.

"Abram. Hoffman."

The pitch of Cassie's voice interrupted Abe's desires and rang in his ears. He spun around to see his best friend standing before him, tucking her auburn hair behind her ears. She stood, a grin as eager as a kid on Christmas, looking every bit as beautiful as he remembered.

"Cass!"

Abe's bear hug lifted Cassie off her feet until she squealed with laughter. The sound immediately brought him back to childhood, sitting with Cass on her parents' deck, as the two giggled while tossing old tennis balls to the Montgomerys' clumsy black lab, Cocoa.

"I see you've met Jared," Cass said, pointing to the Adonis.

"Oh my God," Abe said. "Jared!"

Abe inexplicably went in for a hug as big as the one that enveloped Cassie. Before he caught himself, he felt the strong arms of Jared squeezing him back.

"It's nice to finally meet you!" Jared exclaimed, still holding onto Abe. "Cass won't stop talking about you."

It was a bit of an awkward hug for two guys who'd known each other for less than a minute. When Jared finally let go—after what seemed like an eternity—Abe tried to stealthily examine Cass's newfound love.

"So, how are you? How was Vegas?" Abe asked, determined to steer his mind to a more suitable location. "Happy New Year!"

"Well, we actually have some news," Cass said, her wide smile curling at the edges. "That U-Haul out there? It's ours. I got a job as a literacy specialist at Niagara Falls Middle School. I start Monday!"

A half laugh escaped Abe's mouth as he began to process the news. A fully caffeinated brain would have shouted "Congratulations!" followed by a line of proper questioning. Instead, he stood motionless, darting his eyes back and forth between Cass and Jared. All he could mutter was a breathy "What?"

Cassie and Jared both moved forward, arms stretching out wide, going in for another hug.

"I'm moving home, Abe!" Cassie whispered as she nuzzled into the side of his face. Abe could feel her breath changing and knew she was sobbing the tears of joy that inevitably come when you finally reach a goal you've had for years.

A set of tears formed in the corner of his eyes, too, drying ever so slightly as Jared's bicep pressed on his shoulder blades. He didn't care if Cassie saw him cry, but he didn't want to look like a wimp in front of Jared. When the three finally parted, Abe could sense Jared's eyes intently focused on him.

In any other instance, Abe would have been flattered and, perhaps embarrassingly, maybe even a little aroused. Jared was an impressive specimen, the kind of guy the Cassandra Montgomerys and Abram Hoffmans of the world dreamed about. And there he was, standing in front of Abe, just...staring and smiling and staring and looking remarkably sexy.

Abe stopped the metaphorical drooling and reminded himself of New Year's Resolution number three: don't judge a book by its cover.

More precisely: don't assume every attractive man is gay.

"New Year, New Abram!"

Maybe.

Two: Clare

Clare never thought all material possessions of her sixty-six years of life could be so effortlessly separated, but there she was expeditiously plopping everything she owned into three distinct categories: Keep, Throw Out, Think About.

Another one of her restless nights meant another early morning, and continuing this exercise in simplification seemed like the natural thing to do at 5:00 a.m. The key to sorting through decades of randomness, she told herself, was to trust her instincts. She would only give herself about a half second of thinking before selecting in which pile to put each artifact.

Clare looked at the boxes and felt proud of her progress over the last two days. She'd started with the hutch in the kitchen, moved to Caleb's room, and had now made her way to Cassandra's room. Clare laughed as she remembered her path over the last day—these rooms hadn't been Cassandra's or Caleb's since they both moved out fifteen years ago!

Organizing everything became a bit of a fun game. Clare approached every item in her house with a fresh perspective, as if she were an appraiser stepping into an outsider's home, determining what had value without any sentimentality getting in the way.

The golden yellow vase on the dining room table, filled with silk sunflowers and baby's breath? *Throw out.*

The sign hanging in her hallway that read, "Bless this Home with Love and Laughter" she'd crocheted after Caleb was born? *Throw out.*

The toaster oven? The spice rack? Her French press? *Throw out. Throw out. Throw out.*

It only got a bit tricky when she found bins or boxes of things she no longer even knew she had, which was the current case from the thirty-gallon tote she lugged out of Cassandra's closet.

A vinyl copy of Carole King's *Tapestry* album? *Keep.*

A set of coasters from her and Charlie's trip to Erie, Pennsylvania in 1978? *Throw out.*

Her mother's beautiful, but tarnished and bent mirrored jewelry tray?

For the first time during the purge, Clare didn't make a split-second decision. Her cloudy reflection stared back at her, the coating of dust almost making her wrinkled skin appear smooth, her gray hair blonde. Clare couldn't believe how old the gray hair made her look. She stopped dyeing it *butterscotch* three months ago when the symptoms started. Before drifting further into the abyss of self-disgust, she forced herself to get back to the task at hand.

Think about.

She tossed the jewelry tray in the think-about pile, with the only other item being the baseball from Caleb's game-winning homerun in the 1994 New York State Little League Championship game. Clare yawned as she struggled to pick herself up off the floor. She was so tired. So very, very tired.

Her sleep problems had slowly transformed from a once-a-month nuisance to full-fledged insomnia. Clare had tried every natural method Lilly Langston suggested: spritzing her pillow with lavender, dabbing ylang-ylang behind each earlobe, and leaving a chamomile-soaked cotton ball on her nightstand. Nothing worked. It was another sign of her body telling her something was wrong.

As much as she tried not looking, Clare glanced at the oak, swan-neck grandfather clock (*Keep*) to check the time.

She had convinced herself if 8:30 came and went without getting a phone call, then all the worrying and all the preplanning were for naught. The office opened at 7:00, and she specifically asked Dr. Kincaid to call her immediately with her lab results. She figured an hour and a half was plenty of time for her to be contacted. And, quite frankly, after her meltdown during her appointment last week, she figured they would certainly have the courtesy to call her first thing.

Only three hours to go.

Clare sipped the black coffee from her "I'd Rather be in Maui" mug (*Throw Out*), pushed up the beige roman shades (*Think About*), and peeked out the bay window to see the For Sale sign shrouded in snow on the front lawn. It was hard to believe that after more than sixty years, she was in the final few weeks of calling this place home. The nostalgia began catching up with her, and she wondered, *Am I overreacting? Am I really that sick?* before reminding herself that it wasn't time to start second-guessing.

She repeated her daily mantra in her head: *Listen to your body. It's smarter than you.*

As weird as it was to think about leaving, she was at peace with the thought of moving on. Like most neighborhoods in Buffalo, the Montgomerys lived in a cluster of postwar Cape Cods and ranches, all with very similar styles both inside and out. Clare remembered being a little girl, walking home from school and counting out the nine different styles of homes that existed. Their neighborhood—and several surrounding neighborhoods—were all designed by the contractor team of Wendel & Brackensack, leaving very little variety within a six-mile radius.

Their home on Parker Avenue had been in the family for two generations, and it was truly an architectural prize, not falling into the Wendel & Brackensack pattern. Built in 1954 as a model home by the Canadian architect Pierre-Paul Gagnon, he had hoped to bring his modernistic style to the streets of Western New York. According to Clare's mother, no local contractors appreciated the peculiar design, and after sitting vacant for two years, Gagnon sold it himself...to her father.

Every room, and nearly every detail in every room, had a level of uniqueness Clare had not come across anywhere else. From the moment anyone stepped in the house, so many distinct things stood out. There was the massive stained-glass hanging lantern in the foyer, which reflected fragments of blues, yellows, and pinks with every sunrise. There was the open and inviting sunken living room, the curved wall in the kitchen, the pantry under the stairs, the library complete with rolling wooden ladder—to name a few.

Even the backyard was a suburban sanctuary: a private retreat with flowering dogwoods and tulip trees serving as a lush barrier on all three sides, which Clare admired every summer afternoon with a glass of strawberry lemonade while sitting on the slate herringbone patio. Relaxing underneath the cedar pergola lined with morning glories while the kids played with Cocoa were the moments she missed more than anything.

As Clare's brain overflowed with more memories than she wanted, the sight of glaring headlights pulling up the driveway snapped her back to reality.

Clare slid lightly in her pink moccasin slippers (*Keep*) as she shuffled to the side door, swinging it open to see Cassie and Jared, who looked even better in person.

"Cass?" Clare asked with a confused smile. "What are you doing here?"

Clare was never good at keeping secrets from her only daughter, so it was fitting that the plan to quietly sell the house backfired. She told Cass it was simply time to get a smaller space, deciding it'd be better to discuss the underlying health issues at a later time.

"It's just too much," she said. "Shoveling, yard work, the little repairs. I can't handle it by myself anymore."

It was only partly true. The things Clare used to love were suddenly no longer fun. She'd pinched her sciatic nerve this past summer while picking cherry tomatoes from the vegetable garden, leaving her unable to walk and couch-bound for three days. She assumed it was a fluke, but her body betrayed her again in the fall, when she pulled the same nerve on the same side as she composted and mulched the garden in preparation for winter.

Never one to rush to judgment, Cassie handled the news better than Clare had expected. There were tears, of course, but Cassie wasn't angry and seemed to understand Clare's semi-truthful reasoning. It probably helped that she was distracted, still riding the high of her return to Western New York—a topic Clare was ready to steer the conversation toward.

"Cass, honey, I'm so proud of you. You're finally home!"

Cassie and Clare gave Jared a quick tour of the house, explaining the now and then of every room. The three made their way back into Cassie's old room, where the monumental mess had taken over nearly every square inch.

"What happened?" Cassie asked, pointing to the piles of rubble.

"I'm, you know, organizing! Figuring out what to pack with what," Clare lied. "Getting rid of a few things that I don't need anymore."

There was no need to tell Cassie that a "few" things meant eight full garbage bags. Clare noticed Cassie intently scanning the heaps of Montgomery family relics.

"Oh my God, Beatrice," Cassie said, holding up her childhood teddy bear. "Wait, you're keeping this, right?"

Cassie handed Clare the jewelry tray. Clare grabbed it from her and smiled quickly while lifting her eyebrows halfheartedly. She figured the facial expression was an ambiguous non-answer that would suffice for now.

"And what will you be doing here in Buffalo?" Clare asked, turning toward Jared.

"Well, Mrs. Mont—" he started.

"Ah-ah-ah." Clare cut him off, shaking her finger at him like she was talking to a toddler. Jared had already called her Mrs. Montgomery twice, and Clare warned him the third strike would not sit well with her.

"Sorry! Clare! I promise I'll remember that from here on out," Jared said. He fake frowned and then burst into enthusiastic laughter, showing off his brilliant white teeth. "I'm a psychiatrist working on an interim basis at Buffalo General Hospital with a doctor in their inpatient unit. Fingers crossed it all goes well and becomes permanent."

Clare looked at the elated couple and, for the first time in months, actual happiness swelled inside her. Here she was plotting her end of days, while her beautiful daughter seemed to only be beginning hers. A new job in Niagara Falls, working with children who needed every ounce of help and attention she loved to give. A new boyfriend who was a gentleman in every sense of the word: handsome, polite, intelligent, and kind. He seemed almost too good to be true.

The clang of the phone ringing shot through her ears. Her heart sank, then suddenly started racing. She had been so focused on Cassie's unexpected return home she had lost track of the time.

7:37.

She bolted out of the room and ran back to the kitchen. Startled and slightly out of breath, she realized she still was clutching the jewelry tray in her left hand.

Throw out.

Clare grabbed the phone on the fourth ring, right before the answering machine picked up.

"Hello?"

Three: Abram

He didn't know if it was adrenaline or pheromones, but Abram's elation at Cassie's return to Buffalo stayed with him the entire day, even as Vitality turned into its usual beginning-of-the-year nuthouse.

He grabbed his keys and bounced out of his office to the beat of a P!nk song blaring through the speakers, feeling a small sense of pride as he passed the row of treadmills, each one occupied by someone with a look of fierce determination and satisfaction. For the first time in a long time, Abram was reminded of why he opened the gym in the first place. He found it funny how that notion snuck up on him, especially considering how bitter he had been at the start of the day.

Leave it to Cassandra Montgomery to make life meaningful again. His daylong good mood only gained momentum as she pulled up in her mom's car. She had texted him earlier, asking if they could find time to "talk alone", and with the snow still falling, albeit lightly, Abe asked if she could pick him up from the gym.

"Sassy Cassie," Abe said as he jumped into the passenger seat.

"Abe, my babe," she replied.

Immediately, Abe sensed something was wrong. Cassie notoriously wore her heart on her sleeve, her face never able to hide her true emotions. She currently looked infuriated and indignant with a touch of melancholy in her eyes. He tried to guess the situation that was annoying her and settled on Clare saying something inappropriate to Jared or vice versa. Abe reclined the seat slightly and started an internal dialogue on how he would talk her off the ledge. As much as he loved Cassie, she constantly overreacted and transformed only slightly bad situations into doomsday scenarios.

"What's going on?" he asked.

"My mom's selling the house." Cassie sighed.

"No way!"

Embarrassed by his thoughts, Abe cringed as Cassie's expression turned even more forlorn. Their house was as much a part of his life as his own.

Clare Montgomery was like a second mother to Abe: the mom who watched them after school, the one who picked them up from all their late-night shenanigans, and unlike his own parents, she actually expressed interest in Abe's personal life.

"It's just so unlike her," Cassie said. "It's weird enough that she's selling the house, but then to do it without telling me or Caleb? I don't get it. Something is definitely up with her."

Abe sensed Cassie was internally seething. He wished he had made some sort of effort to see or talk to Mrs. Montgomery after she stopped coming to Pilates class in the late summer.

"Where is she moving to?" Abe asked.

"I don't know. She didn't tell me anything!" Cass wailed, her tears welling up. "She said we'll talk over dinner tonight. But, she's already packed, like, *everything* in the house."

Abe couldn't believe it. The Montgomery house was a landmark in town. He thought for sure the gem would never leave the family.

"I have absolutely no idea what's going on, but now we're fucked for a place to stay," Cassie said. "Jared's out looking at some duplex for rent, but it's in the south towns area and I cannot deal with that commute."

He looked over at his best friend and put his left hand on her forearm.

"Cassie."

"Abe."

"Cassie," he said again, in a long drawn-out pitch that got higher as he extended her name. "You know you don't have to ask."

"Abe. No. We can't."

"Cassie. Yes. You will."

Abe's generosity stemmed from his parents, who never failed to provide him with anything and everything he never asked for. They bought his first car, paid for his college tuition, and helped with the down payment of his house. Even every little stop over to his parents' house ended with the same questions: "You need blueberries? How about apples? What else was I going to give you? You need paper towels?"

The two sat in silence on the way back to his house, except for Cassie's soft, pitiful sniffling. She pulled into Abe's driveway and put the car in park. He wondered how a decade had passed without the two of them missing a beat. How so much had changed in their lives, but so little had changed between them.

"I'll go get keys made for you guys," Abe said. "I only have two conditions. You have to cook healthy dinners three times a week," he said, opening the car door.

"Deal. What's the other one?"

"You won't get mad when Jared falls in love with me and dumps you." He kissed Cassie on the forehead, exited the car, and sauntered up the driveway, feeling euphoric about his best friend—and his mojo—finally being back in his life.

Once inside, he busied himself with finding everything he needed for dinner: stir-fry. With his head stuck in the refrigerator crisper, Abe failed to realize his cell phone had been ringing until the high-pitched ding of a voice-mail notification interrupted his vision of sautéed chicken and vegetables. Abe clicked play on the message and put the phone on speaker as he bounced around the kitchen and riffled through a cupboard for his cutting board.

"Abram Hoffman, this is Daniel McGee. I hope all is well in your world. Can you give me a call back when you get this message? I know it's been a while since we've talked, but there's an opening within my administration I'd like to discuss with you. Hope to hear from you soon."

Abram stopped cutting his green bell pepper and stood dumbfounded. He hastily deleted the message and returned to preparing his dinner, each slice of the pepper producing more questions in his head.

Why now? Why me? Abe grew irrationally angry.

It was one thing to be solicited by Mayor McGee for a potential job opening. It was another to hear his booming voice, which jolted through Abe like a distant, haunted memory he promised never to think about again.

Four: Clare

Clare never learned her lesson when it came to packing. A go-getting overachiever, she constantly had to dig through things she already put away, even if it was for something as simple as a weekend road trip. That night she searched the basement's throw-out pile for her ceramic Dutch oven and blue-and-green paisley cushions for the dining room table chairs because of dinner with Cassie and Jared. What should have been a celebratory dinner for Cassie's new job would undoubtedly be a depressing way to kick off her return home. But she needed to know the truth about Clare's health and her future.

Her plan, admittedly not entirely vetted to her usual standards, was to move into Brighton Towers, the senior-living complex on Fries Rd. The recently remodeled façade caught her eye every time Clare drove by and led her to think, *That would be a nice place to grow old.* She saw elderly women watering flowers on their balconies and elderly men playing tennis on the courts while on her tour of the grounds, so her expectations for the actual apartment were high. Too high. The units were dreary (with very little natural light), small (like a tiny hotel room with a space that acted as a shared kitchen/dinette) and bland (the walls, carpet, blinds all a shade of off-white).

That would be nice place to grow old turned into *This would be a sad place to die.*

But she signed the lease anyway, with a move-in date of February 1, choosing the month-to-month option, obviously.

Clare didn't expect to tell Cassie the news in person, but after the earlier silence on the issue of her health, she knew it had to be done. Clare panicked about the lack of rehearsal time. As she made Cassie's favorite meal—chicken cordon bleu and mashed potatoes with the skins still on—she flipped through the pages of an imaginary script in her head.

"We need to talk" sounded a bit too nonchalant. *"I'm sick"* didn't have enough thoughtfulness behind it. Clare felt bad enough about springing the news about the house on Cassie and knew it would be even worse after delivering a double whammy.

This week last year, she and Charlie had been on the shores of New Smyrna Beach, Florida, celebrating thirty-eight years of marriage. It was phase one of Charlie's plan to start appreciating retirement and taking back control of his life. After spending so many years dedicating any free time to work, Clare had been so happy he'd finally seemed to be allowing his personal life to blossom. Their final night there, Charlie drew a "C + C" with a heart around it in the sand, a memory that would forever be burned into Clare's brain. She never thought watching the tide washing his creation away under a lilac sunset would serve as the omen of what they were about to face.

People always joked she and Charlie couldn't live without each other. And now, as Clare began fighting her own battle, she assumed this was her beautiful fate wrapped in the cruelest of circumstances.

Clare steered her mind back to the dilemma of the day. She decided to wing the conversation once dinner started. She had never, ever, been one to wing it, but things had changed. The Clare of yesteryear disappeared months ago, the final shreds of that strong woman hanging on feebly.

She opened the oven to check the temperature of the chicken. The hot steam hit her face, covering her glasses in condensation. As Clare stood to wipe her lenses, she noted the scent filling the kitchen, the smell so potent she floated back to the first time she had made this meal. It was the spring of 1986, right after Charlie got his promotion at Buffalo Savings Bank. With an influx of cash, the two decided it would be best if Clare stayed home and watched the kids until they both were in school full time, instead of working part-time at the bakery in Super Duper, the local grocery store.

Clare relished her time as a stay-at-home mom, finding no faults with being a devoted housewife and mother—except when it came to her skills in the kitchen. Ask her to bake something, anything, and Clare had no trouble. She could whip up a bundt cake or batches of cookies and cupcakes in an instant, each with the perfect crumb and consistency. But to cook an actual meal was an entirely different, disastrous story.

Shortly after she stopped working, she found a recipe box of her grandmother's index cards in plastic sleeves, full of meals no longer in the spectrum of edibility like liver and onions and boiled beef with turnips. Among the pile of questionable meals stood the chicken cordon bleu index card. Through the flowery cursive handwriting, Clare felt as if her grandmother was in the kitchen with her, holding her hand every step of the way, the precise instructions and attention to detail exactly what she needed. Charlie and the kids requested that meal at least three times a month, and to this day, that chicken cordon bleu still reigned supreme as her signature meal.

Thirty years later, she still felt like it was 1986, expecting Caleb to show up any second and start playing with a Matchbox car at the kitchen table. Clare stood static, looking around at the empty and lifeless space before her. The celestial sounds of Cass saying, "Mommy, I want to help" while tugging on her apron resonated in her ears. It was a simpler, happier time back then. A time she didn't cherish in the moment. A time she would do anything to relive just for one day.

Clare blinked and caught herself by surprise as unanticipated tears fell slowly down her cheeks in unison.

"Mom? Are you crying?"

Through the side door came Cassie and Jared, walking inside in the nick of time to see Clare wipe her tears away on her sleeve.

"Honey," Clare said, contemplating whether or not to blurt out the truth. "I burned myself on the pan."

Each scrape of their fork and knife against the miscellaneous china sliced through the air with a ferocity of a screaming banshee. The dinner had quickly become a bizarre affair, like a bad first date where intermittent talking filled the gaps between long, awkward pauses.

Clare disappointed herself for not being able to spark long-lasting conversations or ask meaningful follow-up questions. She had already asked them to repeat the story of how they met (working as volunteers for the City of Charlotte Animal Shelter) and what Jared's family was like (divorced parents who still talked to each other, three sisters and one brother, all still living in North Carolina). She had always managed to feign interest in any conversation she found herself in, a personality trait she was proud of. But tonight she felt off, partially because of having to talk about the elephant in the room, partially because of the actual effects of the elephant in the room.

Moving home? *I'm selling the house.* New job? *I'm dying.*

With the small talk dwindling, she knew the time had come.

"You guys, I have some bad news." *Really?* That was the exact phrase she had wanted to avoid using, but in the spirit of spontaneity, she let herself continue after spewing it unwillingly. "I haven't been feeling well lately and Dr. Kincaid said there's a small chance it could be something serious."

Lie Number One. There was a big chance this could be something serious.

Cassie, in midchew, stared blankly at her with a frozen expression, while Jared placed his fork down gently and sat back, staring through Clare as if he were seeking more information by peering directly into her brain. Both stayed silent long enough to fill the room with an extra level of unpleasantness.

"I have to have more tests done to determine what's been causing my issues."

"Oh my God, Mom. What issues? Are you okay?" Cassie finally managed, the gravity of the situation catching up to her.

"I don't know." Clare sighed. "The doctors don't know yet either."

Clare explained the morning's phone call from her doctor's office. "The lab work came back inconclusive." Clare had already made an appointment for a second blood test two days from then and rescheduled a follow-up appointment with Dr. Kincaid.

"Clare, if something were that wrong with you, it would definitely have shown up in your blood work," Jared chimed in.

She suspected he meant to say that in a supportive, soothing tone, but it came across as domineering.

"Well, that's why I'm going back," Clare said calmly. "So we can hopefully find some answers."

"How long have you been feeling sick?" Cassie asked, her eyes slowly bugging out of her head.

"Almost two months. It started getting really bad after Thanksgiving," Clare said.

Lie Number Two. Everything had started the end of September. First, it was the fatigue. The ridiculous, out-of-this-world, more-than-just-tired tiredness. Then it was the joint stiffness, the on-and-off fevers, the headaches, and the night sweats. She had honestly thought it was a regular old cold. Every year without fail, she could mark the week on the calendar when she would get sick as summer sailed away and the first signs of fall appeared. Only this year, the symptoms intensified.

Cassie started to speak, and Clare could see the fire on her breath.

"Mom, why didn't you tell me sooner?" Cassie said, each word coming out of her mouth louder and more rapid than the last.

"I was waiting for the right time," Clare said, proud of herself for telling a truth.

"What's even wrong, Clare? Is it a tumor? A disease? Have you had X-rays? An MRI?" Jared asked.

Even though he was a doctor, Clare didn't appreciate the line of questions Jared threw at her.

"Has your doctor given you any indication of what could be wrong?" he asked. "I mean, they had to have given you some sort of idea."

Clare had enough of his dismissive attitude. *Who are you to tell me how I'm feeling?*

"You're making me feel like I'm on trial here, Jared," she snapped. "If I knew what the hell was wrong with me, I'd tell you."

"I'm sorry," he said genuinely. "I only want to make sure you get the help you need."

Cassie stood up from her chair and hugged Clare, her gentle sobs muffled in the nape of Clare's neck.

"Oh, honey, don't cry. It'll be okay. I'll be fine," Clare said.

Lie Number Three.

Five: Harris

Harris expected the queasy, nervous feeling to be fast and fleeting, but instead, it sat stuck in his gut, intensifying by the minute.

This shouldn't be happening. He laughed at the ambiguity of his thoughts.

Being in the spotlight was somewhere Harris had been a thousand times before with his dad: press conferences, inaugurations, public ceremonies, ribbon cuttings. Mayor Daniel McGee never turned down an opportunity to show his face and always—*always*—found an opportunity to parade his family around for the cameras.

Growing up with someone who was a part-time parent and full-time politician meant being "on" at all times, expecting everyday situations to inevitably turn into a media opportunity. Harris had learned that lesson on his tenth birthday, a Saturday morning in August when his parents rented out the local batting cages for his party. Harris distinctly recalled several television news crews showing up in the middle of the party to interview his dad about a piece of proposed legislation on noise ordinances or zoning regulations or something stupid and boring that totally could have waited.

Harris spent the morning patiently watching and cheering on all of his friends during their chance at bat before he finally walked into the cage, put on his helmet, and stepped into the batter's box. He couldn't wait to show everyone his new and improved swing. But after hitting a few balls—all of which would have certainly been home runs—he turned around to see everyone clamoring for a chance to be in the background of his dad's interview. He remembered that sinking feeling as neither his friends nor his father seemed to care how he hit.

It happened as he yelled out to the group to redirect their attention back to him. Harris could still hear the sound of the ball cracking his nose. He could still hear the screaming cries of his friends and the frantic shouting of the other parents as he was being carried away by his father, who was running with him to a patch of grass next to the parking lot. And, of course, he remembered three gigantic video cameras hovering above him, the bright-red light of the record button overshadowing the bright-red blood oozing from his face.

In the end, it wasn't even a big deal. It was just bloody. But it would have never happened had his dad been a lawyer or an accountant or something normal. More than twenty years later, he was still sour over everything that had happened that day.

At least at the end of that torture, he had gotten a hug from his mom.

God, I wish she was still here.

Despite his definite comfort in front of a crowd, Harris never had an event quite like the one before him. And as much as he didn't want to be there, he knew it was his duty as a son.

Well, as a gay son. There was no way in hell his father would ever ask Ethan or Tim to give this speech.

Dan McGee was moments away from being honored as the Buffalo Pride Center's Ally of the Year. Thinking about that title made Harris shake his head with slight befuddlement. It stung to see his dad rewarded for his support of the LGBTQ community when, really, he had never been supportive of Harris.

The introductory speech stipulations were basic, but strict: no more than five minutes and mention how the recipient was an ally to you. The time wouldn't be an issue. The sincerity of his message? That was a different story.

Harris toyed with the idea of incorporating the true stories of his father's past into the speech. He wanted to mention how he constantly heard his dad say, "Hey, fella!" in an exaggerated falsetto every time a character of questionable sexuality was on TV. Or the time in college when he called Harris's first boyfriend "lover boy" to his face the moment they met each other. Or the moment this past Christmas when Harris implied he wanted children while he was holding his new niece, Abigail. "Good luck with that," he'd heard his dad mumble under his breath. The list went on and on. And on.

He snickered at the prospective aftermath in the crowd if he dropped these truth bombs: murmurs galore, followed by everyone stunned, sitting with their mouths agape.

Harris reminded himself to be happy his dad asked him to give this speech. After all, his father finally had done something other than ignore his sexuality. Still, he couldn't help thinking that his invite to the gala was simply a tactic in pandering to the political left ahead of the looming battle against Darryl Samuelson, his likely New York State Senate opponent.

As his knees knocked lightly together, Harris felt his phone buzz for what had to be the seventh time in two minutes—a sign that his latest tweet had struck gold. There was no time to check his notifications, though, as the show was about to begin. Standing halfway behind the black stage curtain, he stared at his father, who returned the look with his patented and renowned wink-smile combo.

Harris reminded himself that his dad was a good guy. And this *was* a big deal. By winning this award, his dad would become the first African-American to receive the honor in its thirty-year history. And though he had his faults, he had done a lot for the gay community as a whole. Daniel McGee supported gay marriage in New York before it became legal, strengthened punishments for hate crimes in the city, and pushed the visitor's bureau to encourage LGBTQ-friendly businesses in order to brand Buffalo as a "gay-friendly" destination for travel and tourism.

The crowd inside the Buffalo Marriott politely applauded as Harris walked up to the microphone, feeling anxious yet confident, thanks to his new Armani suit. He cleared his throat, still unsure of exactly what he was going to say.

Here goes nothing.

"I know many of you in this room will agree with me when I say growing up gay wasn't easy," Harris started, feeling the focus of the crowd shift solely in on him. "In my mind, I never had an ally."

It was true. His dad wasn't his ally. His dad was barely a dad. But tonight wasn't about Dan McGee's parenting skills. And Harris knew if his father had any shot of winning the state senate seat next year, he needed to get the positive momentum started.

"Instead, I was lucky enough to have a dad, who accepted me with open arms the moment I decided to accept myself."

Feeling tipsy after his fourth whiskey and ginger, Harris floated around the ballroom, mingling with everyone and anyone who would talk to him. He felt loose and free and unexpectedly loquacious. It was probably the hard liquor, which he never drank and only chose tonight for fear of stained red lips resulting from his preferred Pinot Noir. Nevertheless, Harris was pleasantly surprised by how pleasantly surprising the night had become.

The crowd had loved his speech, the bacon-wrapped scallops were delicious, and there was plenty of eye candy to scope out, including Alan Smith, the Pride Center's PR and Communications guru. The two had had some flirty email exchanges before the event, and Harris loved that the tone was matched in person.

Alan wasn't exactly his type; a little too skinny, a tad too old. But he was incredibly nice and the two had a very chummy rapport, making small talk about the night's event, the weather and, of course, men.

"I'm not really dating anyone right now," Harris said, feeling only a tinge of guilt for Grant and Kenneth, the two guys he was actually dating right then.

"Well, I'm not surprised," Alan said. "I hear you're keeping busy doing some nice work on the East Side."

It might have taken thirty-three years, but people were finally starting to take him seriously. Harris was rocketing up the ladder of importance at Beautify Buffalo, the grassroots organization he had been working with since the summer. He'd quickly become known as someone who wouldn't stop until the job was done. The only reason? He couldn't leave anything unfinished. It physically made him sick to see a half-painted room or a kitchen without a completed backsplash.

His official title was Landscape Coordinator, but after many long days, nights, weekends, and holidays doing work when no one else did, Harris was put in charge of the East Side Renaissance Project. The project was ambitious, but not out of reach. Beautify Buffalo had raised enough money to buy vacant properties being sold by the city on the East Side and, in turn, would pay to demolish the run-down homes and build new, affordable housing. The simplicity in the plan should have been a no-brainer for approval.

Instead, since they were all at least 100 years old, the city council voted to temporarily classify the homes on William Street as historical landmarks. Councilman Chris Coyle called the preservation effort "an opportunity to reestablish the area as a preeminent neighborhood," but everyone recognized this was an irrational and uneducated decision. For every dozen homes on the East Side that were vacant, there was maybe one—two, tops—that could actually be rehabbed into something livable.

The double buzz of a text message vibrated against his thigh. Harris's phone had been going off all night, but he couldn't exactly whip it out and check it without feeling rude. He split with Alan and headed to the bar, where he bumped into Ronald Young, the city's commissioner.

"Hey, Mr. Young," Harris said.

"I saw your latest tweet, Harris," Ron said indignantly. "You've got some nerve."

Harris didn't have time for this. He smiled politely, grabbed his drink, and then maneuvered through the crowd to join his father at their table. Everyone at Beautify Buffalo understood that a groundswell of public support for their demolition plan would be key for everything to come to fruition—and it was a task Harris gladly accepted.

He had spent the past three weeks taking pictures of the abandoned houses and posting them online. The conditions of the houses were laughable; most were decades removed from anything salvageable. It became quite evident as the pictures spread that the general public recognized the audacity of the city's plan, and so it came as no surprise that the city council scheduled a special hearing on this issue for the following day.

Harris had returned to the East Side right before the gala, determined to make a big impact the night before the hearing. He decided to change his tactic a bit once he saw the eyesore near the corner of William and Clinton. Harris noticed the side door slightly ajar, and took the opportunity to sneak inside. After all, it was one thing to see desecration from the outside, seeing it from the interior took it to a whole different level.

Walking inside, Harris had guessed the home was newly vacated. It proved to be every bit as wretched as he expected: tattered curtains covering cracked windows, exposed plumbing in the kitchen, brown UFO-shaped water stains all over the drywall and carpet. He swore he even heard something crawling in the walls. Rats, most likely. Harris snapped a few pictures on his phone and was slightly disappointed that the rotten odor of the house didn't come across in the photos.

When tweeting, he chose his words carefully, trying to be as scathing and powerful as possible.

Is this really worth saving?

He found the wording biting and brilliant.

The vibration of an incoming phone call coincided with someone he didn't know ending a story on something he wasn't paying attention to. Harris had stopped listening when he caught the eye of a waiter with a jawline for days. He excused himself and slipped into the hallway. The call was from his coworker Brad.

"Hey, man, I'm bus—" Harris whispered, before being cut off.

"Dude. Where the hell have you been? You're going viral," Brad said.

"Good! About time!"

"No, it's not good. Somebody fucking lived in that house," Brad said sternly.

"What?"

"That picture you tweeted? Somebody lived there. You broke into someone's house. Channel 3 just ran a story about Mayor McGee's son breaking and entering in a pathetic attempt to defy the city council. It's blowing up!"

Shit.

Brad kept speaking as Harris instinctively rushed to the end of the hallway and down the stairs.

"They interviewed the woman who owns the house. She's a single mother, a nurse's aide at Children's Hospital. She was crying. Dude, it's so bad. Samuelson tweeted about it, too."

He hung up on Brad and escaped outside, pressing himself against the cold red brick with his head in his hands. The wind lashed against him, giving a brief reprieve from the sudden hot flash he was experiencing. His head and stomach spun. His vision blurred. He didn't know if it was the liquor, a side effect of the sudden news, or a combination of both.

Harris stood on the stoop of the hotel's side entrance for the next five minutes, trying to grasp everything in his mind. His brain refused to cooperate, his thoughts uncontrolled, like the ice cubes in his whiskey and gingers: sinking, floating, overlapping, crashing together, evaporating.

How did this happen?

When his phone buzzed for the zillionth time, he willfully chucked it on the icy concrete.

He didn't even look down to see its shattered remains glittering in the snow. He stood unfazed, staring straight out across a half-frozen Lake Erie, hoping and searching for a hug from his mom that he knew wasn't coming.

Six: Abram

First impressions meant nothing to Abram. Well, not nothing. But he always naïvely assumed that everyone was a good person no matter what initial thoughts popped into his head. He preferred waiting until the second, third, and fourth impressions before truly identifying how he felt about someone.

But not for Jared. Not at all. Jared's strong first impression turned out to be no fluke. From the moment he stepped into the gym, Abram had known what a remarkable soul he possessed. The man was flawless. It wasn't merely the obvious, outward character traits that Abe adored. Yes, Jared was a handsome doctor who was friendly and humble with good manners. But he was also detail-oriented, confident, and gentle—internal qualities Abe had observed in the week since Cassie and Jared moved into his house.

Thirty-two years old and living with two roommates. Now that was something Abram had never believed would happen. But he would do anything for Cassie, especially when tears were involved. He kept picturing that mascara-stained face when she'd shown up at his door after finding out Clare was sick. He could still hear her gasping for air as she struggled to speak.

Poor Cassie. No. Poor Mrs. Montgomery.

Her recent round of tests had come back inconclusive, but Cassie mentioned that didn't make things any easier.

"It only delays any treatment from starting," Cassie said, before mentioning her mother had become even more intent on selling the house. The two had spent many hours that week cleaning and prepping for this weekend's open house, where Mrs. Montgomery hoped to personally choose the lucky successors to the renowned family home.

Cassie had promised Abram this new roommate arrangement would be temporary. "A few weeks at most."

The situation wasn't ideal in the slightest for Abe. His three-bedroom, one-bathroom ranch didn't exactly lend itself to three adults. The two of them had so much: boxes and books and more boxes and clothes and bigger boxes. And despite their best efforts to stay tidy, Cassie and Jared's randomly scattered stuff around the house had begun to bug Abe.

He couldn't find the diplomatic way to tell Cassie it was annoying how she left her coffee mug in the sink before going to work for the day or how to tell Jared there was room for his shoes in the closet, and he didn't have to leave them at the side door entrance.

The structured, rigid routines Abe had built for himself throughout the day were also slipping away. With two roommates, there was no opportunity to blast Demi Lovato at 4:00 a.m. before work to pump himself up and no more privacy for a nightly yoga session and bath to wind him down—three things he desperately missed.

His selfishness scared him. Abe reminded himself that these two just uprooted their lives and were living out of boxes.

Congratulations, Abe. You're an asshole.

To combat his egocentric mindset, Abe left work early to visit his parents, whom he hadn't seen nor talked to since Christmas. Rich and Patty Hoffman had moved from the suburbs of Buffalo to "the country" six years ago. The hour drive to their house in the tiny town of Pomfret was filled with peaks and valleys along Route 20, small corner stores and family-owned restaurants occasionally lining the way. They'd moved because they wanted "more land and more privacy"—something he didn't quite understand but accepted.

Walking into their new house always felt a little off. For almost thirty years, the only home Abe had known was the one he grew up in back in Tonawanda. Their new place stood on almost two acres of land and held a much more cozy and woodsy vibe in its interior. This time around, Abe quickly heard the booming sounds of cable news from the TV in the living room and the shuffle of his mom's slippers down the hallway.

"Abey!" his mom roared, her gusto always providing a little boost to Abram's mood.

Abram never felt the power of mortality quite like he did when seeing his parents. Each time they looked a little older—grayer hair, their skin starting to sag. Their attitudes had shifted slightly too. The Hoffmans used to take weekly Sunday jaunts around Western New York, which had turned biweekly a few years ago and bimonthly in the last year. It's not as if Abe didn't expect this. Their incredible pace as forty- and fifty-somethings was admirable; his parents took road trips regularly, visiting places like Watkins Glen, Presque Isle, Put-in-Bay, and every other hidden gem they could find within a five-hour drive. It was exhausting to Abe. He couldn't imagine how exhausting it was to them! Time and age weren't on their side, but at least his mom still had her patented enthusiastic attitude.

"Hi, Mom," Abe said, giving her a brief but meaningful hug.

"How are you doing? Want anything to eat?"

"I'm good! And no food for me, thanks," Abe replied. "Hey, guess who moved back."

His mom picked up her wineglass off the counter, took a sip of her Chardonnay, and shouted, "Paula Rizzo!" as if Abe had any idea who Paula Rizzo was.

"No. Cassie!"

"Cassie Montgomery? That's great news, how is she doing?"

"She's good. She got a job as a teacher in Niagara Falls. But, her mom is sick."

"Oh no. Cancer?"

"They don't know yet."

"Clare's a smoker, isn't she?"

"No, I don't think so," Abe said, wishing that the answer to Mrs. Montgomery's problem was that easy to diagnose. "She's selling their house too."

"Oh, God, she's going to make a fortune, because that house is gorgeous. That makes sense, though. What the hell does she need that giant house for? She's all alone."

"Would you give up that house?"

"I wouldn't want to, but I wouldn't be able to handle it by myself, that's for sure."

"Yeah, I think she finally realized that after Charlie died. Anyway, Cassie moved here with her boyfriend Jared, and they're going to live with me temporarily."

"Why the hell are you going to let them live with you?" his father chimed in from the recliner in the living room.

"Hi, Dad. It's only temporary."

"That's nice of you, sweetie. But we all know how you are with roommates."

His mother gave him the eye, insinuating that Abe wouldn't be able to handle living with two other people. He didn't argue. Living with people never had been his strong suit, but he wanted to believe things would be different this time around. He was older, wiser, and had learned not to sweat the small stuff.

"What's new with you guys?" Abe asked, determined to listen to everything they had to say and stay engaged. He had the habit of immediately daydreaming during every conversation he started with his mom, who would casually babble through a series of topics, populating each story with facts Abe wasn't sure were true.

But, this day was different. He grabbed a glass from the cupboard, filled it with water, and sat down at the kitchen table.

"Did you hear about Anna Delmonte's plastic surgery?" his mom said.

Abe didn't really care. He didn't really want to hear it. But he smiled back at his mom—a real genuine smile—thankful that he even had the option of listening to her tell one of her ridiculous stories.

"No! She had plastic surgery? Tell me everything."

An unusual feeling filled Abe as he exited the highway and made his way back into his neighborhood. Truthfully, he hadn't been this happy in years. The minute Cass had returned home, something potent ignited inside him. A charge had developed within him—like he finally had a purpose—and he vowed to remember that fact every time a random mug or shoe irritated him.

The week since Cass and Abe's reunion had been filled with every emotion imaginable. Joy over Cass returning home, excitement for her new job, fear for a sick Clare, incomprehension over seeing her childhood home up for sale. Abe found it fitting that after ten years apart, adulthood had forced the two of them to quickly realize that life in their thirties was nothing like life in their twenties. No bottle of Riesling or episode of *Grey's Anatomy* could delay the inevitable.

Abe had even started inadvertently marking milestones in his head for the first time they did something together as roommates. Tonight, the trio sat around Their First Fire, masterfully assembled by Jared, having just finished Their First Homemade Dinner of roasted rosemary Cornish hens with wild mushroom, potato, and artichoke ragout. All expertly made by Jared, of course.

Abram felt a bit foolish, fawning over an unattainable man like this. He repeatedly dismissed his blossoming crush as harmless, equivalent to how teenage girls feel about Justin Bieber. Yet, he wasn't dismissing the fact that the barbed wire around his heart had suddenly loosened with the addition of Jared into his daily life.

Outside, the quintessential Buffalo winter night took shape, with the snow's fat flakes falling in a slow, steady pace, draping everything in glistening white. The three sat in silence, as Jared glided his fingers across the keys of his piano.

Of course Jared plays the piano.

Abe couldn't be happier hearing the piano finally come alive. Ever since they hauled it into the house, he had been dying to see Jared in action. Abram and Cassie looked at each other, smiling. Abram deliberately directed his eyes at Jared and then back at Cassie, before arching his right eyebrow and slowly mouthing the words "he's perfect" to her.

"He's mine," she mouthed back.

Cass and Abe laughed, causing Jared to abruptly stop in the middle of a flawless rendition of "Always on My Mind."

"Keep playing, babe," Cassie instructed.

Perhaps an effect of what was happening with her mom, Cassie had towed out one of her plastic bins in an attempt to start organizing. This one included mounds of old pictures that stretched all the way back to middle school. Abe shuddered as he sifted through photos of the most awkward moments of his life. He hated looking back at times when he was shoved deep in the closet, with his long mushroom-cut parted in the middle and his oversized clothing hanging off his gangly frame.

"That hat! I love that hat," Cassie said, interrupting his self-loathing thoughts. "Why don't you ever wear it anymore?"

She handed Abe a picture of the two of them—a selfie before it was called a "selfie"—walking through a winter wonderland in Delaware Park. Abe had on his patchwork newsboy hat, which was from his it's-so-ugly-I-can-pull-it-off collection. Even now, he still enjoyed the alternating leather and khaki twill wedges.

"He still has it," Abe replied.

Cassie winced. She knew they didn't talk about *him*. Abe was never going to be okay talking about *him*.

A cartoony whistle to the tune of "Don't Worry, Be Happy" emerged from Cassie's phone and filtered through Jared's piano playing.

"It's my mom, sorry," Cassie said and then answered her phone and walked into the kitchen.

Abe wished he could be more communicative with her about her mom. He couldn't quite find the right words to convince her that everything would be fine. Truthfully, he didn't even believe everything would be fine and didn't want to lie to her face.

Jared stopped playing and exhaled loudly as he stood up from his position at the piano. He flashed his killer, sexy smile at Abe. "Abram, do you mind helping me out? I need an extra set of hands."

Sounds X-rated.

Jared pointed to the nail beds on his left hand, which were bruised and caked with dried blood.

"Oh my God, what happened?" Abram asked.

"It's from glissando-ing," Jared said.

"Huh?" Abe said, instructing Jared to follow him to the bathroom.

"A glissando. It's what they call when you slide from one pitch to another, and it shreds my fingers when I play."

This was exactly why he liked Jared. He'd known the man for only a week and already Jared had succeeded in teaching him new words and explaining things he had never even thought of or heard of. Pre-Jared, there was no knowledge of glissando, no familiarity of *carpe noctem* (Latin for "seize the night"), and no awareness that chewing a piece of gum while cutting onions prevents crying.

The two had spent nearly every morning of that week together at Vitality, with Abe acting as Jared's personal trainer of sorts. Per Jared's request, Abe had created an interval training routine for him—half cardio, half free weight and kettlebell exercises—to help tone his (already toned) body. Abe, the personal trainer, had a hard time separating himself from Abe, the gay man, while working out with Jared. It wasn't only his attractiveness—it wasn't as if Jared was the first good-looking man Abe ever had to train. It was his charisma, his demeanor, and his focus. Every morning, Jared entered the gym like an elite athlete, determined to conquer whatever fitness task Abe threw at him.

As dumb as it sounded, Abe secretly wished Cassie would pull him aside one of these moments and tell him everything was a charade. "We aren't really dating," he wanted Cassie to confess. "I found Jared for you."

When the two walked into the bathroom, Abe searched the vanity drawer for bandages. Cassie was still on the phone speaking in a calm and comforting tone. It caught him by surprise that Jared closed the door behind them.

"I need to talk to you about something," Jared said.

Oh my God, it's happening. Tell me you're in love with me.

"I really could use your help."

Stop talking and tear off your clothes.

They made eye contact as Jared grabbed Abe's right wrist. Despite the battle wounds, his hands were smooth and strong. Abe knew this discussion was serious when the smile that had lived on Jared's face the past week morphed into straight-laced despair.

"I'd really appreciate if you could do me a favor and not tell Cassie. Please, Abe."

Abe froze, his inappropriate feelings falling away to the frantic thought of having to keep something from his best friend. Jared clearly sensed his apprehension, not giving Abram any time to respond.

"It's about Clare," he said, lowering his voice.

"Oh. What about her?"

Abe didn't want to talk about Mrs. Montgomery. He didn't want to hear the words that were about to come out of Jared's mouth. Cancer. Tumor. Chemo. Terminal.

"Is she..." Jared hesitated. "Do you know if she has any history of mental illness?"

Abe half gasped, stunned. He caught a glimpse of himself in the mirror as his face turned a noticeable shade of red.

"What? Mrs. Montgomery? No! No."

"Shh. Please don't raise your voice."

"Jared, what are you talking about? I've known the Montgomerys my whole life. Clare Montgomery is not mentally ill."

Jared flicked his hand into Abe's chest and pushed his index finger to his lips again, trying to quiet him down. It was as if Jared was attacking his own mother. The two were officially having Their First Fight.

"Where the hell is this coming from?" Abram demanded.

"I'm trying to figure out what's going on, why apparently none of her lab work is matching her symptoms," he said.

"So you immediately assume she's insane?"

"No, I didn't say that, Abe. I'm just trying to figure out what's wrong with her."

Abe placed both hands on his hips and shook his head, unable to look at Jared.

"Hey, hey. Don't get mad," Jared said.

The blasphemy of Jared's comments left Abe speechless for a moment. "I mean, I know she was on antidepressants after Charlie died, but other than that, there's never been anything off." His hostility kept rising as Jared went in for an unnecessary hug.

"This is hard on all of us," Jared said. Abe didn't want to enjoy it, but Jared's arms felt warm enough to melt the shield of ice he had so carefully encased himself in all these years.

Abe knew he was the one losing it—not Mrs. Montgomery. It had been three years since his last relationship. Three years since he'd even come remotely close to letting love in again. He had only been on four dates since the big breakup, each one driving him further and further into a life of loneliness. And there he was, falling for an astounding man—a heterosexual man—who happened to be his best friend's boyfriend.

The harsh chime of Abram's doorbell caused the two to separate.

Expecting it to be Ingrid, his eighty-four-year-old nosey neighbor, Abe begrudgingly ran to the door and opened it, the cold rush of the winter night blowing in on him. A man stood on the porch, his back turned away from Abram.

"Can I help you?" Abe asked.

Through the soft white wind, the man turned around, and Abe caught a glimpse of the patchwork newsboy hat in the moonlight.

"Harris?" Abe squeaked out, barely.

"Abe. Can I please come in?"

Seven: Harris

All dressed up, and nowhere to go.

Upon leaving the gala, it was obvious Harris's life had become a series of sad clichés.

By the time he pulled onto the street of his apartment complex shortly before midnight, there were already two different news crews parked outside. No stranger to the way the media works, Harris slyly drove past his complex, avoiding the reporters. He thought this decision was a clever ploy, but he should have just parked his car, put on a brave face, and made a statement.

Hours after this shit started, though, his mind was a cloudy mess, full of semidrunk, sleep-deprived ideas. Harris knew if the media was at his house, they were certainly going to be at his dad's house, so he avoided that trap until it was safe. Faced with the choice of heading to Kenneth or Grant's apartment next, he chose Grant, the less infatuated of his two current boyfriends.

Grant lived downtown in what used to be a warehouse for the old store AM&A's, which ruled the retail industry long before the Macy's and the Walmarts of the world took over. Harris wasn't entirely sure what he liked more: Grant or his loft. It wasn't simply the exposed brick or the cathedral ceilings that interested him, but also the enormous history inside a building that was Buffalo's first department store. Plus, an extraordinary oasis existed on the rooftop of the building, with a lush garden in the summer and a year-round hot tub that hardly anyone but Grant used. To Harris, there were very few things better than enjoying a cocktail on the roof while in the hot tub with a cute guy, watching a slice of the sunset over Lake Erie.

Grant swiftly swung open the door upon Harris's arrival, the stench of tequila on his breath slapping Harris in the face.

"Harris!" he shouted, clearly intoxicated but looking very adorable with his dimples showing. "Look at you in that suit! How was your daddio's thing?"

"It was...interesting."

Harris entered Grant's loft with the explicit goal of immediately explaining everything that had happened. But as Grant clumsily danced to the laundry detergent jingle blaring from his TV, Harris realized this man was drunker than he had ever seen.

"Actually, it was really nice."

He knew Grant wouldn't remember anything in the morning, so what was the point of wasting his breath? After lots of buzzed small talk in his living room, Grant suggested that the two crack open a bottle of champagne and hit the hot tub, and Harris had no objections to that plan.

Ignorance is bliss.

The Queen City's lights flickered as Harris popped the bottle, the city absolutely sparkling below as the two undressed and jumped directly into the hot tub—which was exactly what Harris needed. Something nice and relaxing where he could live inside a bubble and imagine his blunder didn't exist yet. The two spent more than an hour up there together, talking, laughing, flirting. In the driver's seat for most of the conversation, Harris learned how much he didn't know about Grant. That night's surprising facts included finding out Grant was left-handed, had a set of sisters who were triplets, and planned on spending two weeks in March at an orphanage in Costa Rica teaching children English.

Everything was going swimmingly until Grant, on his fifth glass of champagne, moved toward him with googly eyes that were inadvertently pointing in opposite directions. Harris lightly pecked him on the lips, nearly gagging at the strength of the tequila-champagne combo seeping from Grant's pores.

"I love you, Harris," Grant said, slurring his name so badly it came out like "Harrish."

"Grant, darling. You don't love me. You barely know me."

Harris didn't want Grant's love—he didn't want anyone's love. Grant slowly sipped his champagne before again coming within a few inches of his face.

"I tell you that I love you—" He paused slightly before taking another sip. "I tell you that I love you and that's your response?"

"Grant..."

"Don't tell me who I do and don't love!" he shouted, grabbing Harris's champagne flute from his hand and heaving it fifteen feet over the roof's ledge.

"Get out!" he bellowed, sounding like Oprah announcing a new car giveaway. "Get out!" Trying to stand up, he splashed wildly like he was stuck in quicksand.

"Grant, no. Listen." Harris tried to grab Grant's arm, but slipped and ended up with a mouthful of chlorinated hot-tub water. He nearly threw up until Grant turned around and leaned over the back edge of the hot tub, vomit freely ejecting from his mouth. Harris immediately went into babysitter mode. He dragged Grant out of the hot tub and told him everything was going to be okay. The two were a giant mess of rubbery, watery flesh. He dried Grant off partially, wrapped a towel around his waist, cupped his head with his left hand, and gently laid him down on the ground.

Harris threw his suit back on, then lugged Grant into the elevator, and hit the button for the sixth floor. Fearful a stranger would think he had roofied Grant or something, he prayed the elevator wouldn't stop and that no one was in the hallway. The ding of the elevator rang out—success! No one was around. Harris fidgeted with Grant's keys, walked him straight to his couch, and placed his kitchen trash can next to his face.

He contemplated stealing an outfit from Grant but decided against the future guilt trip, fully knowing this would definitely be the last time the two of them would ever see each other. Harris kissed Grant lightly on the forehead, wiped the drool from his chin, and walked away, taking one last look at another man erased from his life.

The demons of paranoia overtook Harris's body as he drove to his dad's house. Instead of taking a straight shot down Main Street, Harris took the long route, driving out of his way to Niagara Street, and hopped on the interstate to catch the Scajaquada Expressway, devising a plan along the way to stay clandestine. When he arrived at his father's neighborhood, he parked his truck three streets over along Delaware Park, sifting through the back seat for a winter hat or something to obscure his face. Only able to find a weird old cap of Abram's, he put the hat on and began his incognito trek.

Harris decided to get to the house on Middlesex Road via Nottingham Terrace by cutting through backyards. He carefully chose the poorest-looking house on the street—not an easy task in this neck of the woods—to try to minimize the chance for security cameras or outdoor motion lights catching him. It never really occurred to Harris how ridiculous it might be if someone actually caught him traipsing through the snow in their yard while wearing his Prada loafers, Armani suit, and wool L.L. Bean peacoat. But, there didn't seem to be a soul awake at quarter to six, and Harris was relieved to see no reporters waiting for him as he finally arrived on his dad's back steps.

Perhaps their reaction would have been a bit better than the one that came from his father.

"Your little stunt could cost me big-time," his dad said from the recliner without lifting his eyes from his newspaper.

"Tearing down dilapidated, vacant properties and building affordable housing isn't a stunt, Dad."

"You need to learn to take accountability for your actions, Har," he replied. "This is now a crisis."

It was no surprise his father immediately put this development into a language he loved, as everything in his life came with a set of PR consequences. There were an abundance of events in Mayor McGee's life that he labeled as "good press" or "bad press," but Harris hadn't heard his father utter the word "crisis" since three interns accused his former Deputy Mayor Joe Smyczek of sexual harassment two years ago.

"Harris, you have to leave."

"What? Dad, I can't go home, there are repor—"

His father cut him off.

"Harris, I know you didn't mean to do anything wrong, but I need to distance myself from you. We can't be seen together until this dies down. I cannot—I *will not* be connected to you with this."

"Dad, please, I need your advice. I have no idea what to do."

"You are thirty-three years old. You can handle this on your own. Now, please, you have to go."

He was too tired to be angry and too delusional to protest.

"Fine."

"Like all crises, Harris, this too shall pass," his father said and then patted him on the back, grabbed his shoulder and practically pushed him out the door with that canned, rehearsed response. Harris walked away from his dad's house, bleary-eyed, exhausted, and not one ounce closer to knowing what to do.

At 6:00 a.m., Harris attempted a return to his apartment. He pumped himself up as he headed there, referring to episodes of *Alias* in his head as preparation to ward off an unwanted media sneak attack. He took extra precautions upon his arrival, driving around the block three times and then the parking lot four times, scanning specifically for any unusual people or vehicles. The coast appeared clear as he finally parked his car in spot 14B. Relief washed over him as he gingerly pushed open the door and walked up the steps to his apartment on the second floor. He found it odd that his downstairs neighbor, Judy Lorenzo, still had her Christmas lights on a week into the new year, his attention lingering for a few seconds on her front door. That's when he caught a glimpse of Jennifer Jefferson and her crimson-red lipstick hustling toward him with her *Action 7 News* microphone in hand, the clicking of her heels echoing like daggers in the hollow peace of the morning. Slightly stunned, Harris backpedaled and jogged toward his car. He couldn't figure out what triggered him to run, but it was too late to turn back, so he increased his stride, his legs both lifeless and spirited, like he was about to cross the finish line at the end of a marathon. He clicked the wrong button on his key fob and accidentally set off the alarm. The deafening rhythm of the honking silenced the questions Jennifer shouted as her overweight cameraman struggled to keep up with her.

Harris quickly reversed his F-150 and sped off. The snow-slicked streets prevented a full, pedal-to-the-metal getaway, but Harris was determined to lose them. He peeked in his rearview mirror where their white SUV followed closely behind, Jennifer holding her phone up to the windshield to snap a picture of Harris driving away. He was apparently the target of a good old-fashioned, low-speed witch hunt a la O.J. Simpson. But in this case, Harris was innocent.

Angry and annoyed that everything was working against him, he wondered if Keith and Dennis had tried contacting him or if the media had been bothering them.

While Harris was stopped at a red light, Jennifer got out of the car and walked toward his truck. He seized the moment and made an illegal left on red, losing the news crew when they got caught behind a city bus. He hopped onto the I-190 South and cruised past the Peace Bridge, inherently knowing where he would escape to next.

The Saturday morning calm enveloped his soul as Harris felt a small sense of freedom for the first time in hours. The chill at the city's Outer Harbor felt exhilarating. The air was crisp but pleasant, cold but not unbearable. Chunks of ice rushed past him with a roar he wished he had inside him.

He looked out over Lake Erie, always amazed at its vastness even though he was lucky enough to see it every day. The sapphire water stretched on endlessly, and like so many moments over the past day, Harris thought of his mom. When he was a little boy, probably six years old, his parents had promised to take him to the Outer Harbor one winter day for what they called the Festival of Ice. Harris distinctly remembered hearing that term for the first time and picturing a winter fair, complete with a huge crowd converging on rides, food stands, and carnival games. Turns out, the Festival of Ice was no festival at all, just he and his parents getting as close to the water as possible, tossing stones and rocks onto the mini icebergs. Six-year-old Harris might have been disappointed, but thirty-three-year-old Harris found it sweet.

For the first time since his whiskey-and-ginger-fueled grins at the gala, Harris cracked a smile. It'd been seven years since he'd said goodbye to his mom. It never got any easier—despite what some said—but he still found joy in the little memories that so often popped into his mind. It seemed both shorter and longer than seven years, if that were possible. Truthfully, he stopped consciously counting at five years, imposing a new rule in his life that he would only observe the number of years they had together instead of totaling the years she had been dead. And hey, they sure fit a hell of a lot of good memories in those twenty-six years.

He was sad she wasn't there to see the city's blistering resurgence since she was always a champion of Buffalo. He pictured the two of them trying the countless new restaurants downtown, skating on the fresh ice of the rink at Canalside in the winter, and going for walks at new paths along the Outer Harbor.

Hoping to summon her thoughts, he asked himself how she would handle this situation and what advice she would provide. Monica McGee held the innate characteristic of always knowing what to say and how to say it. She'd listened to Harris's stories intently, processed the facts immediately, and provided an intelligent, eloquent answer to whatever problem he faced.

Harris felt idiotic for getting himself in this stupid quandary. Social media was ruining the world one person at a time, and he happened to be the latest victim. As his self-pity kicked in, a chill traveled down his spine. Maybe it was the blistering wind skirting off the lake, but Harris chose to view it as a divine symbol from his mom, urging him to regain control of his flailing life.

Harris blinked slowly, the madness of the last ten hours finally catching up to him. Yes, he knew what he had to do. He just wasn't quite ready yet. Crawling into his car, he reclined the seat back as far as it would go, closed his eyes happily and fell asleep for the first time in more than twenty-four hours.

Adam Levine asking him for opinions on a new tattoo. Giving a presentation on the solar system in middle school. A juicy chili cheeseburger. Kayaking along Irondequoit Creek. Those are the things he dreamed of in sequential order at the Outer Harbor, each one more inexplicable than the last, except for the burger. The dreams combined with the short, deep rumbles in his stomach were enough to persuade him to prop up his car seat, shake off the groggy feeling, and head back out in search of some food. He felt like a gazelle among a pack of lions, carefully plotting when and where to go without being preyed upon.

Harris didn't know if he was overreacting or if his evasive actions were justified. He grabbed for his phone to search for the closest fast-food joint before he remembered shattering it the night before. He felt wholly disconnected, a bizarre turnaround from his typical mood. Going with the kill-two-with-one mentality, he decided to head to the Walden Galleria Mall to grab some lunch and pick up a new phone.

After devouring his breakfast and lunch—two combo meals of General Tso's, pork fried rice, and egg rolls from the food court—Harris walked up to the cell phone kiosk, feeling uneasy. He'd have to give the worker his name. *What if they saw my tweet? What if they ask me about my dad?*

"How can I help you?" said the pretty sales associate—Hayden G, identifiable from his name tag.

Harris told Hayden he needed a new phone, noting a diamond-studded earring in his left ear and his Gucci watch, both of which immediately put him at ease. It wasn't as if Hayden was screaming *"I'm gay!"* or something, but he certainly wasn't screaming *"I'm straight!"* either. The slight infatuation with Hayden provided a nice distraction for Harris, until the phone turned on, coming to life in his hand with the iridescent illumination and vibrations arriving fast and furiously as notifications popped up one after another. He had sixteen texts, twelve missed calls, and five new voice mails. He pressed play on the latest message.

"Harris, it's Dennis. We've been trying to call you. Keith even went to your apartment this morning to tell you this in person," the voice mail began. Dennis spoke laboriously, as if he were having trouble breathing while reading unrecognizable handwriting. *"We've terminated your position, effective immediately. I wish we didn't have to do this, but there's really no other option. I'm really sorry, Harris. You know we think the world of you."*

Harris lost himself in a cloud of despair on the way to Kenneth Willer's place. He tossed his intuitive spy sense out the window, no longer afraid of any reporter or cameraman. He just wanted to see Kenneth to talk to someone who would actually listen and care. The two had been seeing each other for about two months, and for the first in a long time, Harris actually was developing sincere feelings. Their relationship—like most of Harris's—started out physical, after the two met while posing as fill-in members of Beautify Buffalo's kickball team, Talkin' Proud. To Harris, their physical chemistry only scratched the surface of their relationship's potential. He sensed Kenneth wasn't exactly gung ho about jumping into a full-fledged partnership, so he tried to remain casual as things progressed. He assumed Kenneth, so levelheaded and mature, would be willing to overlook Harris's actions and offer the comfort and conversation he so desperately craved.

He spotted Kenneth in the window, waved, and walked to the front porch, expecting him to open the door. He stood for about a minute before knocking three times. Sick of feeling helpless and scared, Harris made it a point to turn on the charm, flashing a smile and manufacturing a twinkle in his eye as Kenneth opened the door.

"Hey," he said, drawing out the word with softness.

"Did you get my texts?" Kenneth asked, barricading the doorway with his broad shoulders. His body language spoke loudly. Harris noticed Kenneth staring at the bridge of his nose, not actually looking in his eyes.

"My phone broke. Can I come in? It's freezing out here."

Kenneth hoisted his arm and pushed it into Harris's chest. "I don't think we should see each other anymore," he blurted out. "That's what my texts said."

"You're kidding," Harris said, almost adding *You're* dumping *me?!*

"You're a great guy, Harris, but I don't need this kind of drama in my life. I'm thirty-five, not nineteen."

"Ken—it was a mistake. Please, I can explain. I haven't been home since yesterday afternoon. I need a fucking place to crash. Please."

"I'm sorry, Harris. I don't need this." It took every ounce of restraint Harris had left in him not to deliver an uppercut straight to Kenneth's gullet. He didn't care that this was apparently the end of their relationship; he cared about the way it was happening with Kenneth tossing him aside like some old shoe. "You deserve someone who wants to be there for you through these things. And I can't provide that."

Harris didn't have any energy to respond. He nodded and walked away with a rage inside of him he hadn't felt in years.

I'm so sorry. This is all my fault and I take full responsibility. It was an error in judgment and I sincerely apologize to everyone. My actions don't reflect the thoughts of Beautify Buffalo or my father.

Harris sat in the parking lot of a gas station on Sheridan Drive for more than an hour, crafting his words carefully. He hit Send and the email with a subject of HARRIS MCGEE STATEMENT was in the inboxes of all three television stations and *The Buffalo News.*

Harris anticipated a sense of liberation to swathe him with that click. Instead, he felt jittery and helpless about the firestorm he had created. He feared the statement was too little, too late, but his father was correct. He needed to take accountability for his actions. And thanks to the heaven-sent advice from his mom, this started his path toward resolution.

Desolate, unemployed, hungry, and still somewhat afraid, Harris couldn't face going home to an empty apartment where he would stew in his own unhealthy thoughts. He needed to see the one person who had never let him down.

He needed to see Abram Hoffman.

He couldn't believe after successfully avoiding each other for nearly three years that this was how they'd met again, with Harris practically begging Abe to allow him to spend the night in his house because he was shit out of luck otherwise. Harris hadn't showered or really slept in nearly forty hours, leaving him feeling like some miserable, delusional vagrant and surely smelling like the dumpster at Tin-Tin Chinese Restaurant. And he'd had on Abe's dumb newsboy hat! He hated how that thing made him look like a cheap imitation of LL Cool J, but it was the only thing he could find in his truck that covered up his greasy, disheveled hair. At least he was still wearing his Armani suit, which never ceased looking marvelous despite the deep wrinkles.

Unable to get out of bed, Harris yawned as he locked his elbows and knees tightly, stretching his body out as far as he could. By his estimation, he had slept a full twelve hours, though after almost two days of being awake, he didn't feel refreshed. He barely felt functioning. Everything had spiraled so far out of control that Harris didn't know where to begin or what to do next.

He stood up and pulled back the turquoise Jacquard curtains of Abe's meticulously decorated and ridiculously trendy spare bedroom. After a four-day absence, the sun had finally returned, reflecting intensely off the dense white pillows of snow. He lay back down on the bed, unsure if it was ten in the morning or two in the afternoon.

Nothing could have prepared him for the backlash of his William Street tweet. In a social media-obsessed world, Harris had learned the unfortunate lesson that going viral wasn't always a good thing. He had no one to blame but himself and felt ashamed and awful that an honest mistake appeared to have such horrible consequences.

Harris pressed pause on the replaying of events in his head when he heard a cough outside in the hall.

Abe!

Smoothing things over with him was priority number one for the day, as Harris barely had gotten a chance to explain anything. Abe, as expected, let him in the house with little hesitation but played a strong game of passive-aggressive disinterest with their conversation. Harris tried every angle to make things go as smoothly as possible with Abe, first acting nonchalant, and then apologizing, and then cracking jokes. Abe wanted none of it, not interested in hearing anything Harris had to say, ushering him away within seconds of entering his house like someone with a highly contagious disease he didn't want exposed to his friends.

I should have just gone home.

But Harris didn't want to be home. And he didn't want to be alone. He needed someone—anyone—to simply acknowledge him and listen to him and make him feel like he had one other human being in the world who was actually capable of feeling empathy toward him.

That's why he'd chosen to come there. Of course, he had always known Abram would let him stay over. Saint Abram would never turn an old friend away, no matter how much that person hurt him or how much that person wished they'd never broken his heart.

Harris cautiously opened the door, his feet softly sliding across the wooden floors, hoping to stay quiet enough to catch Abe off guard so he wouldn't have time to disappear. As he glanced around the corner, he discovered the guy Abram so rudely failed to introduce him to last night.

"Oh, hi. I thought you were Abram," he said, staring at the attractive stranger, who looked like the younger, more attractive brother of Ryan Gosling. "I'm Harris."

"Jared." The two extended hands. Harris accidentally hit his ring finger and pinky on Jared's hand, which resulted in a dead-fish handshake. "Let's try that again," Jared said, as the two firmly shook. "Nice to meet you. Abe's at work.

"Sorry to barge in on you guys last night. I'm just..." He struggled with how to put his predicament into words. "I'm just a mess."

"So I hear! Abe spent all night googling you."

Harris laughed and then sighed when Jared laughed back, his perfect teeth glowing and biceps bulging through his navy crew-cut T-shirt. How did he not know that Abe had an enchanting, endearing boyfriend? No wonder he'd never sought out a reunion.

"So, how long have you two been dating?" Harris asked, even though he didn't really want to know.

"Since the spring. April fourteenth will be our one year!" Jared said, his eyes glowing with adoration. The news hit Harris hard.

"Wow. Not even a year yet and you guys are living together?"

"Ha, well, only for about a week now. We're looking for a place together."

A sudden wave of intense nausea tumbled through his stomach. Somehow, Harris ended up on the wrong side of love lost. The paths he and Abe had taken since their breakup were as divergent as could be, and Abram clearly had the upper hand in life. He'd not only had capitalized on his love of fitness by parlaying that into a super successful and meaningful job, but he had gotten to do it with an incredibly hot and friendly boyfriend by his side.

Abe had it all. Harris had nothing.

Always the bridesmaid, never the bride.

"Do you need a change of clothes?" Jared said, looking Harris up and down with a slight stink-eye.

"That would be fantastic," Harris said. "I've been wearing this suit for a better part of the last two days."

"You know, I'm doing my laundry right now, so here," Jared said, lifting his arms over his head and removing his shirt. "Take this."

Harris stood in awe as this Prince Charming literally gave him the shirt off his back—a broad, sculpted, beautiful back.

"Are you sure?"

"Yeah, I have some sweatpants in our room, too."

Jared walked down the hallway and entered the room next to the bathroom.

"Do you want gray? Or black?"

Harris walked to the room, surprised to see the disarray of suitcases, duffel bags, and bins overflowing.

"Wait, you guys use this room?"

"Yeah, this is our room. Abe's room is at the end of the hallway. Did he switch rooms since you lived here?"

Harris stood silent for a brief second, the wires beginning to connect inside his brain. As he pieced the puzzle together, a million thoughts began whizzing through his head. *Abe isn't dating Jared! Jared is dating Cassie! Is Abe single? Is Jared straight?*

"Right, sorry, I'm a little out of it," Harris replied, the news slowly hacking away at the pessimism inside him.

"For what it's worth, you should stick around to talk to Abe," Jared said. "Cassie and I were talking about everything last night, and it sounds like you two have a lot of unfinished business."

"Yeah, I think I will."

Every dark cloud has a silver lining.

Jared's cell phone vibrated loudly atop the dresser, and he apologized as he stopped their conversation to answer it. Still grasping the fact that Abe and Jared weren't dating, Harris drifted away, lost in his own thoughts. A brief glimmer of optimism crept into his devastated psyche when Jared slammed down his phone.

"Harris, can you help me get to Sisters Hospital?" Jared asked frantically.

"Yeah, of course, is everything okay?"

"No, I've gotta meet Cassie there. Her mom just collapsed."

Eight: Abram

He refused to travel down that road again. Absolutely refused to head down the highway that led him into a deep depression where he had questioned every moment—no, every minute—of their relationship. Harris had drained him of desire, left him devoid of wanting, needing, and expecting love. More than three years later, the two still had never had a proper conversation of where things went wrong. Abram only somewhat blamed his stubbornness. He wasn't the one who fucked up, so why should he try to be the bigger person?

Since Harris showed up at his front door, Abe hadn't allowed himself to process their reunion. Harris needed a place to stay; Abe gave him a place to stay. That would be the extent of amiability toward his ex. He had no plans to make this a reunion to remember.

For what felt like the hundredth time, Abe scrolled through the text messages from Harris, each of which seemed sincere.

—*Thank you for letting me crash. Do you mind if I stay until you get back from work? I'd love to talk to you for a few minutes.*

—*I really, really, really appreciate it. You have no idea what my day has been like. Or maybe you do? lol.*

—*I understand if you don't want to talk. I hope you can find it in your heart to give me five minutes.*

—*Abram? Please. We need to talk. There's so much I have to say to you.*

—*I'm going to go head back home now. I hope life is wonderful for you. Thank you again for letting me spend the night. And trust me, I'm reading you loud and clear, Abe. But please know that I miss you. xo.*

Abe exhaled, annoyed at himself. He'd started and stopped his responses to Harris at least twenty times over the last twelve hours because he couldn't quite come up with the words that signified his true emotions. How could he accurately convey *"You broke my heart. You ruined my life. I have spent every day over the last three years trying not to think about you"* without sounding like a pathetic, desperate loser? He couldn't. And that's why he didn't respond.

He knew it was a dick move that essentially kicked Harris while he was down. Abram had read every article and watched every news clip about Harris breaking into that house and his idiotic tweet that'd cost him his job and created a firestorm for his father. Abe wished he knew why Harris hid for a day without owning up to everything. But to find out that answer, he'd actually have to speak to him. And that had not, and would not, happen.

His hideout for the day was the gym, his retreat for the past seven years. Within those walls was where the lion inside of him emerged. It was there he had his personal breakthroughs, hiding his regret inside the sets of seated bicep curls and weighted lunges. The whole night after seeing Harris's face became nothing more than a retrospective of his incorrect choices, swaying Abe from his lionlike mentality to that of a sad mouse, sniffing a piece of cheese in a trap before realizing exactly what was happening as the metal clamp snapped down on his neck.

Attempting to recapture his poise pre-Cassie and Harris's return, pre-inappropriate feelings about Jared, pre-life thrown into chaos, Abe stacked his day with task after task, leaving no time for the thoughts of Harris to sprout inside his brain. He started by organizing his office and creating the employee schedules for the next month, followed by teaching a Body Pump class, then a personal-training session with Seth Boccini. He then ran a quick five miles and made small chitchat with some girls on the ellipticals, before retreating back to his office to sift through the mountains of paperwork waiting for him.

Abe shut his office door, sat in his chair, and puffed out his chest out, feeling accomplished for climbing to the top of his kingdom and avoiding overthinking the previous night's events.

The lion had returned.

Or so he thought.

Without delay, the strong sense of disregard to Harris he portrayed on the outside cracked and fell away the second he was alone. His need to speak with Harris gnawed at the barrier of suppression that lined his heart. He stared at his cell phone, debating if he should call Harris or not. But Abe reminded himself this was what he did best. Like an alcoholic who avoided any situation with alcohol, Abe tried his damnedest to circumvent any thoughts he knew would suck him into that black hole of emotion that was Harris McGee.

A knock on the door came at the exact right moment, forcing Abe to escape the pull of his past. He swung the door open and stood stunned, saying nothing.

"Abram. You never returned my call."

Abe's immediate response was only a blank face, like a toddler who had been caught stealing out of the cookie jar. Each attempt at speaking ended before it began, the gap of silence that saturated the hallway becoming uncomfortable. Abe cleared his throat and mustered a reaction.

"Mayor McGee. Please. Come in."

Hearing Mayor McGee over the phone the other day had sent an icy chill through Abe. Seeing him in person again didn't leave any better impression, as a sour feeling climbed up his esophagus and his insides became twisted and wrought with nerves. He hadn't been face-to-face with him since that day three years ago—and he honestly would've liked to keep it that way. Abe immediately assumed Harris summoned his father to Vitality to demand a response to his son's numerous requests to speak. But his assumptions for the mayor's visit vanished almost immediately as he realized it all pertained to business. Mayor McGee outlined his vision for Abe joining his staff as the city's Health and Wellness Manager.

The job entailed overseeing wellness activities for the city's employees and developing programs to raise awareness and motivation of an active lifestyle, helping to create wellness initiatives for Western New Yorkers, and planning and executing public fitness events. Each duty the mayor described sounded right up Abe's alley. He had been searching for that spark for quite some time now, one he discerned might not be possible to find in his current employment situation.

"Is this something I'd be able to do part-time? Weekends and evenings, maybe?" Abe asked.

"I don't see a way you can continue to work full-time here and work for me too."

A familiar feeling of conflict sat in Abe's chest. This job had consumed his life for years. He had never pursued another opportunity in the slightest.

"You don't need to answer me today. I understand this will probably take some time to consider. Just know I truly believe you could make a remarkable difference in this city."

Abe was skeptical, fully aware Mayor McGee had been trying to distinguish himself as a well-rounded, left-leaning, worthy senatorial candidate. His likely opponent, downstate businessman Darryl Samuelson, had recently come under fire from the media for his donations to several corporations that didn't support "protecting religious freedoms" aka supporting anti-gay policies and laws. Abe fully presumed that part of Mayor McGee's plan to win the election would be to play up his nice-guy image and have several staff members by his side who could subtly prove his tolerance.

"You're not only doing this because of your potential senate campaign, are you?"

"This has been in the works for years, Abram."

Abram realized he had to be blunter.

"You're not asking me to take this job so you meet some *gay* quota, are you?"

"You think you're the only fit gay guy in Buffalo?" The mayor laughed, causing Abram to giggle. His offer seemed genuine and the job sounded like a dream come true, but it all seemed like too much to wrap his mind around at the moment—a fact the mayor noticed.

"Take your time," he said as he walked out of the office. "Call me when you're ready. And Abe?"

"Yeah?"

"I'm sorry."

"For what?"

"For what happened between you and Harris. You didn't deserve that."

Poached, shot, gutted. That statement left the lion inside Abe lying on the ground, gaping wounds now exposed, bleeding profusely, much too raw and too massive to stitch up and repair.

Nine: Clare

Clare's Realtor, Julie Duncan, said it was "frowned upon" for owners to be present at their open house, but Clare wasn't one to listen to rules anymore. And lately, nothing was more important than meeting the potential buyers of her home. "It's like a family heirloom," she had told Julie. "I just want to ensure it falls into the right hands."

Clare fully understood that staging the house perfectly would be crucial to guaranteeing a quick sell to the appropriate buyer, so she and Cassie had spent the week leading up to the open house painstakingly perfecting every detail. With all Clare's clutter gone, there was nothing left to encase the house in its immaculate charade. The walls were dirty, the rooms were dusty and dull, and while Clare knew it was from decades of being effusively lived-in, she had made it her mission to revitalize the space in an attractive and cheap way.

After thoroughly cleaning every square inch, she and Cassie had tackled painting the walls in each room, aiming for a neutral, earthy vibe throughout the house. Clare's room had turned from mauve to sun-kissed sand, the bathrooms each got two coats of southwest nutmeg, the hallways brightened from a dark tan to calico cream, Cassie's old room got a fresh pink coat courtesy of lily petals, and they went fairly trendy in Caleb's room, painting it country moss, a gorgeous shade of green. They used sienna sunrise in the kitchen and the adjacent dining room to make both rooms appear as one elongated space, a trick Clare had learned from an old episode of Martha Stewart's talk show. A few new accent pieces and some bright lamps for the bedrooms finalized the brief but effective renovation.

"We did a kick-ass job, Mom," Cassie said after completing their whirlwind makeover.

"That's because we're a kick-ass team!" Clare replied, wrapping her right arm around her baby girl.

As much as it saddened her to think about saying goodbye to the place she had called home for her whole life, Clare felt slightly relieved. Cassie's return home and selling the house served as such nice distractions to Clare that she'd almost forgotten how awful she was feeling. The inability to sleep, persistent aches and pains, and headaches were all still present, just temporarily nudged to the back of Clare's brain. She'd promised herself once the weekend was over, she would refocus her energy on her diagnosis, or lack thereof. She would be seeing Dr. Kincaid on Monday, and already crafted a disparaging speech in her head that she would deliver to him. He had been so lackadaisical with her health. And though she knew it wasn't intentional, she needed someone to take the extra time and carefully analyze her body, her blood tests, her symptoms.

Monday, she'd told herself. Monday would be the day to start the process of finding that doctor.

Among the two dozen or so people that had shown up to the open house, Clare believed the successors to 837 Parker Avenue were Brandon and Marcia Swiatek. The Swiateks stood out from the others for their friendliness and congeniality, complete with a golden aura that filled the house from the second they'd walked in the front door. Julie told Clare that Brandon was a mechanic, while Marcia ran her own cake business from their current home. The couple, along with their daughter Harper, had spent the afternoon eliciting candid gasps as they made their way through the Montgomery home. Already feeling an intangible connection to the strangers, Marcia had solidified Clare's early feelings when the two talked in the kitchen about what kind of home the Swiateks were looking for.

"We've lived in three different apartments over the course of the last three years, so we want something that we love and can settle into," Marcia said. "I want a home with history, Brandon is dead set on something unique, so that's what drew us to this house. Even though it's way over our price range."

Her palpable earnestness had tugged at Clare's heartstrings. She didn't want to lower the asking price one penny. In fact, she had honestly hoped a bidding war would emerge. In real estate terms, Tonawanda's Green Acres community was a gold mine. The perfect mix of reasonably sized and reasonably priced houses, an adequate school system, close to all major highways, and equidistant to Buffalo and Niagara Falls. Julie had told Clare that the house was a stroke of genius that would surely sell at the highest price per square foot the town had ever seen.

"This probably sounds so unoriginal, but from the second we walked in here, it just felt like home. I love everything: the location, the layout, the curb appeal. It's hard not to fall in love with this place!"

As if that declaration weren't enough, there was something about the glow in Harper's deep-brown eyes, the slight gap in her front teeth, and those messy auburn pigtails that reminded Clare of Cassie.

"What's your favorite part of the house, Harper?" Clare asked the little girl.

"The window cushion!" Harper howled with glee, grabbing on to her poufy red dress and throwing her arms up into the air.

The "window cushion" was actually the built-in window seat in Cassie's room, still covered in the champagne-pink fabric from the eighties, which Clare wanted to replace but had never had time to get to.

"That window seat could be yours someday!" Clare said, smiling.

If only she had known that would be her last smile for days.

"It was a pleasure meeting you, Marcia. And it was so great to meet you, Harper."

Clare had spit out the words before everything gradually dissolved into a black abyss. She could feel herself falling, struggling to speak and grasping to hang on to the countertop. She wanted to cry out for help as she slid to the floor, but her mouth wouldn't move as she landed with an astounding thud, staring into the eyes of Marcia, Harper, and Julie as they looked on horrified.

Clare acknowledged where she was the second her eyes opened, staring at the beaded ceiling tile and listening to the melodic beeping of medical machinery. Sisters Hospital held the distinct notion of being the only place Clare both celebrated life and mourned death, the dichotomy not lost on her in this moment. She gave birth to both Caleb and Cassie on the second floor in the maternity ward and watched Charlie wither away in hospice on the third floor.

"What floor am I on?"

That was the first thing she said out loud after waking up, believing an answer of "the third floor" would be akin to a death sentence.

"Mom? Mom! Hey. Hi, do you remember what happened?" Cassie rushed over to Clare's side. She placed her head on Clare's chest, unequivocally shaken.

"Yes," she said, her voice straining inexplicably on such a short word. "Am I okay?"

The initial look on Cassie's face said everything Clare needed to know—and everything she previously assumed. Clare had never witnessed the mix of wrath and worry that swept over her daughter in that hospital room.

"Mom," Cassie said in a nuanced manner. "Why didn't you tell me how sick you were?"

The question left Clare speechless. The truth was she had no answer. It had been months since she'd started feeling abnormal, but it wasn't exactly something she wanted to share with her children. Besides, she had been proactive in her health. She had gone to Dr. Kincaid, gotten several blood tests, and planned for the post-Clare Montgomery world. Notifying Cassie and Caleb of her health issues wouldn't prevent her from being sick. It would only make the two of them scared and panicky.

Cassie stared into Clare's eyes, expecting an answer that never came.

"I'll go grab the doctor," she said, obviously aggravated.

"Cass, what floor are we on?"

"The third," Cassie said, leaving the room and heading to the nurse's station.

Lying in that bed, Clare allowed the feeling of liberation to build inside her. She was ready to hear whatever the doctor had to say, ready to face her fears straight on.

The news from Dr. Andrew Johansen took the runner-up award for Saddest Moment of Her Life, second only to hearing the words "inoperable" from Charlie's doctor about his liver cancer. Always in sync, Clare found it comical that their bodies began rebelling against them roughly nine months apart from each other.

The snow had lost its luster, officially transforming from a fresh, white gloss decorating the earth and turning to sporadic patches of brown and gray, serving as a filthy shell over the entire city, soaking the roads—and Clare's mind—with a film of everlasting, mucky sludge.

The drive home from the hospital took an eternity, as Cassie unluckily hit every red light down Main Street. Clare grumbled inside each time the car stopped, just wanting to be alone already. She caught a glimpse of herself in the side-view mirror and was mortified with what stared back. Such a sullen, miserable woman who hadn't smiled in two days, even when she thought she was. Clare began to think the muscles in her face were permanently stuck in a hideous, droopy scowl meant to broadcast her sorrow to the world.

Partially upset and annoyed, partially feeling like a zombie, Clare hoped Cassie understood why she didn't want to talk. She looked over at her daughter and felt terrible that she was already missing a day of work her second week on the job. Cassie had been so upset inside the hospital, the mood advertised even further on her face in the car. She looked at Clare, who tried to smile, tried desperately to contort her lips from that straight line to a semicircle, but it still never formed. If Charlie were there, he'd make light of the situation, telling her to stop copying him and to find something better to do with her time.

Nine months felt like yesterday. The afternoon they received Charlie's diagnosis, the two of them had barely said a word to each other. Clare had tried to remain a beacon of optimism during dinner, jabbering on about unrelated, foolish topics like, "I think the Martins got a new dog; I've seen Wendy walking a small schnauzer-looking puppy the past two mornings." She'd brought up so many of these random conversations to fill the empty silence during dinner that Charlie politely asked her to stop. Clare obliged, still not knowing what to say or do. Nowhere in the manual of marriage she carefully shaped over her life did there exist a chapter titled *What To Say To Your Husband When You're Told He Has Weeks To Live.*

Feeling helpless, Clare had quickly cleared the table, loaded the dishes into the dishwasher, and grabbed Charlie's hands. She led him into their room, where they crawled into bed, held each other, and cried together. They just stared into each other's eyes, wiped each other's tears, kissed each other's lips, and held each other's hands. No words were necessary to communicate their feelings. That same scenario played out numerous times over the following five weeks. Each time Clare tried to initiate a goodbye speech, Charlie halted her, telling her there would be no goodbye.

"I won't let you say goodbye to me, Clare Bear," he said. "There's nothing you can say to me that I don't already know."

With that bittersweet sentiment as a guiding principle, the two spent his last weeks alive never bringing up Charlie's cancer, never talking about the End.

Clare could only hope Cassie would be the same way with her, as she helped Clare get situated on the couch, complete with a blanket, two pillows, and a cup of peppermint tea—none of which was asked for or necessary. The two hadn't really said a word to each other since leaving the hospital. Though it was awkward, Clare truly believed it was what both of them wanted.

"I'm going to go grab a few things from Abe's and I'll be back to spend the night," Cassie said, finally breaking the silence.

"Sweetie, you don't have to do that." What she should have said was, *"Sweetie, please don't do that."*

"Yes, I do," Cassie said as she kissed Clare on the forehead. "I'll see you in an hour."

As Clare heard Cassie's car reverse out of the driveway and zoom down the street, she thought about ending it all that second. How simple it would be to fill the bathtub, pop twenty muscle relaxants, and head into an eternal slumber where she would be reunited with Charlie, her parents, and her sister, Kathleen. What a wonderful world that must be. Free of pain, free of suffering, with no worry and no loneliness.

Benign. Chemotherapy. Malignant. Surgery. Low-grade. Radiation. High-grade. The words swirled together in Clare's head like a tornado of straight mush, none of them holding any significance or meaning. The doctors could throw as much medical jargon at her as they wanted, but she firmly established her stance. She had a brain tumor, plain and simple. There was no other way to put it, nothing else to believe.

She was dying.

Dr. Johansen's diagnosis wasn't as cryptic. They found the pineal tumor in the MRI and took a biopsy later that afternoon, the results of which would come tomorrow. Knowing if it was cancerous or noncancerous would steer the course of her treatment. Dr. Johansen wouldn't even speculate what would happen next, telling Clare the tumor could range from the least serious to the most serious, with chemo and radiation likely possibilities. She didn't know why she chose to immediately believe the tumor equaled a fast track to the afterlife, but she found it to be both logical and suitable.

Clare walked to the bathroom and stared at herself in the mirror, a reflection of a woman she no longer recognized or respected stared straight back her. Clare was losing control. And if there was one thing she absolutely hated, it was losing control. And there she was, succumbing to the solemn, pathetic lifestyle of an incapacitated, ill woman.

"Live like you're dying."

She scoffed at that statement as she said it said aloud with an acerbic tone. She *had* lived like she was dying by organizing and putting the house up for sale, getting rid of everything she loved while preparing for life to be over. That was no way to live at all! And though there was no crystal ball to provide a clear picture, no easy way to tell if survival was at the end of this chapter in her life, something finally clicked in her head.

The thought of dying, strangely, made Clare feel more alive than ever. The news she got was gratifying. For the last three months, she had been living in fear that something was wrong with her. And now that she knew what it was, there was no way in hell she wouldn't fight this battle with every ounce of determination she had. She didn't care if it spread through her, ravaging her body like wildfire. No brain tumor would be gaining the upper hand on her.

Quickly, she rummaged through the drawer of Charlie's belongings that would forever be in her *Keep* category. Clare had opened his drawer only once since his death, unsuccessfully searching for the tiny screwdriver they used to tighten their eyeglass frames. She riffled through the sad, beautiful randomness and grabbed Charlie's beard trimmer, plugging it in while popping on the clip guard. His scent—a mixture of his aftershave and cedar chips—still lingered on the metal blade.

While Charlie had no choice, Clare had every option still available to her. She could choose to lie down and take it or play the game on her own terms. In that moment, Clare made her decision.

Clare raised the trimmer defiantly, flicked it to the On position and pressed it right to the center of her forehead. The loud drone of the device reverberated throughout the bathroom. With a deep breath, she pushed backward on her scalp, shearing a line down the center of her head, her gray locks free-falling to the floor. Clare repeated the motion at least ten more times, gaining more confidence and clarity with each movement.

As she finished, she examined her buzz cut in the mirror.

Finally.

A smile.

Ten: Harris

Harris had been waiting two hours for Sabrina Rowell to get home, and his patience waned faster than the sun rapidly setting over the row of battered oak trees and run-down houses to his left. Gumption turned to apprehension as day turned to night, and though Harris contemplated speeding away before she arrived, he forced himself to stay put.

Besides, it was not like he had anything else to do. His days had become as boring as they were humbling, each hour's pace passing as if he were perpetually stuck in the waiting room of a doctor's office or in line at the DMV. Harris hadn't ever felt as insignificant and unappreciated as he currently did, with nowhere to go, no job, no perceptible sense of direction or purpose. The first few days after the whole episode died down, he'd strolled around his apartment in a near-comatose daze, inert and detached, passing time eating Lean Pockets and falling asleep on his couch to the phony laugh track of *Roseanne* repeats.

His previous go-to time waster was no longer an option. All the hate on social media had forced Harris to shut down his accounts, at least temporarily. It was bad enough reading the comments about his gaffe; it was even worse with all the Internet trolls stalking every picture he ever posted, every tweet he ever sent. The comments were vindictive and threatening, and Harris knew no other way to stop them than to simply leave his online identity in the dust.

Feeling sorry for himself and playing the victim were the last things he wanted to embody, but he couldn't resist the natural urge to ask the question *Why me?* time and time again.

Jared had said these moments would come often for anyone emerging from a stressful situation. The two had been texting on and off since the weekend, with Jared giving him little tidbits of psychological motivation throughout the week. Cassie Montgomery had found herself a hunk of humanity in that man. He was an angel, really, first offering to help Harris out, and then actually following through with practical, useful assistance.

Jared had recommended several steps to overcoming the anxiety Harris was experiencing, including avoiding exaggerations, not beating himself up, and understanding that time would have to pass to heal the emotional pain. He knew it was important to remember the entire city didn't hate him and not everyone continued to harp on his mistake, just a small sector. The guidance allowed Harris to gain some clarity and take control. Each time the pitiful thoughts of self-sorrow and frustration pierced through his shield of mental strength, he repeated relaxation techniques and said a positive affirmation to try to overcome his negativity.

Breathe in. *You can do this.* Breathe out. *Everything happens for a reason.*

Harris knew it was a lame, bohemian technique, but it truly helped him navigate through the emotional mess he had created.

Jared's most effective piece of advice had nothing to do with Harris and everything to do with the bigger picture. "The world is more than you and your problems," one of his texts said. "Start to appreciate the simple moments happening all around you." Harris took this to heart and immediately noticed how useful it became to clear his mind. He had a newfound gratitude during several instances that week, most recently that afternoon as he walked past two kids in his apartment complex, making a snowman on a small patch of grass near his mailbox. The joy in their laughter made him laugh, the smile on their faces brought on one of his own. The display of pure innocence was exactly what Jared had mentioned—those moments in the day that prove, despite its challenges, life does indeed go on.

At least once an hour, Harris told himself to forget about his misfortunes, to stop dwelling on the shit he couldn't change. It wasn't easy to toss aside something incredibly unnerving, but he pledged to take a cue from the media, which had finally moved on. Harris had officially become yesterday's news. Five days before, the story of the "Beautify Buffalo Bully" with the "East Side ego trip" was top story, front-page news. He had since dwindled into a nameless noun—"the mayor's son"—in a story about his father's favorability rating.

His dad was the one person Harris hated to disappoint, yet even he seemed almost pleased that his son's mistake produced some publicity. After his rather harsh initial reaction, Mayor McGee had pushed Harris to embrace the situation, to turn the negative into a positive by speaking out about his passion to breathe new life into the East Side.

Harris attempted to follow his father's suit, starting to envelop the mindset that things weren't as bad as they could be. Except with Abram. If possible, things with him were even worse than before. Despite his continual attempts, Harris hadn't seen or talked to Abe since the night he'd slept at his house. He had assumed Abe would be the stubborn, steadfast man he always was, but he'd never expected Abe to completely ignore him. His communication was entirely unreciprocated, a one-sided attempt to build a bridge and be adults shot down with utter silence. The only thing Harris wanted was a nice conversation and a chance to catch up on what Abe had been up to over the past three years. He wanted to say thank you for being there in a huge time of need. He certainly didn't want to rehash the past or try to rekindle anything. Harris pushed all thoughts of Abe to the back of his mind for the time being. If Abe didn't want to take thirty seconds to acknowledge him, then Harris would respond in the same manner.

Besides, he truly had bigger things to worry about, like when Sabrina would return home. He waited so long for the chance to talk to her and explain everything face-to-face. Thanks to the endless news reports, Harris knew everything he needed to know about her life—and more. She was a single mom, living with her five-year-old daughter, Charity, and her two-year-old son, Maxwell, working as a nurse's aide and studying to become an RN. The Rowells received an outpouring of support from the Western New York community, none of which Sabrina asked for or accepted. She requested anyone who wanted to donate money or clothes to give to her church or the Buffalo City Mission, insisting she had just moved into the house and things weren't as bad as the pictures made it seem.

One quote of hers in *The Buffalo News* especially stung Harris. "My grandma always told me 'A house is made of wood and stone, but only love can make a home.' That's how I live every day. With unconditional love for my children. This house will be a home, I promise you that." As soon as he read that quote, Harris vowed to help make her house a home.

Sitting in his truck on the East Side, he immersed himself in his vision for the neighborhood. He had such hope, so many ideas and plans that hadn't yet come to fruition. On his way to Sabrina's street, he'd driven by the house where his great-grandmother had lived, a few streets over on Fillmore Avenue. The neighborhood—once so vibrant and bustling—stood in shambles, littered with vacant homes and empty plots of land. Her house had lost the magnificence he remembered as a child, its brick dirty and decaying, the gutters dented and drooping, the shrubs in need of a good pruning. It pained him to know he had ruined his chance to somewhat restore the glory days of the East Side. His long conversation with Dennis and Keith two days before provided some closure. He'd learned they were abandoning the project, at least in its current state, and were working on bringing affordable houses to areas other than William and Clinton Street areas while the city figured out what they wanted. Smack dab in the middle of a sticky situation, neither gave Harris any indication they'd consider rehiring him. He had spent a good part of the last forty-eight hours wondering what would have happened if he had fought to stay or brainstormed some other way to continue with a modified version of the East Side Renaissance.

A black Labrador puppy frolicked on the sidewalk on the opposite side of the street, forcing Harris's focus to shift to the present. The dog had such a spring in its step, its happy-go-lucky attitude becoming so addicting to watch that Harris almost missed Sabrina finally pulling into her driveway. He had parked four houses away, enough to still see Sabrina but not obvious enough for her to notice his truck. Not wanting to bombard her, he vowed to wait at least twenty minutes after she arrived home to knock on her door.

That wait became more excruciating as the digital clock on his dashboard seemed to take an eternity to reach even sixty seconds, so he shut off his car to block his access to time. In his head, he repeated different ways to say phrases like "I wholeheartedly apologize" and "Please find it in your heart to forgive me." He knew it would be a longshot to get Sabrina to hear him out, but he still had a series of categories that he wanted to tackle throughout the speech: introduction, apology, explanation, and offer to help.

Harris gave up on his self-imposed twenty-minute wait, the nerves bubbling inside of him too much to ignore any longer. His thoughts became clear as he walked down the street and up Sabrina's driveway. He didn't expect his knock on the door to be the thudding force it was, but he chalked it up to nerves and his semifrozen limbs.

Sabrina came to the side door, opening it up halfway. Harris interjected before she had a chance to say anything.

"Hi. I'm so sorry to bother you. My name is Harris McGee."

Sabrina stood, arms crossed, glaring straight past Harris.

"I'm the guy—the idiot—from Beautify Buffalo who broke in here and posted that picture of your house. God, I can't believe I did that." Harris stammered, fashioning a self-deprecating smile and a slight laugh, hoping to ease the tension emanating from Sabrina's stone-cold stare.

"I know exactly who you are. I really don't have anything to say to you," Sabrina said, annoyed, as she started to close the door.

"I know," Harris said and blocked her from shutting him out. "I know you don't have anything to say to me. But I have so much to say to you. I'm here to apologize. I feel horrible for doing this to you."

"Honey, you don't have to worry about me. I'm a big girl."

"Do you have a few minutes?" Harris asked, blowing on his hands and motioning inside to Sabrina's kitchen with his head. She stood still for a few seconds, looking standoffish and somewhat scared. Harris realized he had to turn off the robotic charm that had suited him so well throughout his life and simply talk to her unaffectedly.

"Listen. Sabrina. I'm incredibly sorry. And I really would appreciate if you gave me the chance to explain myself."

Unfazed, Sabrina shook her head, looking like she was about to tell Harris to take a hike.

"I waited for you for almost three hours," he said, a final attempt to win her trust.

She looked him up and down, debating in her head what to do before opening the door fully.

"Come on in."

The home had been in Sabrina's family for decades, most recently owned by her aunt, who had been renting the property since 2002. Before that, she explained, Sabrina had lived there with her mother and four sisters. The two sat at her dinky dining room table and drank coffee like they were old gal pals. She accepted his apology with little forethought, seeming to realize the whole thing was a huge misunderstanding.

"Thank you again for forgiving me and allowing me to explain," Harris said.

"Remember, when you forgive, you heal," she replied. "And when you let go, you grow."

The message immediately stamped an imprint in his heart. Harris loved that saying and hoped others in the community wouldn't hold his foolish mistake against him.

"You're lucky you caught me on an off night. Usually I'm either working, at school, or have the kids here," she explained, stating that Charity and Maxwell were with their father's grandmother for the night. "I wish their father was more of a father. It'd certainly help me out."

"Were you two ever married?" Harris asked.

"Who? Me and Boots? For two years. And that was about a year and nine months too many!" She laughed.

"Boots? That's his name?"

"Bruce. His name is Bruce. Growing up, his little brother could never say his name properly. It always came out Boots. The nickname stuck. He makes his buddies call him that now and tries to get the kids to call him that instead of Dad. He even has a tattoo of 'Boots' on his arm."

"Does he see the kids often?" Harris hated to pry, but Sabrina's warm and inviting spirit seemed to welcome the conversation.

"I wish. It would make things so much easier. He loves his kids and they love him. We're working on it. But Bruce needs to grow up, get sober, stay out of trouble, get a decent job, and be a man," Sabrina said, counting the list off on her fingers. "He's a good father. Just needs to be a better man."

Harris gave an understanding nod and looked at his surroundings, noticing that Sabrina had definitely done some work in the week since he was there last. The place actually looked lived in, with some trinkets sprinkled throughout the house and new curtains covering the windows. Sabrina caught his wandering gaze.

"I know I have work to do. It'll get done."

"That's actually why I'm here," Harris started, encouraged by her warmth toward him. "As you know, I'm out of a job. And I really owe you. Big time. I'd like to help fix some of your issues here."

"Oh, that's not necessary."

"Please. Let me help. It's the least I can do. I promise I won't be a distraction."

"Harris, I told you, I'm a big girl," Sabrina said. "I know there are some things I need to fix in this house and I'll get to them, eventually. I'm saving little by little."

"Sabrina, without sounding like a jerk, I know people. I can get all the supplies you need and have all the resources to help. And I'm warning you, I'm not going to take no for an answer."

He sensed Sabrina hemming and hawing in her head. Her uneasiness had dwindled a bit, her body language slowly appearing more natural.

Harris recognized an opening to get her seal of approval, so he rose from his chair and began his demonstration.

"You see these cracks?" Harris said, pointing to her bay window. "That's likely a stress crack, which I can fix with a double- or triple-paned window. And if I put that in, it'll keep this room warmer, too."

He walked over to the brown and amorphous stain on the drywall.

"You've got a leak somewhere in here and that's why you have these marks. I can tear this down, fix the leak, and put up new drywall. And if you want to pick out a paint color, I can paint the whole room. It'll look good as new."

Sabrina stood silently.

"I'll tell you what. I'm going to come back in the morning and fix the easy things, take some measurements. I'll start with finding the leak and then work on the windows. If all goes well, I promise to be in and out in a few hours, okay?"

"Harris. You don't have a job. You don't need to be spending money on me."

Money wasn't an issue for Harris—at least not yet. He had enough in the bank to last him a few months, and he truthfully didn't imagine being unemployed that long.

"Sabrina, you have turned down so much help over the last week. It's okay to say yes this time." Harris stood and extended his hand to shake Sabrina's.

She grabbed his right hand and clutched it. "Thank you, Harris."

"Hey, it's the least I can do."

"You know, you really don't have to do this."

"I know I don't have to. I want to."

The two smiled at each other as Harris put on his jacket and walked down the stairs. They exchanged a few pleasantries, and Harris shouted, "I'll see you in the morning!" as he exited her side door.

The brisk air felt refreshing on his skin. If his goal of revitalizing the entire East Side couldn't be achieved, at least he would be able to help someone in dire need. And selfishly, at least, the woman he inadvertently thrust into the spotlight forgave him and was allowing him to feel like a slightly honorable human.

Harris stopped at the lip of Sabrina's driveway, waiting for a car to pass. He still had his doubts with her house. There looked to be foundation issues and he was hopeful learning the location of the leak wouldn't lead him to discovering mold.

"Hey, man, you got a problem with my girl Sabrina?"

Harris spun around, alarmed at the way the tone of the question carved through the tranquil night.

"Who, me?" Harris turned around to face the man. "No, no. Sabrina is lovely."

Lovely? Harris hated his word choice. Why in the hell would he use that word? He should've kept walking. Instead, the man self-assuredly marched up to him, standing mere inches from his face. Harris could smell the whiskey on his breath.

"Hey, hey. I know you," he said, smiling. His eyes were incredibly bloodshot, entirely red except for a patch of white in each corner. "You're that asshole that broke into Sabrina's house and called it a piece of shit."

"I never said that."

"So, it is you! The asshole who wants to demolish the neighborhood!"

Harris began walking across the street, knowing there was zero chance this would end well. His steps became faster, now heading toward his truck in a half jog, half walk. He remembered the hockey stick in the back of his truck that he could use as a weapon if need be.

"Why you running away?"

The man successfully blocked Harris from any escape, leaving his only recourse to stay and try to talk this out or run, backpedaling toward Sabrina's house. He made the choice to stand his ground, having had enough of running away from his problems.

"Dude, I'm working on fixing her house."

The man laughed loudly, a roaring, sarcastic exhale visibly floating through the cold air like powder.

"You're gonna fix her house?"

"Look, I apologized to Sabrina, okay? I made a mistake," Harris said, trying to diffuse the situation. "Go ask her yourself."

"Aww, isn't that nice of you. Well, guess what? Your pity isn't gonna work on me, pretty boy."

The man grabbed Harris's shirt, his fury causing Harris's hands to shake uncontrollably, his breath becoming short and spastic as his brain bumped and bumbled, trying to think of a way out of the situation. He wanted to scream, to disappear, to wake up and feel the relief that this was nothing but a nightmare. As he headed toward his driver's side door, he wiggled out of the man's clutch, struggling to find the right words to say, getting lost so deep in thought it took him a moment before he felt the stinging crack of the hockey stick on the side of his face.

The kicks were swift and powerful, the punches heavy and vicious. The quickness of the attack provided no chance for retaliation. The voice from his attacker became muffled as his ears pulsed with pain. His whole body burned deeply as he languidly writhed toward his door in a failed escape.

The attack stopped abruptly. The barrage of hits had finally ended. Harris blinked, his eyes opening to a red-tinged world.

Staring up into the sky toward the infinite blackness, Harris saw no stars shimmering above, no planes slowly zooming by, no faint wisp of the wind blowing a tree branch in his direction. He heard no footsteps echoing, no cars driving nearby, no dogs barking or people talking in the distance. He tried to call out for help, but his voice disappeared, leaving him softly moaning and gargling a throat full of warm blood that began seeping out the side of his mouth.

Half on the sidewalk, half in the street, he lay there unwillingly motionless, falling in and out of consciousness, wishing for one of life's little signs that he was still alive.

Eleven: Abram

Abe sat at a picnic table inside Niawanda Park, looking out toward the Grand Island bridges across the Niagara River. The day had turned pleasant—at least by the standards of a Buffalo winter—with temperatures climbing into the upper 40s and the sun shining brightly. While most of the snow had melted away, the Harris blizzard inside him only intensified.

Of course this place would make him think of Harris. After all, this was the spot where they had their first date back in college.

Abe shook his head and remembered that moment he first laid eyes on Harris. The two were waiting for their drinks inside Perks, the coffee house on UB's campus. Abe had been standing at the end of the line reading his calculus book, not even noticing the sexy, fashionable guy in front of him. The barista shouted out, "Hey, man, your latté is ready" and Abe sprang forward to grab the drink, whisking it off the countertop and hurrying toward the library.

"Hey, latté stealer, I think that's mine," he heard a voice say. Abe still recalled spinning around and being blinded by Harris's beauty. "Yours is the one with no sugar added, right? Mine is caramel so, you know, extra sugar."

Their first conversation ended with Abe's apology, but for the two days after, he couldn't get their meet-cute off his mind. Thinking Harris stopped to Perks before his 11:00 a.m. class on Tuesdays and Thursdays, Abe headed back to get a latté on Thursday at the same time. He made sure to wear his nicest casual outfit: a pair of Guess jeans with a Banana Republic blue-and-white checkered button-down shirt. He even got his hair cut Wednesday night so he'd look extra sharp for their second encounter. The preparation was useless, though, as he never came across Harris that Thursday, or the following week, or the week after. Abe gave up after five unsuccessful attempts, begrudgingly assuming that fate had no plans for the planets to align for him and Extra Sugar.

It wasn't until Cassie forced Abe to go to a frat party at the Sigma Phi Epsilon house a few weeks later that the two crossed paths again. Abe clearly remembered not wanting to leave his dorm that night, instead preferring to stay in and watch *American Pie* or *Varsity Blues* before calling it an early night.

"You are such an old man!" Cassie said. "Live a little bit, jeez. I swear we'll be home by midnight. If you go to the party with me, I promise we can play tennis tomorrow."

Cassie always delivered the perfect one-two punch of a harsh insult followed by a quick bribe she knew Abe would find too enticing to turn down.

"Fine. But you better not drink too much," he responded. "You know you suck at tennis when you're hungover."

Every step to the Sig Ep house came with a discernable plod from Abe, who grew more annoyed the farther they traveled away from Spaulding Hall. His aggravation became more apropos after a half hour at the party, when Abe found himself standing alone with his cup of lukewarm Keystone Light as Cassie won game after game of beer pong with her roommate Deanna. He knew there would be no competitive tennis match in the morning—sadly the only reason he was socializing that night—so he quietly tried exiting the room to head back home when he slammed into the back of a guy standing in the doorway of the kitchen.

"Oh, sorry, man."

"Latté stealer?" Harris asked, spinning around to face Abe.

"Extra sugar!" Abe replied, thrilled to see the handsome stranger.

The two planted themselves on the gross yellow love seat in the Sig Ep house and talked for two hours that night. The obvious differences between them—Harris, a social butterfly, Abe an uncomfortable wallflower—couldn't overshadow their instant attraction. Abe loved everything about the moment, like Harris's tight-fitting, sky-blue V-neck T-shirt, the way his left eyebrow arched every time he spoke, the glow of his dark skin and how they both seemed nervous but entirely comfortable.

Nothing came close to defusing their electric connection until a delightfully inebriated Cassie interrupted them by completely disregarding their conversation and asking Abe to take her back to the dorms before she got sick.

"It was nice to finally talk to you," Abe said, being pulled slowly away by Cassie. Harris stood up and followed Cass and Abe.

"Hey, I planned on going to the river tomorrow to get some ice cream at Mississippi Mudds before it closes for the year. You wanna come?" Harris asked.

"Yeah, I'd like that. What time?"

"Meet me there around two o'clock?"

"Sounds good," Abe said as Cassie dragged him out of the room. "See you then!"

Abram still remembered the crazy sexy smile Harris flashed as he walked away, and the even sexier smile when he looked back a second time. He would've made a third attempt, but Cassie grabbed at him flamboyantly.

"Abram, I'm absolutely not going to be able to play tennis tomorrow."

"No biggie. I actually think I have a date with that guy."

That was the moment he came out to Cassie, the whole conversation wonderfully nonchalant and organic. Cassie never flinched at the news, never made Abe feel anything but exhilarated at his potential new romance.

"Tell. Me. *Everything*!" she'd shouted with an infectious, drunken enthusiasm.

Abe rubbed his temples and flashed forward to real-time. Coming to the river was intended to be a chance to clear his mind and process new feelings, not travel back in time. Obviously, the wistful memories of an eighteen-year-old in love for the first time would be coated in an overwhelming recollection of favorability. He needed to determine what, if anything, to do now.

This train of thought was so typical of Abe. To figure out what to do in the next fifteen minutes, he traveled back fifteen years. The overanalyzing had taken control of his life, preventing any spontaneity, any true show of emotion. Each and every serious conversation or important moment had to be thoroughly evaluated in his mind. If only he knew the way to cure this analysis paralysis, maybe life would be better.

While most men focused on bulking up in the winter, he had aimed to cut down his muscle tone for a more slim physique and was right in the middle of an eight-week program. His routine included circuit training with high reps and free weights and high intensity cardio, which included running, followed by sprints. Abe looked at his watch. 5:05 p.m. He had enough time to squeeze in his quick run before heading home for dinner with Jared. Since Cassie had been justifiably MIA since Mrs. Montgomery's tumor diagnosis, spending every free moment with her mother, Jared and Abe had been left alone together—not that Abe was complaining. Jared turned out to be everything Abe wanted and needed in a roommate: an early riser, a healthy eater, a dedicated fitness advocate, and a Demi Lovato lover.

The past week had solidified their budding friendship as they spent almost all of their downtime together; working out in the morning, eating dinner together in the evening, spending lazy nights in the living room watching a movie or chatting and getting to know each other better. The time he spent with Jared was the only solace for what was happening to Mrs. Montgomery, and to a lesser extent, his friendship with Cassie. Abe hadn't seen her in two days, though they did spend an awful lot of time sending cat pictures and amusing GIFs to each other. Their relationship hadn't yet reached the blazing heights of the olden days despite this newfound way of communication.

Abe finished his sprints and began the ten-minute drive home. Sweaty and out of breath, he wondered if he'd have enough time to shower before dinner. It was his night to cook, and he wanted to impress Jared by creating some healthy alternative to comfort food. Tonight's special would be a broccoli and chicken casserole without any butter, cheese, or creamy soup. Jared seemed to appreciate his culinary skills, though Abe knew Jared had little to compare it to, as Cassie couldn't make toast without burning it.

Seeing the lights on inside when he arrived home brought a smile to Abe's face. The driveway was now the temporary home to the *Dreamboat*, Jared's aptly titled whaler boat, which was pulled all the way back to the garage. He would keep it in the driveway until fishing season started, something he couldn't wait to experience along the Niagara River and Lake Erie. As if Jared didn't have enough going for him with his looks, his career, and his personality—he also had highly enviable hobbies that took intelligence and persistence.

The two made small talk as Abe entered the kitchen and prepared the casserole.

"Any word from Cass?" Abe asked.

"Not yet. She likes to wait until Clare is asleep to give me the updates."

Abe wondered how Jared was handling everything. A new city with a new job and a distracted girlfriend. Did he feel trapped? Did he feel annoyed? Was he pissed he had to spend all his time with Cassie's best friend?

"It's a shame you don't drink, my friend," Jared said. "A coworker gave me this bottle of Merlot from Bordeaux."

Bordeaux. The word flickered through the air before dropping swiftly and walloping Abe's skull. He felt the blood rush out of his head, seeping down to his feet, his skin losing all color.

"Hey, you okay?" Jared asked.

"Bordeaux," he muttered, the lump in his throat coming to life in his voice. "It just brings back bad memories."

Jared took a sip from his wineglass. "Mmm. Well, there is nothing bad about this," Jared said, while raising his glass. "Want some?"

"I shouldn't."

"Why not?"

"I haven't had alcohol in two years! I'll die."

"You will not!"

"Well, I'm afraid to see what would happen."

He belted out some Kelly Clarkson to remind Abe that he'd only be made stronger by things that don't kill him, before trailing off into a humming mumble. The inadvertent peer pressure began to claw at Abe. He absolutely hated the way alcohol made him feel the day after drinking, but would one glass really kill him?

"You are a bad influence," Abe said, pulling out his cell phone as it vibrated. "Oh my God! He's calling again!"

Abe slammed his palms down on the granite countertop.

"Who? Harris?"

"Yeah, he must be at his dad's house. This is third call tonight. Leave me alone already."

"Dude, you have to talk to him."

"It's not that easy," Abe said, launching into a discourse that served as a timeline of their relationship. They blissfully dated for all four years of college, tried things long distance when Harris lived in Chicago, broke up after six months of that, and ultimately got back together two years later when he returned to Buffalo. Altogether, Harris and Abe had been boyfriends for nearly nine years.

"So, what the hell happened between you guys?"

Abe never talked about their relationship. Instead, he relied on a memorized speech he kept carefully tucked in the back of his mind. "*We started drifting apart*" was a phrase he often used. "*We both decided things weren't working the way they used to*" was another one of his favorites. Sometimes, if he was feeling sassy, he even threw in "*I decided it was time to move on.*" That one was probably the most truthful. The breakup didn't come after an explosion of hatred or jealousy or anger. It slowly fizzled, shriveling from full bloom to barren and dry.

"We were on vacation in Bordeaux," Abe said, pointing to the wineglass, "And we decided once and for all we were just going to do it. Just get back to Buffalo and do it."

"Do what?" Jared asked, listening intently.

"Pour me a glass," Abe said, shocking himself. "Hurry up! Before I change my mind."

The two laughed as Jared feigned panic filling up the glass.

"I really hate talking about this—us. It's painful."

"Hey, if you don't want to share, that's fine," Jared said. "But, maybe I can help?"

He handed Abe the glass of Merlot, which smelled delicious. Abe stared across the room at Jared and once again got lost in his steel-blue eyes. All Abram could think of was the *Dreamboat*—it was a name that perfectly summed up Jared. Abe didn't know why this man he barely knew stirred up such a strong feeling inside him. He didn't know why this man compelled him to drink a glass of wine and spill the secrets he held so close. Perhaps most telling? Abe didn't care why. This was one portion of his life he definitely didn't feel like analyzing.

"Harris always hated how much I loved to plan everything, so when we got back from France, I decided to throw him the ultimate surprise."

Abe thought his impromptu marriage plan was whimsical and foolproof. A week prior to that fateful day, he approached Mayor McGee and bit the gay bullet, asking for his blessing to marry Harris. The relationship between Abe and Harris's dad wasn't frosty, but it wasn't exactly welcoming, either. Mayor McGee caught Abe off guard when he overwhelmingly approved of the idea, hugging Abe and stammering with excited approval. Abe then outlined the rest of his plan to the mayor, whose help he desperately needed. He wanted to surprise Harris and make him think the two were having a casual Friday night together, when in reality, he would lure him to Buffalo's City Hall to propose and get married on the spot. Even in a perfect world, Abe recognized this was an insane idea, but he had embraced that rare instance of spontanaiety.

Abe didn't realize his plan had a few unforeseen glitches, which Mayor McGee nicely said he would circumvent. New York State law said all couples have to wait at least twenty-four hours after obtaining a marriage license to wed, unless they have a judicial waiver. The mayor assured Abram he would obtain the waiver while also volunteering to be their witness.

"With all the logistics worked out, I moved on to the romantic part of the idea," Abe explained, pausing to sip the delicious Merlot. "Our City Hall has this amazing observation deck on the twenty-eighth floor." He began feeling the tingling of the wine in his bones.

Decorating the observation deck took creativity, with the entire outdoor space enclosed by a ten-foot wall of plexiglass. Abe printed out dozens of photos and gathered their relationship souvenirs he had been holding onto, deciding to string them up with gold ribbon around the entire circumference of the building facing the appropriate direction. Toward Niagara Falls, Abe strung up pictures from Harris's nineteenth birthday at Fallsview Casino, along with a parking stub from a random visit in 2010. Straight below City Hall toward Lafayette Square, he hung up a wristband from a Thursday in the Square concert for Grace Potter & the Nocturnals. Toward Hamburg, he carefully positioned the stuffed Rastafarian banana Harris won for him at the Erie County Fair a decade earlier. Toward Amherst, he displayed their UB graduation program. Toward Lockport, he placed the ticket stub for *Spiderman 2*, which they watched together at the Transit Drive-in. Abe had been holding on to these items all that time, waiting for the perfect moment to utilize them.

"I even set up the inside part of the observation deck to look exactly like this restaurant we adored in Bordeaux."

Abe and Harris ate at Le Bistro du Musée every day while vacationing in France. They had discovered the lovely little place on their first morning there as it conveniently sat near the chateau they'd rented. Not only did the bistro offer stunning views of Bordeaux's City Hall and the glorious Bordeaux Cathedral, but there was something about the atmosphere there that produced a passionate sentiment inside of them. Feeling slightly awkward for their lack of French, Abe and Harris sat in silence for most of their meals there. It was enough to simply hold hands under the table, soak everything in, and smile at each other. To match the décor of the restaurant, Abe printed French quotes about wine like *La vie est trop courte pour boire du mauvais vin* or Life is too short to drink cheap wine. He even ran an extension cord for a space heater that had those fake orange flames on the façade to mimic a fireplace. He had hoped the romanticism of that trip would be surpassed that night, as the two finally became husbands.

"I planned to bring him up there first and propose," Abe said. "When I say I thought of it all, I mean it. I truly thought of it all. I remember feeling really anxious and nervous, but so excited."

"What happened?" Jared asked.

"He never showed. He told me he fell asleep!" Abe said, now shouting and gulping his wine in a fury. "That he *forgot* we were supposed to hang out that night. There I was, planning to fucking *marry* him and he was taking a nap. Or so he says."

"You think he's lying?"

"I don't know what I think anymore. I just know that nothing was ever the same. I instantly started questioning everything about our relationship. We are two totally different people and nothing was ever going to change that. I completely shut down after that."

"You never told him?"

"No way. Do you know how embarrassed I was? How humiliating it was to stand there with his father for an hour while I waited and waited and waited to hear from him? How crushing it was to clean up the observation deck and look at piles and piles of memories?"

The wine was working, speeding viciously through his bloodstream. Abe felt lightheaded but relaxed. The guillotine in his mind that constantly cut off his thoughts, preventing his true emotions from showing slowly deconstructed.

"I've never told anyone this before. Not even Cassie. But, I haven't...been with...anyone since him, if you know what I mean," Abe said, his cheeks flushing as Jared's eyes widened. "And, honestly, I doubt I'll ever feel that way about any man ever again. He completely ruined me."

"Abram, I'm so sorry."

"Hey. Whatever!" Abe said, giggling, his brain pulsing with a hypnotic energy.

"You have to talk to him, man," Jared said. "And that's Jared, the human, speaking. Not Jared, the doctor. You need to talk to him."

"And say what?"

"Ask him to meet you for a quick chat. You can worry about the details of what you'll say later."

Abe looked at Jared longingly. Before him stood an amazing man whose beauty was only surpassed by the heart of gold he had inside. Every hair on Abe's body stood on end when he looked at Jared, a man who got him to finally admit what had been eating him up inside for the past three years.

Maybe it was the liberation of finally coming clean about his wounded heart; maybe it was simply the wine. But Abe honestly felt like a new man.

"I'm going to text him. Give me my phone."

"Atta boy! Abram Hoffman making big moves, everyone!"

Only a slight hesitation existed inside Abe. Jared pushing him to talk to Harris and his wine-induced carefree attitude proved to be precisely what he needed to take that leap he had been postponing.

"Okay, okay, let me read this to you and make sure it's acceptable," Abe said as Jared refilled his glass, finishing the bottle of Merlot. "Harris, sorry for the delay in returning your texts to you. Are you free sometime over the next few days to talk?"

"Add 'in person.' You need to talk in person."

"Good idea."

"Hit Send. Now."

Abe obeyed.

"I feel better." He exhaled. "I really do. I don't know what the hell I'm going to say to him, but I feel better."

The moment had been building inside Abe for ages. He felt alive and proud. There were very few moments in his life over the past couple of years where he had achieved a personal victory—and certainly none as momentous as this one.

"Let this be a lesson. Sometimes you have to do things in the moment and deal with the consequences later," Jared said. "That's the whole point of life! You're so afraid of what will happen if you make the wrong move that you don't even try to make the right ones."

"I know."

"Stop being so scared."

"I'm going to start trying," Abe said. "I really am."

"Well, try harder, Abe. Your happiness depends on it," Jared said. "I mean, you have—"

Abe cut Jared off by grabbing his shirt and pulling him toward his face. He leaned forward with confidence, cupped the back of Jared's head with his right hand, and drew him close.

The Merlot tasted even better on the tip of Jared's tongue.

Twelve: Harris

Sabrina's screams inside the emergency room startled him, each one a ferocious directive that resonated throughout the sterile walls. Harris truly couldn't believe such a soft-spoken woman could yell with such authoritative gravitas.

"Get this man to an OR now!" she instructed. "Hurry!"

He had the urge to carefully tug her arm and whisper in her ear, "Calm down. Everything's okay," but kept his mouth shut, figuring if anyone knew what to do inside a hospital, it'd be Sabrina.

The pain that first stung with a sizzling force now simply cloaked his body with a throbbing numbness. The rapid shouting of medical terminology—words like ventriculostomy—hurt more than his battle wounds did, confusing his mind as he listened for Sabrina's next set of instructions. The voices of a dozen strangers twisted in his head, not a single one of which belonged to her. Harris couldn't believe he didn't confirm what time he'd start working on her house in the morning or get a chance to say goodbye to her. He wanted to turn around and shout back toward her, but missed his chance as the hospital staff had already rushed his gurney down the hall.

After a long nap, the steady stream of visitors began, starting with his father, who had been shouting the entire time he'd been inside Harris's room.

"This is a fucking hate crime!" his dad yelled to two people Harris couldn't recognize. "Jesus fucking Christ, any idiot can see that!"

Harris wanted to blurt out "I don't think this is a hate crime, Dad," but didn't feel like fighting with his father, whom he knew wouldn't listen to a rational explanation in his irrational state.

He overheard the doctor—whose name Harris didn't catch—giving his father the latest update. "The brain swelling is down, which is a good thing, but we'll continue to monitor it closely. We removed his lacerated spleen and he's scheduled for a blood transfusion in a few hours. And the break here was a doozy. It should heal in about six weeks, but we're not out of the woods yet."

He hated how they talked about him as if he wasn't there, but he didn't want to point this out like some petulant child.

"We're going to find that son of a bitch," his dad said as he stroked the top of Harris's left hand, the quiver in his voice growing. Harris hadn't ever heard the high-pitched tremble currently escaping his dad's mouth, not even when he delivered the eulogy at Monica McGee's funeral. "And when we do—" His father paused and gulped audibly. "—when we do, he will pay."

Harris didn't know how to react, but he definitely did not want this to be the knock-down, drag-out fight it looked like his father was prepared to enter. This wasn't an eye-for-an-eye situation to Harris. If he had his way, that guy kicking his ass would be the final chapter of this miserable, pitiful week in his life. His dad gave an outline to the other men in the room, and it sounded like they were furiously scribbling every word he spoke. Harris could only make out segments of sentences: "Sabrina Rowell found him," "It's on William near Clinton" "...because he's gay."

For a brief moment, a surge of happiness overtook his body. It always annoyed Harris how his dad often disguised his sexuality—he had forever introduced Abram as "Harris's friend" to strangers—but his attitude now was a complete one-eighty. His voice had an air of significance behind it, as if he was implying he was finally able to accept his son was gay. He wasn't sure whether to be pleased it finally happened or sad it took so long and something so awful to produce this feeling.

Replaying his father's conversation with the doctor in his head, Harris wondered why he didn't feel pain, but knew it was likely a temporary, medically-induced state. And despite the vanity of his thoughts, what Harris really wanted was a mirror. Even without touching his face, he knew it was puffy, battered, and bruised. All he could taste was a hint of blood in the back of his throat. *When they ask me what I want. I'll politely ask for a mirror and a toothbrush.*

No one ever asked, though.

Harris lost all sense of time in that bed. He had no clue if it was day or night, Saturday or Monday, if two hours had passed or if two days had come and gone. Maybe it was the morphine, the dopamine, the fentanyl, or the thiopental—names he'd memorized from the plethora of nurses and doctors surveying his room—that caused him to go in and out of a cogent awareness, remaining entirely oblivious as the guests came pouring in and out of his room.

His aunt Jodi and uncle Bill were the first guests after his father to visit, awkwardly sitting hushed the entire time they visited, except for the occasional dejected tsking, heavy sighs, and inaudible muttering. They were followed by college housemates Keri and Carolyn, who spent their entire visit only talking to each other about nonsense, which was typical. Then Keith and Dennis arrived, and for the first time since his dad left, someone actually talked to him, albeit in questions that had no answers.

"Who did this to you?" Keith asked.

"Is this all our fault?" Dennis followed. "Because I feel like it is."

If Harris could've lifted his arm, he would've slapped Dennis and said, *This is not your fault. This is entirely my fault.*

He couldn't see them, but he smelled roses, carnations, and gardenias on the shelves above and next to him. The aroma of all the different types of flowers mixing together in the dank room bothered Harris, but he didn't want to say anything, fearful the nurses and doctors would think he was being petty and ungrateful.

The flowers only started Harris's intense nasal sensory perception. His sense of smell seemingly grew stronger, the plastic from his IVs and the stench from carts of food carrying soup and roast beef circulating down the hallway filling his nostrils with a sickening blow. As he desperately struggled to stop the scents from permeating his skin, footsteps came toward him.

And then it hit him: a whiff of cinnamon toothpaste and spearmint lip balm.

Abe.

That man is such a creature of habit.

Three years later, he still used the same toothpaste, still wore the same ChapStick. Harris never quite figured out why or how someone would love a hot mouth and cool lips, but that was classic Abe: a unique man who somehow made strange routines a staple of his daily life.

The screech of chair legs angrily gliding across the tiled floor almost made Harris cringe, but he forced himself to sit stone-faced, waiting for Abram to make the first move. After all of Harris's attempts to talk to him over the past week, he felt a little miffed that it took the presence of a savage beating for Abe to finally show his face.

He understood why Abe still had his doubts. He understood why Abe had trouble expressing whatever it was he was feeling inside. He understood that Abe owed him nothing, and he owed Abe everything. But he didn't understand why Abe refused to talk to the man he supposedly loved for nearly a decade.

As Abe cleared his throat, Harris thought this was finally the moment Abe would bare his soul. Whether it was good or bad, positive or negative, Harris was prepared to handle Abe's words. But as he lay there waiting for them to start flowing, all that he heard were faint, soft whimpers. Abe grabbed Harris's forearm and placed his head on his torso, the whimpers gradually turning into deep, drawn-out wails. The irritation first brought on by Abe once again failing to speak to him quickly turned into sympathy, as Abe's exposed, raw emotions were on full display.

He had zero idea how to react and felt relief when he heard Cassie and Jared arrive shortly after, each of them reassuring Abe everything would be fine, the sound of one of them rubbing Abe's back in a circular motion to provide comfort as they hovered over Harris with a purposeful stillness. Their breathing was strenuous, like a bunch of characters in a horror film narrowly escaping a serial killer. They were all being so quiet that Harris felt weird disrupting the lull in the room, so he kept his mouth shut, not wanting to cause an unnecessary fuss.

It didn't take long for the three to zip up their coats, preparing to leave. Irate, Harris wanted to howl at Abe, demand him to say something—anything—to him. But he wouldn't do it, he wouldn't be the one to continually be vulnerable and put himself out there first, only for Abe to shut him down with his failure to be an adult and have an actual conversation.

His inner furor served as an unfortunate distraction, because without warning, the wet glaze of lip balm pressed to his forehead and was left there by a kiss from Abe. By the time he recognized the gesture, it was too late to respond. Abe was gone.

Harris snapped out of what had to be a days-long drowsiness, the room finally coming into focus, despite something covering his right eye. He tussled with the sheets, trying to prop himself up in bed and catching the attention of a nurse walking by.

"Harris, sweetie? Are you awake?" she asked.

He tried opening his mouth to respond, but his lips were stuck shut and all that emerged was a muffled grumble. Harris's gaze followed the nurse as she hurried with an excited skip to the door of his room.

"Janine? Janine, can you page Dr. Morphy? Harris McGee just woke up."

He immediately noted that her short, inverted bob with straight-as-an-arrow bangs and bright pink uniform were the perfect way for a fifty-something woman to appear fun in an age-appropriate manner.

"Harris. My name is Maureen. I'm your nurse."

He recognized the tone of Maureen's voice, which matched her motherly appearance.

"Squeeze my hand twice if you understand me."

Harris squeezed twice. Confused, he could feel his brow furrowing to question the nurse.

"You're at ECMC in the ICU. We're so glad to finally see you're awake."

He blinked his eyes in rapid succession as if to say *"Please explain what the fuck you are talking about,"* hoping Maureen comprehended his improvised medical Morse code.

"Hi, baby," she said in a sweet, slightly fake tone like she was Jennifer Lopez initially trying to soften the blow of a contestant's negative critique on *American Idol*. He could sense bad news on the horizon.

Harris lifted his arm to his face, the wires and IV cords traveling with him, the breathing tube pinching his nose. With gauze wrapped around his head, he was unable to muscle the strength to ask what the hell was going on.

"Oh no, honey, don't touch your face there," she said, pushing his arms back to his side. "Your jaw was broken in two spots. The doctor had to wire it shut."

His tears were almost immediate.

"Harris, aww, don't cry, dear. You should be happy."

He wanted to scream at her at the top of her lungs *"What's so happy about this?!"* but as he hunted for the correct number of rapid blinks to convey his question, Maureen gave him his answer.

"You've been in a coma for eleven days."

Thirteen: Clare

Less than twenty-four hours post-shave, Clare found out that her tumor, a slow-growing grade II tumor, was indeed cancerous. She had prepared herself for the worst—the same fate as Charlie—and believed that her tumor would offer no options for treatment. But Dr. Kincaid said there was hope this time around, suggesting radiation as the first plan in their series of attacks. Losing her hair from that recommended treatment would be likely, thus solidifying her premature head shaving as the correct move. Clare impressed herself with being so accurate that she made a promise to herself to trust her inclinations more from then on.

It delighted her that after sixty-six years, Clare Montgomery had finally started turning heads. In the grocery store, during yoga class, stopped at a red light—nearly everyone, definitely everywhere—gave her an obvious double take, craning and winding their necks during botched shots to stare surreptitiously. She smiled back at each set of eyes garishly gazing upon her with a subtle hint of confirmation. *Yes, I have cancer,* she tried conveying with a brief nod. If the look from strangers lingered long enough, she switched from the slight smirk to a confident grin to signify *Yes, I will beat this* with the same confidence in her eyes.

It's not as if she offered any other assumptions, proudly shouting to the world she had cancer with her bright orange-and-pink bandanas in bold chevron and paisley patterns. The newfound poise took some getting used to. Clare had spent the last year internally processing Charlie's cancer but never allowing an emotional exodus about him or for herself. Charlie didn't want to talk about anything regarding his cancer, so she stood by him as his muted better half, obeying his desires. After partially hiding from the truth with him, she knew that wouldn't be the route to follow this time around.

Clare felt like a mix of every bald woman who ever made headlines, possessing the meek moodiness of Sinead O'Connor, the robust power of Demi Moore in *G.I. Jane,* and if she were being honest, the crazed, illogical behavior of Britney Spears in meltdown mode.

She tiptoed around the questions of her sanity, which filled her gently intricate conversations with Cassie, Jared, Caleb, Dr. Kincaid, and her new therapist, Dr. Jordana Bihar. Their first session came at the strident recommendation of Dr. Kincaid, who told Clare she had the "unique opportunity to fully digest the physical and emotional toll cancer has on a human."

The month since her diagnosis had been some of the most eye-opening days of Clare's life, even as the news didn't hit her in the way she'd assumed it would. What Clare thought would feel like a dark weight resting on her head, waiting to crash down any minute, instead felt like a light vapor she could either blow aside or breathe in whenever she preferred.

Her recent attitude didn't go unnoticed, nor did it sit pretty with Cassie, who resorted to manic questioning of every decision her mother made since her initial return from the hospital. The shrill shriek of "Mom, what did you do?" and the vision of tears cascading down Cassie's cheeks flashed through Clare's mind each time she saw her daughter. That quizzical look had been permanently stuck on Cassie's face ever since that day, and she wasn't the only one.

Everyone thought the screws had finally come loose, that Clare had punched a one-way ticket to the insane asylum. The exact thought often passed through Clare's mind, too, since the task of being able to articulate what influenced her to shave her head proved impossible. She had no words for the feeling that pumped through her veins that night, no way to express the yearning inside of her to gain the upper hand on her condition.

Since the cancer confirmation, her life followed a schedule of doctor appointments and phone calls from friends and family she hadn't spoken to in years. Hearing from people like her cousins, her nieces and nephews, and Charlie's sisters felt refreshing at first, and she appreciated their well wishes and concern. But after a while, the conversations with the same sentimental platitudes left her longing for peace and quiet—which is exactly why she didn't mind her daily radiation sessions.

Clare was in the middle of her seven weeks of treatment, which entailed about an hour every Monday-Friday inside an oncology center on Harlem Road. Cassie so kindly volunteered to take Clare every morning after rearranging her schedule so that her free periods and lunch were the first three classes of the morning, ensuring she wouldn't miss any time at work. Her daughter had become her caretaker, her confidant. In her free time, if Cassie wasn't with Clare, she was calling or texting, checking in on her undesired patient. The stress and fatigue building in Cassie became palpable, the bags under her eyes growing deep and dark. Each time Clare attempted to tell Cassie to take some time for herself and let Clare handle things, she was shot down with a gentle, yet stern resistance.

"If I couldn't do this, Mom, I wouldn't," Cassie said. "I'm glad I can be here to help you through this. I know it's tough on you."

The radiation itself was anything but tough, needing no effort from Clare other than showing up. Each visit to the oncology center took no more than forty-five minutes, with the actual treatment lasting only a fraction of that time. The instructions were simple: lie on the table without moving. The only difference between these moments and taking a nap were the lasers shooting into her skull and the fact that Clare covered herself with a mesh mask they'd molded from her face. In that short amount of time, so many thoughts and emotions surged through her head. Despite her best efforts to remain a pillar of positivity and the Queen of Current Events, she often found herself in the depths of her own darkness, contemplating if all this treatment was pointless. Dr. Bihar assured her this feeling of mortality wasn't out of the ordinary.

"Anxiety and distress are factors that come into play with a cancer diagnosis," she told Clare. "Everyone deals with their diagnosis in different ways. Some people get depressed. Others choose to completely ignore it."

Every Tuesday and Thursday afternoon for the past three weeks, Clare had been meeting with her new therapist, an intelligent young Indian woman whose best ability might have been the way she forced Clare to question her own motives with the simplest of prodding. It wasn't so much the questions she asked, but the way she asked them—with her affected inflection, stressing certain syllables and pausing in certain places.

"Why," Dr. Bihar stressed by holding out the end of the word, "do you think the treatment is worthless? Once you get your next scan, you'll be able to determine if it's working or not."

"I have this weird hunch. I think this could be it," Clare said. "And I'm just not ready to admit that I'm old or near the end." She failed to mention her instincts had been on fire lately, extending beyond the obvious head shaving. She had purchased a scratch-off lottery ticket on a whim—something she hadn't done in decades—and won fifty dollars. And on the way to see Dr. Bihar the previous week, she'd had a gut reaction to avoid Sheridan Drive and successfully avoided a terrible car accident.

"You don't have to admit that, because cancer doesn't mean the end is near. Age is all relative, Clare, and you are fighting."

Clare shifted in her seat, still uncomfortable hearing others describe her as a "fighter." They only considered her a fighter because she actually had the opportunity to beat this. Clare found that position an incredibly lucky one, but that didn't mean she should be dubbed a fighter. Charlie was the fighter. He had worked all his life, scratching and clawing to make something of himself, working day and night to take care of his family. He'd fought every single day, but never got the invitation to show up for the one bout that meant the most. She grabbed the tissue stuck inside her sleeve and dabbed the inner corner of her eyes.

"I know a fighter when I see one, Clare."

Dr. Bihar had become an unexpected force in Clare's life in their six meetings, inadvertently succeeding in persuading Clare to delay the sale of 837 Parker Avenue—at least until her strength returned. It was one thing for Cassie and Jared to question Clare's intentions; it was another for a completely impartial, nonentity in her life to plant seeds of doubt without even trying. Dr. Bihar had simply asked her, "Is there any outside sources of stress and anxiety that you think can eliminate to help you get through the radiation?" and Clare immediately shouted, "Yeah, I could not sell my house!"

She honestly was half joking, but the thought of staying in the house crept into her mind. For the time being, the house was still on the market, with Clare sifting through the offers that had been trickling in. She'd asked her listing agent to inform all the Realtors of her condition, which she hoped would make potential buyers understand it might take time to hear a reply. It's not as if she second-guessed her decision to move, but Clare already noticed the typical side effects of being drained and weak that came along with radiation. She tried her own methods of fighting that worn-out feeling, mainly stocking up on activities like crossword puzzles, word searches, and Sudoku books. It's exactly what they did for Charlie during his final days to try to distract him.

Fully knowing that Charlie's death dictated such a prevalent amount of Clare's life—especially recently—Dr. Bihar encouraged Clare to attend group grief counseling.

"It seems as if you've never truly had a release, never had a chance to express your feelings about Charlie."

"Well, we can talk about it all you'd like. Where do you want to start?"

Dr. Bihar leaned forward in her chair, removed her glasses, and folded her arms on her lap. "Clare, you know I'm absolutely here to listen to everything you have to say. But I'm not married. I've never had the connection you and

Charlie had. I think you would benefit from hearing from other people in similar situations. Outside of such a clinical, formal setting."

Clare repressed an eye roll as she stared through Dr. Bihar, extremely irritated at the suggestion.

Dr. Bihar evidently sensed the anger and apprehension stemming from Clare's mind, quickly following up her recommendation with, "I've had several clients who have found their time with these groups invaluable."

Reluctance grabbed Clare quickly. Nearly a year had passed without Charlie. The pain she kept inside hurt more than anything she'd ever experienced in her life and she couldn't imagine what would happen if she actually permitted herself to speak freely and openly about his death. For the first time since she started seeing Dr. Bihar, Clare felt uneasy, suddenly picturing herself as the main subject of an intervention. Dr. Bihar might have been accurate in her assessment of Clare and Charlie, but the sheer idea of exposing herself and her feelings in front of a group of strangers terrified her.

I shouldn't be forced to do this. It makes me so uneasy. As soon as she started to say those words, she stopped abruptly, a familiar feeling bubbling inside of her—the same feeling she'd had months ago about her health, the same feeling she'd gotten about her lottery ticket, the same feeling she'd had to switch up her commute.

Dr. Bihar handed Clare a pamphlet for the grief-counseling group "Share Sorrow, Have Hope," which met a few times each month at local churches in the Western New York area.

Clare shook off the hesitancy and agreed to check things out. "This is something I should probably do."

Overjoyed, Dr. Bihar erupted into applause. "I'm so happy to hear you say that, Clare. I really believe you will find this beneficial."

"Beneficial" wasn't exactly the term Clare would have used to describe a gathering of sad people with communication issues, but she wasn't about to let the miniscule seeds of doubt overgrow the instinctual feeling that this group therapy would become a necessity for reasons unknown.

Churches had always given Clare the heebie-jeebies, and this experience was no exception. She remembered feeling this way ever since she was a little girl, being forced to sit inside New Covenant Tabernacle as her mother sang in the choir at two masses every Sunday morning.

Other than the scent of pierogis and a hint of bleach filling the air, the basement halls of St. Amelia's were empty and silent. If Clare hadn't promised Dr. Bihar she would give this a shot, she would've turned around the moment she walked in the door. She adjusted her white bandana with dark purple polka dots so it sat evenly on her head and quietly tried to calm her breath, inhaling deeply through her nose and exhaling quickly through her mouth.

She entered room 104 where there were only six other people, one of whom was Margie, who introduced herself as the group's facilitator.

"This may be a bit unstructured, but there aren't any firm rules here," Margie explained. Clare studied her closely, pegging her for a sixty-year-old, semi-retired grandma who liked watching soap operas while snacking on chips and dip. "You can introduce yourself if you'd like, but if you don't, that's not a problem. It's all up to you. We ask that you please be respectful of all the participants. And, please, keep everything you hear here confidential."

Clare smiled politely at Margie, knowing at one point or another, Margie probably suffered a devastating loss. Clare had done her research on group therapy and knew that the benefit of such a session was being surrounded by people who just "get it" in the saddest way possible. These people would be the unfortunate souls forced to find alternative ways to shrink the looming black cloud hovering over them, unable to deal with a loss of someone they loved.

"Thank you, Margie. I'm a bit nervous but thankful to be here," Clare said, with Margie's sympathetic no-teeth smile making Clare realize the sentence had an unexpected double meaning. She had meant thankful to be in the room and starting to deal with Charlie's death, not thankful to be alive. She patted her head slightly and smiled at Margie, not feeling the need to say anything further.

Clare positioned herself on the uncomfortable wooden chairs in the middle of the half-circle, still unsure of what she would divulge to the group of strangers who looked her up and down. The bright fluorescent lights in the room hurt her eyes as she turned her head left to right, squinting to scope out the others in a nonchalant manner.

Margie started the session. "Who wants to start us off?"

The vibe in the room had been understandably eerie, and Clare sensed Margie had no method at her disposal to make things more smooth or open. Finally, one gentleman stood up and Clare had a chance to learn the lay of the land. The group listened to Louis talk about losing his twin brother to a sudden heart attack. The story was undeniably sad, but Clare honestly drifted in and out of concentration as she prepared what she would say.

"Who wants to go next?" Margie asked, about to launch into the question again after a ten-second pause left the room silent once again.

A feeling of fearlessness surged through Clare as she stood up, cutting off Margie's stammering.

"I'll go. My name is Clare. About a year ago, I lost my husband of thirty-eight years to liver cancer." Her voice started unsteady and her knees knocked together, sending the edginess straight to her vocal cords. "It was very unexpected and he went very quickly." She stressed the second *very* harder than the first. "I've tried to remain strong for my family—my kids mostly. But there's this giant lump in my chest. My heart feels like a rock without him." Clare looked around the room, all eyes staring straight at her. "I've never really shared that with anyone, so thanks for allowing me to."

She quickly sat down with an incredible sense of pride. Never before had Clare been so open with a group of strangers. She felt woozy and delirious, but in a good way, as her fellow grievers nodded their heads slowly toward her with acknowledgment. *Damn, Dr. Bihar is good.* She already felt a bit of relief from her thirty-second speech. She shifted her attention back to the group as a young man who looked awfully familiar stood up. His hat covered most of his face, but Clare swore she knew him. *One of Caleb's friends*, she thought as he began speaking. His staccato pattern of speaking struck Clare; her own thoughts filled the silence when he paused.

"My mom died in a car accident years ago."

Oh, how terrible.

"I still sometimes have nightmares about the final seconds of her life and what was going through her brain."

How much she loved you.

"Was she scared? Did she know what was happening? Was she in pain?"

She went peacefully.

"I was in the hospital for a while six weeks ago and I realized that I can't keep this in any longer. It's never been easy for me, but it's only getting harder. And I think it's because I've kept it bottled up inside."

I know exactly how you feel.

"So, I don't want to say I'm happy to be here, but I'm hopeful that this experience will be beneficial for me. For all of us, really."

Your mother must be so proud of you.

Each participant in the room delivered a similar story of love and loss, the examples marked with sadness and regret. The session proved to be exactly what Clare needed, providing the one route she hadn't allowed herself to travel down. She found it unfortunate that such dire circumstances made her feel as if she were blooming after a year of dormancy.

Before leaving for the night, Clare walked up to Caleb's friend and offered a compassionate stare. She promised herself she would try to soften the pain of him losing a parent by offering her two cents.

"Hi, I just wanted to let you know that I appreciate you telling your story to all of us. Your mom is watching and she is definitely proud of you."

He went in for a hug, and Clare wrapped her arms around him as if he were her own child. As they separated, she introduced herself, officially.

"My name is Clare Montgomery. It's very nice to meet you."

"Mrs. Montgomery? I didn't recognize you. I'm Harris McGee, Abe's ex. I hope you don't mind me saying this here, but it's so nice to see you again!"

Fourteen: Abram

Stretching the limit had taken on a whole new meaning for Abram, as he hit the gym at a sickening pace over the previous week. When he felt tired on his daily run, he had pushed his body past the soreness, running eight miles instead of his typical five. When the weight of his barbell on the bench press became too heavy, he had pushed through the weakness for three additional reps after reaching the original point of fatigue. The intensity left him sweating and nauseated—exactly what he wanted. No stranger to testing the confines of his body's abilities, Abe impressed himself by reaching these new heights. The impetus behind his fervor in the gym wasn't the usual superficiality that encased most of his workouts. This time, Abe viewed the extra push in these workouts as something that came from sheer necessity. Though he hated to admit it, he had never felt this vulnerable and scared.

He supposed that's what happened after watching someone you once loved barely pry themselves from the tight grasp of death. The attack on Harris had spun Abe's complacent mindset to one of pure vehemence. *That could have been me.* It might have been a bit far-fetched to think, but Abe wanted to be prepared in case he ever found himself in the same situation. So each time he almost stopped running or didn't want to lift another weight, he pictured Harris, bloody and catatonic. His beautiful face looked remarkably peaceful inside that hospital bed, and Abe had honestly thought Harris's time was up as he said his goodbyes in his head while sitting by his bedside.

I always thought we'd have a proper goodbye, Har. I'm so sorry I didn't return any of your calls or texts. There's so much I never got to say to you and still so much I want to ask you. But none of that matters now. Just know that I'll never love anyone again the way I loved you. We had a fantastic ride together. I'll forever be grateful for you. And I'll never, ever be loved by anyone the way you loved me. Thank you for everything. I love you. I love you. I love you so much.

The sentiment behind the mistimed message stayed with Abe for days, causing him to fully realize the severity of what had happened to him in that moment. He'd involuntarily shed the anger and resentment he had held toward Harris, his soul awakening with a new outlook on their relationship. Since Harris's release from the hospital, the two had opened the lines of communication—as much as possible when Harris's jaw was wired shut—and had plans to finally meet in person.

As things with Harris trended toward an amicable reconciliation, Abram had turned his focus to having a sound mind in every aspect of life—and that not only meant finding some version of closure with Harris, but also coming clean with Cassie about kissing Jared. Abe's anxiety over the kiss had reached an unhealthy apex since it happened, as he obsessed over every moment leading up to it, every word spoken after it, and every interaction between the two of them since. Coming clean would bring him one step closer to eliminating all the destructive energy he had been holding onto. He hadn't had to conceal anything like this since his days in the closet, and being back in that frame of mind felt suffocating and toxic.

Abram fully expected Cassie to be upset for this betrayal and planned on taking full responsibility for his actions. If she was to ask him why he kissed Jared, Abe would massage the truth a bit. He didn't want to imply that Jared provoked the kiss, but that's partly how he felt. And despite his rather drunken state that night, he wasn't entirely sure Jared disliked the kiss. For a split-second, it had felt like Jared's lips puckered back, his tongue delicately searching for Abe's. Jared appeared so blasé over the incident that Abe didn't even feel ashamed for what he had done, even though he apologized mere seconds after stopping the kiss. In reality, he really wasn't sorry and only wished he didn't pull away so quickly.

"I'm sorry. I've had a little too much to drink," Abe had said that night, as the two awkwardly laughed and wiped their lips.

"No worries," Jared replied.

If only that statement were true. In Abe's head, there was nothing but worries—everything from how Jared would treat him to whether or not he would ever conquer this burgeoning attraction toward an unrequited love.

Abe wasn't about to question Jared's sexuality to his face—or to anyone else for that matter. If anything, his kiss provided a perfect chance for Jared to take the bait and confirm things one way or another. Still, so many little signs pointed toward Abe's theory on Jared being correct. Each time Jared practiced his piano, the songs seemed inspired by lyrics of longing for love.

"You Belong With Me" by Taylor Swift and Bob Dylan's "Make You Feel My Love" were the two he'd continuously practiced since their lip-lock. Abe fully knew the songs could have nothing to do with Jared's real life or could pertain to Cassie, but he couldn't figure out why Jared chose those, knowing Abe was the only one who could hear him.

Things definitely had changed between the two of them in the days after the kiss, which featured little to no communication. Jared's schedule changed to the midshift, ending their morning workouts and evening dinners together. The two subsequently started what Abram thought was an adorable habit of leaving haikus for each other. Abe would write his in the morning, Jared would respond in the evening, and then Abe would write another before bed, and Abe would find a new one from Jared in the morning. The cycle had been repeating itself for a week, with the haikus always carrying a flirtatious quality. Abe's most recent poem read:

> Miss you at dinner
> Well, miss you drying dishes.
> Change your shift back! Please?

Jared's retorts played off Abe's tone and theme.

> I miss you, too, Abe.
> Well, mostly miss the free food.
> I would if I could!

Abe wished Jared would have been appalled and angered over the kiss to say something to Cassie, just so the news could be out in the open. Instead, Abe had let it sit inside, bubbling up and sinking down night after night.

Cassie—and Cassie alone per her mother's insistence—had been staying with Mrs. Montgomery since her diagnosis, but that night was different. Almost two months since her return home, Abram and Cassie had finally had the opportunity to properly relive their youth by scheduling a non-date night full of PG-13 activities—no boys, no parents, nothing but the two of them lounging in their sweats, relaxing, and watching a ridiculous Lifetime movie (tonight's feature was *My Mother's Other Lover*, the best worst title Abe ever heard).

As soon as Cassie entered his house, Abe felt simultaneously at ease and tense. Her presence in his life had always been refreshing, and that didn't change even in the midst of her mom's cancer and a new job. Her cheery disposition might have been slightly muted the past few weeks, but she leaped into his house with an effervescent smile chiseled on her face.

"I miss you!" she shouted as she wrapped her arms around him in a giant hug.

"I miss you more. How's work going?"

"Ugh, it's fine. But can we please not talk about work tonight?"

Abe winced inside. He had hoped to prolong the inevitable kiss conversation as long as possible by filling the night exchanging small talk on every detail of their lives.

"Okay, how's your mom feeling?"

"She's good, I think," Cassie said, sounding slightly annoyed as she unloaded ice cream sundae goodies from her reusable grocery bag. "I mean, I can never tell anymore."

"What do you mean?"

"When we got here, she was, like, suicidal. No joke, Abe. Purely despondent and withdrawn. I was so worried about her I had Jared talk to her doctor. And that was when she didn't even know what the hell was wrong with her. And then, *before* she finds out she has cancer, she *fucking* shaves her head."

Cassie's rambling venting actually made Abe happy; these were the everyday interactions he had been expecting—and missing—since she returned to Buffalo.

"You know that she didn't handle your dad's death well, so maybe it was cathartic for her?"

"It must have been because now she's like the Dalai fucking Lama. I don't ever remember her being this happy!"

"You can't be mad at that, though."

"Oh, trust me, I'd rather her be happy and crazy than sad and sane. She's even going to group therapy, which is so unlike her."

Cassie dished out ice cream for herself, sending Abe back in time. After all these years, vanilla ice cream drenched in rainbow sprinkles with a touch of chocolate syrup was still her go-to stress reliever.

"Hey, how's Harris?" she asked.

"He seems to be doing really well, all things considered."

There were many times over the past few weeks where Abe blamed himself for Harris's attack. If he would've just agreed to meet with him, perhaps nothing would've happened. Abe's mind sloshed all over the place when it came to Harris, traveling to every possible point of every possible scenario. He had started the year with zero desire to see his ex but pictured some idyllic situation in which the two might end up together. The thought was premature, improbable, and an effect of Abe's overactive imagination.

"We're actually going to meet up next week," Abe said.

"Holy shit, seriously?"

"Yeah, it's time, don't you think?"

"I guess so! How could you not tell me this sooner?"

"Sorry, I've been a little preoccupied!" *by kissing and obsessing over your flawless, gorgeous boyfriend.*

"Have you decided yet about the job offer?"

"Cass! We aren't talking about work. Besides, I can't even think about that. I'm not selling the gym. I know that much. I've worked way too hard to walk away at this point."

Clearly preoccupied with what happened to his son, Mayor McGee understandably hadn't contacted Abe about the Health and Wellness Manager position in a few weeks—a fact that Abe appreciated. The job seemed too good to be true, and although Abe didn't want to leave the gym behind, he also didn't want to let a golden opportunity and new challenge fall to the wayside.

"What is this?" Cassie asked, holding up Abe and Jared's haiku pad.

"Oh, that's from your boyfriend."

"You mean *your* boyfriend."

The statement froze Abe, visions of their kiss blinking brightly in his brain. Abe's curiosity kicked into overdrive. *Did Jared already tell her? Is my attraction to him that obvious?*

"What do you mean by that?"

"He's acclimated himself so well here, and I feel like everything that motivated me to come back is being stolen from me—including you!"

"Cass, what are you talking about?"

"Things aren't great, Abe. Jared and I barely see each other, and when we do, it just feels like the spark we had in North Carolina is gone. I thought moving here would strengthen our relationship, but now there's this distance between us and we bicker nonstop."

"You do? What about?"

"Everything! Most recently, I questioned if he started seeing someone on the side."

"What would make you think that?" Abe asked, again slightly scared she knew of their mini-tryst the other week. "You know he loves you." Abe tried to quashing the ideas in her wandering mind.

"It's really hard dealing with a dying mother, a distant boyfriend, and a nonexistent best friend."

I have to tell her.

"So, you better start hanging out with me more," Cassie said.

He had no words available to calm her, so he held her as she took deep breaths.

"Okay, okay, no more boy talk," she said, blotting the tears in her eyes with a tissue.

"Deal." He looked across toward Cassie with a pensive stare.

Here goes nothing.

"Cassie, there's something I have to tell you. It's really kind of embarrassing." Abe sighed twice, his face turning a subtle shade of red. "The other day—"

Cassie's cell phone rang in the kitchen.

"Hold that thought. I bet that's Jared," she said as she stood from the recliner and ran to the kitchen.

"Hey! No boys allowed!"

"Calm down, Babysitter's Club. He's on his one break at work for the night. I can't ignore him."

Cassie walked toward the opposite side of the house to have the conversation in private, but Abe still heard her calling him Dr. Feelgood, which was her sort of cute, but mostly awful pet name for Jared. As disrupting as the phone call was, Abe felt relieved he received the perfect segue to accomplish his sole goal for the night.

This is it. Tell her.

"He wants to talk to you," Cassie said, returning to the living room holding out her phone for Abe, who reluctantly grabbed it.

"Hey," he said hesitantly.

"Don't say a word until we talk."

"What?"

"Cassie. Don't mention anything to her until we talk. Got it?" Jared's tone came off as more of a threat than a gentle, nudging suggestion.

"Okay," Abe responded, trying to sound as nonchalant as possible.

"Promise me, Abe."

"Yeah, you got it," Abe said, tossing the phone to Cassie.

He grew angry at the notion that anyone had the right to tell him what to do as a grown man, especially when he had already made up his mind about telling Cassie. He wished he had the chance to ask Jared exactly what he wanted to talk about.

"What did he want?" Cassie asked. *Fuck if I know.*

"Oh," Abe hesitated, searching his brain for a believable fib. "He asked me to throw out some lettuce in the fridge that went bad."

Abe felt himself retreating back into the proverbial closet, the door slamming shut and locking tightly. He wouldn't attempt an exit again until Jared came with the key.

"So, what were you going to tell me?"

"You know? I can't even remember." He paused and fake laughed. "Let's just watch the movie."

As he fidgeted with the remote, a thought immediately sprung to mind:

He's delusional
And clearly in love with me.
Poor, poor, poor Cassie.

Fifteen: Harris

There are the inexplicable moments in life when people are in the wrong place at the wrong time. The statement changed from a simple idea to a pure fact for Harris, clearly evident as his cloudy memory traveled back to that night in front of Sabrina Rowell's house. If only he would have left thirty seconds earlier or thirty seconds later. He tried his hardest to push those thoughts out of his mind, recognizing he was one of the lucky ones. After all, he lived to see another day when so many others never got that second chance he had been gifted.

Harris's mind parked at this mental crossroad while at an actual crossroad, standing on the corner of Transit Road and Main Street. The visions of that pickup truck speeding, running a red light, and striking his mom's sedan as she carried on cluelessly with her commute home spun through his head. Witnesses told the police Monica McGee had done nothing wrong, a detail everyone repeated to Harris in the hours and days after the accident, as if it was supposed to make him feel better. It only strengthened his anguish to know his sweet, loving mother lost her life due to a random occurrence and the mistakes of another human.

He had avoided this specific intersection for seven years at all costs, taking roundabout ways—like Wherle Drive to Harris Hill Road—to get where he needed to go without actually traveling past that corner. The way he specifically circumvented this part of town served as a metaphor for how he navigated through life, with his mom and Abe mainly: always avoiding anything painful and never really coming to terms and acceptance or taking accountability.

Harris had previously promised himself that he would never visit the site of the accident. He didn't want to allow a location to personify the site where such a vibrant woman met an unlikely and unfair demise. But this exercise was something Jared suggested would bring some closure, some sense of acceptability with his past that he obviously needed.

"What would your mom want you to do?" he asked Harris.

"She'd want me to man up and live my life."

"And how do you get to that point?"

"By starting to do the things I stopped doing once she died."

Harris took three deep breaths, remembering the specificity of the location of her final breath didn't matter. He tried desperately not to picture her lifeless and bloody body trapped inside a mangled pile of metal. As he watched the traffic zoom by in typical, robotic fashion, Harris wondered if what he felt inside was closure. Heavy and dark, the feeling hung in his stomach like a brick tied to his internal organs, dragging everything down with a dull ache. It was not therapeutic or freeing in the slightest.

"It's starting to rain."

Lost in a despondent fog of gloom, Harris hadn't noticed the tiny, ice-cold droplets stinging his cheekbones.

"I think we should get going, Harris."

Clare extended her hand to Harris and kept quiet as they slowly jogged back to his truck. Once inside, their silence continued, leaving Harris with a subdued felicity he never really experienced before. Only someone like Clare understood the importance of refraining from filling the soundless void with weightless words.

"Thank you for coming with me," Harris said.

"Of course, Harris."

Harris shook his head to signify *You have no idea what it means to have you here with me,* and Clare smiled back at him, fully picking up exactly what he tried to convey. The two had only known each other a little more than two weeks but had already forged an unlikely friendship after their paths crossed inadvertently at group therapy. After their third session of therapy together, they had gone out for coffee where Harris learned of her intense radiation treatments. He remembered watching her that night and admiring how she fought through the obvious pain and fright.

"Why don't I take you to your treatments from now on?" he asked her.

"No, no. Cassie is taking me. I would never expect you to do that for me. I still have two weeks left!"

"Call Cassie right now. Clare, please, I have all the time in the world. I'll take you. It'll actually give me a reason to get out of bed in the morning!"

Harris viewed a commitment to Clare as an opportunity to do something nice for someone who seemed to appreciate his company. And with that, their unlikely friendship had forged together, as random and inexplicable as it was logical and fathomable.

He couldn't imagine things otherwise, as the two tackled the difficult journey of overcoming grief together. It wasn't only the group therapy that helped but also their daily, run-of-the-mill conversations. Both had suffered tragic losses and were reeling from their bodies going through tremendous amounts of discomfort and shock.

Though scary for them at first, Jared's idea of visiting a painful place became something they pledged to do together. After the ten-mile drive to the restaurant Tully's, Clare broke the silence.

"How are you feeling?" she asked, leaving the ball in Harris's court.

"It's hard to put into words. I don't think we're supposed to feel something extremely positive right away. So, don't expect that to happen."

"Trust me, I'm not," Clare said as the two exited his truck.

Tully's was the place Clare and Charlie spent multiple days every week since Charlie retired. Clare told Harris since they usually ate there every Tuesday and Friday, the staff knew them as regulars. Clare always ordered the turkey club sandwich with no mayo, Charlie the all-American burger cooked medium with an extra pickle on the side. And on special occasions, the two would split a cookie-dough smash for dessert.

"I'm not sure I'm ready for this," she told Harris as they entered through the front door.

"We can do this some other time if you'd like?"

"I'll never truly be ready for this, Harris. Besides, you did your thing, now I'm doing mine," She pulled open the door and turned toward Harris, whispering, "We're in this together."

A hostess Clare didn't recognize led them to a table in the back of the restaurant before Clare politely asked to sit at the two-person booth that split the upper and lower sections.

"That's our booth," she whispered to Harris.

Immediately upon sitting at "their booth," a tear streamed down Clare's left cheek. Harris returned the favor of saying nothing, something he hoped Clare appreciated.

"I'm sorry," Clare said.

"Don't apologize," Harris said calmly.

"It's just that—" Clare started before a shriek came from out of nowhere. "Clare!"

A waitress bolted from the other side of the restaurant, her long, curly brown ponytail flying behind her, the sound of loose change and pens in her apron pockets clanging loudly.

"Rachel!"

Clare stood up and Rachel hugged her tightly. The jubilant reunion between a twentysomething waitress and a customer of Clare's age mystified Harris, though he understood how Clare's infectious personality could produce a May-December friendship.

"We have all missed you so much. How are you doing?" Rachel asked, politely not bringing up the white bandana with fuchsia roses on Clare's head.

"I'm doing...okay, thanks. As good as can be with this, really!" Clare said, pointing to her head, making no mention of her tumor.

"I thought you'd be here with your kids!"

Clare laughed. "No no, Cass is working and Caleb is still in Seattle. This is my friend, Harris McGee. Harris this is Rachel."

Rachel turned to look at Harris, her eyes widening as she scanned his face.

"Harris McGee? My God, it's so good to see you out and about." She hugged him almost as tight as she hugged Clare. "We were all so worried about you!"

"You were?"

"Yes! The whole city was worried sick you weren't going to pull through."

Her admission left Harris speechless. He had heard from a few close friends how they were waiting with bated breath to see if his condition improved, but he hadn't thought complete strangers actually cared.

"Don't worry. Your dad will find whoever did this," she said to Harris.

Harris groaned internally. His father had been working overtime lately, pushing Police Chief Al Reynolds to keep the pressure on to find the culprit. Harris gave a handwritten description of the attacker to the police sketch artist the day after he woke up from his coma. His charcoal "face" was all over the news, in the newspapers, on billboards, all over the Internet. While he appreciated his father's concern and dedication, it seemed to become an obsession to find him, rather than a wish. Harris didn't want his life to hinge on putting a man in jail, however badly he deserved to pay for his actions. He simply wanted the next phase to start and to put this sad, painful story behind him.

"Here are some menus. You two take all the time you need deciding. I hope you won't mind, Clare, but I'm going to tell everyone you're here." She placed the laminated sheets in front of them and skipped away gleefully.

"She sure loves you," Harris said to Clare, who was stai
menu. "We are definitely getting a cookie-dough smash." H
to find Clare sobbing. She attempted to catch her breath sever.
avail, her sob turning into a complete shake and shudder of hei

Out of the corner of his eye, he noticed Rachel come back to   .able.
Not wanting her to see Clare in this state, he sprung from the booth and cut
her off before she reached the table.

"Do you mind giving us some more time?"

"Sure, I was just bringing over some popcorn!" Rachel said, holding the
basket up to show Harris. He whisked it away from her and said thanks,
racing back to the table to find Clare a bit more composed but clearly
affected by her return to this place. He didn't know what to say, so he
decided saying nothing was the best thing he could do.

Clare and Harris didn't speak again until Rachel returned to the table to
take their order. Clare, of course, ordered the turkey club with no mayo and
Harris opted for the "world famous" chicken tenders.

"I'm sorry," Clare said again after Rachel scooped up the menus and
headed to put their orders in.

"Stop apologizing!" Harris said warmly.

"It's that damn cookie-dough smash," she said with half a chuckle.

Clare explained to Harris that lunch at Tully's was the final date for her
and Charlie before he passed away. They typically only ordered the cookie-
dough smash—three half-baked chocolate chip cookies inside a skillet,
topped with vanilla ice cream and whipped cream—on special occasions
like birthdays and anniversaries.

"But, Charlie knew we wouldn't be back. And he couldn't resist that
damn dessert," Clare said. "Rachel kept asking what the happy occasion
was, and Charlie played it off, telling her he had a craving. Well, a bunch of
the girls decided to have fun with me and kept implying it was my twenty-
ninth birthday."

Clare told the story as she alternated between sniffles and laughs.

"They ended up coming out with candles stuck in the middle of the
cookies and sang their 'Happy Birthday' song to me, complete with hooting
and hollering and clapping. I looked across our table at Charlie that night
and he showed no signs of anything being wrong. He stared back and
laughed at me, joining in with the clapping and the singing."

She popped some popcorn into her mouth.

It was the last time I saw him happy. Well, actually, right after he finished the dessert. *That* was the last time I saw him happy."

Harris looked across the table and stared at Clare. Her lively spirit shined through the sadness, but Harris suspected her spirit was much stronger than her body. She appeared extremely exhausted and a bit frail, surely an effect of her radiation. He admired the brave face she put on, knowing how much pain she was in both emotionally and physically.

"He's just as happy up there seeing how strong you are right now. You know that's true, too," Harris said.

"Oh, Harris. I wish I knew that," she said, a smirk forming on her face as she changed subjects. "I probably shouldn't say this, but I can't see why Cassie doesn't adore you."

Harris harrumphed. "Yeah, well, Cassie was never my biggest fan."

Things between Cassie and Harris had started off so smoothly, his integration into the Cass-and-Abe dynamic a fast and furious lesson in the straight girl/gay guy friendship. He had kept his distance early on and learned that certain traditions of their friendship would not be broken. He couldn't come over on Thursday nights during their *Grey's Anatomy* and wine nights. He couldn't be around Sunday morning for breakfast when they cooked western omelets and chatted about the previous night's shenanigans. And he didn't dare interrupt their BFF traditions, like pumpkin carving or egg dyeing or whatever silly activity came with every holiday throughout the year. But as things developed between Abe and Harris, Abe insisted he join them in each and every situation—something Cassie didn't enjoy. She never explicitly expressed disinterest in Harris, but she also never warmed up to him.

After a year or so together, Cassie and Harris hadn't grown any closer and neither of them—nor Abe—tried to bridge the gap that existed. He took a back seat on the days she was around, knowing it wasn't worth fighting with her for the attention of Abe. Harris never told Abe, but he always believed Cassie moving away was the best thing that ever happened to their relationship. None of the dismissive, insecure qualities Cassie possessed were mirrored in her mother.

"Cassie always held a soft spot for Abe. She is extremely protective over him," Clare said.

"Then please don't tell her I'm actually meeting him for dinner this weekend."

"Oh, really? Good for you! You two should patch things up."

"It will be nice to talk to him."

"What even happened with you guys? You were dating forever. He never wanted to chat about it so I stopped bringing it up."

Harris hated hearing that almost as much as he hated hearing his mom's death wasn't her fault. To this day, he had kept the reason for their breakup to himself. He debated telling Clare the truth but wasn't quite sure he could trust her not to tell Cassie.

"It's a long story."

"Well, if you ever want to share, you know I'm here."

Harris valued the respect and symbiosis between the two of them. Clare Montgomery would never be a replacement for his mother, but she certainly had proven herself to be someone he could confide in. They ate their meals without further talk of Charlie, Abe, or any other serious issues. Harris sensed Clare's mood gradually lightening, the pressure of the moment lifting away.

"I'll be right back. Going to head to the bathroom," Harris said as he left the table, making sure Clare couldn't see him. He found Rachel and hoped the plan he was hatching wouldn't make Clare revert to her sobbing, pre-lunch ways.

For the first time that day, Harris acknowledged how important a breakthrough both he and Clare had made. For seven years, he had bypassed the place his mother died but finally pushed aside whatever fear he still held to conquer whatever fear he had instilled inside himself.

When he got back to the table, Clare had already put on her jacket.

"We're not going just yet," Harris said, as Rachel appeared from the kitchen.

"Here you go, guys. This one is on the house," she said, placing the cookie-dough smash with two flickering candles in the middle of the table.

Clare looked at Harris with tears—happy tears—in her eyes.

"It will never be the same, but they will never be forgotten," Harris said, lifting his spoon up and holding it toward Clare. She picked up her spoon and clinked it against his. "On three, we blow out the candles and make a wish. Deal?"

"Thank you, Harris. Deal."

"One...two...three."

As the two simultaneously blew out the candles, Harris's phone vibrated on the table.

"It's my dad." He scooped up a spoonful of vanilla ice cream in his mouth and answered the phone. "Hey, Dad. I'm out to eat, can I call you back?"

"Harris, get to the police station as soon as you can."

"Why?"

"Good news. I think we got him."

"We got him."

Harris had heard that enthusiastic line before from his father, giddily calling him to indicate his assailant had been caught. He hated being at the beck and call of his dad, who had summoned him to the police station six times in the past two weeks. Catching Harris's attacker became nothing more than a witch hunt, with the police searching for tips that weren't coming and the media pushing a narrative that didn't exist.

It wasn't the first time his high-profile status in the community backfired against him, but it certainly held the most significance. For being the actual victim in this case, Harris felt guilty. He simply wanted the next phase of his life to start and to put this sad, painful story in the past.

Walking into Buffalo Police Headquarters bothered Harris. The last time he was inside the cold, dingy building pushed him to his breaking point. It was during his first sit-down interview, one day after the wires on his jaw were cut. The interview was supposed to be a "few questions" of "fact-finding," according to Detective Bill Kagan. Instead, it turned into a full-blown debriefing where Det. Kagan and his pudgy counterpart, Lieutenant Roy Rivera, continually questioned Harris at a spitfire pace in an effort to get him to remember details of the night.

He'd sat across from them in a gray-walled interrogation room, feeling like a criminal. Harris supposed it was impossible for anyone in a police station to feel at ease, no matter the circumstance. Even still, he had answered every question in the same half-hearted mutter.

"What was he wearing?" *I don't remember, I think jeans and a black jacket and a black winter hat.*

"Did he have an accent?" *Yes, a Buffalo accent.*

"How old was he?" *Hard to say. Midthirties? Maybe younger, maybe older.*

"Any distinct tattoos or facial features?" *He had really, really bloodshot eyes.*

"What else can you remember? What else did he say?" *Just that he knew of my comments about Sabrina's house online.*

As annoying as it was to answer the basic questions, nothing ticked off Harris more than the softball questions lobbed at him toward the end of that interview.

"As you know, Mr. McGee, this is being investigated as a possible hate crime," Det. Kagan said. Harris hated the patronizing way the officers were talking to him, especially how they made it a point to call him *Mr. McGee* time after time. "Is there anything you can remember to corroborate that? You have to let us know."

"I've already told my father—and both of you—that I don't think this was a hate crime. He didn't even know who I was."

"Mr. McGee, you are well aware that everyone in this city knows who you are and what your...lifestyle...is. And that's part of the reason this has been branded as a hate crime in the media."

"I don't give a shit what the media says. I'm not going to embellish what happened to satisfy some false account."

Det. Kagan and Lt. Rivera looked at him, stone-faced, surprised their implications weren't met with more compromise.

Harris had become all too familiar over the past few months with the ways the news industry in Buffalo worked. They latched onto a story and squeezed it dry, looking for the juiciest droplet to bottle up and then spill out into a puddle that stretched on for weeks. If he thought his exposure was heavy during his faux pas with Sabrina, he thought wrong. Nothing compared to the nonstop "Justice for Harris" stories that appeared in the newspaper and on TV. The media had seemingly interviewed everyone who ever had anything to do with Harris, covered every angle possible, even the ones that made no sense, like "Did Harris McGee's assailant hack into his cell phone's GPS to figure out his location? We'll talk to an expert, next at 11." There were stories with his father crying at a podium while giving a press conference, sit-down interviews with Sabrina where she described every detail of what she saw from her house that night, and quick clips with his high school principal, Judith Wilkinson.

The worst part of all the coverage was seeing the picture his dad had taken the day after the assault, his body lying there in the hospital bed, unrecognizable. Harris couldn't believe how he had no recollection of eleven days of his life and how swollen his face had been. Every time he thought of that picture, he touched his jaw, feeling the bones to ensure the healing process was still working. He touched his face numerous times a day no matter where he was, whether it was in his apartment, at the grocery store, or even inside the interrogation room.

Det. Kagan and Lt. Rivera caught Harris with his hands to his jawline as they entered, extending a handshake to Harris.

"It's good to see you again, Mr. McGee."

Harris shook their hands and remained silent, only offering a brief nod. *It's bad to see you again.*

"We have another lineup for you," Lieutenant Rivera said.

"So I hear."

"This one's not a photo lineup, though. Follow us."

Harris followed the officers into another section of the precinct, scared about the prospect of staring his attacker in the face. The officers guided him into a dark narrow room about seven feet long and three feet deep, his pupils immediately dilating due to the blinding white light shining through the two-way mirror.

"If you see anyone you need a closer look at, let us know," Det. Kagan said.

The men filed in one after the other with each one looking like the next one's doppelgänger. Staring at the line of men, Harris didn't feel anticipation about this lineup, instead, he slowly grew concerned. The men looked dejected and angered, and he swore the last one to enter the room wasn't a day over fifteen.

"Where do you find these guys?" Harris asked.

"It depends. Some are from the county's holding center, some come from local jails, others we recruit off the street. In this case, most are from the East Side where your assault occurred, brought in on minor offenses."

It bothered Harris that the cops could simply pick any identifying characteristic—in this case, "black adult male"—and force these men to be part of a lineup for likely no other reason. His defenses rose while he fully recognized how fortunate he was never to be subjected to this. He was one of the lucky ones, growing up in a well-off family, part of a political dynasty that helped alter the racial stereotypes of black men in power throughout Buffalo. His soul ached for these men.

"Well, Mr. McGee, what do you think?" Lt. Rivera asked, sounding annoyed that Harris didn't initiate the talking.

"Oh, I don't know," Harris said as he scanned the lineup of seven men. "Number four, maybe."

Lt. Rivera picked up the beige phone receiver on the wall.

"John, have number four step forward please."

Harris watched as number four took two small steps his way, closer to the wall. The man kept his head down, making eye contact impossible.

"Can you ask him to look straight toward us?" Harris asked.

"John, please have number four pick up his head and stare straight ahead," Det. Kagan said.

As number four picked his head up, Harris spotted them immediately—the red eyes. His breath became shallow as a sick, tumbling feeling turned in his stomach. Harris forced himself not to look away, despite his initial reaction. *It's him. It's definitely him.* He could still see the hate pulsating in the man's eye sockets, still smell the stench of liquor seeping from his pores. Being face-to-face with him carried Harris back to that night, his mind revolving as he remembered his fear and his confusion. Harris didn't want to see this guy thrown in jail, he simply wanted to look at the man and ask why he'd had to do this. "Well, Mr. McGee?" Lt. Rivera asked.

Harris was over all of this. Sick and tired of the lineups, the news coverage, the inane talk of a hate crime. Everything felt so off-putting to him. He held no morsel of vindictiveness. He only yearned for an end to this source of madness. And here it was.

"Mr. McGee?" Lt. Rivera asked again, louder this time.

Harris looked at his attacker again, trying to confirm 100 percent that this was him. As he observed him up and down, he quickly ran through what this man's life was like. It was a life he likely hadn't chosen. A life with no education. A life full of zero opportunities. A life full of drugs and alcohol. A life made up of violence. A life he couldn't escape. A life Harris was about to send further into the depths of adversity. As Harris gently opened his mouth to confirm this was indeed who was responsible for the assault, number four lifted his arm and scratched the back of his head. It was then the dark ink became visible.

Harris's indifferent examination of number four's body suddenly turned razor sharp as his eyes fixated on the word "Boots" that were blazoned across the man's forearm.

"Boots," Harris whispered.

Oh my God. Sabrina's ex.

"Mr. McGee, is this who attacked you?" Det. Kagan asked.

"Sorry," Harris said as he turned away from Bruce and toward the officers. He found himself unable to speak, unsure if he was even still breathing. He pictured Sabrina with Charity and Maxwell taking a family trip to the prison to see their father. He imagined Charity never having the joy of a daddy-daughter ritual, Maxwell standing on the front lawn with no father to play catch with. Harris looked back at Bruce, whose eyes pierced through the two-way mirror with an air of apathy.

"That's not him," Harris gulped. "I really appreciate all you two have done, but I can't go through one of these again. I'm finished wasting my time."

Harris walked backward and grabbed the jacket that he'd placed on a chair, his limbs shaking after his omission of truth. He briskly exited the room, the rapid steps of his shoes ricocheting down the hallway. He hoped neither Det. Kagan nor Lt. Rivera noticed his legs wobbling when he stopped just outside the door and spun around.

He couldn't help but wonder if it was the worst mistake of his life, one that offered an opportunity for Bruce to savagely beat someone else, but there was little he could do. In the interest of buying time and figuring out how to turn this worst-case scenario into the best-case scenario, lying was what he had to do.

Harris lamented his choice as he ran down the concrete steps of the police station that were freshly speckled with spring raindrops, but he couldn't go back on his decision.

Caught in a wave of remorse, he thought back to the night he had met Sabrina. Not the attack, but the words of wisdom she'd passed on.

Remember, when you forgive, you heal. And when you let go, you grow.

Sixteen: Clare

The radiation fought the tumor. The short naps lightened the fatigue. The corticosteroids hydrated the dry skin. The buzz cuts hid the hair loss. The 5HT-3 inhibitor capsule combatted the nausea. Every ailment had a cure. Every side effect had a solution.

So, why did she hate to admit she was winning this war?

Clare should have been ecstatic that her seven weeks of radiation came to an end that morning. After all, the actual cancer diagnosis and its aftermath had been much easier to deal with than the anxiety leading up to it. The poise she'd gained over that time period refreshed her mind and reenergized her soul.

She needed to focus on the task at hand on this mild, sunny morning as she stood in her vegetable garden. Positioning the rototiller in the far left corner, Clare looked back on the giant stretch of soil and grass, rebuffing the notion of another summer passing by without taking full advantage of her backyard. Everything had been derailed last year because of Charlie. Everything had been delayed this year because of her treatment. There was no more time to waste. Buffalo winters were notoriously long—the snow sometimes starting in October and ending in May—so, on this warm April morning, Clare sensed a wave of opportunity in the air.

Her treatment had finally ended a few hours earlier. Seven weeks. Thirty-five days. The time simultaneously flew by and felt like an eternity— and the experience wasn't even over yet. She would have her CAT scan on Monday, which would either end or extend her foray into the world of cancer. Everyone from Harris to Jacki, the receptionist at the oncology center, treated her with a delicate touch of optimism during her final session. Harris bought her a container full of gold-wrapped chocolate coins. "It's your pot of gold at the end of the rainbow," he'd told her. The gesture had invoked the only tears Clare cried on this memorable day.

Thank goodness for the distractions. She'd mapped out her selection of veggies in advance, determined not to fall prey to her whims at the farmer's market, which is exactly what happened with the Great Failed Eggplant

Experiment of 2013. This year there would be an array of tomatoes (plum, cherry, beefsteak) and rows of zucchini, summer squash, English cucumbers, and banana peppers on the far half of the garden. The side closest to the gate would be devoted to berries (blue, straw, rasp), along with basil, parsley, and cilantro. To get to that point, though, she had to fix the soil first. A year without tilling a garden felt like thirty years without getting a haircut. Everything overgrown, tough, and mangled. There was crabgrass, chickweed, dead leaves, dandelions, and other unidentifiable vine-like greenery that created a deep cover over the soil. She couldn't help imagining the obvious metaphor of her garden being equivalent to her brain; something so amazing and boundless covered in something so treacherous and harmful. Clare hated thinking about this. She was so much more than cancer, so much more than a brain tumor.

The piercing slam of the back door on the patio caused Clare to snap her head back.

"Let me know when you want me to bring these over!" Cassie shouted, dropping two ten-pound bags of mushroom compost on the concrete right outside the back door of the garage.

"You can start lining them up here, Cass!" Clare shouted back.

Clare had never tilled the whole garden herself; it was always a joint effort between her and Charlie. Being the thoughtful, observant daughter that she was, Cassie had suggested the two of them tackle this project together, a suggestion Clare happily accepted. She would rototill the garden as is first and then dump the mushroom compost on and mix that in, followed by a few bags of a new garden soil on top of that. The combination and process had worked wonders years previous, the Montgomerys' garden a bountiful source of vegetables for the whole summer every year since they started planting in the early nineties.

Though painstaking and difficult, the tilling was finished an hour later— and well worth every ounce of effort. The garden appeared almost as good as new, the morning's cracked, light-tan dirt riddled with spiky green intruders turning dark-brown and smooth.

"Well, what do you think?" she asked Cassie, opening her arms as if to say *ta-da!*

"Looks great! How are you feeling, Mom?" Cassie asked.

"A little tired," Clare said. The pool of sweat dripped from her red bandana and down her forehead as she crinkled her forehead while responding. "But, I'm happy to be doing this."

"I meant overall. How you're feeling about everything."

Cassie always breeched the conversation of Clare's health with the precise amount of caution and concern, never harping on Clare to discuss details of her physical and emotional well-being—something Clare appreciated more than Cassie would ever know.

"Cass," Clare said, "I feel good. I'm ready for whatever comes my way."

Cassie shot her a look.

"Honestly."

"Good. You're going to be fine, Mom."

"You're right. I am," Clare said. "Even if the cancer is still there."

Cassie rested her head on Clare's right shoulder, causing Clare to notice the freckles forming on her nose. She was the only one of the Montgomerys who had freckles, sunlight so effectively darkening them, it altered Cassie's face to the point she looked like a new woman. Their reappearance drew Clare back thirty years to the morning she had first seen them materialize on Cassie's face. It was a textbook spring day. Warm, but not hot. Sunny, but not scorching. Clare, Caleb, and Cassie were all in the backyard, playing in the sandbox, when Caleb screamed that Cass had something on her face. Panicked, Clare scooped her up and noticed the dots on her face. Immediately thinking Cassie was having some sort of allergic reaction, she rushed the kids into the house and began wiping Cass's face with a warm washcloth. Only under the fluorescent lights of the bathroom did Clare realize what was actually happening. She laughed at the story and viewed it as her clueless parenting at its peak. Clare still felt clueless as her daughter sat next to her. Once a gawky, speckled girl, she had turned into a beautiful young woman. If only their present problems were as simple as a case of mistaken freckles.

"Let's go make something to eat. Is Jared coming over?" Clare asked.

Cassie shrugged her shoulders in an indifferent manner as they stood up and walked into the house.

"Trouble in paradise?"

"No. We're fine. We're better than fine! I think we're at that point...that turning point."

"What do you mean?"

"You know, where we either take the next step or go our separate ways."

"And which fork in the road are you leaning toward?"

"I think you know, Mom. I'm ready to settle down. Stop the ticking of my biological clock."

The insinuation of grandchildren made Clare's heart jump. She had wrongly assumed at this point in her life there would be several babies for Caleb and Cassie—an incorrect assumption considering Caleb hadn't had a long-term relationship since he broke up with Jessica four years ago and Cassie bounced between boyfriends so often that things could never reach a level of seriousness. Though he might have come on a bit strong during their initial meetings, Jared Pfeiffer was a man who checked off all the boxes of approval: successful, smart, handsome, kind. And Clare wondered if she was watching her daughter let him slip through her hands.

"Well, Cass, that boy is definitely a catch. He and Harris have been checking in on me all week, and I don't know where I'd be without either of them."

"I really don't want to talk about Harris."

"Oh, please, honey. He's been an incredible friend to me."

"Yeah, he's incredible all right. An incredible asshole."

"Cassandra!"

"Mom, he absolutely crushed Abe. And for what reason? We don't even know. The guy is a cold-hearted dick."

The chime of the doorbell tersely cut Cassie off. Expecting it to be the mailman, Clare opened the door to see Marcia Swiatek standing there meekly, faintly sweaty and looking scared.

"Marcia! What are you doing here?"

"Clare, I'm so sorry to bother you. Do you mind if I come in?" Marcia asked.

Thinking of Cassie, Clare spun around to see her daughter waving the two in.

"Marcia, this is my daughter, Cassie. Cassie, this is Marcia Swiatek. She was here when—" Clare stopped talking.

Cassie knew exactly what she meant. "It's nice to meet you, Marcia. I don't mean to be rude, but I was just leaving."

"Cass, are you sure?"

"Yeah, I got a text from Darcie at work. I think I'm going to meet the girls out tonight, so I want to go home, rest up, and shower."

"Okay, I love you, honey. Call me later."

"Will do. Nice meeting you, Marcia."

"I'm so sorry to interrupt, Clare," Marcia said with a palpable sincerity.

"Nonsense. Sit down. What brings you here?"

Two cups of Earl Grey tea later, Clare found herself in near tears for Marcia, who was unexpectedly pregnant with the couple's second child in the fall and facing the trials and tribulations of owning her own business.

"The doctors said I could be on bed rest starting in the third trimester, which means no cake baking for me. Brandon has me almost convinced that stopping the business altogether is for the best."

"Oh, really?"

"Yes. We're having such a hard time finding a place that he's even contemplating moving somewhere warmer down South near his parents, maybe trying to open up his own shop or something."

Clare sat in silence. If there was one thing she had learned in therapy, it was that sometimes the stream of conscious venting worked wonders. Marcia had clearly been keeping this in.

"I constantly fantasize about finding that spectacular house that we can afford that would change his mind. I don't want to uproot Harper's life here or our lives. I'm probably just hormonal and completely out of line for asking this," Marcia started. "But if you...oh God, this is so selfish, Clare. I'm so sorry for asking. But if you think you'll be selling soon, I ask that you please let us know. We want this house—I want this house—so badly."

Clare didn't respond right away, fully knowing what Marcia implied. Her brief abstention from thinking of her condition didn't last long.

"Marcia," Clare said, before Marcia butted in with a rebuttal.

"You don't even have to respond. I know it's a lot to ask and I'm unsure of where your head is at, you know? If you're selling, if you're staying."

"Even I'm not sure about that, Marcia!" Clare said, laughing. A small smile showed on Marcia's face. Clare wanted to explain how her treatment just ended, how her brain was a literal jumbled mess, her future more unknown than ever. "Tell you what. Give me a few days and let me think about it."

She knew that was a cop-out, the type of answer she hated to give. Truthfully, she didn't want to think about it. Yet, she knew she had to—with or without Marcia's request.

"Thank you so much, Clare. I better get going. I told Brandon I was out running errands. He's going to put an APB out for me if I'm not home soon."

The two exchanged some more small talk before Marcia carefully skipped down the front steps of Clare's house. When she got to the sidewalk, she turned sideways toward Clare and gave a big wave with her whole arm. Clare admired Marcia's effervescence, wishing some of it would swing her way and stick to her bones.

She walked back into the house, poured a glass of lemonade—complete with both fresh and frozen strawberries—and made her way to the backyard, tore off her bandana, and soaked up the sun under the pergola. It felt glorious and refreshing to relax in her chaise lounge. She opened her eyes a hint, squinting through the sun to see a freshly tilled garden resting under the dogwoods, which were almost completely white. This scene would normally cause Clare's nostalgic memory to go haywire, to drift back to a different era where things were austere and elementary. But not this day. Thoughts of the past weren't sprouting up; she only visualized her future. For the first time in seven weeks, there was no answer to this dilemma. No pill, no steroid, no haircut, no nap would help Clare anymore. She sipped her lemonade and contemplated what to do. Selling the house cured nothing for Clare, but it certainly would alleviate some ailments in Marcia's life.

It felt a bit uncomfortable for Clare to view Marcia as the one in need more than her own daughter, but she knew it was the truth. Cassie and Jared had no use for a house other than using it to put a roof over their heads. Despite any sentimental attachment Cassie likely had toward the house, she made no mention of actually wanting the house. Besides, both she and Jared were too young and too clueless about homeownership for Clare to seriously considering signing it over to her daughter.

She envisioned the logistics of selling, quickly recognizing it wouldn't take much more than a simple decision. After all, everything was mostly packed, so it wouldn't be hard labor. Emotionally? That was a different story. But Clare was aware there was a chunk of the house she rarely entered anymore. And, of course, there was the fact she faced a future she wasn't sure she'd even be a part of.

Here she was again, only thinking about herself. Clare sighed, aware of how narcissistic she had been since her diagnosis, how greedy the cancer had made her. It wasn't as if she had a choice, but it still didn't make her feel any better. She put down her lemonade, plucked her cell phone out of her pocket, and dialed Julie's number.

"Red Carpet Realty, this is Julie. How can I help you?"

"Hi, Julie. It's Clare Montgomery."

"Clare! How are you feeling? Oh, it's so good to hear from you. Listen, I'm walking into a showing right now. Can I call you back when I'm done with my clients?"

"Absolutely, but please call back today," Clare said, pausing briefly. "I've found a buyer for the house."

Seventeen: Harris

Harris approached his destination on Crescent Avenue with as much enthusiasm as someone attending their best friend's funeral. His father had called six times that morning, waking him up out of a dead sleep shortly after 8:00 a.m.

"I need you to meet me at Forty-seven Crescent. There's something I want you to see." When pressed for more information, his dad's voice became agitated but with a slight sense of excitement. "Just get here."

What a wake-up call.

He wrestled from underneath his down comforter and rolled out of bed with limbs like lead, a side effect of being unemployed and wounded. Harris had grown accustomed to sleeping in, staying up late, lounging around, and being all-around inactive and lazy, which was a fact he wasn't proud of but accepted. Weeks after the attack, Harris fought a daily war between recuperation and restlessness. His body wanted to move at a much quicker pace than his brain did, and even when the two joined forces, he rarely had anything pressing to accomplish or attend. Daily chores like cleaning his bathroom and grocery shopping elevated from normal tasks to ones that satisfied his desire to complete a mission.

Harris had no clue what his dad wanted but knew better than to wage a war with him. The two were in a good place, arguably the best place they had ever been. His dad had been understandably different since the attack—more attentive and more present in their conversations, more aware of his presence in the community, and more passionate about the issues in the city and those surrounding his political identity.

Still, the little seeds of doubt about his father's authenticity had crept in throughout the week, and Harris assumed that being summoned to Crescent Avenue was part of another carefully crafted publicity opportunity. This week alone, his dad had asked Harris to accompany him to the after-school program for at-risk teens during his speech to the students and their parents, and then he had Harris march by his side during the kickoff of the year's Food Truck Tuesdays at the Larkinville building. His dad's potential senatorial campaign was firing on all cylinders, but with a brilliantly subtle force. Daniel McGee wasn't making news, he was actually part of it—and he knew his son was exactly the way to keep his face front and center. Where Harris went, the media followed. They didn't pester or stalk, they simply wanted to check in on him, respectfully keeping their boundaries for once.

Too bad boundaries meant very little to the Buffalo media elite, forever believing their position in the city's structure of importance fell at the top. Instead of demanding answers, the reporters asked in a nicer, but still demanding, way. *"Can you tell us how you're feeling?"* Each one probing his thoughts with that same question numerous times simply worded in different ways. *"I feel good, thank you"* was his standard response. He engaged with them as little as possible, but enough so that they wouldn't hound him at inappropriate moments. Harris, whether he liked it or not, had finally learned how to play the game.

Over the last two weeks, he had worked hard to take possession of what happened to him. He fought with himself to refer to it as "his" attack, not "the" attack. Since being released from the hospital, he had inadvertently separated himself into three distinct beings: the Harris before the attack, the Harris who was attacked, and the Harris who survived the attack.

During their last conversation, Jared suggested developing a different mindset in regard to what happened, arguing the moment was truly life-changing. He told Harris no denial or sarcasm or disbelief about that night would change the fact that he had suffered a brutal beat-down and was lucky to be alive.

No matter what he did to accept his fate and move on, he couldn't. Like a water balloon dropped from a rooftop, the sudden fear that his father and Detective Kagan figured out everything about Bruce popped into Harris's head, his mind flooding with possibilities of how angry they would be and how much trouble he would be in. He pictured showing up to the house and seeing both of them there to question him why he had inexplicably let Bruce go free. Truthfully, even days later, he still couldn't even answer that question himself. He would have no idea what to say to anyone who called him out on it.

Letting Bruce off the hook was a necessary short-term, quick fix while Harris filled his free hours searching for the long-term solution. Did he want Bruce to get off scot-free for nearly killing him? Absolutely not. But did he want Bruce to go to jail for years because of his attack? Not really. The man needed help, not incarceration, and Harris needed to set the record straight about the whole hate-crime nonsense. He wasn't sure how to convey this message to the police, to the media, and to the community—all of which wanted a juicy payoff to the year's hot story.

Getting in contact with Sabrina was Harris's highest priority. He called her hours after his encounter with Bruce in the police station, but she was about to start day one of four twelve-hour shifts in a row. With seventy-two hours to think, Harris was actually a bit relieved he hadn't had a chance to speak to her. His first instinct had been to disclose everything. *Your ex was my attacker. I let him go.* As much as it pained him to think it, he questioned how much Sabrina knew. Was she aware Bruce was the one who had attacked him? Did she only take Harris to the hospital after watching the father of her children beat him into a bloody pulp? He wanted to give her the benefit of the doubt, but that sentiment proved far more difficult to attain than to wish.

As he pulled closer to his destination, the heavy thoughts of his attack were overtaken by the sweet signs of summer flourishing around him. He had cracked open the windows on his truck, enough to feel the warm morning breeze brush against his skin as the bright, budding green leaves on the trees fluttered in the even brighter glow of the sun. In typical Buffalo fashion, people were mowing their lawns, washing their cars, and wearing their shorts, despite the fact that it was hovering right above sixty degrees. Crescent Avenue wasn't far from where Harris had grown up, a literal hop, skip, and a jump from Delaware Park. Being back in this neighborhood always brightened his day—especially when the weather turned nice. The park was *the* spot to be on a sunny spring day, filled with golfers, runners, walkers, and families heading to the zoo. The noticeable energy in the air was contagious enough to inspire much of the city's population to embark on an adventure. No Buffalonian ever let a day like this slip by without appreciating the outdoors in some form. This city might have had a downside with its winters, but it made the spring and summer that much more vital to enjoy.

Harris hesitantly glided down the street, searching for the house. Finally, he noticed his father's black SUV in a driveway and there were no other cars around. The sole vehicle served as a sign that there wasn't anything beating-related waiting on the inside. Harris eyed the house up and down from his car, its mustard-yellow shake shingle rotting. Once he stepped out of the car, he noticed how uneven the driveway was, how jungly the lawn and gardens appeared. The decaying wooden steps creaked as he hopped to the front porch. Opening the storm door proved to be a struggle with its hinges so tight that Harris had to use both hands and his brute strength to prop it open on his hip. He heard his father shout "Come in!" after his knock on the rotted wood door, which had a pane of glass missing in four of the nine vertical rectangles.

He entered the house and stared into a vast nothingness. The house was bare, ripped down to the studs. Sheets of opaque plastic covered the windows and staples from freshly removed carpet still clung to the floor, pieces of yellow matting still caught inside most. The guts of the kitchen cabinets still hung on the walls, but there was little else aside from some pipes, wiring, and outlets.

"What did you want to show me?" Harris asked. His voice was hollow and roaring in the empty space.

"What do you think?" his father replied.

Harris hated when people answered questions with a question. It was his biggest pet peeve, by far. So he decided to answer the question to his question with another question.

"What? What am I supposed to be seeing?"

Harris walked farther into the space, the floorboards squeaking with each soft step, poofs of dust squirting out underneath his sneakers. The stench of wet wood and stale air wafted throughout. He couldn't tell where one room ended or started, the intersecting wooden beams playing games with his eyes. The only thing he knew was that the house felt dank, creepy, and slightly unsafe.

"It's yours," his dad said, a porcelain smile painted on his face.

"What?"

"This house. It's yours, Har."

Harris wrinkled his face. "What are you talking about?"

"Flip it. Fix it up. Live in it. Sell it. It's yours now, Harris. I don't care what you do. It's time you did something," his dad said, tossing two keys on a "Buffalove" key chain his direction.

The keys hit Harris's chest and landed on the subfloor with a thud. "Dad..."

"Shh. You've had a hell of a few months, kid. I know whatever you do in here is going to be amazing. I can't wait to see how it all turns out."

Harris still hadn't moved his feet. They were temporarily cemented to the board he stood on. He had a difficult time wrapping his mind around the whats and whys of the news. *This is mine? He bought me this?* He recalled the conversation they'd had last week at dinner, when his dad pressed him to reveal what he would want to do with his life, in an ideal world.

"I'd want to live in Bordeaux, renovating chateaus in a modern way but preserving their architectural integrity," he said.

"There are a lot of homes that need that here, Harris," his dad replied.

That was the extent of any conversation the two had had about fully restoring any homes.

Buffalo, New York, was not the south of France.

Crescent Avenue was not Bordeaux.

This home was no chateau.

Harris immediately felt defensive and unaccepting. He didn't ask for this house nor did he want it. There was nothing to preserve here. It was all already gone! He almost objected but knew that wouldn't go over well. Harris wasn't trying to act like an ingrate. He was genuinely perplexed. It felt like that Christmas when he was nine years old and asked Santa for a Sega Genesis, only to receive some pro-wrestling action figures and new street-hockey equipment. Yes, the gifts were nice, but they weren't what he wanted.

"Go," his dad said, pushing him toward the back end of the house. "Look around, get some ideas. I've got to head out, but I told your brothers you'd be here today so they might be stopping by."

It surprised Harris to see his dad depart so soon after offering this wonderful, grand gift, and he only blamed his laziness for having such little time with him. At least he would have some time alone to process his thoughts.

"I'll see you at the anti-violence symposium tonight, right?"

Shit. The anti-violence symposium was the one and only event of his father's where he actually wanted to show his face.

"Wait, Dad. No, I don't think so," Harris answered.

"Harris, don't you think it's important for you to be there?"

"Yes, I do. But I'm actually going to meet up with Abram tonight."

The audible admission finally made the thought a reality. After all this time, Harris and Abe were finally going to see each other and have a nice, adult-like evening together. Harris stopped short of referring to the night as a "date" in his mind, not wanting to get ahead of himself there. Even his father seemed to acknowledge the scale of importance their meeting held.

"Wow. I didn't realize you two were talking again," his father said.

Harris and Abe's communication over the last two weeks was friendly, albeit entirely electronic. Emails and texts had replaced the face-to-face heart-to-hearts and the early-morning whispers in each other's ears. They were pleasant, virtual interactions, each filled with a civility they hadn't shared since the end of their relationship. Harris believed Abe wouldn't have the guts to bring up the past—at least not tonight. He could predict exactly what their conversations would entail. They would chat about the attack, obviously, and then segue into Abe's life at the gym, how things were going with Cassie and Jared, followed by what new DIY house projects Abe was working on and what summer plans were on the horizon. And since Abe lived on a schedule tighter than a toddler, he and Harris would separate by 9:00 p.m., certainly much too early for any serious discussions to take place.

"Everything that happened..." Harris started. "I think it's made us realize how much we care about each other."

That was the truth. As much as the assault weighed on Harris's mind, one of the positive outcomes was the bridge he and Abe had repaired since. He not only missed the physical things he had grown accustomed to, like Abe's caring, chocolate eyes and ridiculously chiseled abs, but also the small, unremarkable things, like the way Abe played with his watch when he got nervous and how he smiled and tried to stop and pet every dog that crossed his path. Harris couldn't wait to experience at least three of those things tonight—and maybe even some abs if things went *really* well.

"If it comes up, tell him I want his answer on the job. Good luck, Har," his dad said before thrusting the screen door open and leaving him standing all alone inside what was, apparently, his house. Through the screen door, he ominously said, "I hope you're ready for this."

"I am. I hope Abram is, too."

His dad got into his Range Rover and reversed out of the driveway. Harris turned around and stared at the nothingness in front of him, feeling minuscule and insignificant in the cavernous, undesired house.

His cavernous, undesired house.

Eighteen: Abram

"Cassie doesn't deserve this. You know she'll go berserk," Jared said.

Jared and Abe waltzed around the kitchen while preparing lunch on a sunny Saturday morning—their first conversation alone since Jared's faintly demanding request for Abe to shush about their random smooch around Cass. As he chopped the freshly baked chicken for their southwest chicken salads, Abe stared into Jared's eyes—really stared—trying to decipher if his most recent appeal to stay quiet was one that came from total honesty or one that was part of a cover-up plan arising from complete fear. Jared's blue eyes elicited little information, and Abe was simply transfixed on their deep pull. The man had a way to make his heart melt, so Abe had been forcing himself to shut off his emotions and view everything from an objective perspective. If the kiss was a red flag, his wish to stop Abe from telling Cassie was a burnt-orange flag—and he still wasn't sure if he was going to oblige.

"Jared, I don't think you understand just how much her friendship means to me. I have to say something."

"Trust me, Abe. I know how much she means to you. I know how much *you* mean to *her*. But, she's going through enough as it is with her mom and her job, and I don't want to keep dumping on her."

Jared had a point. Never one to conceal her emotions, Cassie's unyielding demeanor in the face of confrontation and adversity often triggered a reaction that affected so many aspects of her life. One time in their junior year of college, Cassie had a complete psychological breakdown during the fall semester after she caught her boyfriend Todd cheating on her with one of her Sigma Kappa sisters. She stopped eating or sleeping and would study all night long, failing to show any interest or emotion in anything but schoolwork. She ended up coming down with a serious bout of pneumonia and failed two midterms as a result of her inability to deal with what was happening around her. The weight of her expectations and the outer pressure of attempting to look perfect broke her. Abe could see her once again spiraling into this world of desolation and despondency if he were to tell her about what happened.

But, God, that kiss. It was as passionate as it was unexpected, as sexy as it was scary. Despite their ability to ignore the lip-lock, nothing that happened between them since had provided any clarity to Abe. Their moments together were sparser than they had been, but the two had made the most of their time, carrying on with the underlying flirtation that had defined most of their friendship.

"I get that. I don't want to dump on her either," Abe said.

It wasn't easy to talk to Jared about this. If the situation were to have happened with any other guy, he would have made it a point to never see him again, never talk about it in general, and certainly never talk about it *to* him while *seeing* him.

Abe so badly wanted to have a more earnest conversation with Jared, so badly wanted to be blunt and humbly ask, "Are you gay?" in a perfect, nonchalant moment. But he knew that question carried a significant implication, and he still didn't know if his thoughts were part of a misplaced erotic fantasy or rooted in something serious. There were minor signs: Abe swore Jared glanced a little too long at him when he was in his towel after a shower—a terra-cotta flag—and found it strange that every time they ate dinner together since that night, Jared suggested the two of them should drink wine again—a magenta flag.

Yet, for all the questionable choices Jared made, he combatted them with the loving way he treated Cassie. Feeling her frustrations putting a strain on their relationship, Jared upped his game, buying her flowers or candy, packing her lunches for work, checking in on Clare every day and holding Cassie close every night.

It was nothing but love.

It was everything Abe wanted.

"Fine," Abe said. "I won't tell her. I know that's better for her." He stuffed the need to tell Cassie into a vault somewhere in the back of his mind, disregarding his hesitancy. Abe's skepticism of Jared's intentions had spiked and sank so many times in the past few weeks, but he truly believed Jared was coming from a good place this time around.

"Thanks, man," Jared said. He went in for one of his patented hugs—a salmon flag—but Abe pretended he didn't realize and brushed him off, walking to the sink to wash the lettuce. He couldn't continue to flirt with Jared, to constantly wonder if this man was hitting on him; Abe knew he was setting himself up for disappointment. He constantly tried to convince himself that Jared wasn't gay, he was simply friendly. And even if he were gay, he'd had every opportunity to tell Abe and act on it. He hadn't. Abe pledged once and for all to wave the white flag and surrender, quashing his desires to pursue anything further about Jared's sexuality.

"Do you have any idea what you and Harris are going to talk about tonight?" Jared asked, changing the subject.

"Not really," Abe said. "I don't even want to talk about it, just want to go with the flow once we're together."

"Well, I wish you luck. But remember: only a fool would turn down a handsome stud like you."

Abe smiled at Jared and kept quiet while assembling the salads, his head categorizing that statement as a deep, vibrant, blood-red flag waving so flamboyantly he couldn't believe Cassie could overlook something so obvious.

Abe stared at himself in the bathroom mirror and lifted up his arms, flexing to make sure his muscles popped and his shirt showed no sweat stains.

"You can do this." He exhaled, slapping his face lightly to psych himself up.

A night three years in the making carried the lumbering burden of perfection and the euphoric sensation of expectation. His clothing combination of dark denim jeans and a forest-green Henley marked outfit choice number six for the evening. Abe acted as indecisive as the weather outside, which fluctuated between the harsh remnants of winter and the promise of spring's bloom. A sliver of sun squeaked through the bathroom window and illuminated a rectangle on the marble tile—a sign Abe equated with warmth. He determined his outfit was finalized and brushed his teeth. He looked in the mirror again to see his body showing the first sign of a revolt—his right eye twitching uncontrollably, a symptom of nervousness he had never been able to regulate.

You can do this.

He mouthed the phrase to himself over and over again, hoping each attempt would singe the words into his mind and leave him with no choice but for them to become reality.

You can do this.

Abe planned to lay it all on the line at dinner, to speak his mind on every last detail he'd held in for the past three years, to expose the rawest nerve right there at the table, unafraid of the outcome. If Harris's attack proved anything, it was that life was short, time was finite and the end could be near for anyone at any moment. His existential way of thinking had been in the forefront of his brain ever since the day he'd seen Harris's lifeless body lying in that hospital bed surrounded by machinery, tubes, and IVs.

Abe adjusted his hair one last time, threw on sunglasses, and grabbed his phone from the charger, noticing he had missed a text from Cassie.

—Abe, my babe. I know it's a big night for you, so good luck! Call me as soon as you get home! Unless Harris is with you, then call me in the morning after he leaves. I love you!

Her brief message brought a smile to his face, as always. The dichotomy of his current situation was not lost on Abe. While he planned to go all-in with Harris, he kept his cards close to his chest regarding Cassie—per Jared's somewhat reasonable request.

As much as keeping a secret from Cassie weighed on his conscience, most thoughts of Jared had been overtaken by the anticipation of seeing Harris. They agreed to meet for their "date" at Mississippi Mudds, bringing them back to where things had started. Abe arrived fifteen minutes early on purpose and picked a booth on the perimeter of the restaurant that overlooked the grassy knoll leading into the Niagara River. The weather had been slow to change, the warmth of spring struggling to permeate winter's grasp on Western New York. But that night, the sun shone brilliantly, a giant swath of yellow engulfing all of Niawanda Park. Abe scanned the crowd, searching intently for any sign of Harris.

He immediately transported back to the weeks and months after they'd broken up and Harris had moved out of their house. He remembered purposely running his errands and heading to places like Target and the bank when he'd assumed he'd see Harris. Abe longed for that one interaction where he'd see Harris, play it cool, and the two would begin communicating again before eventually patching things up. The pathetic plan had never worked out (despite Abe's numerous attempts) and the contact between the two ceased completely. If Abe could do things differently, he wouldn't let Harris out of his life without full knowledge of why things had ended in a plume of smoke. Instead, he'd lived for the last three years in relationship purgatory full of distressing ache and innumerable, unanswerable questions.

Preoccupied with thoughts of the past, Harris finally caught his eye as he walked toward the restaurant. Abe felt like a predator in a hunt, eager and ready to pounce, as Harris slowly trod in his direction. Abe assumed he moved a little slower because of the attack, but remembered it'd been years since he had watched Harris from afar. Maybe the mobility issue wasn't because of the attack. Maybe it was another sign they were growing older.

The moment Harris approached the table, Abe stood up, grabbed him, and hugged him tightly for a longer-than-normal time, towing the line between cute and uncomfortable. Abe got emotional as Harris's chest moved in and out against his with each deep breath he took.

"How are you feeling?" Abe asked.

"I'm doing all right. My jaw kills me every now and then, but that's to be expected. How have you been?"

How have you been?

"Where do I start?" Abe laughed. *Well, let's see. Visiting you in the hospital made me finally admit to myself I never really got over you. I think about you all the time. And, oh. I just kissed Jared. You know, my best friend's boyfriend—whom I live with—and I'm pretty sure he liked it. And your dad offered me a job in his administration, which I'm leaning toward taking but am a bit hesitant to toss aside everything I've worked for.* "I've been good, thanks."

Abe chose to be succinct in this instance, not wanting to make their reunion entirely about him. Anything he was going through paled in comparison to Harris, who still faced the battle of returning to routine after being assaulted.

"You gonna grab a burger and fries? Or ice cream?" Harris asked.

"Actually, I was going to get a grilled chicken sandwich with no bun and a side a guac."

"What?" Harris laughed. "What is that shit?"

"I eat clean now, Har!"

"Oh, please. A burger isn't going to kill you."

Abe snickered and slouched back in the wooden booth. He stared across the table at his ex and beamed widely. Despite the beating he'd taken, despite age creeping up on him, Harris looked as handsome as ever. He still had all the attractive qualities Abe had first spotted all those years ago. Not only did his mocha skin glow in the waning hour of daylight, his aura projected confidence, charisma, and positivity.

"Well, if you're not going to get actual food, what do you say we get out of here and get to the water? It's a beautiful night for a walk."

"I'd like that," Abe said, happily agreeing. He had secretly hoped that would be the plan, no worries of ill-timed bites, full mouths, or food stuck in their teeth getting in the way of the long-awaited conversation.

Their walk started off with the topics Abe expected, signs of spring all around them.

"Are they any closer to catching anyone or naming any suspects?"

"Not at all. I went to a lineup the other day at the police station, but none of those guys were him. I don't even care anymore. I don't want to deal with it."

"How did he know you were gay?"

"He didn't." Harris paused. "He was pissed at what I wrote about Sabrina's house. It wasn't a hate crime, Abe."

The news spewed out of Harris's mouth indifferently, briefly shocking Abe.

"What? How is that possible? That's all they're talking about on the news."

"They're wrong. I hate to say it, but I think it's my dad's fault."

Harris explained how his father had dropped the hint to the police, after hearing Sabrina Rowell's version of events. She had watched the whole thing unfold from her front window and told police she heard the words "pretty boy" before the attack.

"I still can't believe everything that happened. I was trying to make things right with her, Abe."

"I know you were."

"Speaking of my dad...he keeps asking when you're going to make up your mind about his job offer."

Abe made an exaggerated sigh and threw his arms up in the air. Leaving Vitality and working for the city crossed his mind at least once an hour. He had tossed around every option imaginable and made pros and cons lists for each possibility, settling on two choices: selling the gym completely or finding a managing partner who would oversee day-to-day operations.

"Ugh, Harris, I don't know. I think about it nonstop, but..."

"But you don't wanna give up the gym?"

"But I don't want to give up the gym!" Abe loved that Harris knew exactly what he was thinking. "Do you blame me?"

"Hell, no. You worked your ass off to get where you are today. The only reason you should give that up is if you're unhappy and you actually want to give that up. Are you unhappy there, Abe?"

"I wouldn't say unhappy, just kind of bored." Abe smirked as the moment struck him. This was precisely the get-together he wanted and needed to have with Harris. The two of them completely at ease and enjoying each other's company, discussing the things that meant the most to them. After nearly ten years together, three years apart felt excruciatingly lengthy and agonizing.

The sun began to set behind the Grand Island bridges in the distance. The desire to pick at Harris's brain grew stronger as it dropped.

"Listen, I know things have been rough for you lately and I swear I'm not trying to pick a fight or anything, but I can't drag it out any longer without asking." Abe looked at Harris, his skin glowing as the setting sun reflected off the water into his eyes. "What happened between us?"

It was the question that haunted Abe's life since they officially ended things, staying with him like a bowling ball handcuffed to his body that he dragged around every day.

Harris scraped the tip of his right shoe across the blacktop of the bike path. He tenderly replied, "Abe," as if to imply the foolish question would be better left unanswered.

"Harris, honestly, I don't care anymore. When I saw you in that hospital bed, all I kept thinking was how much we should have told each other the truth—no matter how hard it might be. I'm prepared and ready to hear whatever it is." Abe impressed himself with his calm tone in the face of an apathetic Harris, whose silence sent a clear message. "I had it all planned out. I wanted to marry you. And then, just like that. You were gone. Just like that. You completely checked out."

"Abe," Harris said it again, this time in deeper key and much more curt.

"You owe it to me to tell me. You owe it to us." Abe's eye twitched wildly, the entire upper right quadrant of his face pulsating. He assumed Harris wouldn't be eager to divulge all the details of whatever reason inspired him to walk away, but Abe promised himself he wouldn't give up without trying as hard as he could to get Harris to speak.

"Har, I haven't moved on. I *can't* move on! Okay? So, please, I don't care what it was. I don't care if you met some guy or you got sick of my shit or you didn't want to get married. But I need..."Abe struggled to speak as he looked down, fighting back the need to shake Harris and beg for the truth. "I need to know. Please."

Harris looked past Abe and out onto the water for a good twenty seconds, no reaction appearing to register in his mind or cross his face. The orange haze of the sunset enveloped the two as they stood still amid the sea of roller bladers and joggers and dog walkers and runners. Abe sensed Harris holding back but watched closely as he gulped slowly and his lips began to part.

Abe's stomach tensed as he waited for the words to release from Harris's mouth. He meant every word he'd told him; Abe was ready—good, bad, ugly, or any combination in between. He needed the truth. Harris turned his head slowly and locked eyes with Abe, who drowned out the screech of the seagulls and the soft sounds of waves splashing against the rocks.

"I..." Harris began. "I really don't know what you want me to say."

Nineteen: Harris

"You don't know what I want you to say? I want you to tell me what the fuck happened! That's what I want you to say."

Abe's simmering, white-hot rage boiled over exponentially, his wound open and painful. Harris had expressly made two goals for the evening: no yelling and no tears. Each of those was an ambitious objective to accomplish with Abram Hoffman. Abe cried so often in the most random events of their relationship, no matter how insignificant the situation. Harris had forgotten to buy sour cream for the fajitas on the same night Abe accidentally burned the peppers and onions? Dinner was ruined. Tears from Abe. A rabbit ate the freshly sprouted sunflowers in the garden? Tears from Abe. There was an unexpected thunderstorm and they'd left the windows open at the house? Tears from Abe. These weren't full-on outbursts of crying, just an effect of annoyance and irritability. On the other hand, Harris struggled to cry in even the most serious of moments, his emotions and tear ducts apparently not hardwired in the way most humans were—and certainly nowhere near as sensitive as Abe.

It hurt him more than Abe would ever comprehend to stay muted, unable to create a sentence to both satisfy the inquiry while stifling the hard truth. His body and his mind needed to collaborate quickly to develop the response Abe unquestionably deserved; he needed to find that exact right technique to soak up the blood still unmistakably dribbling from Abe's broken heart.

"Abram," Harris started gently, pulling Abe by the bulging bicep of his left arm and guiding him over to the bench sitting parallel with the water's edge. "In the hospital, I knew you were there. There are no words to describe how much it means to me that you were by my side."

Harris would never forget it was Abe who had come to his bedside and not any of his boyfriends since. Not Ryan, not Joey, not Christian, not Dan, not Aaron, not Travis, not Grant, not Kenneth. As he rattled the names off in his head, Harris couldn't believe how many frogs he had kissed and still managed to be incapable of finding his prince.

The "date" had started off so promising, though wholly nerve-racking for Harris, who felt a rush of blinding heat at seeing Abe sitting inside the restaurant. It had been years since he'd gotten a nice, long look—and the result was better than he'd anticipated. Abe had clearly used his anger at their breakup to his advantage, pouring his heartache into time at the gym. In an odd way, he looked both more muscular and thinner, definitely having bulked up in his shoulder and chest area, but thinning out in his face and midsection. Abe's physical prowess impressed Harris, who had spent the period between the dissolution of their partnership slowly gaining weight and rapidly losing muscle. He couldn't believe Abe still hadn't found a man to make him happy!

This topic was destined to arise eventually, Harris knew; he hadn't expected it on night one of their latest reunion. This night was supposed to mark a new era of their often-torrid relationship, one without melodramatics and speculative accusations—a destination they would never reach if they continued to take this route. Harris immediately switched into competitor mode, the same mindset he encompassed during his cross-country track meets in high school. *Always move forward. Put one foot in front of the other. Focus on the finish line.*

The only problem? Harris had no idea where the finish line was, and he would never get there without looking backward first.

"I'm so thankful that I'm here and for us to get this chance to get reacquainted," Harris said as he wilted under the pressure this conversation brought forth, speaking without really saying anything in an effort to try to buy time.

Ever since the attack, his brain hadn't worked quite the same. No longer did the words flow superfluously; each sentence was a bloody-knuckled battle, a melee of the mind that repeatedly resulted in a muddled mishmash of words sometimes only making sense to him. Harris forced himself to concentrate on Abe and envision clarity, which only produced thoughts evenly divided in two categories. He would either use his bare hands to tear Abe's heart out of his chest and tell him the truth, or he'd find a temporary plug to stop the bleeding and keep the real reason for their breakup tucked away under lock and key as he'd done for the past three years.

"Do we really have to talk about this now?" Harris asked half joking, half serious.

Facing away from Harris, Abe positioned his knees toward the water and hung his head in an obvious sign of frustration.

"I know I have a lot of explaining to do," Harris said, for the first time debating sharing every last detail. If there was ever a time to bare his soul and speak the truth, this was that time. Harris's initial thoughts of keeping quiet suddenly seemed irrational. This moment between them marked his chance to have a fresh start with the man who meant more to him than anyone in the world. While the news would inevitably crush him, Abe already appeared dispirited and mere inches away from a mental collapse.

"It all started in Bordeaux," Harris said as he slowly turned, massaging Abe's broken heart with his words. "Do you remember how amazing those two weeks were?"

Abe grunted out an amused reply that signified agreement, causing Harris to intently observe his body language, waiting for the opening to partially right the wrong created by not knowing what to say.

"You honestly think I could ever forget that?" Abe said, finally picking up his head, but still staring straight ahead.

The beauty of Bordeaux had forever changed the course of Harris's life, not only with Abe but also with his career, as he left a job as an insurance agent at GEICO to pursue home remodeling and renovation soon after returning to Buffalo. Inspiration never came easily to Harris, who jumped from job to job fully believing he'd succeed in anything he'd ever choose to do. Before Bordeaux, every employment opportunity hinged on all the selfish benefits that were offered to him like salary, vacation time, and the cost of health insurance. Yet, from the moment they pulled up to their rented chateau, something whimsical internalized inside Harris. The architecture was flashy but classy, clearly steeped in culture but with modern touches placed throughout. The front of the house was a lesson in restraint; the only embellishment being the cascading lilac wisteria adhered to the façade, covering about half of the pale-yellow limestone and extending beyond the slate roof.

The inside of the house was no less spectacular, filled with stone walls and exposed oak beams on the ceiling every few feet. Harris and Abe had cherished their time in the chateau. From the dining area that sat inside a cove—which made every home-cooked meal romantic and intimate—to the living space kept warm by a medieval fireplace with a woodstove. And Abe could never forget the breathtaking bathroom, which had a sunken bathtub surrounded by terra cotta tomette tiles.

"Do you remember how we felt the entire time there?" Harris asked.

"We felt alive," Abe replied.

"Alive" only began to scratch the surface. They were inseparably in awe of their situation, both together as a couple and as two young Americans taking in one of the most beautiful destinations in the world. Reminiscing about Bordeaux always brought out the best in Harris, especially in reminding him of his true joy in life. His fascination with the architecture there was something he always strived toward imitating.

"The night we got lost going to the Pont de Pierre and spent three hours walking in circles, only to end up back at the house and then eat cereal for dinner? That was the night I assumed you and I were going to be together forever," Harris said, unsure if his declaration would help or hurt the situation he faced.

Harris and Abram had never shied away from marriage talk, but for the majority of their relationship, it wasn't even legal. Not being an option in New York meant they'd never faced any questions from friends and family and the subject had never hung over their heads like it did with most long-term couples. They had plenty of conversations where they talked about everything from their dream honeymoon destination of Fiji and the names of their potential children (Noah and Rebecca), but it hadn't necessarily meant marriage was the next logical step—until that one night in Bordeaux. It was their ninth night there and an unseasonably warm autumn night. Abe suggested a dip in the pool and Harris happily agreed, pouring giant glasses of wine for the two of them to indulge in.

The backyard had a limestone walkway lining the beautiful Roman pool and was surrounded with an extended garden terrace that overlooked undulating hills appearing to be never-ending. Something happened that night for Harris—something he still had trouble explaining. Picturing Abram as his one and only wasn't hard to do. Every low-key night, every holiday, every dinner out, every photograph together was pure happiness. Though not against marriage, Harris never really saw himself with a spouse, never assumed he'd be a one-man man. Until that night, when he gazed into the bright crescent moon and the iridescent stars and things became crystal clear.

"I remember looking at the sky, thinking all the signs in the universe pointed toward a brilliant future for us."

"Then what happened? You just fell out of love with me, Har? You don't even know how close I was to proposing."

"It's not that simple! Stop making it seem like one day I woke up and decided to leave with no rationale put into anything."

The truth still struggled inside Harris, fighting its way toward the tip of his tongue, as he reminded himself of the promise he'd made never to reveal the truth, never to drudge up the past. But those promises were then. Three years later, Abe might understand. He might actually take the news with aplomb.

"The thing is..." Harris trailed off, the words failing to materialize. Caught in a lose-lose position, he swayed back and forth between finally explaining the real reasons behind their end and extending the years-long omission of honesty. Each minute of their time together now felt like a completed circle around the track, each word they spoke shoving him forward. His breaths became short and heavy as he homed in on the finish line.

"It's just that..." Harris started again, unable to fathom the words that were about to come out of his mouth. He had spent years vowing never to let it slip to anyone, let alone Abe. As the two turned toward each other, Abe's deep brown eyes looked longingly into Harris's, their innocence as potent and as beautiful as the day he saw them.

"Something—" He paused for a brief moment that felt like an eternity. "Something...just felt off."

He couldn't do it.

"Something felt off?" Abe replied, mocking Harris. "Something felt off. That's all you can say? I should have known you'd be too much of a coward to tell me the truth."

Harris became incensed at being called a coward. He wasn't avoiding the truth to make himself feel better; he was doing it for Abe! He tried biting his tongue, but the verbal lashing he'd received caused his legs to shake with rage. Harris could feel the venom shooting to his throat.

"Did you ever think this wasn't my fault, Abe? That maybe whatever reason pushed me away from you stemmed from someone else?" Harris didn't want to toss out this allegation, but he was sick and tired of bearing the brunt of their breakup.

Stunned, Abe looked toward Harris with a blank face.

"No. You never thought that, because you never think you're wrong."

Abe's prior cycle of rage transitioned to Harris, who no longer cared about mending his ex's broken heart.

"You know what, Abe? You didn't fight one bit for me—one bit for us!" Harris pushed his index finger hard into Abe's chest as his voice raised. "You didn't fight *at all*. You let me go without a goddamn care in the world."

The volume of Harris's shouting led the older couple in lawn chairs two hundred feet away to place their books on their laps and turn around. Abe's blank stare turned irate at Harris's accusations.

"To think I thought there was actually a chance we could work toward some semblance of a friendship," Abe said.

"You're a great guy, Abram. And one day, when you finally appreciate our relationship for what it was and put it in the past, you'll realize you deserve somebody really special."

"That attack on you—it scared the shit out of me. But I honestly thought it would make things different," Abe said, his expression alternating between disbelief and outrage. "Assuming you've changed is the saddest thing I've done in a while."

Harris looked into the face of his ex, which had changed so much in the last three years. The youthful radiance, the wide-eyed purity had all faded into a dull and complex mask of indignation.

"No, Abe. Assuming you need a reason from me to actually move on with your life is the saddest thing you've done in a while."

Harris stood up from the bench, realizing he'd not only failed to heal Abe's broken heart, he'd succeeded in cracking his own open. He was tired of hiding, tired of stifling cold hard facts, so he sat back down.

"It was your parents," Harris said calmly as Abe turned his head, his face filled with confusion for the first time that evening.

"What?"

"Why I left. Why I never showed up to City Hall that night, why I immediately became distant, and why I moved out and ended things between us. It was because of your parents."

Harris felt a wild release standing there as the wind wafted against his back, the adrenaline rolling throughout his body. He turned numb but still noticed the sensation of goose bumps popping up. Everything around him came to a standstill, except for Abram, who stared into his eyes, blinking and waiting for him to continue.

"I knew you were going to propose, Abe. I knew we were going to get married. My dad told me everything," Harris said as he bumped his fist on Abe's thigh. After holding the secret so close for three long years, the words flowed freely. "So that morning, I drove to their house to get their blessing, invite them to the ceremony and for dinner after. I figured we were about to have one of the happiest days of our lives, and you went to all this hard work to surprise me, so I wanted to bring a surprise for you."

Abe's face scrunched slowly and turned demoralized as Harris continued speaking.

"They didn't want to come, Abe." Harris's voice began to crack as he recalled that day inside the Hoffmans' house. He arrived with the wide-eyed glee of a child, only to be brought back down to reality by their response. Patty and Rich were never the kind of people who outwardly showered Abe and Harris with affection and attention, but the two would've done anything for "the boys"—as they so often called them. Anything, apparently, but support their son in his marriage to another man. When Harris delivered the one-two punch of the marriage news followed by the wedding invite, Patty and Rich sat silent. She simply ate a bite of her cinnamon-raisin toast, while Rich drank his coffee, not taking his eyes off the newspaper.

"Their lack of reaction set off alarm bells in my head. It took me a few minutes to realize how unhappy they were. I mean, from your dad, I expected nothing. But from your mom? I thought she would scream and hug me and applaud. Do you want to know what she said? She said, 'I think it's best if we don't come.' And when I played dumb and questioned her, she added, 'It's just kind of embarrassing.'"

"You're lying," Abe said.

"I'm not lying."

"She would never say that."

"She did."

Abe's incredulousness stung Harris, who instantly began regretting sharing his side of the story.

"She also told me that they were both raised in a Christian household and held the firm belief that marriage should be between one man and one woman."

Abe had buried his head in his hands, a symbol to Harris that he should perhaps stop talking. But he couldn't stop; he was in far too deep to end the story here.

"Abe, I basically bared my soul to them and assured her how in love we were and how they had no reason to be embarrassed of you or of our relationship. That's when your dad chimed in and said, 'We're not embarrassed *of* him. We're embarrassed for *ourselves*.'"

Abe scoffed. "What the fuck? Why didn't you tell me this?"

"It wasn't exactly the easiest thing to discuss! And I know you. And I know your reaction would've been awful and you probably would've just... disowned them or something."

"You're damn right I would've," he said, his voice soft and slow. Harris expected to see Abe wipe tears from his eyes, but instead saw nothing. No flicker of sadness, no sign of distress. "I can't fucking believe them."

"I'm sorry, Abe. I really am. I never told you because I didn't want to drive a wedge between you and your parents, okay?"

"Well, you did! Clearly. Jesus Christ, I can't believe you ended everything because of what other people think."

"They aren't 'other people,' Abe. They're your parents."

"Stop accusing my family when it's your own damn insecurities that are to blame."

Abe made a valid point. Something about marriage had always made Harris a bit uneasy. The Hoffmans were the overarching reason their relationship ended, but Harris knew they merely opened the door and created the doubt he might have secretly been searching for. Marriage should have been the obvious answer, should have been what both of them wanted. And for the first time, there at the river, Harris recognized that maybe that wasn't what he'd wanted. Maybe he had wanted things to stay the same for as long as possible—something Abe clearly hadn't been content with doing, which had led to the planned proposal years prior.

Harris looked out toward the water, the sun completely lost beyond the horizon. He hated confrontation and always seemed to avoid it with Abe. He evaded City Hall the night of their nonexistent wedding, a move that was the worst—and easiest—choice he could've made. Harris originally had hoped Rich and Patty would bring up their conversation to Abe, but, apparently, that had never happened. By the time he realized Abe's parents were never going to say anything, he had already started the breakup process in his head, making up his mind that he couldn't marry a man whose family wouldn't accept them.

"It wasn't me, Abe. It was your parents," Harris reiterated, trying to justify his behavior, even if it wasn't entirely accurate.

"Yeah, well, fuck them. I always knew they had a problem with me being gay. I can't believe they wouldn't—" He stopped midsentence. "I'm done with them. And, Har, I think I'm done with you. You were never going to say anything to me? I can't believe you."

Harris couldn't respond, frozen in fear of what Abe would say next. His moody logic was exactly why Harris had concealed the real reason for their split.

"I don't need them. I don't need them and you didn't need me. You don't need me. You've made that painfully obvious. And I'm so glad I've finally realized that I don't need you, either."

"Abe, you can be done with me. But you can't do this to your parents. You know they love you."

Abe shook his head back and forth at a violent pace, like a mental patient on the verge of convulsing. The lampposts along the bike path finally illuminated, shining a beam of light that hovered directly above the two of them.

"Why are you doing this? Why do you care? Stop defending them. You should've told me, Harris. You gave up a life with me for this."

"I care, Abe, because I know what it's like to live without a mother. And I didn't want to be the reason you had to live that life too." Harris backed away from Abe before turning around and transitioning into a slight sprint toward his truck, zigging and zagging through the crowd, fighting the burning desire to turn around and hold Abe tightly.

No yelling? That goal was long gone, a failure early on in the evening.

No crying? Harris wanted to turn around to see how Abe reacted to his exit, but he didn't bother looking because he already knew.

The tears were definitely flowing.

Harris just never expected them to be his own.

Twenty: Abram

It wasn't only anger. There was a bit of perplexity mixed in too. Anger, perplexity, and a little dash of rage—all thinly veiled in a cloak of bitterness.

No single word in the English language could accurately describe Abe's feelings as he headed home on autopilot, sacrificing not one thought to the actual task of driving.

He realized how zoned-out he had become when approaching his street, not quite remembering how he got there, not recalling any of the stop signs, rights and lefts or red lights along the way. Arriving home on sheer memory alone, Abe spent all his effort building his wall back up, brick by brick, blocking the night's horrible conversation from being processed within him.

He put his car into park, turned the engine off, and flung his head back on the seat with enough force to send a jolt down his spine. A large fractured breath came out, punctuated by the near onset of a sob. Abe held it together—for once in his life—trying to handle the night's events like a capable adult and not a petulant child, despite the fact that he emerged as a ball of confusion after his time with Harris.

Is he lying? Did they really say that? Would they really do that to me?

Abe couldn't answer those questions himself. He disputed Harris's explanation and felt he deserved to know the actual truth, exactly what caused the one damn thing that had sucked up so much of his energy for the past three years. That was apparently never going to happen, thrusting "Abe and Harris's breakup" on the list of the world's greatest unanswerable questions, landing on the list next to what really happened to Amelia Earhart or who the Zodiac Killer was.

Abe knew he was being overdramatic, but his emotional overanalyzing was an unfortunate side effect of stress that he had spent his whole life trying to avoid. As he sat in his driveway glued to the front seat, his emotionally fragile mind-set suddenly solidified into something powerful. Abe declared that this was officially the end; he was done. Harris McGee, the man downright responsible for so many memories and so much love, would never again enter Abe's life. Watching him walk hastily away from their conversation at the river had been the sad finale of their friendship, their relationship, and their lives together.

He couldn't do this to himself anymore, couldn't watch Harris dangle the carrot in front of his face as he continually fell short of grabbing the prize. And Abe knew what steps to take to guarantee that he removed Harris from his life forever.

Abe tussled with the pocket of his jeans before springing his phone loose, quickly going to his recent calls and dialing the fifth number down. The phone rang in elongated tones as Abe cleared his throat.

He couldn't believe he was doing this without thinking of what to say or how to say it. Typically, Abe would practice these speeches for days on end, trying to perfect every word and inflection, while rehearsing responses to a burst of possible return questions. The phone finally stopped ringing on the other end.

"Daniel McGee."

"Mayor McGee, it's Abe Hoffman."

"Abram! Good to hear from you, son."

His use of the word "son" made Abe wince, especially after what had happened with Harris. Abram's plan started to fray at the edges, temporarily hindered as he envisioned a world where Daniel McGee was actually his father-in-law. He imagined knowing the ins and outs of the state of the city, the pomp of the bigwig political events, the grandeur of the holiday parties, the amusement of the parades, and the endless other activities that he and Harris would've had to attend if they'd actually gotten married. As shameful as it was to admit, Abe wanted that. He wanted to be entrenched in everything Buffalo.

"I apologize for taking so long to make my decision about your job offer."

"No need to apologize," the mayor said. "I take it you have good news."

"Yes," Abe said, pausing for a split-second. He hesitated to say what he actually wanted to. "Good news for me."

Nothing but an awkward silence came through the other end of the phone.

"I've decided to decline your generous offer and stick with things at the gym," As the words came out of his mouth matter-of-factly, Abe's body went limp, the feeling traveling down his arms to his hands and draining out his fingertips.

"Well, uh, wow. I wasn't expecting that, Abram," Mayor McGee stammered. "Can I ask if there's anything I can do to change your mind?"

Abe so badly wanted to tell Mayor McGee everything. *Working for you brings me one step closer to Harris and I can't have that. I have chosen to no longer expose myself to situations where my heart will constantly be shattered.*

"It's too much, too soon," Abe lied. "I can't give up everything I've ever worked for."

"Well, I strongly encourage you to reconsider. If you change your mind, please let me know."

"Thank you, but I won't be changing my mind. Mayor McGee, I really appreciate the offer, but I respectfully decline."

"Abram, I really think that you're maki—"

Abe hit end call on his phone and tossed it on the passenger seat, feeling like a badass for hanging up before the mayor stopped talking, essentially slamming the door on a golden opportunity. There had been disappointments before in his life but nothing quite like this. The truth was that Abe wanted the gig. He'd been bored at Vitality for a big portion of the last year, mired in paperwork, watching fitness take a back seat to business, and finding very little inspiration in his daily tasks. Choosing this career path wasn't supposed to be about making money, managing a staff, and reconciling budgets; it was supposed to be about inspiring people to be healthy, to make fitness fun, to engage each and every person in the community.

He stepped out of his car, expecting to feel awful and irate but instead feeling nothing. Lifeless and empty, he again struggled to find the words to accurately depict the magnitude of his decision.

Abe entered the house and tossed his keys on the counter. The loud clang caused Jared's voice to soar from the living room.

"Babe?"

"Hey, just me. I thought you and Cass were heading out?" Abe asked, not expecting to see anyone home.

"Hey, Abe. Some girls from work invited her to one of those Paint with Wine classes, so she decided to finally be sociable."

"Oh. Fun."

Abe looked around the kitchen and smelled the scent of citrus. The floors were completely clean and reflected the recessed lighting brightly. He'd been so absorbed in his own world with Harris that he'd failed to notice how dirty the place must have been.

"Did you clean?" he asked Jared.

"Yeah, I know you've been busy, so I dusted, swept, and mopped. And I cleaned out the fridge. I hope you didn't want that two-week-old oatmeal!"

A man after my own heart, Abe thought as he entered the living room.

"So, how'd it go?" Jared asked, sitting up from the recliner and flicking the remote so HGTV went on mute.

Abe flopped down on the love seat, hoping his mammoth drop indicated enough to Jared that he could reply without an answer.

"Oh geez, that bad, huh?" he asked, turning the TV off.

"I really don't know what you want me to say," Abe said.

"Well, that's okay. You don't have to say anything. Sorry things didn't go great."

"No, Jared," Abe cut him off before he could walk out of the living room. "That's what Harris said to me at first."

"You're kidding."

Abe loved that with Jared. There was no need to rationalize his thoughts. The two shared the same perspective. Jared understood how irritating that response made Abe.

"Then he gave some excuses that were all bullshit," Abe said, unwilling to drag his family's name through the mud if, as he suspected, Harris's claims of parental homophobia were a bit embellished.

He had hoped the sight of Jared would boost his spirits. For months, he had always been a beacon of hope, an ear to bend, a friend to comfort him. Staring at Jared caused a rush of sadness to fill Abe. Jared was the unbeknownst representative of the many men Abe passed up post-Harris, never wanting to explore any potential connection as he regretfully hoped and waited for a sign from Harris. And with this new sign—whether truthful or not—it was not anything that would bring the two of them back together.

"So, how did you two leave things?" Jared asked.

"It's over. For sure this time. Am I an idiot for thinking things could've turned out differently?" Abe asked, his voice cracking during the second half of the sentence. Jared must have sensed the impending breakdown, as he shuffled across the floor and grabbed Abe, who had managed to abort most of the tears, except for a few.

"Are you okay?" Jared asked.

"I don't know what I am. I'm mad. I'm disappointed. I can't describe it."

Having held it together so long, Abe crumpled in Jared's strong arms, sinking into him. Abe hated how easily the vulnerability spewed from him.

"Sorry for crying," he said to Jared with a slight laugh, dabbing the tears on his sleeves. "Things weren't supposed to end this way." Abe wondered if Jared understood his use of the word "end" not only meant his evening with Harris, but also his life with him. "I'm such an idiot."

"I know, Abe. It's okay. You aren't an idiot. Do you want me to try to talk to him at all?"

The offer was typical Jared Pfeiffer—trying to help where his help would be nothing but a disadvantage. The offer comforted Abe, as did Jared's stereotypical motions to ease Abe's unhappiness—a few shoulder taps here and a rub of the back there.

"It might sound selfish, but I don't deserve this," Abe said, a bit fearful Jared would realize he was holding back the details that made him so disappointed. He pushed back from Jared's snug, warm embrace and sat flush against the arm of the love seat.

"You're absolutely right," Jared said, shifting his body to face Abe by swinging his legs on the cushions and propping himself up on his knees. "You don't deserve this. You deserve a man who appreciates everything about you. Your amazing generosity, your insane commitment to staying fit, your ability to juggle a rough work schedule and still smile ninety percent of the time. The list goes on and on."

"Thanks, Jared."

"*I* appreciate those things, Abe." Abe noticed Jared inching closer, a simmering intensity behind his eyes.

"I know you do."

"I think I've finally realized just how much I appreciate them."

Jared slinked toward Abe lasciviously, running his hands up Abe's thighs before gripping the small of his back and pulling him closer. Abe's initial reaction was to wrench his body backward, but Jared's strength prevented him from moving. Jared's legs—intertwining with Abe's—felt incredibly powerful as he flashed his impeccable smile, which lingered before Abe's eyes as if to say *I'm ready.*

For the first time all night, Abe suddenly had the ability to accurately describe exactly what he was feeling inside.

Sensual. Animalistic. Aroused.

All it took to find those words was the deepest, most passionate kiss Abe had ever had, after which he ripped off Jared's shirt, starting their unbridled, spine-tingling romp on the love seat.

Twenty-One: Harris

After all the longing for a purpose—a chore or a project that would fulfill his undying need to use his brain—he finally had one. Too bad this was one he didn't actually want.

The situation fell squarely in the realm of typical behavior for Harris, as he was acting and feeling like an ungrateful hypocrite. It's something that had stuck with him from childhood into adulthood and how he often felt with everything in life, from toys to food to men. Once he got what he wished for, he no longer wanted it. The personality trait had always been a recognizable source of alarm, but it struck Harris harder than ever this time around, which was why he insisted on devoting his Sunday to devising a plan for his new home on Crescent Avenue.

Easier said than done.

When he arrived at the house that morning, he'd sworn to sketch out the first encouraging idea he had. Listlessly staring into the cavern of wood pillars and intermittent, shorn pieces of pink insulation, his mind felt barren; no brilliant ideas coming to life, no inspiration in his meandering thoughts, no grandiose visions to replicate on paper.

The lack of spark in generating any beautiful and luxurious blueprint to strive toward disappointed him. Unlike his ingratitude, this characteristic was not a usual part of Harris's know-it-all repertoire. His attack had surely taken its toll, but he could no longer use that as an excuse for the absence of cogent thoughts.

The trendy styles were obvious options for renovations nowadays. An open concept would be a no-brainer. Harris pictured the back left corner to be an all-white kitchen with a farm sink and a bold backsplash—perhaps a deep red or a vibrant teal. The front entrance to the house would lead to a larger-than-normal mudroom, with heated floors and barn doors to cover the closet space. And the stairwell to the second level would feature open-riser stairs with a clear glass railing.

These were all attainable design decisions, each guaranteed to generate a serious wow factor. Still, Harris wasn't in love with the designs. Having never done so before, he didn't want to start simply following the trends.

But there were no spirited signs of anything else being cultivated. Taking a step back, Harris went simplistic and began rattling off interior-design styles in his head. Arts and Crafts. Contemporary. Mediterranean. Mid-century modern. Industrial. Victorian. Each conception merely a bead in a kaleidoscope, only present for a brief moment before transitioning into something else entirely.

Not that this surprised Harris. There was little focus in his life currently. Maybe it was because getting the house was so unexpected. And the fact that this would be the first project in a home he *owned* certainly played a factor.

At least that was what he kept telling himself.

He knew it was really because all he could think about was Abram.

All About Abram.

That could be the title of the last decade of his life.

The grenade had been launched at Abe twelve hours prior, and both watched carefully as it exploded into a cloud of anger and disbelief. Being able to delicately express to Abe what his parents said was never going to be a successful venture for Harris. And Abe's reaction—the wholehearted suspicion that Harris was telling the truth, the ire at Harris taking three years to tell him—turned out to hurt more than he had expected.

Digesting their conversation the morning after only reaffirmed his choice to suppress the long-awaited truth. Yet, Harris began to experience extreme guilt for placing Abe in a predicament regarding his parents. Harris wondered if he would even bring it up to them or if he'd let the "secret" stay hidden for eternity, pretending it never happened. That's the course the Hoffmans had taken—and Abe didn't fall too far from the tree.

The hours since he and Abe had parted at the river had Harris shifting between feeling resentment toward himself, absolution toward Rich and Patty, and vice versa. Stuffing aside his personal apprehension, he again placed the blame squarely on the Hoffmans. Their behavior and principles were despicable, but not outwardly virulent. Three years removed from the conversation that changed everything, Harris shook his head at how much it showed their true colors. Their true, horrible, foul, bigoted, old-fashioned colors.

Abram didn't deserve their closeminded intolerance. Of course, maybe they felt they had been accepting all along. Their response to an interracial gay relationship wasn't terrible—at least not to Harris and Abe's faces. But the underlying demons of selfishness and homophobia had left them unable to accept Abe for what he was.

Harris laughed to himself for how much he had been thinking about Abe. The morning wasn't intended to be a soul-searching, cathartic trip down Memory Lane. Though it wasn't obvious in the moment, the second he and Abe separated, something had captured Harris. Something that filled the gaping void in his life. Even after all that time apart, there was still love there. That certain sense of comfortability and the reciprocity of warmth, humor, and respect between them. All things Harris hadn't come close to reaching in his life since they were together.

Figuring out a plan for the house wouldn't be his most difficult task moving forward. Figuring out where to go next with Abe would be an even more time-consuming, dangerous cat-and-mouse love game.

The wishful thinking of a romantic reunion died after last night's breakup bombshell. He hadn't just put the final nail in the coffin. He'd built the coffin, clocked Abe over the head, placed him in the coffin, hammered all the nails in, dragged it to Lake Erie, and tossed it off the side of the proverbial boat. In spite of that, Harris still wanted to get back into Abe's good graces, to have a chance to prove to him that their love had reached a zenith that wouldn't be touched with anyone else. He hoped it wasn't too late.

A knock at the door cracked his shell of self-absorption.

Harris quickly looked at his reflection in the camera of his cell phone, and the effects of working all morning were evident in the beads of sweat dripping down his face. A silhouette of someone behind the door holding flowers materialized in the sunlit stained white curtain covering the front windows.

Wow, these neighbors are legit.

After unlocking the door, Harris swung it to see a familiar face smiling behind a glass cylinder vase of purple, yellow, and red tulips.

"Sabrina! What...what are you doing here?"

Even with her beaming smile in his face, the bloodred stare of Bruce's eyes flickered in Harris's brain, the pain of each punch suddenly aching in a ghostly throb throughout his body.

"You didn't think I was going to miss the opportunity to bring you a little housewarming gift, did you?" she asked, pushing the vase toward Harris.

He invited her in and quickly realized the gesture might not have been the appropriate thing to do with the unequivocal mess inside. The weight of the door closing kicked up swirls of dust that left Sabrina struggling for fresh air. As he set the flowers down on a windowsill, a groundswell of shame suddenly swept over Harris. He had ignored her calls for days, unable to muster the courage to tell her about Bruce and unwilling to have a conversation about anything else.

"How the hell did you find me here?" Harris asked.

"I saw your father at the anti-violence symposium last night. I'm sad you couldn't make it."

"Sorry, I had plans with an old friend that I couldn't break," he replied, proud of himself for holding back from uttering *Sorry, I was too busy ruining my ex-boyfriend's life.*

"This place is..." Sabrina struggled to find the proper word.

"A dump? Not what you expected? Eerie?"

"Full of potential. Have a little optimism!" Sabrina slapped Harris's shoulder, and he giggled, wondering how someone like Sabrina could ever love a monster like Bruce.

"I *am* excited. It's just all a bit overwhelming."

"I have no doubt you're going to create something beautiful. You certainly have the space to do anything you want!"

Harris wished he could be like Sabrina, so idealistic even when sheer nothingness was staring her straight in the face. She saw through the emptiness and pictured a fabulous finished product existing inside the vacant space. If only he could form building blocks in his mind that outweighed the deserted catacomb in front of him, maybe he'd be that cheerful too.

There he was again—wishing for something he didn't have.

"Is everything okay? You seem a little down. I thought you'd be thrilled about this place," Sabrina said, extending her arms upward and waving them back and forth to signify the giant opportunity before him.

"I'm okay. I saw my ex last night and things...did not go well," Harris replied.

Sabrina leaned in, her eyes practically begging for Harris to continue.

"We almost got married a few years back, and last night I finally told him the reason I walked away." Harris was unsure of how deep into the story to go.

The two carefully walked through the guts of the house, to the backyard where a picnic table sat under a towering oak tree. Sharing an abbreviated version of their fairy-tale beginning and ill-fated ending made everything seemed so trivial. And telling the story to someone completely removed from the history of their partnership made Harris realize how absurd it was to end things the way they had. While he blamed himself for most of their downfall, Abe was no angel either. His stubbornness and lack of passion had made walking away easy.

"Sounds to me like you aren't over Abram," Sabrina said.

"I'm not. And I think I'm ready to admit that now."

"I am no relationship expert, but it sounds like Abram has no idea what you're feeling. You reenter his life after years away and you haven't actually said what you want."

"I don't know what I want. That's the problem," Harris said. "And at this point, even if I do figure it out, I'm not sure I'll ever have the chance to explain it to him."

"My advice to you is simple. Prove to him how much he means to you. Show, don't tell," she said. "Do something that gives him no other choice but to understand how much you mean to him."

Whether she realized it or not, Sabrina had a point. Abe was always a glutton for big, romantic productions. Before getting lost in a brainstorming session on how to impress Abe, Harris decided to focus on the woman in front of him.

"How did the anti-violence symposium go? I haven't talked to my dad yet today," he asked as the two began making their way back through the dank, dark house.

"You will be proud to know that they sought out volunteers to be in charge of their neighborhoods. You're looking at the new cochair of the East Side committee! No one is ever going to have to go through what you went through, Harris. Mark my words."

Her words shone through the chalky air with a sweet layer of authenticity. This woman had no knowledge of who attacked him, had no clue the father of her children was likely a vicious sociopath. She radiated unadulterated joy about making a difference in her community. Harris wrapped his arms around her in a congratulatory hug, regretting ever thinking she was aware of what Bruce did.

"Thank you, Sabrina."

"Your dad said there's really nothing happening with your investigation, which is such a shame. Anytime I see one of my neighbors, I bring it up, Harris. I ask everyone if they saw anything that night or have heard anything through the grapevine," Sabrina said. "Someone besides me had to have heard or seen something. Someone knows something. And I will find out and bring you justice."

"Thank you. I appreciate that. But, I actually hate thinking about that night."

"Understandable. Sorry I brought it up. I should get going anyway."

"No, Sabrina, it's okay. My mind is all over the place today," Harris said. "You say you've asked people about the night I got attacked. What about Bruce? Any chance he saw anything?" Harris hoped his ploy of dropping Bruce's name would hint at the truth of that night. He wanted Sabrina to associate Bruce with that night. To begin to fathom that he possessed a violent streak. For her to confront him and garner an admission, which would lead to her forcing him to confess and turn himself in. But that wasn't about to happen.

"I already asked him. He was at Anchor Bar that night watching the hockey game." Her dismissive response proved how uninformed she was about Bruce.

"You sure about that?" Harris asked.

"I've turned a new leaf about Bruce, Harris. I'm done suspecting everything he tells me is a lie. To be honest with you, things with him are back on again."

The news pierced through Harris like a carbon arrow flung from the crossbow of a hunter lurking in his house. Unaware of whether his face matched his emotions, Harris muttered a response.

"What do you mean by that?"

"We're trying to work things out. Together. As a couple."

"Oh, Sabrina," Harris said, a lump leaching upward from his chest into his throat.

No, no, no, no, no, no.

"Charity hasn't been this happy in years, and Maxwell's face lights up every time he sees his dad. I owe it to them to make this work."

Picturing Sabrina with Bruce made him queasy and crestfallen, his insides rejecting her news with a fierce fight.

"Please be careful," Harris said, his tone threatening and out of context.

"How many times have I told you that you don't need to worry about me?" Sabrina smiled at Harris with an understated confidence. This woman was strong, poised, and ready for anything that came her way. Looking at her made him feel as at ease as possible in the situation. If anyone could handle Bruce, it was Sabrina Rowell.

"I wish you luck, Sabrina." To him, his response sounded artificial and vacant.

But Sabrina sprung forward and kissed Harris on the left cheek. "Thank you, Harris," she replied. "I really do have to get going. Good luck with the house!"

Sabrina carefully traipsed down the stairs and ran to her car. He needed more than simple good luck to figure out his game plan. But at least things were finally starting to align in his head.

A schematic plan for the house? That was far from reality.

What to do about Bruce? Absolutely nothing. Sabrina's happiness meant more to him than his own. He had already made her life miserable once. He wasn't about to interrupt the reintegration of Bruce into her family.

A way to broach a new conversation with Abe and prove to him they belonged together? Well, he needed some help with that one.

Harris picked up his cell phone, scrolled through the contacts, and took a deep breath before hitting send.

It was time to wish for one last thing.

He sure hoped Cassie wouldn't ignore his call.

Twenty-Two: Clare

The weather matched Clare's mood that Sunday morning, more dark and dreary than it had been all spring. The wind slapped her shoulders with brute strength. The chill in the air fused to her bones. Everything around her and within her was mere seconds away from bursting; the clouds filled with water, her eyes brimming with tears.

One year had passed. Everything was different. Nothing was the same.

It was hard to fathom in her mind, even harder to comprehend in person. For 365 days, she had been a widow, alone for the first time since her twenties. Most of the year had flown by with a heavy fog, as she struggled to find her footing in a world without a man who had become her world. Charlie's headstone looked empty and forgotten. The overflowing bouquet of yellow calla lilies and white daisy poms shook in her hands, their vibrant colors so strikingly distinctive in a sea of gray, black, and brown. Despite her hesitancy to fully participate in this visit, Clare stared ahead at the inscription on the tombstone.

It wasn't easy. She didn't want to be there. For so long, she had refused to visit Charlie's final resting spot in Mt. Olivet Cemetery. Though it was only a five-minute drive from home for Clare, it might as well have been five hours away. She hadn't been back since his burial. There had been no desire within her and no bravery that existed for her to return. Thinking of Charlie's lifeless corpse underneath her feet was too much and too heartbreakingly real.

Dr. Bihar suggested the visit, implying that leaping over this hurdle was another part of the mental makeover Clare needed to undertake. She had come so far from her lowest point; there would be no turning back. This was paramount to the metamorphosis that was so vital to moving toward a healthy mind.

Their whole life as a couple she pictured Charlie knowing all the feelings she possessed when they weren't together. And immediately following his death, she had believed he was somewhere out there watching her, fully aware of her mood each day since he'd left her. Assuming he was an ethereal figure invisibly attached to her side each moment throughout every day was a preferred approach—at least until the past few weeks.

She got lost searching for Charlie's tombstone, circling the cemetery four times, scanning for any semblance of something recognizable from that horrific, yet beautiful, morning last year. The temperature had hit sixty-seven degrees that day, the sun warm enough to eke out some uncomfortableness among the formally dressed guests situated on the lawn in the east section of Mt. Olivet along St. Gabriel Drive. Sixty-seven was a number Clare would never forget; it was one Charlie would never see, having died a few months shy of his sixty-seventh birthday. On her fifth attempt circling the cemetery, she caught a glimpse of the grotto hidden by some overgrown shrubs and quickly mimicked applause by tapping her hands three times on the steering wheel.

"Jesus," she muttered.

Clare couldn't believe it had taken her so long to remember where her husband was buried. Feeling embarrassed, she parked her car and breathed a sigh of relief. Charlie's spot was about fifteen paces to the left, behind the grotto. The only reason she remembered this was because she had leaned against it after they buried him, her heaving body barely holding up as she pressed against the amorphous concrete stones.

Expecting her visit this morning to be full of pensive contemplation about Charlie, Clare instead began reflecting on her own life and how everything had changed for her in the last twelve months. She had gone from weak and needy to a carefree adventurer.

In the past few weeks, she had done a wine-tasting tour in the Finger Lakes, ziplined in Ellicottville, and learned how to ice skate at Canalside, each a compelling experience she had never dreamed of doing with Charlie. Each thrilling activity made her crushed sense of self blossom. She didn't want Charlie to see that. She didn't want Charlie to see her happy. He wouldn't understand how she could be happy without him.

But Clare hated thinking back on how dependent she had become in the months right after Charlie's death. Dependent on Cassie for comfort. Dependent on her doctors to provide a course of action. Dependent on Harris for rides to her treatment. Dependent on Dr. Bihar to provide a mental map of guidance. Dependent on the radiation to zap the cancer inside of her. Clearly, everything happening with her cancer had failed to help her stabilize emotionally after Charlie's death, but the worst was behind her—temporarily. The moment of truth wouldn't happen for a few weeks until she had an MRI to determine what, if anything, was left of the tumor and the disease in her brain.

And so in this moment, Clare let the last remaining remnants of her painful year evaporate from her body. The anguish from having her spouse ripped away from her? The doubt that her tumors were gone? Each tossed aside with unorthodox composure. Never one to believe in spirituality, she strangely sensed she was fully cleansing her soul on her trip to the cemetery, purging all of her lingering fear and anxiety, involuntarily burying it alongside Charlie. She knelt down and placed the bouquet beside his headstone, deciding to let the weight of the world slide off her shoulders.

"I love you," she said as she kissed her hand and pushed it on Charlie's headstone.

Everything was different.

Nothing was the same.

And for the first time in 365 days, Clare accepted that fate without question.

Her transformation, though not whole, was one step closer to completion.

"Your house is a masterpiece!" Harris shouted with delight as he hopped down the staircase with the gait of a happy child, staring up at the ceiling toward the lantern and rubbing his hand along the rainbow reflection of the stained glass. Harris had spent twenty-five minutes exploring every nook and cranny of her house, commenting on everything from the stain of the hardwood floors to the stones lining the patio. "Can I move in?"

"You have your own house now, Harris. Unless you want to see if your dad will buy this one, too?" Clare giggled, hoping Harris understood her joke. Her mood had brightened alongside the afternoon sky, Mother Nature and her demeanor once again in sync. "Thank you so much for coming on such short notice."

"Not a problem. What happened between you and Cassie? Everything okay?" he asked.

Harris had arrived shortly after Cass stormed out, severely upset about the house being sold to the Swiateks. Clare expected the unhappiness; she did not expect the personal attacks from her daughter.

"You're scaring me, Mom. You're acting bipolar! One minute you want this, the next you want that. Are you sure this is what you want to do?" Cassie shrieked.

Clare had never been more certain about anything. It was time to let the house go—just like she let her plights go early that morning. There were no doubts, only a slight trace of nostalgia as Cassie's gaze shifted around the house, her eyes covered with a thin wall of tears about to crumble. Clare's face reflected in Cassie's eyes, moments away from sobbing, a zillion thoughts churning through her head. It was exactly how she had looked throughout much of the past year. Like mother, like daughter—in its truest, most authentic form.

Reasoning with Cassie was never easy. She tended to shut down immediately and grow more defiant as time wore on. Resorting to the same tactics she'd used when Cass was a toddler, Clare spoke in a soothing voice to assuage her pain and bribed her with offers of bigger and better things to come.

"Cass, without the house, we can start doing everything we've always talked about. We can travel more, you know? Finally head to Italy. We can give my condo a top-to-bottom remodel, maybe even try to do one of those home makeover shows!"

Of course, all future plans hinged on the results of her upcoming MRI, but Clare chose to ignore the possibility that her cancer wasn't cured.

"I'm doing the right thing, Cass. I know it. Your father would be so happy this house will be left in good hands."

Cassie rotated toward Clare, bracing her arms behind her on the countertop as she inhaled deeply. "He didn't want you to sell this house, Mom."

"What?"

"Dad. He didn't want you to sell the house."

"Cass, stop. You don't know that."

"Yes, I do. He told me. We had a conversation about it during his last Christmas. A long conversation," she said, stretching out the vowel in the word *long*.

Clare stopped dead in her tracks, her back to Cassie. Per usual, her daughter was testing her. Numerous times after his diagnosis, Clare attempted to talk to Charlie about the future. They went through every detail of his will—including the house. Charlie left it all up to Clare. The house was her house, technically, having been handed down from her parents. She had asked him time and time again what he envisioned as she got older. He said he didn't have a vision! There was no way Charlie would talk to Cassie about his plans for the house and not her.

"I said stop it, Cassandra. I get it. You're upset. But stop making up stories about what your father said."

"He tried to convince me to move back to Buffalo so I could live in the house when you two moved to Florida."

Clare looked at Cassie and puckered her lips in a mocking fashion.

"He had a broker and a Realtor down there, Mom. He was going to surprise you with a condo in New Smyrna." Cassie spit the story out so coolly that she had to be lying.

"I said stop it!" Clare hollered louder at her daughter than she had in decades.

"No, Mom. I've had it. I've been tiptoeing around everything with you since the second I got back to Buffalo. I'm sick of it."

"What are you trying to prove, Cass? You want me to tell Marcia 'too bad' and let you and Jared move right in here? That would sure make you happy, wouldn't it?"

"You don't get it, do you? I just want *you* to be happy," Cassie said. "And it seems all you care about is pleasing other people. This shouldn't be about Marcia and it shouldn't be about me. Stop making all your decisions on what other people want and start doing something for yourself."

With her angry, yet kind outburst, Cassie grabbed her purse and left the house, leaving Clare alone to gather everything up, haul the boxes out of the basement, and finish the minimal packing she had left.

The process of selling her house and moving out was indicative of Clare's eternal desire to finish what she'd started in the shortest amount of time possible. Julie had been a godsend and worked on Sunday to get the paperwork primed and ready, which was waiting for Marcia's signature that would come in the morning. The moving van was rented, the boxes had all been labeled, a condo overlooking Ellicott Creek in Williamsville had been rented. Most importantly, her spirit had returned to its desired location. Inklings of death—whether Charlie's or hers—were nowhere to be found.

Harris had arrived less than an hour after she called asking for help, a testament to their still blossoming friendship.

"I think we're okay," Clare said to Harris. "She told me Charlie didn't want to sell the house."

"Whoa, really?"

"I think she's lying to get me not to sell. He and I talked about a few things when he got sick, but he was adamant that the decision to stay in the house or sell the house was mine. I think Cass is distraught. It's not easy to leave this place. I mean, even you see how special it is and you've only been here a half hour!"

"Is there a chance Charlie didn't tell you the truth?"

"Doubtful. Maybe he said those things to her in passing. He always wanted her to move back. But we never kept any secrets with each other. That's the key to a good relationship, Harris. Always tell the truth."

"Yeah, well, telling the truth didn't help me and Abe this weekend."

Clare felt like a fool going on and on about herself without asking Harris how his date with Abe went.

"Hold that thought," Clare said. "I'm making you a sandwich and then you're sharing every detail."

Nearly everything fragile in the kitchen had been swaddled and neatly packed in boxes. Clare would be making the move in a few days, her refreshed life taking on a new setting. The hollow home felt unusually warm to her, maybe an effect of the sun setting on the back of the house, maybe the continuation of her body finally feeling energized. She scanned the cupboards one final time and had started to wrap her glassware when she heard Harris shout her name from down the hallway.

"Clare?" he asked. "I found this in the bathroom. In the bottom drawer."

Walking toward Clare, he emerged holding out an off-white envelope as she continued bubble-wrapping the last of her pint glasses.

"It's probably an old warranty or something. Do you mind opening it and seeing what it is?"

Harris tore the envelope open and read the first few lines with zero inflection, clearly not comprehending the words on the page. "Clare Bear, I miss you already and I'm not even gone. I can't say goodbye to you. I will not say goodbye to you. But there's so much I have to tell you."

Clare dropped the final pint glass and froze.

"It looks like a letter from Charlie."

Her eyes widened automatically, a curious gaze forming. "Where did you find this?" she asked frantically.

"It was stuck beside the leather case for a pair of clippers."

That sneaky bastard.

Harris folded the paper back up and handed her the letter tucked halfway back into the envelope. Clare hesitantly snatched it out of his hands, her fear permeating her skin. Unfolding the paper ever so slowly, her hands trembled. She scanned the page, gauging the handwriting to confirm the accuracy of the note. Sure enough, it was Charlie's chicken scratch.

Clare Bear,

I miss you already and I'm not even gone. I can't say goodbye to you. I will not say goodbye to you. But there's so much I have to tell you.

I'm writing this to remind you how wildly in love with you I have always been. You are the sole reason I consider my life one that was well lived. I have spent so many nights wide awake recently, questioning the reason why I was put here on earth. It pains me to say that in my final days, I don't yet have an answer. But I have figured out why you are here. And that was to create this wonderful, picture-perfect life for me and for us and for Caleb and Cass. No words exist to convey all my love for you. You are an astounding woman, a remarkable mother, an amazing wife and friend. Each day with you only strengthened my love for you.

I imagine you reading this in the fall at the start of your annual spree of organizing the house. By this time, you've probably done everything we never talked about like giving away my clothes, throwing away all my junk in the garage, and finally painting over that color in our bathroom you always hated.

My final bit of advice for you is easy. Don't spend the next few years getting ahead of yourself. As saccharine as it sounds, please live in the moment. Do everything you want to do and do it now.

I had it all planned out, Clare. You and me in our new place in Florida, with Cass back at the house, keeping the Montgomery monarchy in existence in Buffalo. But we never even got a chance to talk about my dreams, let alone live them out. That's my only regret in life. Not being able to do all the things I had planned for us to do.

So, go out there and live, Clare bear. You have more verve inside of you than any person I've ever met. Embrace that. As they say—go forth and set the world on fire. And when things get tough, which they inevitably will, don't give up. Don't you ever, ever give up.

Though I am no longer me, I am now part of you. I am now part of Caleb and a part of Cassie. I am now part of this home. As long as you're here, I'll be here, too. Please don't ever forget that.

I'll see you when I see you.

I love you. I love you. I love you.

Forever yours,
Charlie

Her transformation immediately halted. Like a butterfly in reverse, her wings closed and fell off as she spun and stuffed herself back into her cocoon.

"Cass wasn't lying," she said in a whisper, clutching the letter to her chest. "He didn't want me to sell the house."

Twenty-Three: Abram

He sure had a penchant for picking men capable of lying so easily.

First with Harris who, although not *technically* a full liar, lied by omission, failing to mention the real reason behind their breakup. That confession still seemed a bit too convenient for Abram to believe 100 percent, but no matter which way things ended up, he would have no choice but to classify Harris as an expert deceiver.

And there was Jared. Sweet, beautiful, confused, and closeted Jared. The silence from him since their rendezvous together on the couch wasn't what Abe had anticipated. As a hopeless romantic, Abe had finally somewhat opened himself up to the idea of life with a partner again. When it came to Jared, he'd wondered if this was merely lust or the blissful beginning to their potential life together. However strong the chemistry between them was as friends only seemed to multiply on the couch as they'd let their desires take control—and Abe had envisioned that bond only strengthening if things continued to evolve between them. But, no, he couldn't and wouldn't do that to Cassie.

Despite trying to quell any attraction to Jared, chills ran down his spine as he thought of Jared's insatiableness that night, his strong hands grabbing at Abe's face and body, pulling him in closer every time Abe backed up slightly. Prior to that sensual moment, Abe had tried to conceive of a reason for Jared's mixed signals.

He's not gay. He just likes attention.

He's not gay. He's just horny.

He's not gay. This is all in your head, Abram.

But after what happened? There was no second-guessing. No reason other than the obvious. Jared *was* gay. Or bi. And if he tried to deny that he felt something between them that night, Abe would absolutely call him out. Because Abe had definitely felt *something*—and that something undeniably indicated that Jared was enjoying their time together. Everything was naughty, unanticipated, and wrong. And, at the same time, it was lustful, pleasurable, and fun. Being wrapped in Jared's arms brought

Abe a level of affection he hadn't known he was missing. For the first time in years, he yearned for that intimacy, the desire to be that closely connected to someone again. As Jared had broken down the barrier of his sexuality, Abe had bulldozed through one of his own, finally acknowledging that he wanted this again. He wanted a man to call his own, a man to hold and a man to hold him, someone to share every meal and every dumb story with. And he truly wondered if Jared could be that man.

Abe's recent pleasure would, regrettably, mean Cassie's pain—and the fact that he'd be the one causing it left his body rejecting sleep, food, and rational thinking for forty-eight hours. It was one thing to be upset over what occurred, but it distressed Abe even further that he wasn't the one who stopped it. It was Jared who separated their bodies, telling Abe that he couldn't go any further.

"Abram, you know I think you're amazing. But..."

"Ah, the dreaded 'but,'" Abe replied.

"Cassie."

Without sharing another word, the two had decided to stay cemented on the couch, finally partaking in a cuddle session that was five months in the making. Abe, a mix of sleepiness and giddiness, felt right at home on Jared's broad chest as he listened to the rippling pitter-patter of Jared's heartbeat in his left ear. After his whirlwind evening with Harris, Abe felt lucky to be so peaceful. All thoughts of the argumentative blaming session with Harris left him as he became enveloped in Dr. Jared Pfeiffer. It was a bit early to assume he and Jared would instantly win the title of Buffalo's Cutest Couple, but he questioned whether or not he'd waste an opportunity to try to get there.

That potential scenario would certainly be unattainable until Jared told Cassie the truth. Abe broached the subject head-on, threatening to destroy the perfection of their cuddling.

"You have to tell Cassie," he told Jared without lifting his head off his chest.

"I will. Trust me," Jared replied, his tremulous voice showing his apprehension, but acceptance.

"Jared, if you want me to tell her, I can," Abe offered.

"It's probably best if I tell her, don't you think?"

That wasn't an easy question to answer. Cassie would be devastated no matter which of them told her. Abe pondered the situation and all it entailed. Would she be upset? Does she know? She had to know. *She's probably always known. Deep down inside, every woman knows.*

They parted ways that night with a quick, but sexy, peck on the lips, and Abe told Jared to decide. He could tell Cassie if he wished, or Abe could tell her. Abe even suggested they take her out to dinner and tell her together. It was a very generous, non-pushy proposition. The last thing Abe wanted was for Jared to feel pressured coming out to her. But if it were up to him, they would have waited until Cassie came back that night and told her the truth point-blank. There was no sense holding things in any longer.

Sitting at the foot of his bed two days later, Abe was still holding things in, no closer to figuring things out with Jared, no closer to Cassie knowing the truth. Every pure part of him understood how awful and inappropriate their encounter on the couch had been—but he couldn't deny he had enjoyed every second. Abe didn't really assume Jared would unequivocally embrace his newfound interest in men, but it had been more than two days! Jared had been MIA and was only answering Abe's texts with the effort of a prepubescent teenager responding to their parents' annoying questions. There had been lots of "yeahs," a few "yeps," and an occasional "lol." Abe thought maybe his questions incited those curt replies, so he threw the ball in Jared's court.

"Did you talk to Cass yet?" he asked, already knowing the answer.

"Nope," Jared replied.

That single word jumped off the screen of his phone like swords stabbing Abe's eyes. Jared's obvious avoidance sent a strong signal that he was either ashamed of what happened or unsure about what to tell Cassie. The situation was a once-in-a-lifetime form of awkwardness, yes, but Abe was not about to get caught in another incident where a secret would slowly burn through his life for years until it detonated at an ill-timed occasion.

That first kiss came back to Abe. The tipsy smooch they both played off as an innocent, inebriated mistake. Had that been the turning point for Jared? Had Abe's lips sealed the deal? So many questions ran through his head, but one thought soared above the rest.

Jared had said he would be the one to tell Cassie and he hadn't.

It stung Abe with a dull, persistent throbbing. Like Harris, he was indirectly lying, shoving everything down further and further. Jared's prolonging would only weigh heavier on him and Abe until it became suffocating and lethal, so Abe decided to fix this situation himself, no matter how shitty it felt. Outing a grown man was not something he looked forward to doing, but he refused to sit idly by, watching his best friend have her heart broken by a clearly gay man. The next time he talked to Cassie, he would tell her everything.

Like Jared, Cassie had been nowhere to be seen since Saturday, but at least her texts were a little more forthcoming. "I can't wait to hear about your date with Harris," she texted Saturday night during the couch tryst, which was closely followed by "Sleeping at Karla's. I'm having a great time. So drunk!" They had briefly chatted Sunday while Cass was hungover, but Abe had tried to be as casual as possible, assuming that Jared would break the news any minute that night. Again, he'd been sadly mistaken.

Annoyed with himself for obsessing over this, Abe decided to do something he hadn't done in a few years. After searching in the basement for a good half hour, he finally found the old VHS tape marked in cursive handwriting with "News" on the label. Abe popped the tape in—the VCR making the kind of whirring noises that sounded both perfectly normal and also seconds away from explosion—and intently watched the news clip from when they'd saved Olivia Davidson's life outside the Dairy Queen. They were just kids then. Their outright innocence jumped through the TV screen and grabbed ahold of Abe, strangling him with its perfect and sincere simplicity. Simultaneously smiling and cringing at the footage, each passing second drove him further and further into the time warp. They were so innocent and so youthful. A noticeable longing to go back and return to that world of childhood wonder grew inside him exponentially.

Abe watched the news report six times in a row, rewinding instantly as the story ended and transitioned to that day's weather forecast. By his seventh viewing, he had memorized the words and mouthed along as Lisa Van Sant read the script in her obnoxious newswoman voice.

"Two high school juniors from Tonawanda are being hailed as heroes tonight after saving the life of a six-year-old girl. It all happened outside the Dairy Queen on Brighton Road, when a first grader began choking on a piece of a bubble gum.

"Action 7 news reporter Terry Livingston has all the details on how these two teens sprang to action to help a stranger in need."

"Tuesday started off completely ordinary for Cassandra Montgomery and Abram Hoffman, who say they were working a normal day at the Dairy Queen."

"Cass was out front, putting away the ice cream cakes she just made. I was in the back, because Tuesday is shipment day. I was unloading the boxes that were delivered when I heard her gasp."

"At that minute, unbeknownst to Cass and Abe, six-year-old Olivia Davidson had left her house on her bike and was headed to her grandmother's two blocks away when she started choking on a piece of bubble gum."

"I saw her hop very weirdly off her bike. It almost looked like she hit something and then fell, but she was jerking back and forth while standing like she was in pain."

"Olivia stopped breathing and fell to the ground. Her body lay there lifeless, right outside the exit door."

"I immediately hopped the counter and Cass called 911. When I got outside, she was blue. It was obvious she was choking. I pulled her up to a sitting position and started the Heimlich, hoping that whatever was stuck would dislodge."

"Cass then began administering CPR—something she says she learned while working as a babysitter. Her kneecaps—which were seared on the scorching blacktop—show how desperate and dedicated these two were to make sure this story didn't end tragically."

"They hurt, yeah. But nothing would have stopped me from saving that girl."

"Olivia's family wasn't available for an interview tonight, but did send in this statement into Action 7 News."

"We want to say thank you to everyone in the community who has sent their well wishes today. Olivia is still a bit shook up, but we are so grateful she will be fine. Thank you to the EMTs, the staff at Kenmore Mercy, the police officers who arrived on scene, and most importantly, to Cassie and Abe. It is only because of them that our little girl is still with us. We will never be able to adequately thank them for what they did."

"That same sentiment was shared by the town of Tonawanda Police Chief Sean Terragnoli."

"Without these two young heroes, Olivia might not have made it. They really deserve all the credit in the world."

"Just don't go into the Dairy Queen and say that word in front of Cass or Abe."

"We aren't heroes."

"Abe's right. We're regular people. And we happened to be in the right place at the right time."

"As for anyone who finds themselves in a similar situation? Abe says the key is stay calm, cool, and collected."

"I reminded myself to breathe, not to panic, and to figure out a quick plan of what I needed to do without freaking out."

"That's sound advice from a sixteen-year-old we could all stand to learn from. Reporting in Tonawanda, Terry Livingston, Action 7 News."

The story only lasted a minute and thirty seconds, but that fleeting break from reality was exactly what Abe needed to clear his head. Everything lately had felt far too real. He still hadn't recovered from the flirtation with mortality from Harris's near-death experience and Mrs. Montgomery's cancer. The possibility of selling the gym still existed and the supposed truth about his breakup with Harris hung over his head like a halo of doom. And, of course, the most startling segment of reality was the pickle he and Jared had gotten themselves into—and the effect it would have on his best friend.

Abe looked at his phone, hoping for a text from Cassie or Jared. But as it had been for what seemed like an eternity, the screen was blank. Abe winced and shifted his attention outside, where spring was rapidly transforming to summer. The trees all had their leaves, the temperatures were in the eighties. Sure, it could snow next week, but summer had gouged its way into Western New York. Wanting to break out of his funk, Abe slipped into his flip-flops and skipped out the front door.

If anything could tame his overwrought analyzing, it would be the beauty existing in every corner. His flowers—peonies on the left side of the house, zinnias and snapdragons on the right—were in full bloom, adding a faint fragrance in the air and a delicate touch to the curb appeal of his house. The warmth of the sun seeping into his skin transferred him back twenty-five years. He pictured everything from the afternoons of his youth: Swimming and riding bikes with Susannah, watching episodes of *Saved by the Bell* and *Who's the Boss?*, helping his mom cook dinner inside, and both he and his sister watching and waiting for their father's Oldsmobile Cutlass Sierra to turn the corner so they could run outside and hug him as he walked up the driveway after a long day of work. The precious nostalgia slowly overpowered the overthinking, sending Abe into a brief descent of sadness. He would do anything to go back to those days, to feel carefree and buoyant once again.

It was so easy to want things to be anything other than what they were currently. The grass had always been greener—and would always be greener—to Abe. What would it take to finally be happy with things as they presently were? *When do I finally get what I deserve?* As he combed through his mind for answers, his phone vibrated.

He halted his walk on the corner of Fairlane Avenue and Marion Drive and picked the phone from his pocket, the reflection of the sun making it impossible to read. He frenetically searched for shade, transitioning to a jog before settling alongside a parked FedEx truck.

The words were cryptic. "When are you coming home? I need to talk to you about Jared."

The period at the end of Cassie's text startled Abe, signifying the conversation would be serious. Cassie rarely ended her texts with any punctuation other than an exclamation point.

He told her. Abe's jaw dropped.

Relief that Jared had finally told her hit Abe. But he was also annoyed Jared gave him no heads-up that the deed had been done—something he had specifically asked Jared to share as soon as it happened. His annoyance faded to respect as he recognized how monumental this had to be for Jared. Coming out, coming to terms and being true to yourself, was no small feat; he was proud Jared could be man enough to admit the truth.

Turning around and heading home, a Zen attitude swelled within him, one that could only be beneficial as he prepared to have one of the most difficult conversations of his life. In a way, this felt worse than coming out to his parents. At least in that scenario, he wasn't betraying a friend and wasn't the cause of a relationship ending.

By the time he reached his house, Cassie was sitting on the front porch in the orange Adirondack chair—she had dubbed it "my chair"—her arms crossed and her legs stretched out showing off her patriotic Ralph Lauren flip-flops. Abe hypothesized her mentality in the moment, empathizing with the fragility she likely possessed.

"Hey, stranger," he said, slowly sitting down next to her in his chair—the navy blue Adirondack chair.

"Hey, Abe," she replied, her voice neither angry nor excited.

How to start the conversation had been a subject of debate for some time for Abe. Was it better to say *"I'm sorry"* outright, to hug her first and foremost and then grovel? Or should he let her bring up the subject organically and ask for forgiveness later?

"How have you been?" Abe asked, settling on the latter.

"Well," she started, lifting her head with what appeared to be slight tears behind her sunglasses and a quivering smile. "I have to move out."

"Cass. No, you don't. Listen, I'm so sorr—"

"Yes, I do," she said, slowly shoving her arm into Abe's chest, before lifting her hand up to his face. "Because Jared and I got engaged!"

The sparkle of an apparent engagement ring glistening off the sun charred his soul and blistered his brain. Her celebratory shout knifed through his ears, leaving him lifeless and frozen. She jumped up and down, screaming with delight, pulling Abe up with her. His knees began to buckle as he stared at her beaming face. His breathing stopped.

Breathe, Abram.

Don't panic.

Don't freak out.

Figure out a plan.

He became disoriented, unable to change what was happening, his limbs and his mind paralyzed with fear. Trying to suck in air, Abe sensed his face turning bluer than Olivia Davidson's that fateful afternoon seventeen years ago.

He needed a hero to save him.

Twenty-Four: Harris

She could be hotheaded, mean-spirited, and downright harsh, but Cassie Montgomery did have a few redeemable qualities. Her inability to be a bullshitter always impressed Harris. He never had to guess where he stood with her. If the world was as honest as she was, there might not be as much graciousness, but no one would waste a single second guessing how another person felt. Harris always assumed she had other girl-next-door characteristics that made her as popular as she was, but he never was a witness to those. Her only other trait that he'd found pleasant was her unwavering loyalty to Abram. Their friendship was admirable—it was not easy for a gay man and a straight woman to remain close while standing the test of time thousands of miles apart. She supported him like a wife supports a husband, a mother supports a child. And that was the entire reason he had asked her to meet him for coffee.

The hipster music inside Tipico Coffee filled the unspoken tension between them while Harris waited twenty feet away as the barista whipped up Cassie's grande Americano. They positioned themselves at the stools lining the windows facing Fargo Street, the open air fanning in the scent of the crisp spring evening. The whizzing and plinking sounds of the helicopters dropping in droves from Maple trees provided a nice accompaniment to the acoustic guitars and lilting voices.

The new coffeehouse stood on the corner of a residential street, a vibrant and welcomed sign of rebirth in a building that had stood vacant for years. It was the epitome of what Harris attempted to accomplish as part of the East Side Renaissance project. The inside had an industrial, yet homey feel, with half of a brick wall covered in different-colored textured paints sitting juxtaposed to a tiled wall with a funky black-and-white zigging pattern. The hype surrounding Tipico was huge, pushed largely at first by a viral blitz on social media. It hurt him to think that his social media stupidity botched his plans in their early stages and his fear of another encounter with a maniac like Bruce stunted any potential future ideas. Harris knew the focus needed to be on what brought him together with Cassie—and she made sure not to sugarcoat things, jumping right into the conversation.

"He has no desire to ever see you again," she said. "So if I were you, I'd probably just respect him and stay away."

Without Abe in the picture, he and Cass were a mismatched pair of socks; they could work together only if they had to, but it was not ideal. Having never had a Cassie to call his own, Harris realized his jealousy likely affected his feelings toward Cassie and prevented him from fully understanding her relationship with Abe.

"I figured that's what you were going to say," Harris replied. It was the exact reason he'd called Cassie. If anyone could hack into Abe's brain, it was Cassie. He hated to admit that he needed her, but he did. And it was time she knew that. "I really need your help, Cass. No ulterior motives here. I want Abe to know how much I care about him."

"He doesn't believe your story, Harris," she said, blowing gently into her white ceramic mug. "He doesn't think his parents would say that. *And* he doesn't think you'd end a good relationship because of what they think."

With her omittance of the word "marriage" or "engagement," Harris surmised she didn't know the full story, didn't know how close they were to getting married or how impactful the Hoffmans' comments were. Abe was funny like that, never wanting to reveal too much of his personal life, even to his best friend. It had been a sore spot of their relationship together too, forcing Harris to speculate (often incorrectly) what was bothering him. It was something Abram worked on diligently to correct, but when it involved a stressful or significant situation, the walls went up automatically. And, to Harris, being told your parents think being gay is "embarrassing" and wouldn't support your marriage qualified as a stressful and significant event.

"Cassie, I'm not lying. And there's more to the story than you think. But it's all irrelevant," Harris said, not about to prove her wrong by disclosing all the details. If anything, that would make Abe angrier at him. "What I need your help with is how to get through to him. Over the last three years, has he changed at all? I mean, I know the odds are against me here. But, do you think there is anything I can do?"

"Look, you know Abe almost as well as I do," she said. "He isn't going to forget about this any time soon."

"Cass, trust me, I know. Why do you think I waited so long to tell him? I honestly thought I'd take this secret to my grave. Do you think I should try talking to Patty and Rich?"

"God, no! That is the *last* thing you should do. He's probably not even going to talk to his parents about it."

"Well, then, what do I do? Or is this an exercise in futility?"

Although fruitless, Harris believed this was the most agreeable conversation they'd ever had. It was nice to see Cassie had grown up a bit, softening her hard edges and appearing willing to find a solution that would be best for her best friend.

"Okay, here's an idea. In college, we both had to read the book *The Five Love Languages*. We were obsessed with that book!" she said, laughing to herself before slowly sipping her Americano.

"What's your point?" Harris asked, a bit bothered by her half-hearted suggestion.

"The five love languages are: gifts, quality time, words of affirmation, acts of service, and physical touch. Which one do you think fits Abe the most?"

Harris didn't pretend to comprehend her question.

"What the hell are you talking about?"

"Just think about it, Harris! I can't do everything for you. Which love language fits Abram the best?"

"What are my choices again?"

She responded by holding up her fingers on her left hand as she counted them out, starting with her thumb.

"Gifts. Quality time. Words of affirmation. Acts of service. And physical touch."

As she said the words "acts of service," he saw the ring.

"Wait!" Harris said, grabbing her left hand. "Does this mean what I think it means?"

"It does!" she replied, smiling meekly. "You're looking at the future Mrs. Dr. Jared Pfeiffer."

All talk of Abe subsided as they went through the details of the engagement. It happened mid-Tuesday while Cassie was at her job, sitting in her classroom working through her lunch creating study guides on *Where the Red Fern Grows* for some of her problem students. Jared unexpectedly popped in with an orchid—her favorite flower—and a gift wrapped in silver-and-gold paper. Cassie told Harris she knew it was a book and was a bit annoyed Jared would be obvious with his presents. ("Getting a reading teacher a book? It's like buying Abe a set of dumbbells. It's unnecessary.") But when she unwrapped the gift, there was a picture of the two of them designed as a book cover that was titled, *Our Story Starts Here.*

"I was actually still irritated when I saw the cover." She laughed. "I had no idea what was happening and I really wanted to finish the study guides."

When he encouraged her to open the book, she found the center of the book hollowed out and a white-gold, split-shank engagement ring with two princess-cut blue sapphires in the middle. And when she looked up at Jared, he was on his knee, asking her to be his wife.

"I couldn't say no to that," she said.

"Wow, Jared came through on the proposal," Harris said.

"He certainly did. It was so unexpected, but he said he had been waiting to propose for weeks."

"How did your mom react?"

"Ha! Who knows? She is all over the place these days."

For the first time that morning, Harris noticed sadness in Cassie. Long gone was the Cassie from college—the one with the youthful enthusiasm and a flouncing gait that left her ponytail bouncing with each step she took. The years had caught up with her. Though her everyday-girl panache and attitude still prevailed, it showed signs of cracking when she started talking about her mom.

"Moving back home was supposed to be the dawn of a new day. I finally ended my struggle to get back to Buffalo and it's been nothing but a challenge."

"I'm sorry she sold the house without talking to you. She had no idea what your dad was planning, you know."

"Of course she didn't! She never once asked me or Caleb about her decision. Not that she needed to, but this is what happens when families don't communicate."

Harris wasn't one to judge. His father had bought him a house without saying a word—and was that really any different or better than selling a house without asking?

"It really is a beautiful piece of property. At least she knows it wasn't what you wanted," Harris said. "Try to remember she's going through such a hard time. Your dad, her cancer. She isn't the woman she wants to be and she's working on that."

"Oh yeah? How does selling the house get her to the point where she's who she wants to be?"

"That's something only your mom can answer."

Cassie sighed.

"Anyway, she's fine with the engagement, already planning on how to help with the wedding even though we don't even have a date set. Funny enough, it's Abe who has been the weirdest."

"How so?"

"When I told him, I thought he was having a heart attack. He stopped breathing!"

"Holy shit, really?"

"He claims he was faint and had low blood sugar or something. But, I honestly think the news shocked him. And I'm not sure he's happy, which sucks."

That didn't sound like a typical response from Abe, who had always put Cassie's happiness above his own. And the man was a picture of perfect health, his meals and snacks planned around his workouts and classes to ensure sufficient levels of every nutrient and vitamin known to man. Cassie had always thrown things out of whack for him, but there had to be a logical explanation for his uncharacteristic reaction.

"You're his best friend, Cass. He probably just doesn't want things to change between you two."

"I suppose," she said with a shoulder shrug.

"Jared's a fantastic guy," he said to her. He meant it. The man had been there for him from the moment they met, offering advice and support to a complete stranger without hesitation. "Abe knows you're a lucky girl. He really hates his routine disrupted."

Their conversation continued as the sun began its descent behind the neighborhood's architecturally brilliant old row homes. It became a casual encounter touching on everything from Harris's health ("As good as can be expected") to Cassie's job ("Not perfect, but better than North Carolina") until they walked outside to their cars and Cassie put the kibosh on their newfound amiability.

"Whatever you try to do, make it count. Think about what makes Abe happy, what reminds him of your good times," Cassie said. She then turned stern, looking Harris dead in the eye with a fierce glare. "Because, as much as you and I don't see eye to eye, he really did love you. And he probably always will."

Harris looked at her and pulled his lips to the right side of his face in a side smirk.

"I'm serious, Harris. Treat this is as your final chance. I'm not sure how much more his heart can handle."

"Thank you, Cassie. Congrats on your engagement. Tell your mom I say hello."

"I will. But chances are you'll talk to her first!" Cassie said as she reached her car, placing her lower body in the driver's seat before popping back out. "If you need any other help or anything..." Her sentence didn't materialize, but Harris enjoyed that she was extending an olive branch. In their fifteen years of knowing each other, it was by far the nicest she had ever been to him.

Harris turned around toward his car with some pep in his step, in part because of the caffeine but also because of his conversation. If he had success in getting Cassie to be that nice to him, he predicted Abram wouldn't be far behind.

He flung open a cheap comforter and placed the tan side on the floor with the maroon side facing up, then pulled out a sleeping bag, unrolling it on top of the puffy foundation he'd laid out. Lying dead center in the middle of the empty space, his head sunk comfortably into two pillows as he let out a weighty sigh. Forgoing a return to his apartment, Harris decided to sleep in his house, trying to transfer his good mood post-Cassie into inspiration for what to do with the space. If he was going to be inspired at any time, it was likely this moment. After weeks and months of several appalling events, it was time he grabbed life by the horns and turned motivation into action. He had made some progress in the house that week, going through a thorough cleaning and sweeping of the inside and a total scrub down of the porch. The backyard, which was mostly encased in overgrown shrubs and weeds and featured several piles of hot, plastic garbage, looked a bit more livable with a little work.

Crafting a plan for the inside was Harris's main goal for his overnight stay, but all thoughts, unsurprisingly, led back to Abe. Cassie's words had glued themselves to his brain.

"Think about what makes him happy, what reminds him of your good times," she had said.

Although the bad times were amplified most recently, there were innumerable good memories between them. There was their first apartment together in the Elmwood Village on Norwood Avenue—which included an epic housewarming party that was still talked about to this day, the trip to Los Angeles where they were asked to be extras on an episode of

The O.C. and their behind-the-scenes tour of the Buffalo Zoo where they got to hold and play with the baby ocelot kitten Indira when she was only three weeks old.

And, of course, there was Bordeaux. His recollection of Southern France was possibly misguided and placed on an undeserved pedestal in his memory, but it was everything that a vacation should be: romantic, exhilarating, relaxing, charming, educational. He and Abe had always been happy together, but Bordeaux intensified their connection. Everything fit together there and they both felt their commitment solidify—at least, until the Hoffmans weighed in.

If only they could get back to Bordeaux, maybe things would be different.

The thoughts continued to flow in his head, this time concentrating on Cassie's idea about deciphering which love language fit Abram the best. Harris decided it was either acts of service or quality time—and seeing as he couldn't even get near him, quality time was crossed off the list. That's when it finally hit him.

He sprang up to a sitting position and shouted, "The house!"

His voice echoed in the hollowness. How had he been so oblivious? The house! Why didn't he think of this sooner? His eyes darted from corner to corner, all the pieces connecting into a well-thought-out strategy.

This was it.

This was how he'd win Abram back.

Twenty-Five: Clare

She was as ready to say goodbye as she'd ever be, staring blindly into the backyard, her eyes unable to pick a focal point to lock in on. Everything around Clare was either blurry or completely clear, each object transitioning from one to the next and then back again. The heat and the constant activity of the last few days had taken its toll, her body merely a sputtering vehicle for her powerful mind, pushing forward against the obvious signs of a necessary slowdown. She hadn't taken a moment to relax the entire week, frantically jostling boxes up and down the stairs and from room to room, neatly organizing piles to load into the moving van so that they'd be unpacked in a sensible order.

This was another new side of Clare, one with no hesitation or second-guessing. All that mattered was that the choice had been made. She was selling her house to Marcia and Brandon Swiatek. That was that. End of story. There'd be no sense living in the house until it became "official" from the bank. Her new condo was ready to move into, so it was time to leave. Delaying the inevitable was the old Clare. Working through the difficult moments with the dedication to fully complete her task as quickly as possible was the new Clare. She wasn't going to stop until everything was packed and everything was moved.

Besides, if she stopped, she'd start thinking about that letter Charlie wrote.

And she was *not* about to start thinking of that letter.

Instead, Clare took a few deep breaths and walked toward the vegetables she'd planted. Slowly, she regained her composure, the faint feeling disappearing as she placed her arms on the fence posts. That's when it hit her. This would likely be the last time she'd stare at the sun shining so brilliantly on her garden. What started as a gigantic, rectangular patch of dirt when Charlie and Clare got married had yielded so much for the Montgomerys—an embarrassment of riches, really. So many years, they were forced to throw out the cucumbers and tomatoes they couldn't eat any more of—there was only so much cucumber tomato pasta salad a family could eat—and freeze the zucchini they failed to give away to friends and neighbors. If she inhaled deeply enough at any point during the year, Clare could smell the aroma of the freshly baked zucchini bread she made every winter with her frozen leftovers filling the downstairs of the house. This year, the crop was once again poised to deliver. The flowers on the zucchini were bright yellow and generous, the tomatoes already had their first fruit forming, and the blueberries and strawberries were already full of buds, though in desperate need of some bird netting to keep out the pesky robins that would devour each and every berry with free access. Of all the things she'd miss in the house, the vegetable garden stood at the top of her list. The backyard had been her sanctuary. She'd flourished in the space, which seemed to exist in a different portal than the real world. With numerous tasks to tend to in the backyard, she had often wandered to the space where real problems melted away and were replaced by backyard problems: grass creeping under the fence from the adjacent property, mold spores forming on the leaves of the squash, rabbits worming their way into spaces they shouldn't be and eating things they shouldn't be eating. The backyard took definite work and dedication, but it was a much-needed haven during several eras in her life.

What would be her new escape? Clare looked back at the house, admiring the structure from her point of view in the garden. Eight-thirty-seven Parker Avenue was the perfect place to raise a family. The Swiateks were going to love it, surely, but no one would ever appreciate it like Clare did.

In a day, Clare would no longer be a homeowner—and she felt comfortably satisfied about that. The tasks continued to dwindle, with little remaining to do before the moving company packed up the furniture. She had to dry mop the hardwood floors and dust the chair rails one last time, then do one final sweep of the house, ensuring she left nothing behind. Almost completely empty, the house had delivered no additional secret letters from Charlie. She wondered if Harris had stumbled upon the only trick up Charlie's sleeve.

Was that the final goodbye? Were there other surprises she'd find out about later?

"Stop it, Clare," she said aloud, reminding herself that she wasn't going to think about the letter.

It might have been childish, but what was the point of looking backward? The new beginnings were coming fast and furious for the Montgomery women—she with her new condo and Cassie with her new title of fiancée. The thought of preparing for Cassie's wedding left Clare equal parts excited and exhausted. The venue ideas were already flowing (Cass wanted somewhere "rustic" and "unique") and she and Jared had only been engaged seventy-two hours. This was only the start of Cassie's venture into what was sure to be precise planning in pursuit of perfection. Clare tried to calm any premature apprehension and be realistic. She knew her daughter wouldn't be the world's biggest bridezilla, but she would be very particular and set the highest of expectations for her wedding. Merely imagining the process of getting to the big day left Clare's head hurting and in need of a nap.

Having already successfully navigated away from her thoughts of Charlie and the house, she received further distraction after hearing Marcia yell her name from the gate where the driveway and the backyard met.

"Clare? I'm here!" Marcia said.

She arrived promptly at 1:45 that afternoon, precisely as Clare had asked. The two greeted each other with a hug, and Clare led her inside, where Marcia's jaw dropped at the absolute bareness inside. The house didn't look one bit similar to its former state—an entire transformation in just a few days. Marcia intended to continue running her cake business from the house, so Clare had made a concentrated effort to empty as much as possible from the kitchen, wanting Marcia to be able to picture the area as her own. It had been completely cleared of all the magnets, photos, and other personal effects Clare had stacked up in every available space. The pictures were off the walls, the African violets off the plant hangers, and the rugs rolled up and put away. To Clare, the kitchen looked terrible, the curved wall appearing so out of place, the entire room so unhomely and sterile that it made it painful to observe. Marcia didn't see it the same way.

"Even empty, it's flawless, Clare," Marcia gushed.

"Marcia, that's actually part of the reason I asked you to come here today. The house isn't perfect. No old house is! I want to show you a few of the quirks around here," Clare said, motioning Marcia to follow her.

Starting in the kitchen, Clare pointed out the funny things that had always been a little off with the house. There was the one section of tile near the stove that—for whatever reason—caused the metal above the range to creak and clang when stood on in the right spot. And there was the cabinet next to the sink, which featured a handle that never stayed screwed in. ("If the hardware for these weren't antiques, I would've replaced them myself," Clare told her.) The kitchen marked the beginning of Clare's tour of Montgomery Manor, where she made sure to point out every idiosyncrasy she could remember.

"That door doesn't close all the way when it gets above seventy degrees."

"A very earthy smell, kind of like dirt, comes out of that vent when it rains out."

The behind-the-scenes tour of her house felt unusually purgative to Clare. After days of suppressing all the positive memories of her home, the ability to speak of all the little negative things reminded her exactly why she no longer wanted or needed a house. These problems would belong to someone equipped to fix them, like a maintenance crew or her condominium complex super.

"To shut this window, make sure you hold the top part up and slam the other down. Otherwise, it won't lock."

"In the bathroom, the one switch says Heater and the other says Fan but they both go to the fan. I've never felt that heater work in my life!"

Marcia nodded understandingly with each statement, but her nervous laugh made Clare sense the litany of problems had become overwhelming. What had become therapeutic for her seemed to be inducing stress in Marcia. She decided to switch gears and cut all talk of potential complications.

"Listen to me, talking about all the bad things about this place! They aren't deal breakers, trust me," she said. "In six decades of living here, there have been relatively few major issues." Clare felt lucky the two had approached the three-season sun porch at the back of the house, not only because its white brick radiated in the glow of the sun, but also because of her personal connection.

"My grandfather laid the brick in this room. It took him an entire summer to do," Clare said. "And it's also where Cassie took her first steps when she was eight months old. She wasn't a crawler, you know. One day, I was cooking dinner and she and Caleb were playing with blocks. I told Caleb to make sure his sister stayed in that room. She propped herself up on the couch and took off. Caleb was so cute. He scooped her up right away and brought her to me and shouted 'Mom, she won't stop moving!'"

Clare led Marcia to the garage and pointed out the peg board. She removed it from its hooks carefully, displaying a set of tiny slashes in the wooden beams.

"The first set of marks is my height, every year on my birthday from when I was four until fourteen. The second set—on the beam closest to the wall, those are Cassie and Caleb's height."

Clare apologized for the permanent memory etched in the wall before placing the peg board back in its spot.

"Marcia, this place has been nothing short of a treasure," Clare started, surprised at her ability to hold back her emotions. "I'm so happy to pass it on to you and Brandon. You're going to love it."

It was a true statement. After decades of happy moments and sad memories, Clare felt ready to hand the house over to a lovely couple who would continue to love and cherish it. Marcia walked toward the beige tote bag she had brought with her and pulled out a wrapped box, which she handed to Clare.

"This is a little something Brandon and I thought you would like."

Clare gasped as she opened the box. "Marcia, where did you find this?"

Inside was a framed print of the front page of the Lifestyle section of *The Buffalo News* from October 19, 1984. The paper spent a week profiling the most unique homes in Western New York—with Clare and Charlie closing out the series that Friday. In near-perfect condition behind the tempered glass, the newspaper featured Clare and Charlie smiling widely with the house behind their right shoulders. The headline read, "The Pearl of Parker Avenue."

Unable to look away from the article, Clare's eyes and heart swelled with a bittersweet melancholy.

"Thank you so much. I don't know what to say," Clare said while hugging Marcia.

"Just promise you'll come back and visit often. You know you're welcome here anytime. This house will always be your house."

The gift and what it signified were the only things more wonderfully sweet than Marcia.

"Thank you, again."

"No. Thank *you*, Clare. I have to get running and pick up Harper, but I'll see you soon, right?"

"Of course. See you soon, Marcia."

Marcia pranced away with a confident swagger, each step exuding her bubbly demeanor and her pure happiness in being the new owner of this house. Her joy was contagious and provided yet another reason for Clare to believe that she was doing the right thing in selling the house.

Turning around back toward the kitchen, Clare picked up the framed newspaper again and grinned. That picture of her and Charlie felt like it was from a lifetime ago, both of them fearless and ready to conquer the world as new parents and new homeowners. Quickly wrapping the picture back up in the white tissue paper, she walked away and sprawled herself on the couch, hoping to sleep away all her contemplations.

She wasn't going to think about Charlie, because she didn't want to think about the letter. And she wasn't going to think about the letter, because she didn't want to think about the house. There would be a time and a place for reflection, but it certainly wasn't the time.

Clare placed her head on the arm of the chair, closed her eyes, and tried to turn off her churning mind as the warm wind drifted in from the windows, gently blowing away the tears that were starting to roll down her cheeks.

Cassie woke her up when she dropped her keys on the counter, the crash inside the sparseness of the house leaving an earsplitting reverberation in Clare's ears.

"Mom?"

"In here, Cass!" Clare shot up, shifting her shirt around, trying to smooth out the wrinkles on her shirt and her face.

"Oh, did I interrupt nap time?" Cass asked, smiling.

"Very funny, Cass. I'm just worn out," Clare said. "How are you doing today?"

"I'm good. Are you going to get ready for dinner?"

"That's what I wanted to talk to you about, honey," Clare said. "We can't go to dinner."

Cassie's face turned red, her smoldering rage contained behind her beautiful brown eyes. Though a well-adjusted young woman, the hints of Clare's little girl still existed not so deeply beneath the surface. Clare, Cassie, and Jared were supposed to go to dinner to celebrate their pending nuptials, but Clare had bigger plans.

"We can't go to dinner because you need to pack. We're going to Chautauqua Lake! We'll go to dinner this weekend when we're there."

"What are you talking about?" Cassie asked.

"I rented the cottage at Willowridge Estates. The same one we went to all those years as a family. We're going for the whole weekend, Cass!"

Cassie looked up at her mother and ran toward her.

"Oh my God. Seriously?"

"Yes, honey. I'm so happy for you and Jared. You deserve a proper celebration."

She really did. Clare and Charlie had missed so much with Cassie. The distance between them over the past decade meant spending most birthdays and holidays (even some Christmases) apart. The drive to North Carolina was not enjoyable for anyone and flights were often sparse and expensive. It was time that Clare honored Cassie with a party for the ages.

"You know how big that cottage is, so I invited Abe. I hope you don't mind," Clare said.

"Not at all," Cass replied.

"We leave tomorrow after work, so make sure you pack tonight!" Clare said.

"Tomorrow? But you're moving tomorrow."

"In the morning, yes, but it'll all be moved in by the afternoon. And I'll unpack when we get back."

"Oh, Mom. Does this mean you're not upset with me for what I said about Dad?"

Clare hadn't told her about the letter yet, because telling Cassie would mean thinking about the letter. And Clare reminded herself for the umpteenth time that day, thinking about the letter was not happening.

"Oh, Cass. I'm not upset with you," Clare said. "I just really miss your father."

"Me too, Mom. Me too."

Clare held her daughter tightly and rubbed the back of her head like she had since Cass was a newborn. She didn't have to speak—and she didn't want to, either. Cutting off the conversation at this point was vital for Clare. The highly emotional milestone of leaving the only place she had ever called home needed no added dramatics.

She wasn't going to think about the letter.

And she wasn't going to think about Charlie's plan for the house.

And she most certainly was not going to think about the fact that this was the second day in a row she had felt this way—the same way she had all fall and winter. The tiredness. The headaches. Dr. Kincaid had told her to call if she ever felt "abnormal" for longer than a day, that symptoms sometimes reappear and would necessitate an MRI sooner than normal.

Is that what was happening? Was her headache a sign of another tumor?

No. It couldn't be. Logical thinking dictated she was tired from packing and moving all week. Logical thinking suggested she only had a headache because she was surely dehydrated.

Logical or not, Clare didn't care.

Because like everything else storming around her head these days, she wasn't going to think about it.

Twenty-Six: Abram

He wanted her to slap him across the face, kick him in the balls, stab him in the back. Really anything but profess her love for—and lifelong dedication to—Jared. At first, Abe thought Cassie was kidding, playing a cruel practical joke about their engagement after finding out about their sizzling manhandling of each other. But once the oxygen returned to his lungs that afternoon, it all became clear. Jared had proposed and Cassie had accepted. It was the worst scenario imaginable—and had permanently left an extraordinarily stupefied expression on his face. He anticipated by the time Friday rolled around he'd be going on a date with Jared, not contemplating ending Cassie's supposed date with destiny.

These were the thoughts going through his head as each of the two dozen participants in the afternoon's yoga class—Abe included—were in the middle of their Shavasana poses, the time at the end of a yoga session dedicated to self-reflection and the removal of sensory distractions. As he lay on the mat motionless, Abe tried to embody the "corpse" pose in both body and spirit to no avail. Every deep breath, the hum of the lights, and the beat of the music outside the room were audible, infiltrating his crack at resting. In a moment intended to be a complete blank slate, all he could see was Cassie's blinding smile, so excited at the news of Jared's proposal. Unable to shake that image left him feeling like a fraud. There he was teaching this class how to purify thoughts and perfect the art of relaxation when he was on edge, filled with an intense anxiety he hadn't felt in years.

"All right, everyone. That's it," Abe said, pushing himself up out of Shavasana. "You all have a good weekend and I'll see you next week."

It was definitely not the proper technique to abruptly end Shavasana like that, and though Abe felt slightly dishonest about stopping it so quickly, he remembered not every session was going to be textbook perfection. He vowed to make it up to the group the following week.

An aura of dread dripped from his sweat-soaked Dri-fit T-shirt. Heading to Chautauqua Lake with Cass, Jared, and Mrs. Montgomery was the last thing he wanted to do, but he couldn't say no to Clare. How would he justify being absent from one of the biggest events in his best friend's life? Abe also wanted the chance to talk to Jared, whom he hadn't seen alone since the engagement. The weekend was bound to be a shit show.

Inside his office, he saw a note from Brianna, who would be opening and closing the gym while Abe was in Chautauqua.

> *Mayor McGee called looking for you. He asked that you call him back. - Bri*

The calls had happened daily since Abe turned down the job and hung up on the mayor. Any morsel of guilt he had about his actions had withered away with what was happening with Jared and Cassie. For most of his life, Abe had put his professional life above his personal life. *Happiness in your job will equal happiness in life*, he believed. After the news that week, he no longer held that adolescent way of thinking. No job equaled happiness. He would have to figure out ways to find it on his own. Abe left his brief notes for the weekend crew in the office and walked outside to the car.

The GPS on his phone showed the journey to Chautauqua Lake would take a little more than an hour—a straight shot down I-90 for the most part. Hitting the open road with windows rolled down, the radio on full blast and the breeze blustering through his hair often put Abe in a great mood. Not this time, as his mind was soaked in seriousness. What he really needed was to vent to someone who had met Jared, but understood his friendship with Cassie. Someone who could evaluate things about the three of them from an objective point of view. The only person possible? Harris. Abe let out a deep snicker. As much as he wanted to talk to someone about Jared, that eagerness did not outweigh his wish to never speak to Harris again.

Like riding a bike, the way back to Willowridge Estates returned easily. He didn't have to pay attention to the GPS, subconsciously turning to the left at the thruway exit, and then a quick right down Route 60. The Montgomerys had brought Abe every year on their family vacation until he was a teen, and with everything up in the air for the weekend, the one thing he knew would be a definite was the stunning view from the backyard.

Approaching the cottage, Abe didn't have a plan other than the obvious: telling Cassie the truth. If he lost his best friend, fine, but he wouldn't let her become a laughingstock and he wouldn't let Jared steal some of the best years of her life. After crossing through the wrought-iron gate emblazoned in gold with *Willowridge Estates*, Abe instantly noticed Jared cleaning the windows on the *Dreamboat* in the driveway of the cottage. Abe hated that his first reaction was to think, *Damn, he looks good,* but it was only natural. The surrounding area outside the cottage showed no signs of Cassie or Mrs. Montgomery. Finally, he had caught Jared alone. Abe sped up and slammed the car into park, practically bolting out of the car before pulling the keys out of the ignition.

"Really?" Abe said in disgust, marching toward Jared.

"Abram, I'll explain everything," Jared said.

No explanation in the world would suffice. Jared's blatant lie would only destroy Cassie in the long run. Her life would delicately dissolve as soon as he decided to be true to himself. That day when Jared's brain would start short-circuiting after suppressing the pent-up lust of being with a man would come soon enough, and Abe wasn't about to stand by, reticent until its arrival.

"I don't want to hear it, Jared," Abe said, pushing his finger in Jared's chest. "You're making a mockery of Cassie—and marriage in general! What the hell is wrong with you?"

Abe delivered his question with an appalled subtext and turned to walk toward the cottage when Jared grabbed his wrist and pulled him backward.

"You're not telling her anything," Jared said.

"Oh, I'm telling her everything. Every. Fucking. Detail." Abe's venom spewed involuntarily. Even though he knew this was coming, the weight of the wrath behind his words took him by surprise. From the second Mrs. Montgomery invited Abram on this weekend getaway, he'd promised himself he would tell Cassie. The news of their engagement could not continue to be spread; the charade could not linger any longer. The more he analyzed everything the angrier he became. His blood was boiling, each vein in his arms jutting out of the skin, pulsing with fury. Jared's body language stood in complete contrast. His baby blues exhibited a plaintive, sorrowful stare, as if they were saying, *"Please understand me. I'm confused."*

"Abram."

"What's your explanation, Jared? That being with me made you realize how much you love her? That you're only *curious* about men?" Abe asked, flamboyantly making the air quotes with his fingers. "Look, I've been in your shoes, and if you're not ready, there's nothing wrong with that. But you can't go ruining someone else's life because you're incapable of admitting who you are."

"I love Cassie," Jared said. "I really do."

"So do I. But I love her enough to realize I'll never make her happy in the way a husband should. It's time you realize that, too. She deserves better," Abe said. "And so do you."

As much as Abe hated Jared for what he was doing to Cassie, he also hated him for ending whatever existed between the two of them. He had thought their night together on the couch was so much more than physical. Their affinity for each other had been palpable from the onset of their friendship. And whether Jared wanted to confess that or not, he had been an incredible friend to Abe. Predicting this could be the last conversation they would have, Abe decided to lay off briefly and speak to Jared man to man.

"To be honest, Jared, I thought we could have had something real," Abe said.

Jared's reply was simply his dimples showing with a small smile.

Abe assumed that was the closest to a confirmation as he would get. Jared hadn't denied he felt something for Abe, but he also hadn't acknowledged it either. It had become painfully obvious that there would be no more kisses between them, none of the cuddling and hand-holding that Abe believed would be coming, and none of the stuff he stupidly envisioned could have ever been a possibility if Jared and Cassie broke up: no adorable 4:00 a.m. workouts together were in their future, no fun date nights to Canalside, no weekend jaunts aboard the *Dreamboat*—absolutely none of the cute couple activities he had prematurely imagined.

At the very least, Jared had given Abe his answer. What had existed between them wasn't love—it wasn't anywhere close. It was nothing other than unadulterated lust and infidelity in its ugliest form. Abe hated himself for reaching this point.

"Abe, there's something I want you to know," Jared said, his voice stern and authoritarian. Before he could speak any further, the screen door on the cottage slammed shut.

"Abram Hoffman!" Clare shouted. "How are you, buddy?"

She ran toward Abe and gave him a monster hug—and she looked good too. Her hair had grown in a bit more, turning into a very short (albeit chic) pixie cut. Clare had moxie and courage, which was likely a main factor in helping beat her cancer. Abe briefly felt happy to be back there with her after all these years, until she spoke again.

"What are you two boys chatting about?" she asked. "It looked pretty serious."

The tension between Jared and Abe stretched far beyond the driveway of the cottage, filling the atmosphere around them with a soggy turbulence, each sound and action bumping and plodding along in an obvious manner. Jared offered a conciliatory glance toward Abe, who didn't take the bait.

"Jared told me there's something he wanted me to know," Abe said. "So, what is it, Jared?"

Jared froze like an animal trapped by a predator, eyeing an escape, nervously fidgeting and shifting his gaze from Clare to Abe before opening his mouth.

"I wanted you to know—" Jared started, his sentence interrupted by a set of glaring headlights turning toward them. The pickup truck pulled into the driveway and parked behind Abe's car on the grass.

"Hi, everyone," Harris said as he jumped out of his truck and walked toward the *Dreamboat*. Abe's stoicism in front of Jared instantaneously melted.

"I wanted you to know that Harris was on his way," Jared said, picking up the paper towels and the window cleaner with a vigorous, angry swipe.

Clare greeted Harris with the same enthusiasm as Abe, a high-pitched "Hi" and a huge hug. Placing her arm around him, they walked toward Jared and Abe, Harris visibly aware of the discomfort of the situation. Clare, bless her heart, only saw three people she loved, standing before her.

"You boys ready to have some fun this weekend or what?"

Twenty-Seven: Harris

The beauty of a weekend in Chautauqua Lake existed not only in its distance from home—the actual, undulating seventy-five miles door-to-door—but also in the substantially different way of life down in the Southern Tier. All aspects of city life vanished. The highways and people and abundance of shopping plazas were only a memory, their absence filled by green pastures, family-owned businesses, and an overall sense of rural calmness. The atmosphere surrounding Harris should've invaded his soul. It was supposed to be a respite from the arduous week of construction and planning. Life, unfortunately, had other ideas. The weekend started out as anything but calm for Harris the second he set foot on the soil of Willowridge Estates.

"Look, when Clare invited me here, I didn't think you were coming," Harris said to Abe as they walked into the cottage the previous night.

"You didn't think I'd spend the weekend celebrating my best friend's engagement?" Abe's monotone delivery shut Harris up. Abe saw right through his lie. Harris had known he would be there, and Abe knew that Harris had known. Truthfully, being able to clear the air with Abe was the sole reason he had stopped the construction on his house and come down to Chautauqua. Their brief encounter in the front yard proved Abe had still not recovered from the blow Harris had delivered about his parents and it was the main factor causing Harris to toss and turn ever since crawling into bed as he struggled to devise the perfect icebreaker to actually get Abe to talk to him.

Harris began to think it was insane for him to be there. Why did Abram make him such a thrill-seeker? Harris sat up in the bed and yawned before plopping back down on his left side. At the very least, the question deflected his thinking away from his house, which had usurped every minute since his coffee date with Cassie. Only an iota into his vision, the progress was already staggering—but it wasn't satisfying enough. Harris wanted more. He was rapidly falling into the same trap he always did when remodeling: once the design was formulated, he craved it be completed as quickly as possible. In this case, with the lack of communication between him and Abe, time was even more of the essence.

Each tug of the sheets and breathy movement to get comfortable only increased his crabbiness. Sleeping on a foreign bed was never a forte of Harris's—his body never able to adjust quickly enough to slumber peacefully—but tonight's instance wasn't because of his body. Lying wide awake, Harris gave up on falling back asleep and dedicated his brainpower (the minimum amount available at dawn) on the house. Spending an entire weekend away from the renovations was not ideal, and although he enlisted the help of the London Bros., a company he used during his days at Beautify Buffalo, Harris knew he'd fall behind his self-set timeline. In the world of home renovations, nothing ever worked out perfectly; plans that were set to take a month always extended longer, blueprints designed at the beginning of a project rarely matched the end product as ideas and reality often failed to match. Pushing his deadline back a bit and working eighteen-hour days would help, but neither were an optimal solution. Even in these dark and negative moments, he kept the goal of making Abram happy in the forefront of his mind. It felt inherently and entirely productive. When completed, the result would surely beguile Abe. Harris wanted his newly redone house to reflect every happy moment, every joyful memory of the two of them together. He wanted to see Abe's face match the reaction he'd had when they stepped inside the chateau in Bordeaux for the first time—and Harris's aspirations to succeed at this were at an all-time high.

Having seen the inspiration so few times, it was difficult to remember each and every unique facet of the space, but Harris didn't allow himself to stress out because of that. His photographic memory would be advantageous here—he could picture the bathroom, living room, and kitchen space clear as day—and Abram would be wowed, dazzled, amazed, and left with no other outcome than to scoop Harris up, whisper "I love you," and give him the strong, passionate kiss they both deserved.

Harris's anxiety began to disappear as he thought of what he'd undertaken during the latter part of the week. The insulation and drywall on the perimeter of the house had been installed, while the new walls were under construction. The electrical work would be completed in a few days, and the paint colors and tiles were all picked out and purchased. Even the stain for the hardwood floors was narrowed down to Pioneer or American Copper—the final choice to be picked once the floors were refinished and the first coat of paint dried. For days, his mind had become a free-flowing source of creativity, with idea after idea evolving into genuine cogs that would eventually create his masterpiece.

Harris recognized he might have been putting too much stock into his plan, but at least at this hour, he could blame it on the delirium. If he had to guess, he had only gotten about three hours of sleep, but even that might have been a generous exaggeration. Unwilling to sit still inside the cramped bedroom at the front of the cottage, Harris softly crept out into the hallway—determined not to wake anyone else—and tiptoed to the sunroom overlooking the lake.

Close to 6:00 a.m., his whole body ached as his mind trudged along a few paces behind. Even at that ungodly hour, the morning view from the quaint and cute cottage was spellbinding. The whole scene was a level higher than serene, a touch above tranquil. Still visible, the full moon gleamed over the water, delicately fading as the sun rising behind the cottage overpowered the darkness. Feather-like clouds were beautifully etched above, each elongated wisp marking the sky with the fierce purpose of creating a majestic morning backdrop. Steps from the deck led down to the private dock, where the *Dreamboat* rested, gently rocking with the waves of the lake, its ropes generating a rhythmic knocking that created a lovely call and response with the birds singing above.

As his gaze traveled down the stairs, Harris noticed someone sitting on the dock facing the lake, their arms propped behind them, feet dangling over the edge. Harris rubbed the sleep out of his eyes and walked outside to get a closer look with a daintiness to stay sly.

It was Abe!

Of course Abram was up and at 'em this early. He had probably been up for four hours at this point, ready to conquer the day with his foolish morning cheer. Harris stood quietly on the deck as he looked downward, hoping Abe wouldn't hear the wooden beams creaking with each step he took. Harris paused and took a minute to recognize the importance of the moment. Abe had nowhere to run, no room to retreat or car to take off in. If Harris confronted him, his only escape would be jumping into the lake and swimming to the other side. And though he didn't put that past Abram, he decided to take his chances.

Harris gingerly walked down the stairs toward Abram, who hadn't even turned around to see who was walking his way. He squeezed out three large yawns before reaching the end of the dock, sniffing the air to determine how awful his morning breath was.

"Morning," Harris said, trying to sound as sunny as possible without any caffeine. He sat directly next to Abe, their thighs millimeters away from touching.

"Morning," Abe replied, his tone matching that of two strangers saying hello to each other while crossing paths. Abe didn't swivel one bit, his hands still propped behind him, looking straight across the endless water. Harris noticed the earbuds hanging out of Abe's pocket and the remnants of sweat on his skin.

"You've already gone for a run this morning?" Harris asked. "Impressive."

"Just three miles," Abe replied.

Harris adored the way Abe talked about his workouts. This time it was "just three miles," as if any normal person would run more than that by 600 a.m.

"How was the rest of last night?"

While the rest of the gang hung around the fire last night, Abe had gone to bed after dinner, saying he had a migraine. Harris knew it was a lie; Abram didn't get migraines. The real cause of Abram's distance was Harris, and Abe's absence was the first indication that the night would not go as planned. There would be no fun and games around the fire, no s'mores to snack on, no reminiscing to deliver a flicker of normalcy between the two of them. It wasn't as if Harris expected Abe to welcome a conversation with open arms, but he hadn't expected the stagnancy that instead had taken over. It wasn't even only Abram; a weird vibe soaked the entire evening, only growing worse once Clare fell asleep in her lawn chair, leaving no one there to keep the conversation going. Cassie and Jared didn't seem particularly happy with each other either, but Harris tried to ignore the minor uncomfortable connection between them.

"It was fun. Sucks you had to miss it," Harris said, only lying to push the conversation past that topic. "This place is beautiful."

"It really is," Abe replied. "It still looks exactly like it did when we were kids. They need to update some stuff in there. But, this view? It never gets old."

An innocent giddiness filled Harris, who was encouraged by the fact that they were actually talking to each other. Abe's inflection didn't exactly scream *I still love you!* to Harris, but it was promising nonetheless. The two sat in silence, admiring the splendor before them, allowing Harris to ruminate on what had led him and Abe to this point. Two ex-lovers, two ex-best friends, two once-thought soul mates, were side by side as strangers, cumbersomely fumbling toward a resolution of their relationship. For the first time in days, Harris thought of his attack and how much he had wanted to change afterward, how being alive was truly a gift he wouldn't ever dismiss. Sitting next to Abe made him feel like a grown adult. Like a man. Abe motivated him to be a better person, to say what he was thinking, to strive to be his healthiest self. How one person could produce those goals in him, Harris couldn't comprehend. He only explicitly understood making things right between them was a duty he had to carry out.

"Did you want to talk about last weekend?" Harris asked Abe, his voice pleading with a strong hint of desperation.

"There's nothing to talk about anymore, Harris," Abe said, shutting things down once again.

"I'm sorry I didn't tell you sooner. Clearly, I was in the wrong, but coming between you and your family... It's not something I wanted to do."

"You already told me the story, Har," Abe said, continuing his motionless gaze across the lake. The lack of eye contact was somewhat frightening to Harris. "I get it. I totally get it. You've shared your little story and we can all move on now." Abe's repeated use of the word "story" punctured the brief enthusiasm that had started developing in Harris.

"This isn't a story, Abe. There's nothing fictitious about what your parents said. Have you even asked them? Jesus, you need to go talk to your parents."

"You need to leave me alone," Abe said, jumping up into a squatting position. "This is over."

"Abram, go talk to your parents," Harris said.

"No! Stop it. This. Us. All the animosity here. It *needs* to be over," Abram said, finally locking eyes with Harris. "I can't do this anymore. Nothing can change what happened. We can't go back in time, and we can't start over. It's time to officially end this."

The restrained anger from Abe pricked at Harris, leaving him speechless. Abe stubbornly refusing to deal with what had driven them apart left Harris with little to do. Until he actually spoke to Rich and Patty, the options were finite.

"Please go talk to your parents, Abe," Harris pleaded, one last time.

Up on his feet, Abe looked again over the lake, every crescent of each wave shimmering vividly under the sun. Harris stared at Abe as intently as he could under the morning light. It was the perfect setting for an acknowledgment of pitiful excuses from both sides, a chance to transcend the past between them and, together, move forward.

Abram thought differently. Without another word between them, he fished his earbuds out of his pocket, turned on the music from his phone, and bolted up the dock stairs, weaving his way around the patio and toward the front yard, presumably heading out for another three-mile sprint.

There was nothing left for Harris to do except watch Abe disappear to the front of the cottage, literally running away from their conversation, their problems, and their lives together.

There were worse ways to spend a Saturday morning than out at sea aboard the *Dreamboat* with a dreamboat. The only thing more stunning than the sights surrounding Harris was the man by his side. Jared, shirtless and sweaty, had earned his man card for the year in the first few minutes of their fishing trip, handling the slimy worms and stringing bait on their poles.

"Live bait season doesn't legally start for another month," Jared said. "So you're aiding and abetting right now."

"Naughty boy," Harris said, laughing.

They had been on the boat for about an hour, leisurely wading along the water ever since Jared stopped the boat at the northern part and the deepest portion of the lake. The goal of the day, Jared had said, was to capture bass, walleye, or muskellunge.

"Any of them will do," Jared said.

Harris smiled and nodded toward Jared and hoped it would masquerade his apathy toward actually catching something. Still, spending time together with Jared was always nice, and this was no exception. They made small talk on every topic imaginable—the weather, the boat, Jared's job, Harris's health, Clare's health, the cottage, the differences between Buffalo and North Carolina, their siblings, pizza, Weber grills, the Long Island sound—but not Abe, a fact that didn't bother Harris. If there was one thing he had gleaned from their encounter this morning, it was that Abe still wasn't willing to make amends yet. And, to be fair, maybe Harris wasn't either. The house was still in disarray, and Harris hoped that by the time that project was ready, Abe would be ready too. Although Harris gladly accepted the No Abe Zone the boat had become, he felt guilty being together so long without mentioning Cassie.

"So, you are now an engaged man. How does it feel?" Harris asked. He expected stereotypical, positive responses, the things everyone always says like *"Great!"* and *"No different than dating"* and *"We're so excited!"* to come out of Jared's mouth, which might be why he was taken aback by the response.

"It feels weird," Jared said, causing Harris to sit silent for twenty seconds until Jared started speaking again. "I thought it'd be a natural extension of our relationship, but Cassie has immediately changed from 'Cassie, my girlfriend' to 'Cassie, the bride-to-be.' And I'm not sure I like it."

The fairly harsh confession startled Harris. "Jared, she's just excited. You can't blame her." Harris tried to alleviate the apparent anxiety. "She's been dreaming about getting married her whole life."

"I want her to be excited, Harris. It's hard to wrap my mind around, I guess."

As the boat sat languidly on the lake, the gears inside Jared's head were completely the opposite, visibly cranking and spinning madly. Harris felt bad for the guy. In what should have been one of the happiest times of his life, Jared appeared agitated and doleful when talking about his future wife.

At a loss for words, Harris dropped the subject and let the sound of jet skis in the distance and the high-pitched squawking of some mallard ducks nearby fill the quiet. They continued to peacefully drift as they fished, both of them lounging back with their feet crossed over the side of the boat, enjoying the relaxation. The lack of sleep had caught up with Harris and he blinked longer than normal, his limbs drooping ever so slightly.

Harris had no idea how long he was sleeping before Jared's voice woke him up. "Hey, do you have your phone on you?"

"Yeah," Harris said, grabbing it out of his pocket. "But there's no service out here."

"Clare is texting me like crazy, telling us to head back to the cottage."

"Why?"

"I don't know, but I guess we should start packing everything up."

"Is everything okay?"

Jared shrugged his shoulders and removed the bait from his hook. "Oh, hang on, she's calling." Jared slid his phone across the floor of the boat to Harris.

"Hey, Clare, it's Harris."

"Harris, get back to the cottage right now," she said, her voice sounding frantic and agog to see them.

"What's going on?"

"They finally got him!" she screamed. "They got him!"

"Who? What are you talking about?" Harris said as the boat's motor started to rev.

"The Buffalo police arrested a man named Bruce Rowell last night. They say he's the one responsible for your attack!"

Harris didn't respond. He couldn't. The phone fell from his hands as Jared pushed the *Dreamboat* forward, the roaring motor hacking away at the calm morning as they sped back to the cottage. For the first time that day, the water rippled violently in the wake of the boat, its disruption matching the tear in Harris's heart, which was gashed by Clare's phone call.

It took almost ten minutes for the *Dreamboat* to get back to the cottage, the wait feeling like an eternity. His palms and armpits began to nervously sweat, his head screamed for answers—*How did they find Bruce? Do the police know I lied at the lineup? What will I say to Sabrina?*—but his face remained a frozen pillar of puzzlement. He thought mainly of Sabrina and how disappointed and shocked she would be, how dreadful the conversation would be when Maxwell and Charity asked where their dad was.

With the cottage finally in sight, Harris spotted Clare waiting at the top of the dock as they slowly guided the boat to the side, her arms waving back and forth impatiently.

"Oh, honey. They got him!" Clare said as she hoisted Harris up the stairs, before almost pushing him over with her uncontrolled squeeze. "It's over, Harris. It's over."

"What happened?" he asked Clare, half-coherent and half-lifeless, much like the immediate aftermath of his attack.

"I recorded the blurb on the news they showed at the top of the hour. Here, watch."

Clare dragged Harris inside and over to the floral camelback couch and pressed play on the DVR. Sitting at the anchor desk was his friend, Jennifer Jefferson—wearing the same outfit from the day she'd confronted Harris at his apartment—with the words *Breaking News* scrolling across the bottom of the TV.

"Good morning, everyone, I'm Jennifer Jefferson. We have breaking news coming out of Buffalo today. Buffalo police have arrested thirty-seven-year-old Bruce Rowell in connection with the January attack on Harris McGee, which left the mayor's son in a coma for eleven days. This video footage you're seeing is from a little over an hour ago as police led

Rowell into the Erie County Holding Center, where he'll be held until his arraignment Monday morning. Sources tell Action 7 News that police were tipped off by Rowell's ex-wife. We will be covering this story all day and will bring you the latest details tonight at six."

His heart, filled with a fiery bliss, stopped beating. His eyes stayed stuck in a straightforward stare. He couldn't believe Bruce was under arrest.

Clare clicked the television off and wrapped her arm around Harris, pulling his head against hers.

"That Sabrina Rowell," Clare said. "She's your guardian angel!"

Harris turned to Clare, launching a likeness of a smile on his face.

"She is," he said. "She really is."

Twenty-Eight: Abram

"Jared is gay."

The words fell out of Abram's mouth with an alarmingly low rate of consideration. It was the emotional equivalent of a slap in the face. No, its timing and unexpectedness made it much worse, like knocking an elbow against the side of a chair, the funny bone left with an excruciatingly long tingle.

Abe waited to move as he gauged her reaction—which was nonexistent post-outing. He sat up in the hammock and noticed Cass's parted lips and shallow breathing.

She was asleep.

The first delivery from Abe would merely serve as the dress rehearsal. The adrenaline receded from his limbs, his chest beginning to puff up and down again.

They had been sitting in the hammock at the cottage for twenty minutes or so when Abe nudged Cass to wake her up. He needed to buy some time to garner the courage to speak those three words again, so he reminisced about their previous vacations to Willowridge Estates—mainly the final trip there as soon-to-be college freshman, when Charlie got them drunk on sangria.

"Do you remember how he kept sneaking our drinks past your mom?" Abe asked.

"Barely! I was so wasted," Cassie replied.

"Didn't he keep filling those mini water bottles and telling her we were drinking grape juice?"

"She was so pissed," Cassie said. "She's probably still pissed about that!"

Cass and Abe laughed like schoolchildren, their giggles competing with each other for maximum volume and length. The innocence of the location was not lost on Abram. This was once a place where the sole problem in the world was being required to come inside once the sunlight faded away. What Abe wouldn't give to teleport back to that era, when nothing was second-guessed and everything was a breeze. As a flock of birds flew above them, Abe remembered the ways Mr. Montgomery entertained them as kids, most specifically how he told them a family of purple finches lived in the sycamore trees in the backyard.

"Her name is Rita. His name is Quincy," Charlie said during Abe's first year there, when he was six or seven years old.

Every year thereafter, whenever a purple finch flew by, Charlie would make the kids look out the window and tell him who it was—Rita or Quincy. It was the cause of some serious childhood debates between Abe, Cassie, and Caleb, as they forever argued over what bird was who. Even into his teens, Abe never broke through his gullibility and figured out they weren't actually the same birds. Whether it was innocence or stupidity, Abe didn't care. He only wished his brain still worked that way.

"Remember Rita and Quincy?" Abe asked, followed by more laughter.

"God, I miss that man," Cassie said, sighing and picking at a vine from the tree that shook in the wind above them.

"Safe to say we all do," Abe replied.

"I'd do anything if he could be here to see how happy I am."

Cassie's delusion that she was happy made Abe heartsick, the lump in his throat growing larger as he contemplated when and how to tell her the truth. Their morning had not gone according to Abe's plan whatsoever. By the time he'd gotten back to the house after the latter half of his run, they had no alone time. First, Harris and Jared had been by their side for breakfast, and then Clare had been lounging with them for hours, falling asleep next to them in the backyard before finally retreating into the house. He had wanted to spit everything out immediately and expose the truth once and for all, but not with anyone else there. It annoyed Abe that Harris once again had interrupted his preplanned path to honesty. At least he was out on the boat with Jared, far enough away not to be meddlesome.

The anticipation had reached its summit when Cassie mentioned being happy. Her sense of joy only existed under false pretenses, a horribly unaware perspective of life with Jared Pfeiffer. Abe could wait no longer.

"Jared is gay."

Cassie deserved a speech. An explanation. A soliloquy of Shakespearian proportions that wasn't coming. He intently watched Cassie's reaction, looking for a scowl or some negative body language. Instead, she simple gave an eye roll and shimmied onto her left side.

"Here we go again," she said coolly.

"Cassie, I'm serious," Abe said, speaking in a low-toned, but enunciated, whisper.

"Oh, please, Abe! You think everyone is gay," Cassie said.

Abe knew this would be her argument—and it was a valid one too. For years, he had always joked around questioning everyone's sexuality, but it wasn't his fault there were incessant subtle hints with cute guys he came across. Cassie happened to be the person he mentioned every questionable man to, a fact he bemoaned at this stage in his life.

"Cass," Abe said, grabbing her hands and interlocking their fingers together. "Jared is gay. And I don't just think he is. I *know* he is."

The hammock rocked as Cassie turned her body toward Abe.

"Oh you do, do you? Enlighten me." Her sarcastic tone showed the gravity of the conversation wasn't sinking in.

"Last weekend when you were out with your work friends and I came home after my date with Harris...things happened," Abe said.

"Things happened?" her eyebrows arched, mocking him.

"Yes. Things happened. And I feel terrible. I'm a horrible friend for being in this situation in the first place and for not telling you, and you can hate me if you want, but I can't stand to see you so oblivious."

Her face was blank, unrelentingly smooth and patient after Abe's disclosure. She ripped her fingers away from his and jumped off the hammock.

"You're so full of shit, Abe." Her anger was muted; she was more dismissive and flippant than upset.

"Cassie," Abe said while climbing off the hammock and joining her as they stared across the lake. "I know it might be hard for you to believe, but we fooled around on the couch. I'll spare you the details—"

"Stop it, Abe." She laughed in his face. Loudly. "You have been acting incredibly weird ever since I told you we got engaged. And, you know, I assume that you're upset that our friendship will never be the same because you're losing me to another man. But, Abe, I will always be here for you. Be happy for me—for us."

"It's impossible for me to be happy for you in this situation."

"Why, Abe? Why can't you be thrilled your best friend is in an amazing relationship?"

"Because, Cassie," Abe said, shrugging his shoulders. "Jared is gay."

"You're only saying that to piss me off."

Abe stared directly into Cassie's eyes, hoping to substantiate the validity of his words through the uncanny telepathy he and Cass had always shared. She looked back gently but scared, like a doe that had witnessed her whole family murdered. Abe didn't want to say it again, but he saw her mortar cracking, his words finally sinking in.

"Jared is gay." The words throbbed in his mouth and rolled off his tongue.

"Why are you doing this? I don't even know what you're talking about!" Cassie struggled to get out her response, her words and her breaths messily weaving into each other.

"Jared is gay." His inflection didn't waver once during the repetitive use. Saying it again and again chipped away at Abe's self-respect, not only for hammering the words into Cassie's head, but for revealing the truth about Jared before Jared was apparently ready.

"Enough!" Cassie shouted, apparently finally recognizing the severity of the conversation.

"Look, I know you don't want to hear it, but you can't marry a gay guy!" Abe tried to remain calm, but Cassie's hurried retorts left him little time to remember that goal. "Cass, I've had a feeling about Jared from the moment I met him, and trust me, he confirmed that feeling and a *whole* lot more the other night. I'm sorry I didn't say something sooner, but you two can't go on like this."

"I can't believe you. I cannot believe you," she said, her intonation rising with each word.

"Please. You have to believe me, Cassie," Abe said, quieting his voice and trying to quell the brewing battle.

"You know what, Abe?" she asked, pivoting toward him. "You can get the fuck out of my face now."

Abe planted his feet to the ground, determined to work through the rough discussion.

"You're *so* unhappy and *so* alone that you want the rest of the world to be exactly like you." Her words carried a truthful bite; Abe was alone and, for the most part, totally unhappy. The one light in his life over the last few months had been this nonsense with Jared, and here he was tearing apart the life Jared had built with Cassie. Abe was the worst kind of person, a pure narcissist, demolishing her life for no other reason than the small chance to build up his own. He didn't want to continue the conversation, but he couldn't stop and leave Cassie hanging. She deserved him owning his reprehensible mistake.

"You have to believe me," Abe said. "I would never bring this up if I wasn't being 100 percent truthful."

"Why are you playing these games? Can't you just be happy for me?"

"Why do you think I'm telling you this? I want you to be happy," Abe said. "I'm looking out for my best friend."

Cassie was trembling, a tea kettle about to whistle and roar, a pot of boiling water about to explode over the edge. The hope was that Cassie would trust him enough to inquire further, to hear him out fully, where every dirty detail would confirm his story.

That hope was quashed when Cassie stared coldly at Abe, striking her hand viciously across his right cheek. "Goodbye, Abram."

The distinct decisiveness in her voice shot through Abe like ice in his bloodstream. He could feel his face turning white, his fingers turning numb. She started to walk away and Abe struggled for a response. What he wanted to shout was *"You know what's going to happen to you? You're going to end up loving a man who doesn't love himself enough to be truthful. Someone who will tell you one thing but always be thinking about another. I'm just trying to protect you!"*

Abe chose to stay speechless instead. Any supplemental words would only serve as ammunition for Cassie's future use. He walked backward and stared at her overlooking the lake, mixed emotions overflowing. Relief poured out of him, his week-long and months-long secrets no longer constricting every organ. Cassie still appeared beautiful even though her shoulders hunched forward and her head hung down. Her hair swayed in the wind, as wild and free as Abe's soul felt.

"Goodbye, Cassie," he whispered, not yet knowing the accuracy his words held.

Somehow luck was on Abe's side when he went inside the cottage, as Clare was on the couch napping, not disturbed by him hastily rushing to pack his things and leave. Yes, leaving without saying a word to her was the rudest thing to do, but it was also the best-case scenario. She would find out in due time why he'd split so quickly, but not with him around, thankfully. Abe didn't want to be there to witness the dismayed faces of two Montgomery women in one day.

The image of Cassie standing in front of him so unbelievably angry glared like a beacon in his brain. As much as he tried to crush the disconcerting thoughts, he couldn't toss it aside the way Jared tossed aside his desires. It was like trying to stretch a queen-size fitted sheet on a king-size mattress. It wasn't happening no matter how hard he pulled, shifted, struggled, and strained.

Processing the conversation with Cassie began by splitting it up into segments, with Abe putting himself in Cassie's shoes. At the start, she'd assumed he was making another joke by implying that Jared was gay, so she was blasé about his news. The middle—where Cassie likely confronted the possibility that what Abe was saying was indeed true—coincided with Abe assuring her he wasn't fooling around about the two of them fooling around. Abe pinpointed the moment he had grabbed Cassie's hands and interweaved their fingers together as the downfall. Instead of taking the blame, Abe had placed it squarely on Jared's shoulders. He could've found ways to lessen the blow—telling Cassie it was entirely his fault, telling her that he and Jared had perhaps found an actual spiritual connection, telling her he was an incredible man who happened to be refining who he was as a person. All of those superfluities might have helped. Yet, by the end of their conversation, Cassie had dived into a sea of distrust and antipathy. It wasn't so much what Abe had said, he decided, it was that he was the one who'd said it.

At least the expected part of Abe's plan was in full swing. Driving away from Willowridge Estates, he headed down Route 60 destined for his parents' house, which was a mere seventeen miles away. Knowing the proximity to their house—and, more importantly, what confession was in store at the cottage—Abe had warned his mom he might pop in over the weekend.

Undeniably upset about Cassie, Abe also embodied some weird hybrid of a man who was half monster, half messiah. There was a certain aura around him since this news was out in the open, like the one a new haircut brings or like when he spent $450 on a melon-and-basil body polish at the Ritz-Carlton Spa in Los Angeles. The quiet confidence within him grew larger the farther he drove away from the cottage. As awful as it was to shatter Cassie's dreams about her life with Jared, the admission was the necessary first step to ensure she'd actually find what she deserved. He knew someday she would recognize what had transpired as the sweetest way to break her heart.

The solace Abe had found within himself over the unfortunate truth of everything was the impetus to stop thinking about it. He was only a few miles from his parents' house, and it was time to switch gears. Getting away from the Jared/Cassie/Abe/Harris love rhombus that had commandeered his brainpower for weeks on end was both crucial and coveted.

By the time he reached his parents' driveway, Abe had almost completely distanced himself from the fallout at the cottage. The curiosities of what would happen next—would Cassie confront Jared? Would Jared tell the truth? Would either of them say anything at all?—were the final thoughts he had when he approached his dad by the side of the garage.

"Hi, Dad," Abe said.

His father barely lifted his head from the patch job he was doing on a cracked part of the foundation. "Hi, Abram. Your mother is inside."

Ahhhh, Abe had missed the warm, fuzzy welcome home greetings from his dad. Not. He volunteered to help and was immediately shot down, an outcome he had predicted before the offer was even made. Making his way into the house, Abram first noticed the half-full glass of chardonnay on the counter, his mom's fresh lipstick marks stuck to the side. Before he could begin to feel jealous or sad about her day-drinking habits, his mom shouted his name from the living room. The cadence of her voice when she said his name always pleasantly transferred him back in time.

"Hi, Mom," Abe said. He expected a hug, but the welcoming was curt.

"You heard about Harris?" she asked while pointing to the TV with the remote, her question spoken so unemotionally Abe almost asked "Harris who?" before he responded.

"What?" Abe asked instead, a bit puzzled to hear Harris's name come out of his mom's mouth. For their entire relationship, Patty Hoffman had acted like Abe and Harris's best friend; she had been the cool mom who adored her gay son and his boyfriend. But since their breakup, she hadn't talked about relationships with Abe, and she certainly hadn't spoken of Harris McGee.

"Harris. The police caught the guy who attacked him."

Abe's eyes shot open and he stared at the TV, which was showing an infomercial for a two-pack of car dent removers. Instinctively, Abe grabbed his phone, hopped on Twitter, and clicked on the first article he saw from *The Buffalo News*.

He read aloud to his mom, who had started to pull out the iron and an outfit he presumed was for his parents' dinner date later.

"Buffalo Police have arrested Bruce Rowell in connection with the January attack on Harris McGee. The thirty-seven-year-old Rowell was taken into custody in the presence of his ex-wife, Sabrina, who police say is responsible for alerting authorities of her ex-husband's involvement in the brutal beating. Buffalo Police spokesman Andrew Duffy said Rowell has confessed to carrying out the attack that left McGee in a coma for eleven days, but at this time, there is no evidence and no indication this was a hate crime. He is being held at the Erie County Holding Center and will be arraigned Monday morning. Buffalo Police say their investigation will continue. This is a developing story, please refresh for the latest details."

Abram read article after article, looking for more information, but each one held the same information only slightly reworded. He repeated the word *wow* several times, unable to summon the intelligence to use advanced vocabulary.

"Who are these people?" Patty asked.

"Sabrina Rowell owned the house that Harris trashed on Twitter," Abe said, his mom showing no recollection of Harris's social media disaster. "He broke into her house and posted pictures, basically calling for it to be demolished. This guy was her ex, apparently."

"People will do anything to get revenge these days. It's sickening," Patty said. "You should call him, you know, see how he's doing."

"We aren't really on a level like that anymore, Mom. You know that." Abe tried to shut down this topic before it started, hoping not to dredge up their most recent history.

"Well, call him anyway. He's gone through a lot the last few months," she said.

"That's for sure." Abe thought of their lives since the start of the year. While he was dealing with his crush on Jared, Harris had faced some serious setbacks. He started the year unemployed, got knocked into unconsciousness, and was forced to recover in the public eye. He still didn't even have a job, as far as Abe knew.

"You know, I still have no idea why you let that boy go, Abe," his mom said.

The comment floated erratically through the air, buzzing like a moth swarming a spotlight. Its hang time rivaled the punt of a pro football player as it sailed above Abram just begging to be caught and run away with.

All Abe could hear was Harris's urge of *"Talk to your parents, Abe."*

"Huh. That's funny," Abe said. "Harris seems to think you'd know exactly why we broke up."

His mom stood up and crinkled her forehead while messing with her bangs. "You got me!" she pushed out with a laugh while turning on the faucet and filling up the iron.

Abe pondered how to deftly broach the subject—mainly whether or not to insinuate what she supposedly told Harris the night he asked for their blessing.

The fearful side of him wanted to shy away from ruffling any feathers and causing commotion.

The daring side of him remembered that his stats for the day were perfect. Abe was one-for-one and batting a thousand on bringing up things no one wanted to talk about.

"I know what you said to him that day we were going to get married." Much like the start of his conversation with Cassie, the words tumbled out of his mouth with relatively little forethought. Abe decided to lay it on the line, figuring it would be nice to prove Harris wrong—again—for his actions.

Discomfort very obviously surrounded their discussion as Abe and his mother entered new territory; prior to this second, there was never any talk of the near-marriage between Abe and Harris. Until Harris told her, she had no idea what Abe planned at City Hall that night, no idea how much Harris once meant to her son.

"I'm not sure what you're implying, Abram," she replied, plugging in the iron and laying out her clothes.

Abe didn't have to say anything. He simply let his mom respond. He knew she couldn't stand silence.

"It was three years ago when we had that conversation. I'm not going to remember every word I said."

Interesting. That was no denial, no repudiation emerging from his mother. Was what Harris said really true? Had the egotism of his parents been the main culprit of their collapse as a couple?

"Did you say you couldn't support me and Harris as a married couple, Mom? Simple question. All I need is a yes or a no and I'll drop this."

Patty's expression turned solemn. She unplugged the iron and walked toward him. "You know I didn't mean it. We were...not expecting that news that day. We didn't know how serious you two were."

Everything shook and rattled. Abe went momentarily deaf, his mom's reasoning equivalent to someone banging two pots together inside his head. It was entirely evident: his parents were ashamed of him and would rather see him painstakingly alone than content with a man.

Harris wasn't lying. The breakup was a mistake. The three years apart were unnecessary.

A vivid rage inside of him steadily coalesced with these revelations, causing his stomach to turn sour. The taste traveled up to the back of his tongue. His palms began sweating as he clenched his fists and gritted his teeth. Every hair on his body felt electrified, his brain fighting the impulse to vomit and punch something.

Abe didn't want to accept it but was left with no choice. He had let their love die over his parents' abhorrent, reprehensible behavior.

"Abram. You know how your father is. You know how I can be," she said. "I have been nothing but supportive of you since you told us you were gay."

Though she was telling the truth, it did little to calm Abe's fury.

"Which makes all of this even worse, Mom."

She didn't have a response to that, apparently fully understanding no words could solve the problem she herself created. "Abey, honey," his mom said, walking over to him. She rubbed his shoulder and combed his hair with his fingers, a technique that might have worked when he was a child, but only caused image after image of Harris to pop into his head with each brush of her hand. The only thing more prevalent than Harris was the numerous questions somersaulting through his mind.

How could I be so stupid? How could it take so long for the truth to be exposed? How could I not trust Harris?

Abe directed only one question at his mom as he looked her squarely in the eyes. "How could you do this to me?" The question held more gravitas than she would ever know.

Abe made it less than three miles from his parents' house before pulling over in the parking lot of Rucinski's Grocery & Deli to wait for the crying to dwindle. The emotional overload was fitting; Abe had held it all in for an unhealthy chunk of time. Every encounter with Jared and Harris over the past week had left him frazzled with fear, pushed to the brink of a permanent breakdown—and here it was in the flesh. The source of the tears was nothing and everything at the same time: his annoyance at Jared, the resentment toward his parents, his selfish betrayal of Cassie. Running away was the most childish choice to make, but he had no time to listen to his half-inebriated mom explaining her life-altering narrow-mindedness.

"It didn't mean what you think it means, Abram," she shouted as he walked out the door, as if suggesting he was twisting her words made the situation any better.

Abram caught his breath long enough when the sobbing subsided to think clearly for the first time since he'd fled his parents' house in the midst of his mother's pleading retraction.

What he needed to do was as clear as ever; he needed to talk to Harris. Finding him became the objective of the hour, an absolute necessity that couldn't be delayed. It was time for Abe to apologize for it all. For not believing him about his parents, for letting him go three years ago without a fight, and for everything in between. Abram had been an imbecile since that night at City Hall, making mistake after mistake in his quest to find that missing piece in his life. In a way, Abe viewed Harris's ability to keep the secret about his parents as the nicest thing anyone had ever done for him. Harris was being protective and selfless. He had given up a chance at bliss to comply with what he assumed was best for Abe.

As affable as Harris could be, Abe had been nothing but unkind and uncouth to him over the past few years. Harris deserved better than that. He deserved to be treated the way he'd treated Abe—with the generosity and compassion of a saint.

Accomplishing that goal wasn't something Abe knew how to do, but he dialed Harris's number anyway.

No answer.

Crafting a text message was the obvious next course of action, but Abe needed to hear Harris's voice and wanted Harris to hear his. Their relationship could handle no more vagueness; a face-to-face, thorough conversation was the only outcome that made sense.

Abe floored it all the way back to the cottage, his car delicately hugging each twist and turn. If there was a speed limit on the road, he didn't notice, his focus fully on Harris. He wanted to erase the last three years, go back and start over from the day they left Bordeaux, capturing that mood and gradually releasing it into their daily lives in Buffalo. Their partnership had no fitting ending; it was time to give it another go.

After slamming his car into park, Abe bustled into the cottage, which was oddly empty. There was no sign of anyone anywhere.

"Harris?" Abe called out, hoping for a response. "Mrs. Montgomery? Cassie?"

Nothing.

Abe ran to the back room—each step strengthening the anticipation in his heart—when he noticed someone pacing on the dock. He ran outside and skipped across the backyard and toward the steps, only to see Jared leaning over the wooden railing.

"Hey," Jared said.

"Have you seen Harris?" Abe asked. There was no time for platitudes. "I really need to talk to him."

"He left an hour or so ago. They arrested his attacker," Jared said. Abe nodded, signifying he already knew the news. "Do you know where Cassie is?"

Shit. Abe had been so engrossed in finding Harris that he'd nearly forgotten his slap-inducing conversation with Cassie and the reason for leaving the cottage in the first place. "Out with her mom? I have no idea."

"No, Clare walked down to the beach by herself. I haven't seen Cass since we got back from fishing."

The debate on what to tell Jared stirred virulently inside Abe, who both loved and loathed Jared simultaneously. This man had swooped into his life and forever changed it. For better or for worse remained to be seen.

It was easy to fantasize about reconciling with Harris when the temptation of someone like Jared wasn't around, but seeing Jared on the dock smacked Abe right back into reality. Jared represented more than a man who was an impressive physical specimen; this beautiful man could have been his future, as absurd as that might have sounded. If they'd continued along the path set forth last weekend, Abe thought they might have had a chance to create a solid future together—the exact reason why he needed to tell Jared about the awful outcome of his earlier discussion with Cassie.

"Jared," Abe said sensitively. He had messed up his chance to be gracious and resolute with both Cassie and his mom; he vowed to change things around with Jared. "I'm sorry, but I told her."

Abe placed his hand over Jared's, which were gripping the railing with superhuman grit.

Jared sighed, seemingly resigned to the fact that Cassie already knew. "That's really something that should've come from me." Jared faced Abe.

"I gave you a chance to tell her the truth and you proposed without acknowledging anything. So, when we were together, I felt like I had to tell her," Abe said. "She's my best friend, Jared."

"What did she say?"

"She doesn't believe me. Well—she said she didn't believe me. But I'm betting that deep down inside, she knows," Abe said. "She's probably always known."

Jared studied the unruffled water below. There was a confirmation behind his baby blues, a slight signal to Abe that Jared had actually made the admission to himself too.

"It's okay, Jared. The hard part is over. You don't have to hide anything anymore."

Jared pulled Abe toward him, his biceps swallowing Abe, his brute power not allowing an escape. It was difficult to fight against him—and Abe wasn't even sure he wanted to battle back. As Jared moved his face toward him, Abe partially swooned, his body collapsing further into Jared as he immersed himself in the moment. Their lips touched together and Abe's toes tingled as Jared grabbed the back of his head, once again giving in to his craving. Abe partially tried to squirm free, but stopped and gave in to the lust. After all, wasn't this exactly what he wanted? As he closed his eyes, visions of Cassie flickered through his mind. He could no longer justify accepting Jared's magnetism and his raw lust. Though his lips were inviting and tender, this didn't feel like their love seat lip-lock, Abe wasn't comfortable in the slightest, kissing him here. After all, the fates of their relationships with Harris and Cassie hung in the balance. With intent, Abe forcefully broke free of Jared's clutch and backed away, only somewhat regretting the choice the second their lips were a millimeter apart.

A wry laugh oozed out of Jared, who appeared equal parts relieved and distraught. "What the hell do we do now?"

Abe rubbed the small of Jared's back, hoping his gesture would suffice for a response. If an answer existed inside him, he had yet to find it. Abe not only felt guilty for kissing Jared because of Cassie, he also hated doing that while longing for Harris. His conflicted mind was clearly unaware what to do for himself, let alone what they could do together.

"What the hell am I going to say to Cassie?" Jared continued, throwing his arms up in a clear symbol of confusion.

"You don't have to say anything," Cassie said, climbing out of and stepping off the *Dreamboat*.

Abe's heart wrenched at the sight of Cassie, and he wasn't sure if his gasp was heard out loud or only in his head. Cassie's eyes were red with rage, alive with ire. A glassy sheath covered her stare, which hadn't moved from Abe and Jared.

"I can't believe you!" she shouted sloppily, her tears and runny nose affecting her speech.

Abe couldn't tell which of them she was speaking to. Cassie pushed both Abe and Jared out of her way and ran up the stairs, taking two at a time. Jared shouted her name with a pitiful scream and rushed behind her.

Their exodus left Abe standing alone on the dock. He quickly outlined his options: chase after Cassie, comfort Jared, or go find Harris.

Each one of his choices carried benefits and disadvantages, all colliding at every turn. He was the pinball inside a pinball machine, ricocheting up and down, left and right, back and forth, unable to slow down long enough to keep it straight and go in the right direction.

So, for the first time this day, Abe took the easy way out. He didn't climb the stairs to look for Cassie. He didn't scour the cottage and its surrounding areas in search of Jared. And he didn't whip out his phone and furiously text or call Harris. Those interactions would all come eventually—just not at this moment. He slowly marched up the stairs, sat on the hammock, and stared at the sun-stained waves in front of him, hoping the simplicity of Mother Nature would transfer to his brain via osmosis.

Lost in the thoughts of wanting no thoughts at all, Abe almost missed the birds fluttering by his side and chirping in his direction.

A smile quickly came to his face.

The two purple finches were playfully hovering and jumping, forcing Abe to do nothing but sit, stare, and follow their frolicking.

"Hi, Rita. Hi, Quincy. Good to see you guys again."

Twenty-Nine: Clare

Like so much else over the past year or so, things weren't supposed to go this way. Abe and Harris weren't supposed to seethe at the sight of each other. Jared wasn't supposed to permanently depart alone on the *Dreamboat*. Cassie wasn't supposed to be in front of Clare, crying and mulling the end of her relationship.

And Clare wasn't supposed to feel so extraordinarily unwell.

The weekend trip to Chautauqua Lake had been an absolute bust. A failure in nearly every aspect—save for the stunning views and the impeccable weather.

Staring out across the misty hills, Clare reminded herself to take the good with the bad. In this case, the good shone softly onto her skin, the morning's sun beautifully golden and full of life.

The bad? Well, the bad was worse than bad.

Her daughter's relationship had exploded in an instant of unexpected honesty and unfaithfulness. Jared still hadn't explicitly told Cassie he was gay. But it didn't matter.

Cassie had seen his passionate kiss with Abe, which was enough confirmation, apparently.

Clare breathed in deep and looked toward Cassie, who had been sitting silently by her side for a better part of the last twelve hours, trying to find the energy to comfort her.

"Cassie, I can't even imagine how you're feeling, but at least you know now," she said, hoping some additional words of wisdom would pop into her head.

There was no response except a long, slow blink.

And there had been no response from Cassie since last night when she had shared the news about Jared. Clare's heart had shattered at Cassie's play-by-play, not only for her daughter, but also for Jared—and Abe for that matter. There was clearly some cosmic chemistry happening between those three that Clare didn't pretend to comprehend. What she gathered was that Jared was apparently into both Cassie and Abe and had even kissed Abram, causing Cassie to throw him out of the cottage.

Their fight turned out to be a garish, ugly affair that woke Clare up out of a dead sleep.

"He's gay. He's gay! I caught him and Abe kissing," Cassie told Clare through tears and short, rhythmic breaths of madness.

The drama had compounded during Cassie's yelling, which was a mixture of virulence and self-indulgence. The words she'd spewed toward Jared originated from a truly unattractive side of Cassie.

"You're despicable!" she had shouted. "Only someone fucking sick in the head could be so selfish!"

Clare had wanted so badly to go say something to Jared as he glumly walked down the dock and onto his boat, but she knew better. Cassie would never understand why Clare's motherly instincts had kicked in, but they did. He needed support, not a summons to be alone after such a pivotal moment in his life. Tears came to Clare's eyes as Jared left on the *Dreamboat*, disappearing down the lake with no known destination.

Cassie's love life was cyclically depressing, a never-ending merry-go-round of promising lovers-turned-fiancés that flamed out with disastrous spats. The whole ordeal left Clare essentially speechless, but even if she knew what words to say, she'd have to somehow gain the vigor to get them out. The fatigue had reached new heights and was stronger than it ever had been before. It had been easy to ignore at first. Justification after justification hushed the consideration that her health had regressed. Packing and the process of moving had done it, she assumed. Yet, reality quickly sank in as she sat next to Cassie and counted the hours she had slept over the last two days. In a forty-eight-hour span, Clare had slept twenty-five. This wasn't from the move. This was something else entirely, something else she knew all too well. But Clare didn't have the gall to say it aloud.

Her heart ached for everyone—including herself.

In the morning, she would call Dr. Kincaid. He would likely recommend a quick visit to the office, followed by bloodwork and another MRI. The results would show her tumors had grown and multiplied. She would be given the option of additional radiation. The cycle would repeat once again, leaving her spinning out of control on the crazy wheel of life.

Why can't things be normal? Clare asked herself over and over again.

It wasn't just this weekend; it was everything since the day of Charlie's diagnosis. Their life together wasn't supposed to end so abruptly; Clare's life without Charlie wasn't supposed to include her own health scare. For once, she wanted a regular life. One full of coffee on the couch watching QVC, errands in the morning, chores in the afternoon, with reading and baking and visits with Cass and Caleb strewn in between.

Her eyelids felt like steel traps, each blink shutting swiftly and taking an attentive effort to pry open. Thankfully, there wasn't any time to feel sorry for herself. Her daughter needed her. Despite wanting to play fortune-teller and give Cassie a brilliant glimpse into the future, all she could do was sit by Cassie's side as a symbol of support, strength, and solidarity.

At some point, she dozed off as the seagulls circled above her, only snapping awake when Cass started talking.

"What am I even contemplating?" Cassie shot up suddenly and asked. She flung her arms out to the side and laughed in a mocking manner, as if the logic behind her question was the funniest joke in the world.

Once again, Clare nodded and smiled when Cass looked toward her. For the entire morning, Clare had believed there was nothing she could say that would lessen the anguish Cassie currently felt. She needed to vent. But her latest outburst looked maniacal, showing remnants of the feisty little girl that still existed inside. Cassie got up and walked to the fence near the stairs of the dock.

Clare wasn't paying enough attention to notice Cassie winding up her arm and making the throw.

"Cass, no!" Clare shouted to no avail.

The plink of the engagement ring hitting the water echoed so pitifully that Clare wasn't sure if Cassie actually tossed it. Clare mustered enough oomph to spring from her chair and head to the fence, hoping she'd look out on the water to see the ring sparkling below the surface in some easily identifiable spot.

"Our relationship obviously meant nothing to him, so that ring means nothing to me," Cassie said.

Jared being gay wasn't the issue here. The lying and the alleged cheating—those were the qualities she couldn't forgive. In Cassie's desolate stare was a girl who felt foolish for not recognizing the signs when they were right in front of her face. Cassie's heaving cries never reached their full potential as Clare drew her in, wrapping her arms around her baby girl.

"What should we do now, Cass?"

It was a question that Clare meant as much in the present as she did for the future. As much for Cassie as it was for herself.

"I just kind of want to go home."

The word "home" made Clare wince. Where was home for either of them? Cassie surely wouldn't stay with Abe, and the condo wouldn't be enough for the both of them—at least not permanently. The details would be finalized later, once they got out of Chautauqua Lake.

"Okay, kiddo. Let's go home."

Clare decided they would head back to the condo and work toward producing warm memories in a new location. She hugged Cassie and then stared out across the lake one last time. The same seagull flew overhead, gliding up and around with ease, causing Clare to give it a jealous glare.

The weekend had backfired so unbelievably bad, Clare shook her head. In her mind, the old cottage represented everything she loved about raising a family. It was cozy and relaxing, set in a peaceful, yet entertaining area. But after this weekend, those precious memories were pulverized, replaced by infidelity, grudges, and the likelihood of a serious medical issue.

"Are you ready?" Cassie shouted from the back door.

No. I'm not ready. I can't do this again. I don't want to go through this again.

It had been there since Friday night, but she hadn't had the wherewithal to peek at it again since the day Harris found it—until that day. She pulled the piece of paper from her bathrobe pocket and quickly unfolded it. Seeing Charlie's scratchy handwriting made her happy. Covering her eyes from the sunlight with her right hand, she looked down about three-quarters of the way through the letter and read the section that she hoped would give her the inspiration and ability to get through whatever was happening to her.

> *So, go out there and live, Clare Bear. You have more verve inside of you than any person I've ever met. Embrace that. As they say—go forth and set the world on fire. And when things get tough, which they inevitably will, don't give up. Don't you ever, ever give up.*

She reread the last line of the paragraph three times.

Don't you ever, ever give up.

Clare heard Charlie saying those words with his encouraging tone and thought this would give her that je ne sais quoi and that internal inspiration she so greatly needed.

It didn't.

If Charlie were there, she'd sit him down and explain it all. To her, this wasn't "giving up" as much as it was life's most humble compromise. The fighter inside her had given it everything and then some—but it still wasn't enough. The radiation, the group therapy, the regular therapy, selling her house, shaving her head! Every detail of every day since her original diagnosis tasted more acrid the longer she thought about them. Charlie wouldn't want her to go through the emotional roller coaster again. He barely got on the ride himself! And with that thought, Clare accepted that there was nothing left to do.

She made it a point to internalize that she hadn't lost the will to live; she had only acknowledged the destiny written for her. The latest setback was nothing more than the universe grabbing her by the shoulders, shaking her back and forth, and handing her the opportunity to verify that she wasn't supposed to exist without Charlie. It was such an archaic way of thinking; the suggestion that a woman is nothing without her husband wasn't what Clare wanted to project. But she was too weak to combat the truth billowing inside her.

Glancing at the letter one last time, Clare folded it up haphazardly and tore it to dozens of tiny shreds. She walked to the same spot Cassie had stood and looked up, begging Charlie with her gaze to pay attention. Parting her cupped hands, the pieces of the letter cascaded like sad confetti so slowly into the lake.

"Mom? Are you ready?" Cassie's voice caused her to jump and turn around.

Am I ready?

It had been a rationalization in her head the entire weekend—one she hesitated to speak. As she stared at the pieces of the letter wafting unpredictably away from the dock and into the lake, Clare felt the embers inside of her ignite as she gathered the courage to finally say it loudly.

"I'm ready."

Clare embraced the omnipresent aura of inevitability around her. She looked toward Cassie and smiled, completely unaware her body had begun to abandon her, all movement ceasing as she dropped backward, her head cracking against the railing. The deafening blow didn't faze Clare; it was merely a corroboration of her recently accepted fortune.

Clare assumed she was still smiling until she looked at Cassie running toward her and screaming, an arm outstretched and clenching and unclenching in a grasping motion.

She couldn't lift her arm back. She didn't want to. Instead, Clare watched her surroundings slowly fade and fizzle to black, the screams of her daughter dwindling as she plummeted backward, plunging twenty feet into the lake.

Submerged and sinking, she repeated the words just uttered in her head, and then closed her eyes.

I'm ready.

Thirty: Harris

Bruce's eyes weren't as bloodshot as Harris remembered, but they still held an excess of evil as his gaze lurked around each corner of the courtroom, avoiding eye contact with every other human—including his lawyer, Thomas Braunscheidel. The reporters and their cameramen murmured as he shuffled his feet to the chair with shackles around his ankles, their subtle arm movements causing the cameras to pan from Harris to Bruce and back. Well aware of the lens zooming in and out, Harris stayed expressionless, hoping to end this story while conveying an assured and empathetic air.

Harris's attention span wavered as the hearing began. As hard as he tried to pay attention to the legal banter from the courtroom clerk and the judge, he couldn't escape the thoughts of timing. It didn't feel like six months since his Beautify Buffalo fiasco and the attack. It didn't even feel like a month had passed since Bruce's arrest, since he and Abe had restarted their friendship, since Clare almost died in Chautauqua Lake. The full throttle pace of life since the start of the year needed to slow down— and Harris believed this moment was the first step toward achieving that goal.

The weeks since Bruce had confessed were a whirlwind. The media—of course—wanted to know everything about everything. *"Where were you when you found out?" "How does that make you feel?" "Are you happy he's off the streets?" "What do you want to see happen?"* The pestering— normally a nuisance that annoyed Harris to no end—slid right off his shoulders, a temporary irritant he tried not to let it get under his skin. Harris did his best to accommodate every interview request and answer each question with a sturdy and heartfelt response. Like the sentencing hearing, Harris believed closing the chapter on the media involvement with this case would lead him toward freedom from the attack.

Harris got so lost in his own head that the judge's voice startled him.

"Mr. McGee, we're ready for your statement," Judge Roberta Allen said. "Please step forward."

Harris looked at his dad who displayed a clenched fist as if to say, "You can do it." He needed that small nudge to bring himself toward the microphone. Since his arrest, most people had told Harris to make sure the judge threw the book at Bruce. Even his father had encouraged him to speak of the "raw emotional and physical pain" the attack had caused. The advice, though understandable, stood against every fiber in Harris's being. He had never been a true believer in the revenge mentality. Nonetheless, he stepped up to the podium, exuding a quiet confidence, unfolded his prewritten speech, and cleared his throat. The words he had taken nearly four weeks to perfect looked foreign and blurry. Harris sighed loudly into the microphone, cognizant that all eyes and ears were hanging on the words about to leave his mouth. Concentrating on the paper in front of him became impossible, his handwriting transforming into illegible scribbles. Harris gave up trying to force the words to come out. Deciding to ad-lib, he cleared his throat again.

"I am grateful that I am even standing and able to talk about what happened earlier this year," Harris said, speaking entirely off script. He turned his body to the right and stared into Bruce's expressionless face. "Bruce, I feel sorry for you. I feel sorry for your ex-wife. I feel sorry for your children, all of whom now have to live their lives knowing the man they once loved or their father is a convicted felon, someone so cold-blooded that he left another human beaten and bloody and lying in the street waiting for death. But I'm here. I survived. And I'm happy. You? You are obviously the complete opposite. You're a man who isn't one hundred percent present in this courtroom today. And you're a sad, angry man. But, in spite of everything, I don't hate you; I only hate what you did to me. Sabrina deserved better. Maxwell deserved better. Charity deserved better. I deserved better. And you, too, deserve better. So, Judge Allen, with all due respect, when it comes to this sentence, I urge you to be sensible but fair. Get this man the help he needs. Anger management classes, maybe. A stint at a substance abuse recovery program. Something—anything—other than him sitting in a jail cell for years on end, which will do nothing but ruin his life and the lives of his family. We all make mistakes, but we're not all given the opportunity to learn from them. I urge you to give Bruce Rowell a chance to learn from his disgusting, violent, and vicious mistake. Thank you."

He expected Bruce to show some sort of emotion—gratitude perhaps—but he continued on, remorseless. Miffed for a minute, Harris brushed the nonreaction aside. Those words weren't delivered because he wanted Bruce to smile and respect him. He spoke from the heart because this situation called for it. A man's life hung in the balance, and Harris would be damned if he didn't try everything he could to make the sentencing as painless as possible.

The people in the courtroom whispered as Harris made his way back to his seat. He didn't realize how much he was shaking until his dad slapped his knee as he sat back down. The adrenaline rushing through him had only grown stronger when Judge Allen spoke again.

"Mr. Rowell, do you have anything you'd like to say?"

The chains of Bruce's handcuffs rang as he stood up. Harris wasn't expecting Bruce to say anything when he turned around, looked directly into his eyes, and started talking.

"I'm sorry," Bruce said at Harris, the first signal of humanity appearing from the man. "Please tell Sabrina that I'm sorry and that I love her."

The two small sentences were all he said before returning to his chair next to his lawyer. All eyes again shifted toward Harris with Bruce's directive. Unsure of how to respond, Harris kindly offered a small head nod toward Bruce, who reciprocated the gesture. The two men—bonded together by a horribly violent act—had reached some common level of understanding.

"Mr. Rowell, you have been charged with Second Degree Assault, a class D felony, which carries a maximum seven-year prison sentence. You may have received forgiveness from your victim, but you cannot and will not escape the law. What you did was barbaric and inhuman. And I suspect that if I let you off easy, you may carry out another vicious attack one day. If it were entirely up to me, I'd hold you in jail much longer than seven years. You're lucky it's not entirely up to me. I hereby sentence you to seven years in prison..."

Harris tuned out the judge after hearing the number of years, focusing solely on Bruce—who didn't flinch at the sentence, didn't look back at anyone. Harris's father tugged him close, his fingers digging into Harris's shoulder. Clearly excited at the sentence, he looked at Harris and gave a thumbs-up.

"It's over, Harris," he said.

Harris smiled out of obligation. Things with Bruce might have wrapped up, but the residue of the attack remained. And what Harris hoped to accomplish was far from over.

It pained Harris to see the intersection of Clinton and William looking almost exactly like it had six months ago. Nothing had improved. In fact, Harris thought it looked even worse—but thought perhaps the sheen of the snow in the winter had masked much more than he'd imagined. His selfishness caused the grand vision of rejuvenating the neighborhood to implode and apparently no one at Beautify Buffalo had searched through the rubble left behind to build it up in the aftermath.

Sabrina, his saving grace, had been distant and unavailable since Bruce's arrest. A visit to her house directly after the arrest was punctuated by an unanswered knock, though Harris could see her shadow walking around inside. He didn't blame her and resisted pushing a conversation between them—he couldn't fathom what she was going through.

The circumstances surrounding Bruce's arrest came to light shortly thereafter. One night when Bruce was drunk, he had mentioned something about "sticking it to the mayor" this past winter. Sabrina, putting two and two together, pretended like she knew all along that he was talking about beating Harris up. She poured him another drink and asked questions like, "Where did you find the hockey stick?" to get him to spill the details. She buttered him up with more whiskey and told him she had to make a quick pit stop to the police station to file a complaint about noise levels in the neighborhood. She asked Bruce, inebriated beyond his usual state, to come with her for protection. Once inside the precinct, Sabrina asked to talk to a detective and got Bruce to admit to everything. It was a sly move from Sabrina, one Harris knew wasn't an easy decision. The fact that she didn't think twice about turning her ex in made Harris so thankful. But since he had learned all these details, a brief phone call and a few texts were all the two had exchanged.

He had to talk to her, even if only for a minute, to catch a glimpse of the Sabrina he first met months ago—someone against the odds but so full of life.

The attack still left emotional bumps and bruises lining Harris's body; traveling back to this section of the city only amplified their presence. Tempted to get back in the car, drive away, and never, ever return, Harris collected the courage to get out of the car. He wasn't sure what he could accomplish by visiting Sabrina, but he knew he had to see her. There wasn't going to be anything specific he could say to lessen the length or harshness of Bruce's sentence, so he decided to go the symbolic route and bring her a bouquet of lily of the valley flowers. The flowers (so the florist said) symbolized a return to happiness, an essential memento he surmised Sabrina would appreciate. Harris almost picked up an extra bouquet for himself in an effort to truly encompass his personal journey to this moment, but realized his suffering had ended and effectively transferred to Sabrina, Bruce, and their children.

The baking blacktop of Sabrina's driveway radiated through his flip-flops, his stride quick and long to her side door. Harris knocked on the door and grasped the stems of the flowers, for the first time debating giving them to her. It might have been a cheap token—especially mere hours after her ex-husband was sentenced to seven years in jail—but it was the least Harris could do. This woman had saved his life. This woman was the driving force behind Bruce getting arrested. Schmaltzy or not, he had to do anything and everything he could to express his sincerest appreciation.

"Harris," Sabrina said as she opened the door, her gaze holding a melancholy glow.

"I just came to say thanks and to drop these off," Harris said, handing her the bouquet.

Harris added an extra ounce of cheer in his voice, trying to strike a balance between being upbeat and realistic. Sabrina was a woman masquerading as happy, even through the trace of dried tears on her face.

"I tried, Sabrina. I didn't want the judge to sentence him for that long. I'm so sorry."

"Don't you dare apologize, Harris. Bruce made his own bed and now he has to lie in it."

"But your kids," Harris said.

"They'll be okay," Sabrina said. "We'll be okay. It's just going to take some time."

Life had completely turned upside down since his fateful mistake with the click of his camera in her house six months ago. In a way, the idiotic tweet—coupled with losing his job—set in motion a turn of events Harris was proud to arise from. The attack had left him aching and battered, but also tougher and more conscientious.

"You want a cup of coffee or a glass of wine or something?" Sabrina asked politely.

Harris could sense it was one of those uninviting invitations done only out of graciousness.

"I've actually got to get back to my house and put some finishing touches on before tonight," Harris said. "I'm having some people check out all the renovations. You'll have to come by and see it sometime."

"I would love to, Harris," Sabrina said, as she hugged him.

There was conclusiveness in her hug. Harris recognized it as the kind of interaction you have with someone you know you won't see for a very long time. This ordeal pained Sabrina, clearly. Maybe she held contempt toward Harris for getting her involved in this mess in the first place. Perhaps she was ashamed that the father of her children had carried out a despicable, reprehensible crime. Whatever Sabrina was thinking, Harris could feel it in her shuddering breaths against his chest.

"You know I'll always have your back," she whispered. Though peeking out slowly, the old Sabrina was still there.

"And I'll always have yours," he replied. "Thank you. For everything. I owe you."

Harris had that repayment somewhat mapped out. With his house nearly complete, he would shift toward the East Side neighborhood. The East Side Renaissance project floundered without him, but he still had a chance to correct that. Preliminary talks with his father on founding a subcommittee toward revitalizing decaying sections of the city seemed promising—and Harris pledged to successfully push this project through to completion. Sabrina, her neighbors, and all the citizens of Buffalo were due a fair shake.

Harris grasped her shoulders and looked deep into her eyes, both of them holding tears back. No matter what happened from here on out, Harris knew Sabrina Rowell would always be a part of his life. He said goodbye and walked down the driveway, reliving that cold night in January.

Each soft step came with a heavy heart, his memory inching closer and closer to the agony and bewilderment of the beating. Avoiding reminiscing about the attack had been a staple of Harris's mindset since the day he'd come out of the coma—but that wasn't currently possible. He could almost hear the cracks of the hockey stick against his jaw, could almost feel his skin pressing against the cold pavement.

As Harris got to the end of her driveway, a car sped by. A swift breeze shot through him, leaving a chill in the air. Footsteps sounded of someone approaching from behind. The scenario mimicked the exact beginning to that night with Bruce—a fact that was not lost on Harris.

"Hey," the man said as he approached.

"Hello," Harris replied, spinning around and attempting to hide his panic.

Harris immediately got upset for not preparing for a copycat attack. He should've taken his father's advice and signed up for self-defense lessons or started carrying mace. Harris turned and counted the steps in his mind back to Sabrina's side door. A quick run would get him there within five seconds, but if the door was locked, he'd only drag Sabrina into another situation. Harris made a fist, prepared to block any punch with his left forearm and deliver an uppercut if necessary. As Harris moved forward toward his car, his path intersected with the stranger.

"Have a good night," the man said, nodding toward Harris.

Dumbfounded, Harris involuntary responded. "Thanks. You, too." Harris giggled to himself as he got into his car and the man continued walking down the street.

The world wasn't out to get him. Living a life in fear due to an unfortunate, isolated incident was childish and ludicrous. It was officially time to put everything related to the attack behind him.

Driving away from Sabrina's house, Harris looked in the rearview mirror. The scene became small and distant—exactly what he hoped the memory of the attack would soon be. The houses sailed by at shutter speed, but Harris captured the image of each one on Sabrina's block in his memory. He'd need new windows on the blue house and to repair the front porch on the white one. The green one needed a new roof. And on second glance, all of them needed new windows.

His designs were already in motion.

The East Side Renaissance wasn't officially dead. It was just about to begin.

Thirty-One: Clare

Having been around her share of sick friends and family members, Clare recalled how often people described coming back from certain death as a "miracle." That word was used incessantly after her aunt Theresa survived a near fatal bout with meningitis, and when her childhood best friend Mary Lou Smithson barely escaped a boating accident that severely injured her college boyfriend, and also when Charlie's coworker, Julian Kyle, somehow lived to tell of his four-story fall during a hike in Letchworth State Park. Their bodies, left decimated, bounced back with no logical medical explanation. *It had to be divine intervention,* Theresa, Mary Lou, and Julian had implied. "Someone" or "something" was watching after them— and that was the only reason they were still standing.

Clare didn't expect a miracle in her case. And as she lay there at a standstill, she didn't even know if she wanted one.

Her body wasn't breaking down easily, that was certain, but her spirit was mostly absent aside from a dingy sliver of hope that she would soon wake up to find this was all a bad dream. One where she would rise in the middle of the night with a cold sweat and her heart racing, Charlie by her side, the whole debacle merely an elongated nightmare. That scenario would be the only way Clare could envision herself uttering the word "miracle."

To no one's surprise, her emergency MRI conducted after her episode at the lake confirmed a set of tumors had grown back. Immediately, everyone rushed to combat their regrowth the same way they'd handled their presence in the first place. The questions overlapped one another and fell in domino fashion. *Surgery?* This time it might be necessary. *Radiation?* Set to start the following day. *Medicine?* She'd need radiosensitizers, ASAP. *Are there any clinical trials you qualify for? Do you need a ride to treatment? Will you be okay in your new condo?* If anyone took a second to ask Clare what she wanted, she might've had the guts to tell them the truth. But no one—not Cassie, not Harris, not Abe, not Dr. Kincaid, not Dr. Bihar, absolutely no one—asked her what she wanted to do. It should've been flattering; treating an old woman like she was a young ingénue on the cusp of the rest of her life. But, truthfully, it was mildly insulting. At some point, something had to give. Her body had already been put through the ringer once, her brain arguably barely surviving the initial treatment. Was it really compulsory for a second try? She already required a daily nap in the late afternoon and could feel the drive inside of her decreasing daily.

Torn between her ideal (dying) and the expectations of others (living), Clare became a strange mix of apathetic and interested. In her mind, it made perfect sense to end the crusade. This wasn't one of those periods she felt early in her diagnosis; there would be no symbolic rise from rock bottom, no lively reawakening like those from weeks and months ago. The fall into Chautauqua Lake coincided with the most breathtaking moment of her life. The acceptance of death turned out to be rather beautiful and liberating. The fact that she was actually able to find the power to concede pleased her more than she'd ever imagined. No longer afraid of the inevitable future resulted in an unorthodox feeling of harmony for Clare.

She hated not making her feelings known to Cassie while at the cottage. If she had said something seconds earlier, maybe Cass would've let her sink to the bottom of the lake to go peacefully instead of jumping in, pulling her out, and creating life's latest skirmish Clare was unsure how to handle.

Articulating the feeling that existed within her would be a pointless exercise. No one would understand. If only Charlie were still around. He'd get it. After all, he got it! His diagnosis was fast, his health was fleeting. He didn't get lost in the medical mumbo jumbo of how to overcome this and keeping that intact while monitoring this and that. Clare's current situation was another case of humans unhealthily obsessed with prolonging the inevitable. She wanted to look everyone in the eye and shout, *"Let me die already!"* but realized how insane that would sound. So, instead, she stayed meek and mild as she tried to trudge through the long days and even longer nights.

Returning to her everyday routine became a struggle, mainly because Clare had zero idea what everyday life was supposed to be anymore. She and Cassie had been living in her new condo while poorly striving to assemble the life they once had. A month after the madness of that weekend in Chautauqua Lake, her daughter still moped around so upset and depressed over the end of her engagement that it likely appeared Cassie was the one dying.

For Cass, it was all work and no play—actually, all work and literally nothing else. Each day, she went to work, then came home and did more work. Nothing in between, nothing after. Cassie wasn't despondent; she wasn't functioning at her usual level of congeniality. She and Jared hadn't spoken to each other since that evening on the dock—a mistake if they asked Clare. Cassie deserved to know his feelings, however hurtful they could be. She needed closure. She wasn't getting it from Jared and she also refused to speak to Abe, no matter how many times Clare urged her to talk things out with both of them.

Thankfully, school would be ending in a few days, and Clare vowed to bust Cass out of her funk when they had more time together. At the very least, Cassie's attitude produced a distraction that allowed Clare to shift effort toward making her daughter happy. Clare had everything lined up for the days and nights of Cassie's summer vacation, including the newest edition of Scrabble—her favorite childhood board game, a DVD of the sing-along version of *The Little Mermaid* and a sushi-making kit.

Her time alone often included hours of reflection. Clare found it pleasant and particularly amusing that the memories were only of good times: Tuesday night "Pay What You Weigh" dinners with the kids (complete with bottomless bowls of popcorn) at the Ground Round, day trips with Charlie to see musicals in Toronto, Christmas morning breakfasts of eggs and ham—the only day of the year where Clare could stomach warm ham. Random memories, yes, but all entirely enjoyable. Lost in the annals of her mind, Clare wondered what her legacy would be viewed as. For Charlie, his legacy was creating and maintaining a beautiful, successful family. For Clare, it would definitely be the same. Her children were the gift she was so lucky to bring into this world. But beyond that—would she be remembered for anything else? She wasn't only a mother. Only time would tell if others would agree, but Clare was very aware time was the one thing she didn't have.

While she spent her nights internally reminiscing, her days were spent with Marcia, who began to run her cake business out of Montgomery Manor. Clare loved being inside the old house. It was exactly where she needed to be at this period of her life. Marcia had decorated every room sparsely, yet beautifully, a stark change from Clare's style of overloaded knickknacks and photographs. There was little time for reflection when Clare was there, though. Marcia had put her to work mixing, baking, and frosting the cakes. About to pop any day, Clare urged Marcia to take it easy and let her do the heavy lifting, something Marcia only occasionally accepted. Truthfully, Clare's energy level had been near its nadir for weeks. She saved the majority of her strength for the mornings at Marcia's, never wanting to appear weak or in need.

Originally, Clare assumed being back inside the house would be too much for her. There was too much history within those walls, too many spots in the house that would remind Clare of Charlie. She missed the way it smelled, the familiar patches of sun hitting the floor in predictable spots. She missed every part of that house more than she wanted to admit. And the fact that he had never wanted her to give up the house in the first place, well, that was yet another reason Clare thought she should've avoided helping Marcia.

Yet, everything had changed on that dock in Chautauqua. Thinking of Charlie turned into a godsend; it wouldn't be long before she saw him again.

The three brash beeps signifying the end of the session woke Clare up out of a dead sleep. She immediately lifted the radiation mask off her face.

"All right, by the end of the week, we'll be halfway there!" Lindsay, the radiation therapist, said. "See you tomorrow, Clare."

"See you tomorrow," Clare responded while bending down and touching her fingertips to her toes in an attempt to stretch out her back.

As strong as Clare had felt about not wanting radiation, she wasn't as strong as she needed to be. She couldn't look Dr. Kincaid or Cassie in the eye and deliver a firm no to treatment. Death she could handle. Disappointment and disdain from her daughter was different. So there she was in the middle of one more seven-week round of radiation. No matter what the doctors promised or how optimistic everyone seemed, Clare knew the outcome before the treatment even began.

She made her way to the parking lot and hopped in the front seat of Marcia's car.

"How are you feeling?" Marcia asked.

"Not bad," Clare responded.

"Mrs. Montgomery, are you going to be okay?" Harper inquired from the back seat.

"Oh, Harper," Clare said, looking quizzically toward Marcia. How would she tell a six-year-old that her odds of living were the same as the odds of dying? "It's a little too soon to tell."

Clare figured being honest was better than lying and hoped Marcia wouldn't be upset about how she was speaking with her daughter.

"When will you know?" she asked.

"Well, that's the thing, honey. I don't think I'll ever know if I'm going to be one hundred percent okay."

"But you're okay for now?"

The loaded questions from Harper created a stinging sensation inside Clare. Leave it to a six-year-old to actually ask if and when she would be fine when no one else had the nerve to do so.

"Yes, honey. I'm okay for now. And that's all that matters."

Unsure if what she was saying was true or not, Clare smiled at both Marcia and

Harper.

Each had a distinct look in her eyes: Marcia's quick looks to the side said *"I'm sorry she's asking this!"* along with *"You're going to make it, Clare"* while Harper sat straight up wide-eyed and curious, inadvertently dispersing some of her youthful exuberance toward Clare.

"We've got to make a pit stop to the grocery store really quick," Marcia said. "Do you remember what Mommy said she needed, Harper?"

"More sugar and more butter!" she screeched.

Both Marcia and Clare laughed at Harper's enthusiasm.

"Mrs. Montgomery, you're going to help me with the cake, right?" Harper asked.

"Oh, sweetie, I wasn't planning on coming over today. I'm very tired," Clare said, and Harper's face turned from elation to stone. "But if you insist, I'd love to help."

Harper screeched and clapped her hands in a way her that reminded Clare of Cassie almost thirty years ago. Her tiny, chipped pink fingernails sparkled in the sun. She bopped her head back and forth to the beat of the used car lot commercial on the radio and caught Clare staring at her. Immediately, Harper waved her tiny hand at Clare and grinned. Looking back briefly, Harper transformed into Cassie, sitting in the back of their Oldsmobile in the 80s, singing along to the MarineLand theme song blaring through the speakers.

Months ago, an instant like this would've sent chills down Clare's spine and inspired her to fight, push forward, stymie the negative thinking in her head, and pray for that miracle she knew she needed.

That wasn't the case anymore. As Clare waved back at Harper, her little face lit up Clare's soul.

These were her final days, yes. But, surrounded by people she adored? Harkening back to countless wonderful memories?

It wasn't such a bad way to go.

Thirty-Two: Abram

Abe and Jared had only spoken twice (once on the phone and once in person) and both on the same day—the Wednesday after they'd gotten back from the cottage. Their first conversation was succinct and platonic, acknowledging the craziness of what had happened with Cass without ever fully expressing it.

"How are you?" Abe asked Jared over the phone.

"I've been better," Jared replied. "You mind if I stop by the house today?"

"Of course, I'm at work until three," Abe said.

"Okay, great, I'm going to come get my stuff. See you then."

This was the first indication that Jared would be moving on by moving out; his indifference in breaking the news to Abe came as a slight shock, but Abe tried to remain understanding. After all, Jared had entered a new phase in his life—one where he'd move forward as a man who was true to himself. It might have been nearly fifteen years since that had happened for Abe, but he was ecstatic at Jared's late-in-life realization. Was Abe happy? Not at all. But that didn't mean he wasn't fully supportive.

When Jared finally came to the house, Abe immediately clammed up, his nervousness revealing itself in a harried pulse. They exchanged the usual platitudes as Abe awkwardly followed Jared around the house as he packed two empty suitcases full of his clothes and other belongings. Abe didn't want to raise any serious questions, but he also didn't want them to continue on in virtual silence.

"Where did you disappear to Saturday?" Abe ended up asking eagerly. It had been eating him up inside—wondering where Jared had gone after being inadvertently outed by their kiss.

"I needed to get away," Jared replied, masking how downtrodden he was. Abe could see right through him.

"Hey," Abe said, bracing his right shoulder. "Are you okay?"

"Yeah," Jared said. "I'm heading back to North Carolina this weekend. For good."

The news gutted Abe. Greedily, he viewed this as Jared abandoning both he and Cassie. Perhaps it had always been obvious that a relationship between them wouldn't work, but Abe still believed that in a different world, he and Jared might happily end up together in the near future.

Like a lost puppy, Abe followed Jared outside when he'd finished packing. He awkwardly hugged Jared and whispered in his ear, "I'll miss you."

"There's one thing I wanted to say to you," Jared said. Abe's heart bounced up and down, back and forth as he slowly backed out of the hug. He wanted to hear something corroborating his awful behavior, anything to make him not feel like he'd been duped by a smug and handsome stranger. Some confirmation that Jared, too, believed they could've been a perfect couple if some alternate universe existed.

"Thank you," Jared said.

"For what?" Abe asked.

"For letting us stay here," Jared said. "And for understanding why I have to go."

Jared shut the trunk of his car and walked to the driver's side door. Abe couldn't let things end so blasé.

"Jared. Before you go," Abe said, his voice cracking with emotion. "I want you to know how much you mean to me. You're...a remarkable man."

"Thanks, Abe," Jared said, opening the door.

That wasn't the response Abe envisioned. The "Thanks, Abe" was completely unsatisfying. He longed for the reciprocation of prominence within Jared's life. The desire, entirely needy and unbecoming, radiated so strongly within him that Abe couldn't and wouldn't let "Thanks, Abe" stand as Jared's goodbye to him.

Abe recalled the night of their first kiss and how Jared encouraged Abe to speak his mind. *"Sometimes you have to do things in the moment and deal with the consequences later,"* Abe remembered him saying. He couldn't let this moment slip by without hearing Jared say what Abe so desperately wanted.

"Wait. Jared. Tell me I'm not crazy," he said while Jared froze, prompting Abe to elaborate. "It was worth it for me. Us. You. You are entirely worth it. Is it... Was it worth it for you?"

Abe wanted to be breezy and sexy (a combination he called "brexy" in his head) while earning the validation, but his rushed speech and high-pitched voice were exactly the opposite of his goal. Brexy it was not. It was a rudely selfish request—wanting Jared to profess his love. But Abe reminded himself how messy everything with Cassie had become. Abe, a self-centered arsonist, willingly set their friendship on fire over the highest of expectations with Jared. If Cassie was forever removed from his life as he knew it, he needed to know it was over something as significant as quite possibly a once-in-a-lifetime love.

Abe took Jared's old advice a step further and moved toward him, leaning in with the sole purpose of kissing Jared. The two locked eyes for a split second, Abe no longer saw Jared's warmth and energy shining through. His face still exuded the outward beauty it always had, his blond hair glowing in the sun, each wisp of his bangs gently framing his face and producing his patented, yet inadvertent, *GQ* smolder. Jared appeared tired and worn for the first time since Abe met him—the telltale signs of a man in the midst of an internal struggle. Abe dove headfirst anyway, hoping Jared would break down the final barrier and lose himself in Abe's arms.

"I gotta go, Abe," Jared said, pushing back on Abe's chest.

The disappointment fermented inside Abe, a feeling of promise and ecstasy instantly turning to one of regret and shame. He didn't know how to react, but Abe still wanted some sort of acknowledgment that his bad behavior wasn't entirely one-sided. It had taken two to tango, and he had no shame in needing Jared to fess up to his part in their dance.

"Jared. I feel like I deserve to know if you also think that under different circumstances, you and I could've maybe worked things out? I don't want to have to guess on this for the rest of my life."

"Goodbye, Abe," Jared said, ending the conversation by tossing Abram's house key to him and finally getting into his car, shutting the door, and quickly backing out of the driveway.

He didn't glance at Abram once, simply put the car in reverse and drove away.

This latest chapter in his life was an addendum, a detour so out of place and unforeseen that Abram held zero knowledge on how to react timely or appropriately. He shouldn't have been startled; it wasn't as if things were following the preplanned path he had imagined when he was younger. Days shy of his thirty-third birthday, Abe's life had not worked out in any of the ways he'd fantasized as a kid. There was no nine-to-five job, no wife to come home to, no kids, no in-ground pool, no cocker spaniels, no convertible, and no penthouse suite directly on the shores of the Pacific Ocean in Malibu.

Sure, there was a job. And his house was nice enough. But, his story fell far short of the idyllic world he had pictured. Contemplating the life he had once predicted versus the life that was actuality became something Abe did often. He wasn't supposed to be gay. He wasn't supposed to be so distant with his parents. He wasn't supposed to devote most of his free time to his job.

And he certainly wasn't supposed to be single and alone.

That hit him more than ever as he entered his empty house—a house that showed no trace of Cassie or Jared or their time together as roommates, except for Jared's piano, which awkwardly sat in one of Abe's spare bedrooms. Every night after work, he headed straight to the room to see if the only tangible object of the last six months had been removed. Like every other night before it, the instrument stood in the same spot in the middle of the room, an emblem of solitude that struck Abe like repeated jabs to the gut.

As he walked into the room, the resonating buzz of the air conditioner kicking on masked his soft hums of "Always On My Mind," which had been in his head the entire day as he'd traveled back to that winter's night when Jared first played the song on his piano. That night held such promise of a budding friendship between the three of them. Looking back, Abe's feelings toward Jared seemed foolish, a blasphemous attack on his best friend. He had arduously questioned his motives ever since Cassie found out the truth, but still had no concrete answer for pushing the envelope with Jared and pursuing something other than a friendly rapport. For someone inherently goal-oriented and motivated by specific outcomes, his endgame with Jared had never become clear, and therefore, was never attainable. Abe ran his fingers across the ivory keys, the clunk of his hands eliciting an ominous and out-of-tune tone. He found it mildly amusing how in the process of attempting to lessen the hurt for Cassie and grow closer to Jared, he'd actually lost them both. Abe had assumed Cassie would be the first to bend her stubbornness and realize how his confession was made also to protect her. Yet, after a month, he was dead wrong. There was nothing. Cassie's neuroses over relationships had forever been a bit irrational—and this circumstance was above and beyond anything she'd previously faced. Abe understood keeping his distance was the most sensible course of action, but trying to make sense out of this predicament was a losing battle. There were no rules to follow anymore, only a friendship he needed to fix.

Eight attempts. That's how many times Abe had driven to Clare's condo and tried to see Cassie. Each time, he'd brought with him a gift or item with a personal connection he knew Cass would love. All eight times, Cassie had refused to see him. She'd denied Abram the chance to talk to her, showing no interest in the bag of raunchy beach reads he'd bought for her summer vacation, or the half-dozen original glazed doughnuts he had gotten from the only Krispy Kreme in the area—two hours away in Erie, Pennsylvania. His bribes of food and gifts hadn't been meant to be as trivial as they appeared; they'd been meant to be fun, inane icebreakers. After the eighth attempt, though, he feared he was farther away from chipping at her shell than he was the first time around.

Abe avoided acting on the panic building within him. *It's only been a month*, he told himself numerous times. The repetition didn't help, though. The longer they went without speaking, the worse he felt. Time alone wouldn't heal this wound, but clearly, more of it appeared to be absolutely necessary. Trying to balance his wish with his patience, Abe convinced himself he'd only need five minutes face-to-face to begin the process of smoothing things over with Cass. Unfortunately for him, it was entirely up to her when those five minutes would be.

All Abe wanted to do was go in reverse, back to the day Jared and Cassie had shown up at Vitality. Their arrival had rejuvenated him, their initial days living together holding the potential for lifelong memories—*fun* lifelong memories— not these heartbreaking, monumentally upsetting lifelong memories.

The pill was tough to swallow. Ever since he graduated college, Abe had grown accustomed to achieving his goals. All he had to do was set his mind to it—and poof—it'd happen.

Opening and running a fitness center? Easy.

Trimming his body fat to below 6 percent? Simple.

Eliminating all addicting toxins from his diet and daily routine? Effortless.

Getting the man of his dreams to admit he had similar strong feelings? Impossible, apparently.

Not getting what he wanted from Jared had caused a schizophrenic reaction in Abe. There were moments after Jared's departure when Abe lost all touch with reality—thoughts and emotions conflicting with his actions, grandiose delusions of isolation strangling him and whisking him away from reality. He deteriorated both physically and in his personality in the week after Jared left, lost in a horribly unstable outlook.

Thankfully, Abe was pulled out of his murky mindset by Harris, whom he had reconnected with on a level he had never fathomed. Abe's profuse apology for not believing Harris about his parents was met with sincere acceptance from Harris. They were once again actual friends, perhaps the first time in their lives they were genuinely just and only friends. There were no sexual undertones in their three quick lunch dates or their random trips to Home Depot together. Everything between them at the onset of their new amicable expedition together had been purely sexless—but despite that, Abe second-guessed his own intentions. He had drifted through his relationship with Jared by mainly going with the flow, an anomaly for someone who usually overthought every word, gesture, facial expression, and outfit in every situation. There was no explicit objective with Jared; Abe knew there must be one with Harris. Would the two remain only friends? Or would they rekindle the magic that once existed? And how long would it take for Abe to figure it out so he could plan accordingly?

These were the latest questions that would dictate where Abe's story went next, but he had no time to answer them that night. Abe was waiting for Clare in the parking lot outside her condo. The two were on their way to see Harris's newly renovated house—and seconds before she climbed into his car, Abe told himself to take stock of the situation. Abe lost Cassie and Jared—both of whom might eventually end up back in his life. But Clare? She had so much more to worry about than he did. Her health was in decline and her attitude reflected it. She had become uncomfortably numb about her cancer returning. While she'd agreed to radiation, her attitude was different the second time around. Sure, she was attempting to kill the cancer once again, but it was a pedestrian effort, unlike the fierce fight during her initial round.

"Hello!" Abe said cheerfully as she got into the passenger seat.

"Hi, Abe. I made you a little something," Clare said, handing him a heavy plastic grocery bag that weighed. "It's chicken cordon bleu. The chicken is par cooked, so you need to heat at 350 degrees for twenty to twenty-five minutes. And the recipe is in there, too. Just in case...you know." Her words implied this would be the last time she would deliver Abe a home-cooked meal.

"Mrs. Montgomery..." Abe started, before she cut him off.

"And there are a few slices of banana bread and a fruit salad in there too. Don't worry, this is for Harris," she said while holding up a bottle of Shiraz with a silver bow taped to it.

She had always been there for Abe—and continued to be there even more as the strained relationship with his parents continued. He had spoken to his mother a few times by phone since their argument, each conversation basically lifeless—all of which stemmed entirely from him. His mom was keen to move on and bury the hatchet. She apologized for her actions years ago, blaming it solely on shock. Abe appreciated her apology. It was earnest and necessary. But he couldn't forgive and he wouldn't forget.

For those reasons, Abe was even more thankful for someone like Clare Montgomery. She asked the questions his mother never did, knew of the stories his mom didn't even envision. She wasn't his mother, but she was more of a mother than his mom had ever been.

"What do you think the house will look like?" Clare asked, again snapping him back to the situation at hand.

"I have a feeling," Abe said, "but I don't want to jinx it."

Harris McGee was as predictable that day as he was at any point over the course of their relationship. Whenever he wanted to surprise Abe, he had hinted at a subject over and over again at the most unfitting times. And twice that week—once via text and once at lunch—Harris had mentioned something relating to Bordeaux.

"Doesn't this music remind you of Le Bistro du Musée?" Harris had asked while they were eating lunch at Webster's Bar & Bistro—a French-inspired restaurant, which coincidentally happened to be his choice to dine that day. The mention of Bordeaux had caused Abe to squirm. They hadn't discussed Bordeaux since that day at the river when Harris told him the truth about their breakup. In Abe's mind, Bordeaux was a topic off-limits for both of them. There was no sense in bringing up a subject that reminded them of nothing but the idiocy and immaturity of their separation. Yet, here was Harris, willingly and purposely evoking the subject.

Abe had tossed it aside as miscue on Harris's part until it happened again. Clue number two had come via text that morning, when Harris texted Abe with, "Bonjour! See you and Clare tonight at 7:30 for the unveiling! Until then, au revoir!"

Abe was no fool; the house would be inspired by Bordeaux. And he couldn't wait to see how their chateau motivated Harris. If he and Harris could capture one ounce of that Bordeaux feeling here in Buffalo—after months of stress and gloom and sourness—life would undoubtedly turn to the sweeter side for Abe.

He wished he could say the same for Clare, who did her best to put forward a valiant front as she sat beside him. Abe couldn't ignore her demoralized mood or the absence of Cassie.

"How is she doing?" Abe asked.

"She's getting there, Abe," Clare answered. "She's not great, but she's getting there."

To hear that Cassie was still troubled over Jared produced deep pangs within him. Yes, what happened between Jared and Abe was excruciatingly awful and undeniably uncomfortable for Cassie, but a month had passed! Though that amount of time wasn't prolific, it was enough—Abe assumed— for the two of them to at least have one small conversation about everything. After all their years of friendship, after their lifetime together, Abe rebuffed the notion that silence would be the way the story of him and Cass ended.

The feeling of hypocrisy rapidly swaddled him as Abe reminded himself how long it took for him and Harris to work things out—and how he still wasn't ready to truly talk to his parents. How could he fault Cassie for needing additional time to comprehend everything? A month suddenly seemed microscopic in the grand scheme of things.

Approaching Harris's house on Crescent Avenue, Abe grabbed hold of Clare's knee.

"How are you doing?" he asked. She had instructed Abe numerous times to ignore the cancer and treat her as he did all his life.

"I've spent most of the year letting this define me," she told Abe. "I'm not doing it again." After his question this time around, she clasped his hand on her knee and sighed deeply. "I don't want to talk about it, Abram. If you don't mind. I've made peace with everything."

Abe respected her desire not to speak about it when he put his car into park outside Harris's house. From the outside, the home on Crescent Avenue looked no different than the picture Harris had shown Abe weeks ago, but the neighborhood was livelier than he'd imagined. Several families with strollers were on both sides of the street, a young woman with her dalmatian jogged by, and two couples were outside tending to their gardens and lawns.

"You ready for this?" Clare asked.

"I sure am!" Abe said, hoping his feigned response appeared truthful.

Quite frankly, he wasn't sure he was ready for this. If, as expected, the house was a throwback to the better days of Bordeaux, what exactly would that signify?

There was no more time to question everything as Harris greeted them on the front porch with hugs and a smile as wide as Abe had ever seen. He looked positively giddy and entirely in his element.

"Now before you guys head in, I want to explain something to you," Harris said. "This is by no means complete. In fact, I debated postponing until everything was done, but who knows when that is going to be!"

Harris walked toward the door to open it, before stopping and speaking again. "Please know that I tried really hard to make this as beautiful as I remembered, but it's really, really tough when you only see something for such a short amount of time."

He again walked toward the door but turned around once more. "And I want you two to be honest on what you think, please."

"Harris!" Abe laughed. "Let us see already!"

With one swift motion, Harris pushed open the front door.

Abe took one step into the house and his jaw immediately dropped. He tried to gasp but the view left him breathless. "Oh my God. Harris!" Abe said with delight. "How did you do this?"

"You know I have a good memory," Harris answered.

His reply coincided with Clare dropping the wine bottle, the sound of shattered glass shearing through Abe's awe.

"Oh, Harris. I'm so sorry," Clare whispered while bending down, trying to pick up the large pieces of glass swimming in the Shiraz. Abe noticed her hands shaking uncontrollably.

"Clare, don't touch that. I'll go get the broom and a mop," Harris said. "You two head on in. Start the tour yourselves!"

Abe walked toward Clare and grabbed her hand so they could tiptoe around the puddle of wine. Entering Harris's house, Abe knew she would need something—or someone—to hold on to.

It was like stepping into a parallel universe; a sense of déjà vu combined with total consternation.

Much to Abram's amazement, the house was not a duplication of Bordeaux. Instead, it was a near replica of the Montgomerys' former home.

Inside the front foyer hung a stained-glass lantern that matched the Montgomerys' old one almost perfectly, except with a few more turquoise triangles thrown in. A fast glance to the left showed practically every detail of the Montgomery home imitated. The open concept was highlighted by the sunken living room, which like the Montgomery home, was flanked on one side by the combined dining room and kitchen. From what Abe could see, the kitchen had the same curved tile wall and the pantry under the stairs. Abe swore he saw the bindings of several books inside a library on the other side of the kitchen. Even Clare's signature smell of lavender and vanilla seemed to be pumping out of the vents and washing over everything.

"What do you think of Montgomery Manor 2.0?" Harris asked, stretching his arms out and spinning around.

"Harris," Clare said with a voice that wobbled and cracked. "You rebuilt my house?"

"I tried to!" Harris said, dumping the bag of broken glass inside the trash can.

Abe wanted to continue the tour and scope out every room, but his feet stuck to the hardwood floor in front of Harris. His cheeks ached from smiling. It wasn't a precise copy; this house was wider and narrower than the Montgomery home and the abundance of natural light made the cream-coated walls appear much warmer. Still, what Harris had accomplished was relatively indescribable.

Clare ran up from behind Abe and jumped into Harris's arms. Without thinking, Abe tag-teamed Harris and hugged him from behind, their three bodies melting together into one giant pile of tears and laughter.

When the hug ended, Abe once again got lost marveling over Harris's creation. It was immaculate. Magnificent. Ridiculous. Utterly unexpected and the biggest instance of real beauty Abe had ever witnessed. His heart not only beat fast, but it beamed with gratitude and pride for Harris. The man had done something so noble, something that transcended even the highest of hopes.

This Harris McGee was not the Harris McGee of old. He'd developed into an ambitious self-starter creating something inconceivable. Abe found Harris manlier and sexier than ever, his house proving to be a manifestation of all his attractive qualities.

Abe could feel it bubbling and decided to give up the fight. For weeks, he had been projecting his adoration on the wrong man, searching for something in Jared that was never there and would never be there. Without thinking, Abe looked at Harris, his lips mouthing the three words he'd promised himself he'd never repeat to Harris again.

"I love you," Abe said, admitting what he had known all along and officially starting the sequel to their story without an ounce of fear or hesitation.

Thirty-Three: Harris

Connecting the dots of destiny over the previous six months had become a bit of a game for Harris. He loved to pinpoint the exact choices that caused his fate to hopscotch from a preplanned target to unknown territory. Harris picked his tweet and breaking into Sabrina's house as point A and realized that choice caused the chain reaction leading him to his current standing. He suffered through B because of A, lived to see C despite B and made it to Y because of X. He yearned for point Z to arrive soon, for that one moment where the craziness of his life would slide into the regularity he longingly craved.

He would get there soon, that much he knew. The booze-swigging, bed-hopping, entitled, and immature Harris of long ago matched more closely to the life of an evil twin, not the person he actually was. The emotion of everything substantial that had happened since the start of the year jostled around inside him as Clare and Abe stood inside his house. The fact that he had persevered through losing his job, becoming a target of the media, the agony and the confusion after the attack, and the hours of boredom in the aftermath was no small feat—and he was reveling in the glow and satisfaction that came with this night's unveiling. Something in the air soothed and tempered his ever-present anxiety. The aura surrounding him infused his soul with a calmness that had been lost ever since the attack. He couldn't trace its origin, unsure if it arose from the sheen of Clare's smile when he'd opened that door, from Abe's jaw-on-the-floor reaction, or if it was simply an effect of the secrecy from the renovations finally being out in the open.

To Harris, the most unavoidable aspect of adulthood was that with age came disenchantment. Personal accomplishments for people in their thirties were often whittled down to job promotions, how much money was in the bank, marriages, and children. His brothers willfully followed the trend. Ethan had his sons; Tim recently became equity partner at his law firm. Meanwhile, Harris had little or none of the things society said he should have at his age, but he still had a reason to feel fulfilled.

The finished product had turned out substantially similar to how he planned—and even better in some circumstances. Managing to recreate the level of grandiose peculiarity from the Montgomery house had never been an option; it was an absolute necessity. Although his project started as a mission to win Abram back, it quickly became something much deeper. The return of Clare's cancer coupled with Abram's issues with Jared and Cassie played a part in Harris's journey of persistence and malleability. He'd needed to finish this project because he needed Clare and Abram to receive a jolt of happiness and have no additional sadness tumbling through their veins. But those outside factors weren't the driving force behind his never-quit attitude. More than anything, Harris had done this for himself.

As physically taxing as the renovations were—eighteen-hour days, seven days a week—nothing could have stopped him on this personal and professional odyssey. Fixing the house became emblematic of Harris's life. There were the obvious, necessary fixes that anyone could have picked out from a mile away: removing the galvanized plumbing and adding copper pipes, replacing the jalousie windows in the kitchen with something from this century and installing new storm doors in the front and back. But then there were the unplanned problems. Each unexpected twist of his blueprint synced perfectly to the unexpected twists of his year. Much like his life, the basement had foundational issues, its crumbling sections threatening to dismantle the entire base of the house. Much like his life, there were energy issues. The addition of a dishwasher and recessed lighting to the kitchen had thrown too much at the 100-amp electrical box, which Harris needed to upgrade. Much like his life, the painted façade began to show its age, every crack and gap seemingly widening by the passing second. Much like his life, though, there was a light at the end of the tunnel. Harris patched up the wounds of the house like he'd patched up the wounds to his heart. Each aspect of his life he had worked to improve correlated perfectly with the unforeseen issues of the house.

Harris's dedication produced a home, which if not absolutely similar to Clare and Charlie's, came pretty damn close. His photographic memory had certainly helped him thrive—but so did the help from Cassie. He'd held his cards close in his texts to her and hadn't revealed his grand scheme, even when she questioned why he wanted to know the paint colors and decoration placements in their former home.

If there was one thing wrong with the big reveal, it was that Cassie wasn't there by her mother and her best friend's side. Harris didn't blame her. She'd be ready to accept the situation in her own time. He also felt an ounce of remorse for being happy that the house produced tears in Clare and Abe. Clare had seen better days. Not only was she weaker physically, she had hit a new emotional low recently, seemingly content with withering away into an uneventful demise. Yet, that attitude was far and away the opposite from what Harris witnessed firsthand that day. Standing before him, Clare's eyes were alert, her voice packed with joy, her body language spastic and alive.

And to see Abe mouth the words "I love you" in his direction? Well, that was the icing on the cake. It created a billion questions in Harris's mind—did Abe mean he was *in* love with him? And how exactly did Harris feel about Abe? Perhaps that was the more important question, Harris discerned. Since their return from Chautauqua Lake, things had been edging past simple friendship, at least in his mind. Their conversation earlier that month still sent chills down Harris's spine. They'd met on the walkway underneath the Peace Bridge, set on Lake Erie smack dab in the middle of the US and Canadian border. It was Abe's choice to meet there—an apropos location that hadn't surprised Harris.

"We always said we were going to do this," Harris said.

"There's still so much to do on my Western New York bucket list!" Abe replied.

"Let me guess. You still want to hike to the eternal flame at Chestnut Ridge, buy tickets to the Lucy Comedy Fest and the Lucile Ball Museum...and visit that rock park near Olean?" Harris asked, fascinated by his ability to remember all the things he and Abe had never gotten to when they were dating.

Abe had laughed, involuntarily confirming the guesses were correct. It amazed Harris that after everything together, they were still so naturally united. The bad breakup and the years of silence had done nothing to separate their innate bond. No matter what happened in their lives, Harris and Abe would always be inexplicably linked, together forever in principle, whether they were actually together or not.

"I'm really sorry," Abe had said that day as the cars and trucks on the bridge rumbled above them. "I ended up speaking with my mom and...let's just say I should've trusted you. I hate that I assumed you were lying to me and know now that you never meant to intentionally hurt me. So, I'm sorry."

At that point, it had only been three days since their conversation on the dock in Chautauqua and Harris sensed Abe was in emotional tumult. Never before had Abe divulged such personal information so effortlessly. The usual stammering and delay tactics weren't noticeable in his apologetic delivery.

Abram's change of heart had set Harris's heart ablaze. For so long the stupid secret between them had pushed them apart. There were no secrets any longer. Everything that had separated them currently pulled them together. Still, a sense of blame sat with Harris. Being truthful with Abe had caused a large divide between the Hoffmans and their son—but it did bring Abe closer to him. He was very grateful that the two were back in each other's lives and forged ahead knowing full well that he and Abram likely wouldn't cross the friendship line any time soon. In spite of his underlying desires, Harris had stood on that walkway with a deep sense of understanding. Once things settled down for both of them—if that ever happened—maybe there would be time to explore something more. Staying just friends was a crucial undertaking to adhere to.

Nearly a month later, he looked at both Abe and Clare, each with a dumbstruck smirk on their faces. The culmination of his hard work and their happy expressions delighted him. He guided them on a tour of the house, showing off how each room mimicked the Montgomerys' house. Harris tried courageously to match every room layout, every shade of paint, every minute detail he could. He placed the lamps in the same corners of each room, found similar stains of wood for every table and piece of furniture. His success caused Clare to grab a tissue from the bathroom and continually dab her eyes to stop the tears. The three of them strolled around the house with the wide-eyed wonder of children.

"Wait, I almost forgot the best part," Harris said, as he began speed walking toward the back of the house and motioning Clare and Abe to follow. Through a set of french doors (which he'd added, instead of a sliding glass door like the Montgomerys had) Harris led them to the backyard patio. The herringbone tiles looked incredibly bright in the twilight and the morning glories strung along the pergola still offered a faint scent of pleasantness. The backyard was the hardest part to recreate; the space in the city was not as abundant as the suburbs; the soil wasn't as fertile; the sunlight and the shade came from opposite directions. But Harris had made it work as best as he could. He'd spent most of the past week covering the preexisting concrete slab with the slate tiles, which served as a nice complement to the pergola (oak, not cedar like the original), and also planted nearly everything Clare had in her backyard.

The result was not as cozy or as lush as Clare's, but it was fresh and alluring. Showing the backyard off to Clare and Abe presented the first opportunity for Harris to take a step back and digest the panorama before him. Working at an insane pace for the past month hadn't broken his spirit or his body, but it had prevented him from fully recognizing his achievement. What he'd created wasn't merely nice; it was breathtakingly impressive. Having never felt such pride before, Harris was unsure how to react when Clare started screaming.

"You did not!" Clare shouted, her voice muffled by her hands covering her mouth. "You. Did. Not!" she repeated. Despite being veiled, Harris could still see the smile plastered on her face.

"Okay, so everything is still freshly planted, but by this time next year, it'll all be in full bloom," Harris said, pointing to the fence. "There are black-eyed Susans, and hostas, and the bleeding hearts. Oh, and the dogwoods and tulip trees are on all three sides. Who knows if they'll survive, but they're planted!"

Clare held her chest as she wandered around the perimeter of the backyard, her head shaking back and forth in amazement.

"And I started a veggie garden," Harris yelled to her. "It's not as big as yours, obviously, but there are cucumbers, tomatoes, zucchini, squash, and green beans. I have absolutely no idea what I'm doing, so it's going to definitely need your green thumb."

"Harris," Clare said, shuffling toward him hurriedly. "Tending to a vegetable garden is a full-time job! I'd have to be here every day."

Harris's heart swelled at her suggestion. He had toyed with holding off on mentioning his plan, but Clare's statement proved to be the perfect segue.

"I know," Harris said. "That's why I want you to move in."

The smirk melted off Clare's face instantly. She stuttered a bit before she finally spit out her response. "What are you talking about? Harris, this is your house."

"Well, I'll be here, too," Harris replied. He could tell by the looks on Abe and Clare's faces that he needed to complete his sentence, but he giggled at their reactions. "I built an in-law suite in the back of the house. We'd have our own separate entrances and everything."

Leading Clare and Abe to the door at the left-hand side of the backyard, Harris ushered them in, revealing the suite with a bedroom, a living room, a full bathroom, and a kitchen. He had decorated this space more to his liking. The hardwood floors were a dark espresso that popped against the off-white walls, which were accented by the delicate ivory flecks of the designer wallpaper. It was much more modern than the interior of the main house, but still tasteful.

"It's not the biggest space, but it's big enough for me! And either of you can access this part through a door in the main hallway."

"Either of us?" Clare asked.

"You and Cassie," Harris responded. "I want her to be here too."

Clare became weak and rushed to sit down on the oversized sofa. She focused downward, staring at the floor. Unable to determine what she was thinking about, he blatantly asked her to move.

"So, what do you say?" Harris asked, bending down on one knee and grabbing her right hand. "Will you be my roomie?"

All three laughed at his proposal.

"Of course!" Clare said. "You mind if I call Cass? I have to tell her right now. Oh, Harris. How do I ever thank you?"

"You can maybe make me some of that famous chicken cordon bleu I've heard so much about!"

She grabbed Harris's cheeks and planted a kiss on his forehead. The tears were in freefall, absorption not possible, even with the tissue dabbing. Clare hugged him again and pranced away, her body heaving as she laughed and sobbed simultaneously.

They could hear her whispering "Oh my God!" over and over again in the house as they returned to the backyard. By themselves, Harris and Abe gleefully laughed together, each in awe of what Harris had accomplished.

"Harris!" Abe said while playfully hitting his shoulder. "I haven't seen her that happy in years!"

"It's exactly the reaction I was hoping for!" Harris replied.

"I can't believe you," Abe said.

"Yeah you can," Harris said while grabbing Abe's hand and interlocking their fingers.

Over the course of their relationship, Abe had always been the attentive one, the one with the cutesy surprises, who remembered the minutiae of daily conversations from six months previous and turned it into a stellar birthday gift. Harris had captured his chance to do something special—and the results were thrilling.

The two stood silent, hand in hand, as an iridescent goldenrod vapor cloaked the backyard during the sun's half-hearted summer slide. Harris again contemplated what had led him to this point. He arrived here because of a series of mistakes and bad decisions but fully believed that this was it—this was the final stop on his tour of embarrassment, loneliness, and hurt. The saga of Bruce and Sabrina was over, he and his father had hit a new level of appreciation for one another, the city's restoration subcommittee was one meeting away from approval, and of course, there was Abram. Harris marveled over what was currently unfolding. There he was, in the backyard of his new, freshly renovated home with his old boyfriend gripping his hand tight, both of them smiling in stillness. The two men had so much to say to each other; there were three years of silly stories to share, three years of memories to catch up on. This was neither the time nor the place to start those conversations, and that was okay. It became comforting, this newfound slow and steady pace between them. There didn't need to be a crisis or serious discussion between the two for them to coexist.

A tremendous amount of emotion filled the air. Harris and Abe could hear Clare talking a mile a minute and gasping on the phone, her high-pitched cackle causing both of them to chuckle. Harris turned his head to the right, pretending to stare at the edge of the backyard, but catching fast peeks at Abe. He pondered grabbing Abe's other hand and slowly whispering "I love you too." But it had been nearly a half hour since Abe mouthed those words to him and Harris still was unsure if the "I love you" was a throwaway compliment or a statement entrenched in romance.

To bring up such a heavy topic at a time like this seemed inappropriate to Harris, so he didn't say I love you.

As Harris turned his head fully toward Abe, they remained bound together in their silence. Harris had once and for all made it to point Z. The long, ever-winding journey of his year had reached the finish line. And by his side was the one man he would never let go of again.

He loosened his grip from Abram's hand and cupped the back of his head, leaning in for a kiss. It wasn't long and intense, it was short and subtle. In Harris's mind, it marked the end of their relationship as it was—and the start of something much more.

Yet, Harris still didn't say "I love you."

He didn't need to.

Their faces parted but their bodies grew closer. Abram launched another hug and refused to let go, tightening his squeeze around Harris's lower back. Neither uttered the *L* word again that night, but Harris could feel the love in the air.

And as his gaze moved back and forth between the beautiful man beside him and his house glowing in the waning minutes of sunlight, he knew Abram could feel it, too.

Thirty-Four: Abram

Don't depend on anything but yourself to get through the day.

Don't let your past dictate your future.

Don't judge a book by its cover.

New Year, New Abram?

Hardly.

While he never fully admitted to being a failure, Abe's three New Year's resolutions were unequivocally a bust. There were positives, sure, but he found little comfort by prevailing in eliminating caffeine from his life; he had bigger and better things to worry about.

The midyear evaluation of his progress invariably arrived whether he wanted it to or not. Abe knew this was no way to spend his thirty-third birthday—but it had become the norm. Parties or drinking or fancy events never happened anymore. Held inside Bar None when he had visited New York City for the first time, "Abram's Twenty-Third Birthday Extravaganza" (as named on Myspace) marked the last time he'd truly celebrated his birthday. Exactly ten years ago to the day. Abe tried his best to avoid contemplating the rapid passage of time and how he had lost touch with so many people who attended that party.

It wasn't as if he hated his birthday. He just grew up always being reminded his actual date of birth fell short of what could have been.

"If you would have waited sixteen more minutes, you would've been an Independence Day baby," his mom had always said. "But you couldn't wait to come out."

That fact left Abe feeling inadequate as a child, but he was grateful the proximity of his birthday to the Fourth of July still shaped his identity. It resulted in a staunch love for his country that was embodied by a plethora of patriotic clothing, magnets, and other tchotchkes he wholeheartedly revered. It didn't matter that his birthday took a back seat to a national holiday; involuntarily giving up the spotlight to something more important made him feel like a patriot. And that night, the eve of his thirty-third birthday, would thankfully be another low-key affair since he and Harris had plans to go watch the first night of the weekend's fireworks at Canalside.

Abe dared to think that the two of them were hours away from officially becoming official once again—a possibility that stirred around inside him with a distinct thrill. He was stone-cold sober but felt intoxicated with the rush of affection.

They hadn't seen each other since Abe had left Harris's house with Clare shortly after the big reveal. Abe still couldn't quite fathom what Harris had accomplished in his recreation of the Montgomery home. The level of audacity to try to reconstruct that house room for room, color for color, and detail for detail blew Abe away. Harris's success didn't have to be measured in anything other than the reaction he'd produced. Tears. Disbelief. Gratitude. Never-ending smiles. All the worry over Clare's mental state washed away the second Harris had opened the door to his—to *their*—home. Something had clicked inside her head. Abe could hear it in the words she'd spoken and see it in each delicate, but focused, movement of her eyes.

For a moment, Abe had refrained from asking Harris exactly why he'd done it. With a blank canvas, why build a replica of Charlie and Clare Montgomery's house? Abe never questioned an artist's intentions, and Harris, with what he'd just built, most definitely fit in the category of artist.

Wandering around Main Street downtown, Abe fancied all the new cute restaurants popping up with their small sidewalk cafes. Long a desolate stretch, Buffalo's Main Street makeover was stunning. There were freshly paved walkways, new coinless parking meters, a spattering of recently planted flowers—and perhaps the biggest change of all—there were actually people there. Living, breathing Buffalonians purposefully enjoying a Friday evening downtown.

If all the revitalization there produced such a positive reaction in Abe, he couldn't imagine how it affected Harris. His path to rehab the East Side of Buffalo would not be as easy as the Main Street revival, but if anyone could do it, it was Harris McGee. He was currently suffering through a zoning board meeting, attempting to get his subcommittee approved by the zoning board. The support of his father obviously helped, but no relationship would aid him in his climb out of the governmental red tape. So he had to approach the situation like any other person attempting to influence the city's administration by suffering through their monthly meetings. It was a difficult but fair method and one that would hopefully lead to prosperity in the neighborhoods in which Harris planned to start his rehabilitation projects.

The Friday before a national holiday wasn't ideal for a meeting, but Abe assumed tying up loose ends was pertinent for everyone involved before vacations and days off kicked in. Gaggles of inebriated twentysomethings wandered unevenly down the road. One of the girls carried her high heels in her hand and walked barefoot, a birthday crown draped sideways on her head. He smiled at her and her friends as they clumsily passed. Ten years before, that had been him. He was the drunken fool stammering all over the streets after one too many shots. Ten years later, he was here, watching shadows of his former self and snickering as he reminisced.

Failing at his New Year's resolutions hurt, but Abe somewhat admired his current standing. A decade before, right after the worst hangover of his life, he had made his first five-year plan. He'd vowed to spend the next five years saving his money, learning the ins and outs of the business side of owning a gym, and then he would do it. No matter what, he'd open his own facility. And that was what he had done. He made a plan and stuck to it. The hungover dreams of him at twenty-three had become the everyday reality of his thirty-three-year-old self. That success had shaped Abe's life even more than his July 3 birthday. Having a plan and following through had become a drug to him, the feeling so rewarding and pumping him full of exuberance. No goal became too lofty; no idea too ambitious. And that's why he lived life the way he did, with to-do lists and objectives weighing him down each day in every way.

If only that night's schedule would finally go off according to plan. Abe glanced at his watch. Ten to nine. The anticipation to see Harris and get their evening going made its way through Abe's insides like a tapeworm, hungrily hacking away at his patience. The sky had fully evolved from baby blue to a royal azure, a perfect fit for a night full of fireworks. No longer willing to wait for the meeting to end, Abe walked toward City Hall, staring upward at each star shining brightly above.

Obstacles had plagued the first half of the year, derailing any of Abe's planned mental and physical upward mobility. All the unforeseen circumstances left his schedule in disarray. He hadn't cut down on his running, and his diet and grocery lists were not updated to reflect the fact that he'd soon enter the bulking phase of the year. The superficial issues only skimmed the surface of what Abe hadn't yet initiated. Before he could devise his strategy moving forward, his phone vibrated. It was Harris—finally.

"Hey, Har," Abe said.

"Abe, sorry, the meeting just ended. We're never going to get to Canalside on time," Harris said. "Let's go up to the observation deck and watch. Meet me up there?"

Abe agreed to stay put and ran toward Harris, hopping up the steps of City Hall two at a time, swinging his body around the giant art deco columns and hustling through the first set of doors. The elevators were blocked off by the cleaning crew mopping the floor, so Abram backed up and was searching for access to the stairs when he bumped into someone behind him.

"Abram Hoffman," Mayor McGee said. "Nice to see you."

"Mayor McGee," Abe replied, a bit stunned to see him.

It had been weeks since the two had last spoken, Abe ignoring every soliciting phone call the mayor had made.

"I hear it's your birthday," the mayor said.

"Yes, it is. Well, tomorrow it is."

"Are you doing anything to celebrate?" he asked.

"Actually, I'm about to go meet Harris up on the observation deck to watch the fireworks. That's it, though. Nothing special."

"Sounds pretty special to me," he said. "Listen, Abram. I don't know why you changed your mind about the job offer. But I want you to know I'm willing to compromise."

That job offer from Mayor McGee paled in comparison to the major things happening in Abram's life. In fact, since he hung up the phone on the mayor while in his driveway, Abe had assumed the job offer was off the table. *What kind of person wants to hire someone who hangs up the phone on them?*

"What do you mean?" Abe asked, hoping it didn't come out as insincere as it sounded in his head.

"You're a planner. I need a planner. I want someone in charge who will make a roadmap that the city will follow for years. And if that means you need to be a lead consultant or work on a freelance basis, so be it. I want you to be part of my team."

Hearing the words "consultant" and "freelance" appealed to Abe. If he could somehow spend a few hours a week developing ideas that the city could use for its Health and Wellness Manager, then the feasibility became much more possible. But the extra stress? The added workload? Those were things Abe did not need in his life.

"Mayor McGee, that's awfully nice of you. But I really can't fathom how it would work with me and the gym."

"We'll make it work, Abram. Okay? You better get up there and enjoy those fireworks. But, please, call me after the holiday?"

"Okay."

"Promise?"

"I will call you next week, Mayor McGee."

"Thank you. And, Abram, it's about time you start calling me Dan." The mayor smacked his shoulder in a playful manner and chuckled. Abe never considered calling him by his first name. Even if things were to continue down this path with Harris, Mayor McGee would always be Mayor McGee to Abram. The two went their separate directions before Abram realized he still had no idea how to get up to the observation deck.

"Hey May—Dan?" Abe shouted, his voice echoing in the unoccupied halls.

The mayor turned around.

"Which way are the stairs?"

Abram followed the mayor's finger point to the far corner on the south side of the building and booked it. The fireworks would be starting any second, and curious about the status of Harris's subcommittee and the outcome of the meeting, Abe actually wanted to talk to Harris before they began. He launched into a sprint, running up the stairs like an Olympian in the 100-meter dash, huffing and puffing his way uphill. The lethargy had set in, an effect of working all day before heading downtown. Even his advanced physiology had trouble handling the hike up nearly thirty flights of stairs. Running all the way to the top of the building was an incredibly foolish undertaking, but like any physical challenge, Abe powered through and burst out the door onto the rooftop with the power of a tyrannosaurus rex.

"Harris?" Abe called out amid long, deep breaths. There was no response.

Sucking in air, it took him some time to notice exactly what was happening on the observation deck, but once he did, his breathing stopped as he became inert. The circumference of the entire deck was covered in pieces of red, white, and blue ribbon, pictures of Abe and his family, Abe and the Montgomerys, Abe and Harris hanging every three feet or so. Intermittently mixed in between the pictures were fake plane tickets on white cardstock with a destination listed on each one. Abe slowly walked to the closest one and saw "Lucile Ball Museum" written in black Sharpie.

He walked over to the left side of the observation deck, where a picture of him and Cassie from senior year of college wavered in the wind. Next to the picture were two more tickets, marked "Hike at Chestnut Ridge" and "Rock City Park." He picked up the Chestnut Ridge ticket and rubbed his thumb over Harris's handwriting, a tender smile forming.

"Surprise," Harris said quietly. Abe dropped the ticket and stared out across the cityscape. Harris had done it again—creating a charming and undeniably poignant work of art. "I figured you need some new goals to strive for. We are going to absolutely crush your Buffalo bucket list."

Abe said nothing. The two embraced each other and entered into an adoring kiss before Harris broke free to continue talking.

"I know what you did for me up here that night three years ago," Harris said. "And I've been trying to think of a way to pay you back ever since. So, Happy Birthday, beautiful."

Boom.

The fireworks began with a bright white flash. The oohs and aahs of the crowd at Canalside were audible. Abe and Harris stared straight ahead and watched in each other's arms as the show began. Abe drifted back to the last time he had been up there. The night he'd planned to propose to Harris ended so devastatingly bad and set forth a series of events that led to the darkest years of his life. No action by Harris—not even this unreasonably romantic effort—would ever erase the sadness from that night that still charred his heart to this day.

"Happy birthday, Abey."

Crackle.

Abe almost didn't recognize his mom's voice over the inaugural fizzle of the fireworks. When he swung around, both of his parents were there, each smiling tentatively, the guise of hope written on their faces.

"Happy birthday, Abram," his dad said.

Snap.

The glittering sky matched Abram's emotions: free-falling, smoke stained, wonderful, chaotic. Over the past month, he had practiced the speech he wanted to give to his parents time and time again. It included the rather harsh but perfectly accurate phrases, "What you did veered my life so far off course" and "Your selfishness is appalling and remarkably intolerant."

"Harris invited us here and we couldn't say no," his mom said. "We love you so much and wanted to be with you."

Sizzle.

Letting go had never been a personality trait Abe possessed. And, certainly, what his parents did to him would likely forever be a blemish on their relationship. Nevertheless, none of those words he'd envisioned saying to them came to mind as they stood in front of him. Abe walked toward his parents and drew them close.

"Thank you," he said.

New Year, New Abram?

Perhaps.

His parents hugged back, their grip extra tight. In his mind, that additional squeeze meant more than any words in any apology could ever signify.

"I can't believe Harris did this!" Abe said, still hugging them close.

"You shouldn't be surprised," Clare said as she tapped Abe's shoulder, searching for a way into the hug.

"Mrs. Montgomery!"

Abe exited his parents' arms and transitioned into hers. He picked her up off her feet and bent backward, causing a small yelp to escape her mouth as he lifted her.

"How are you feeling?" Abe asked.

"Can I be honest with you, Abe?"

"Always."

"There are moments I feel like my old self. And there are moments when I know I'm slipping away," she said. "Tonight is one of those times I feel like my old self. Happy birthday, sweetheart."

Out across Lake Erie the fireworks continued, the bright-red stars, faded purple trails, and bursts of green spheres electrifying the sky in an endless rainbow. Abe walked around the side of the observation deck facing the fireworks, reading each ticket Harris had created and elatedly perusing through the pictures. The most recent photo he could find was from Bordeaux, Abe and Harris standing in the manicured gardens of Jardin Botanique. The picture produced a bittersweet nostalgia in Abe. He might have started tearing up if it wasn't for the horrendous outfit he'd had on in the picture. Abe often felt like the least fashionable gay man on earth, choosing to wear workout clothing the majority of the time. While in Bordeaux a warm-front caused the temperature to unpredictably hit ninety degrees—and the only breathable shirts Abe had with him were the ones he had packed for his morning runs. The fabric photographed so shiny and shimmery that every picture of them made Abe look like Elton John in concert, all sparkly and bedazzled.

"You have one heck of a soul mate, Abram Hoffman," Clare said, interrupting his self-pity as she came up behind Abe to give him another hug.

Soul mate. Those words hit a nerve within him. As much as Abe understood Harris was the man he was destined to be with, his soul mate was Cassie. Already a night chockful of surprises, Abe somewhat expected her to be waiting around the corner, ready to forgive and forget.

"Abe," Harris said. "There's one last thing I want you to see."

Boom.

He so badly wanted to see Cassie appear from the staircase, arms extended for a hug and ready to have their much-needed talk. Instead, Harris guided him to a ticket dangling on the right side of the observation deck. This ticket was the only one printed on what appeared to be gold matte paper. Harris ripped it off from the string and handed it to Abe.

"Go ahead," Harris said. "Read it."

Abe obliged.

"Pack your bags and go get ready. It's time for our second chance. By this time tomorrow, we'll be back in Bordeaux. That's right! We're headed to Southern France!"

Abe's hands began trembling. "Harris! What?"

Boom. Crackle. Snap. Sizzle.

The finale of the fireworks coincided with a long kiss between Harris and Abe, each explosion syncing to the rhythm of Abe's racing pulse.

"We leave tonight," Harris said.

"You're lying."

"Well, we're taking the last flight out of Buffalo to New York and then a red-eye out of JFK. So we're going to have to cut this shindig short."

Harris led the two of them to his parents and Clare, who were chitchatting like long-lost friends seeing each other for the first time in decades. Abe had a difficult time grasping the last twenty minutes but took on Harris's frenetic pace in saying his goodbyes.

"I hate cutting this short," Abe said. "I love you all. Thank you for coming."

"We'll be fine. You boys go have fun," his mom said.

"Yeah, we've got a lot to catch up on here," Clare said as she winked at Abe. He knew it meant she would be talking to them about their ignorant comments. Leave it to Clare—fighting for her life but still trying to make everyone else's better.

Exiting the observation deck holding Harris's hand, Abe searched for the way to properly thank him for the most memorable birthday celebration he'd ever had. Instead, he filled the ride down the elevator with a million questions for Harris, slightly scared to bog the moment down with logic. *What airline are we flying? How long are we going for? Are we staying at the same place? Do you have my passport already?* Harris avoided answering all questions but one of them.

"Who's going to watch the gym?" Abe asked, panicking.

"I talked to Brianna. Everything is covered," Harris replied. "Stop worrying and start getting excited!"

The car ride back to Abe's house included lots of laughs, but no explanation on how long Harris had been planning this surprise. While they talked briefly about the meeting (Harris's subcommittee was approved!), most of their time was spent shimmying in the front seats. Harris put on the Britney Spears playlist in his phone, cranking the volume to its highest level, and effectively getting the two of them to bust a move as best they could strapped in and driving. Harris used to hate when Abe danced while in the passenger seat, but tonight, he encouraged it.

"You better start dancing!" he told Abe.

Abe began his interpretive dancing in the passenger seat with his patented alternating finger wag and raise-the-roof motion. It didn't matter what the song was, that maneuver fit with every beat and every melody. The two of them swayed back and forth, belting out song after song at the top of their lungs, easily amusing themselves. It was like nothing had changed between them, though nearly everything in every way had. The lightheartedness of the night continued but turned a bit more serious when Harris pulled up to Abe's house and gave him a stern deadline to get in and get out.

"I'll go fill up the gas tank and come right back," Harris said. "You've got, like, ten minutes."

Abe ran in the house, threw his keys on the kitchen counter, and made his way to the spare room. His suitcase, so rarely used, was either under the bed or in the closet. Abe felt like he was in an episode of *The Amazing Race*, his brow sweating as he tried to complete the task as quickly as possible. Entirely occupied in finding the suitcase and packing, it took Abe almost a whole minute to realize Jared's piano was no longer in its usual spot. Freaked out, Abe presumed it could have been stolen and that he'd stumbled into a robbery in progress, until a piece of paper sitting on the dresser caught his eye. He picked it up and recognized Jared's handwriting immediately.

> You deserve to know
> I'm happier than ever.
> It was all worth it.

Abe looked around, half expecting Jared to still be in the house.

He wasn't.

Rereading the haiku again, Abe paid special attention to the last line. "It was all worth it." That referred to Abe's question in the driveway the day Jared left for North Carolina. The dissolution of a relationship, the embarrassment of Cassie finding out, the waste of his move to New York—Jared confessed that his brief fling with Abe made it all worth it. The confirmation made Abe's already beating heart tick a little bit faster. More important than Jared's revelation was the fact that Jared was happy. Abe breathed a sigh of relief. When Jared left, Abe had been demoralized and clearly conflicted. Whatever happened between then and the weeks since must have been positive and liberating.

Abe could've spent all night guessing what had happened to Jared, but he was a man on a mission. He needed that suitcase or he'd spend all his money in Bordeaux buying a new wardrobe. Shutting the light off in the spare bedroom, he ran to his room, hoping to find it in his closet. As he shot into the room and turned the light on, he gasped.

"Looking for this?" Cassie asked, sitting on his bed and holding out Abe's tan leather suitcase, complete with American flag luggage tag.

Abe's stomach rocked back and forth, the sight of Cassie leaving him feeling equal parts sick and confused.

"Cassie? What are you doing here?"

"I packed a suitcase for you," Cassie said. "You cannot go back to Bordeaux wearing those hideous shirts again."

"Hey, how did you know we're going there?"

"I know more than you think I do, Abe."

"Cass, you didn't have to do this."

"Well, I know I didn't have to," she said, getting off the bed and setting the suitcase in front of him. "Trust me. I picked out outfits so nice and so trendy that Justin Timberlake would be jealous. You're going to look insanely handsome."

"Cass, we have to talk. And not about my clothes."

"Abram, you have to get going! There will be plenty of time for us to talk when you get back. But so help me, if you miss this flight..."

He appreciated her brevity about their necessary discussion and appreciated that she understood the inadequate timeframe they had in front of them. But Abe couldn't remain speechless on the subject.

"I can't just leave without telling you how much it hurts me that I hurt you. I'm so, so, so sorry."

Abe grabbed Cassie's arms, but she withdrew her hands from his clasp and stopped in her tracks. What he had done with Jared seemed like an out-of-body experience, something so monumentally unlike him. Abe hated how he had made all the inappropriate things feel acceptable, how he'd allowed Jared's charm and attractiveness to cloud the whole situation.

"Look," she started. "This isn't easy for me to be here. What you and Jared did? I can't even put it into words. Of all people, I never thought *you* would do something like that to me."

Abe wanted to tell her every detail of his feelings toward Jared, every minor flirtation that kept him pursuing her boyfriend. The ordeal was not simply for naught; he truly believed it was a genuine and substantiated fable.

"But when I saw Jared today, he explained everything and told me how much you two cared for each other," she continued. "I didn't realize the kind of bond you had."

Jared's unannounced trip to Buffalo didn't appear to be unannounced to Cassie. Abe was grateful that those two had had an opportunity to patch things up, but he sort of wished he could have seen Jared one last time, if only to gain that desired closure. Nevertheless, the presence of Cassie inside his bedroom outweighed any desire to see Jared. All the closure he needed was standing directly in front of him.

"That still doesn't make it right, Cass."

"You're damn right it doesn't. You could have told me. Secrets have no place in this friendship—even if they're gut-wrenching, terrible, colossal secrets. You could have saved me a lot of misery."

"I know," Abe said, standing up and snatching Cass in for a hug. He missed the warmth of her skin against his, the way her hair smelled like her coconut shampoo. "I'm sorry. I love you, Sassy Cassie."

"I love you, Abe, my babe," she replied. They hugged for what seemed like five minutes, no words between them, though Abe aspired to find the courage to again apologize for his actions. Before he could muster anything acceptable, the honking of Harris's truck in the driveway caused Cassie to break free and literally start pushing him out the door. "Okay, now go! Go, go, go, go, go."

"Did Harris know you were here?"

"Abram," she said. "Harris is the only reason I'm here."

That man out in the driveway was his man, imperfect and flawless at the same time. Something in Harris's soul had changed since they were last together as a couple; he seemed to be dedicating all his free time to finding ways to blow the minds of everyone important to him. It wasn't a characteristic he would likely be able to keep up, but it cemented the foundation of a new starting point for him and for their relationship.

"Oh my God, that house! You've seen it, right?" Abe asked.

"I have no words!"

"Okay, I love you so much. I'll call you the second I'm back—whenever that is!" Abe yelled as he made his way out the side door.

He hurried down the driveway, tossed his suitcase in the back seat, and jumped into the front seat. Before Harris could put the gear in reverse, Abe plunged toward him, kissing him so passionately on the lips Harris accidentally pressed down on the gas pedal, causing an ear-splitting, deafening vroom that made them burst into a loud laughter.

"Thank you," Abe said. "I don't know how you got her here, but thank you. For Cass and for everything."

"Happy birthday," Harris replied.

As they drove away from his house, Abram craned his head around to peer out the back windshield. Cassie's silhouette appeared in the living room, fading instantly as she turned off the lights.

"You guys okay?" Harris asked.

"You know, I think we are," Abe replied.

Abe grabbed Harris's right hand and held it as they made their way onto the highway. This man was Abe's partner in every sense of the word. Not just his boyfriend, but his incredible friend and loyal ally. He had known this all along, even in their years apart, but his recent actions solidified any wavering doubt Abe ever had.

It wasn't lost on Abe that he had no idea about what was happening with their trip to Bordeaux. He had no information on where they were staying or what they'd be doing or if they had a layover or where that layover would be or when they were coming back. It was so far removed from anything he had ever done before in his life.

The pretrip research? Never happened.

The game plan once they landed? No idea.

The to-do list in his head? Nonexistent.

Ordinarily, the lack of knowledge should have been enough to send Abe into a tailspin of anxiety. But as he looked at Harris next to him, a sense of serenity washed over him.

"I love you," Harris said.

"I love you too," Abe responded.

It was the first time in three years they had exchanged those three words with each other. Suddenly, the absence of details or any plan felt quietly refreshing.

New Year, New Abram?

Absolutely.

About the Author

Having little luck finding anything similar to a "beach read" featuring a gay male character, Steve Pacer decided to write one himself. The end result, *New Year, New You*, is his first novel. The former television news anchor and reporter always possessed a penchant for writing but never imagined the satisfaction creating fiction has produced.

When not writing, Steve enjoys obsessing over what to eat for dinner, perfecting his tennis game, and watching reruns of the *Golden Girls*. He calls Buffalo, NY, home, where he lives with his husband Mike and their cats, Glory and Julie.

Email: stephen.pacer@gmail.com

Twitter: @stevepacer

Website: www.stevepacer.com

Also Available from NineStar Press

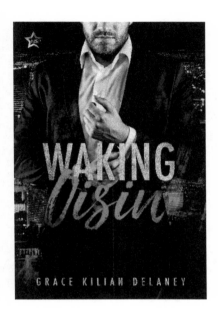

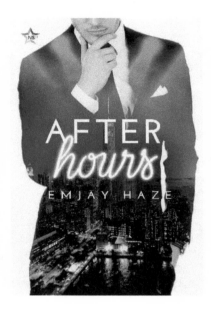

Connect with NineStar Press

www.ninestarpress.com

www.facebook.com/ninestarpress

www.facebook.com/groups/NineStarNiche

www.twitter.com/ninestarpress

www.tumblr.com/blog/ninestarpress

CPSIA information can be obtained
at www.ICGtesting.com
Printed in the USA
BVHW06s0440250518
517262BV00002B/117/P

9 781948 608565